Who Were the
RED BALL PEOPLE?

Dedalus Wildroot

John— There are plenty of
Books that can help
your game. This Aint
one of them. 2/4/16
Chief Tit
AKA SE

Bora Publishing

First printing 2005

ISBN 0-9763099-3-9   LCCN 2004116229

**ATTENTION CORPORATIONS, UNIVERSITIES, COLLEGES,
AND PROFESSIONAL ORGANIZATIONS:** Quantity discounts are available on bulk
purchases of this book for educational, gift purposes, or as premiums for increasing
magazine subscriptions or renewals. Special books or book excerpts can also be
created to fit specific needs. For information, please contact
Bora Publishing, 153 Vierra Way, Hercules, CA 94547.

ACKNOWLEDGMENTS

I would like to thank Mike Lewis, Jerry Vaught, and Bob Swenson for the extraordinary dedication they put forth in editing this book. Thanks to them, some of the best material ever put on paper was yanked out and saved for my next book. My warmest gratitude is also extended to Doctor Larry Foster, author of *Dr. Divot's Guide to Golf Injuries*, for all the valuable guidance he gave me in regard to tempering my expectations.

I also extend my deepest appreciation to Leslie Kahle Designs for designing a spectacular web site—RedBallPeople.com, where readers can order my book without getting out of their pajamas.

In case anybody is wondering, except for Chief Tit, all main characters are composite characters. The composite characters are much smarter, more sober, and a heap better looking than the people I know. In fact, if you are one of my friends and pondering reading this book merely because you think you are one of the characters, let me cut you off at the knees right now. I know what you're thinking. You'll read some insidiously stupid things that my characters say and do, and think to yourself—"he's talking about me!" Well, you're right. In this case—I am talking about you. However, don't kid yourself in thinking that when that same character says something clever or does something socially redeeming that I'm still talking about you…because I'm obviously not. That's why they call them composite characters.

I never met mathematics Professor Daniel Goldston of San Jose State University. As a former student of mathematics, he caught my attention when I read an account of his claim that he solved one of mathematics' most famous enigmas—the Twin Prime Conjecture. Sadly, shortly after his victory celebration for his twenty-year effort, his nifty proof was shredded by his colleagues and he faded back into obscurity. His futility reminded me so much of my golf game and career path, I was inspired to use the Professor's scientific method whenever I needed to stretch my logic, particularly when the desired conclusion wasn't supported by facts. I found the gimmick so handy, before long—it just snowballed on me. By the time I got done with him, his stellar career included stints as: the founder of Gesundheit Psychology; a Nobel Laureate economic model calibrator; a Navy contractor and mentor of the only dolphin to attain the rank of Ensign; and a sound wave expert who proved that snoring effects amplification circuitry and is the ultimate cause of blaring televisions.

Undoubtedly, Professor Goldston is a brilliant man. I'm praying he also has a sense of humor. In any event, my deepest gratitude is offered to Professor Daniel Goldston for helping me discover that futility and imagination are intertwined.

While I completely understand that the point of an acknowledgement is to laud those who helped me, I would like to thank myself on behalf of O.J. Simpson for ferreting out the real killers. For the curious, you will discover in Chapter 17—*The Real Killers*, how Simpson was framed by a ruthless gang of killers that heed to the names—Hank the Hammer, One-eyed Luther, Three-Fingers Pete, and Vinnie the Eliminator …whose modus-operandi is committing heinous crimes tantamount to their level of play in golf tournaments. Thanks to my elaborate proof, the Juice's reputation is on the fast track to recovery.

This book is dedicated to my beautiful wife Deborah Evans, who for some reason, thinks I'm quite talented. At what, she's not quite sure. But like O.J.—she's still searching.

TABLE OF CONTENTS

The Red Ball People Choose a Leader

M y name is Dedalus Wildroot, though no one calls me by that name anymore. They address me by my new name—Chief Tit, leader of the Red Ball People. My new name was constructed by a bipartisan collaboration of people who were abusing Microsoft Outlook.

Most of the collaborators learned long ago that the rungs on corporate ladders couldn't support the weight of a junior executive caught by a superior playing minesweeper on their company's computer. Most turned to their Internet browsers as an alternative to killing time at the office, until some overachieving technocrat discovered that web servers could track the visited sites. Before long, promising junior executives were being summoned into Personnel to defend the business need to visit such sites as buttparade.com and lostpanty.com. Embarrassed technical neophytes soon settled on the company email system as the safest method to meet entertainment needs while arresting productivity.

Unlike minesweeper, solitaire, and porn sites, email entertainment requires the collaboration of a network of individuals with a common interest and a commitment to waste as much time as anyone on the distribution list. Those who fail to live up to the commitment often find themselves excluded from receiving the best images, satire, and political jokes. The associations that yield the most potent entertainment are often those that are comprised of a dedicated core of members who recognize that their primary mission is to heap as much ridicule as possible onto fellow members in regard to their political positions and athletic prowess. Naturally, one of the most combustible associations is the one made up of golfing partners. If an unfortunate member suffers a major pratfall or gets caught fudging his score on his Saturday round, he can spend all day Sunday looking forward to three interpretations of the event appearing in his email inbox on Monday followed by numerous commentaries of those who weren't there but can vouch for witnessing similar behavior.

Mondays and Fridays are the red flag danger days. The former is the preferred day where the agenda is set for the week, often based on recent weekend incidents, while the latter is the preferred day to waste company time. Years of warfare had taught network members that the only way to battle a brush fire before it turned into an all-consuming conflagration was to set a backfire. It was vital that the backfire be set with utmost urgency to prevent an onslaught from all directions, as no other retardant was effective in suppressing the danger. The most potent backfires redirected the advancing digital wildfire back toward the arsonist, although any direction other than upwind was satisfactory. And God have pity on the poor soul who is away on an errand or detained by a business meeting during the first critical minutes of ignition. By the time this unfortunate oaf opens his email, his reputation will be sullied and in extreme cases, he might even be sporting a new nickname as a few of us have learned the hard way.

One victim who was slow to respond to an attack and lived to regret it was my golf pal Johnny McClurg. After failing for the third straight year to perform his assigned custodial duties following the fourth quarter of the annual Super Bowl party, the Nickname Nomination Committee convened and commissioned Johnny with the new moniker of 'Blister' after we all agreed that the name was the most descriptive antithesis of his work ethic.

Chief Tit, leader of the Red Ball People, had its origin in an annual three-day golf tournament that my buddies and I play near the Sierra Nevada town of Graeagle, north of Lake Tahoe. The tournament consisted of eight players whose handicaps varied from seven to twenty eight. I had a particularly dreadful time shooting ninety-nine the first day, one hundred on the second day and ninety-five on the third day at a relatively easy course. Although three or four players had combined scores much higher than me, I was the worst of the lot relative to my handicap. By the third day I ended the round using range balls, having depleted all four sleeves of my Titleist NXTs.

Like most casual tournaments whose participation is restricted to buddies, the focus was more on drinking rare brands of scotch and smoking expensive cigars than it was on being sticklers for rules. By the second day, anyone who had no chance of breaking ninety was conceding their own three-foot putts. Five footers were conceded with regularity if the putt was to save a double bogey. By the third day everybody was colorblind. White stakes were treated as red stakes. Red stakes were treated as unfinished picket fences indicating that the general vicinity was ground under repair where we were entitled to take relief. Winter rules were declared on the second day as the temperature soared above ninety degrees.

By no means was I the most egregious cheater. In fact, Blister topped his final ball into a canyon on the 17th hole on the second day and when everyone refused to offer him a replacement, he finished the hole with an imaginary ball, taking a double bogey.

Regrettably, my transgression was much more unforgivable. I won the tournament and the first place prize of $180.00. Even more galling was the way that I accomplished the feat. Seven other players stood on the first tee for three consecutive days and watched as I set the tone for each round by drilling my first drive into a river, a canyon, and a manzanita bush.

As it turned out, the unorthodox best ball betting arrangement we hashed out treated skill as the least important factor but nobody realized it until the third day. Players rotated to a new betting partner every six holes. It just so happened, when I played poorly, my partner inexplicably played over his head while the opposition played to my level of ineptitude. It was the oddest coincidence that any of us had ever witnessed and by the start of the third day everyone was grumbling about it.

The second gaffe I committed was my spontaneous response to the pro shop attendant who informed me that all three courses had introduced a cart path only rule. The new rules were a very unwelcome turn of events for the six players relegated to traipsing after errant shots over rugged terrain while encumbered by hangovers. However, my riding partner and I were excused from the dreaded restriction when I cleverly dropped my shorts and convinced the attendant that the scar running along my left thigh was the remnant of a hobbling hip injury that could be exacerbated with excessive walking. To the chagrin of everyone except my riding partner, I was granted a coveted blue handicap flag that enabled my partner and me to drive our cart anywhere we pleased.

The practice green burst into pandemonium as players clamored to be my riding partner when word spread that I possessed the magical blue flag. The honor was settled with a series of coin flips preceding each round. The victors were more ecstatic about riding with me than in making birdies, which contributed to the notion that I might be the reincarnation of some mystical omnipotent tribal chief.

The final piece of the puzzle fell into place when tournament players took notice of the whimsical way in which I marked my Titleist balls with a red felt marker. With very little forethought, I had simply blotted out the last five letters of the word Titleist without realizing that the remaining recognizable characters spelled the word—Tit. Unwittingly, I had provided an ample supply of volatile and toxic fuels that could burn for days if left unchecked.

Forgetting that the Monday following a tournament is the unequivocal red flag danger day, I foolishly agreed to have lunch with a potential client in San Francisco. Owing to the ninety-minute commute from my house in the East Bay, I departed at 10:30 A.M. after getting up late following a snap decision to extend my recuperation from the three-day event into mid-Monday morning. My obligation to my reputation to be on alert for upwind email flare-ups had been subordinated by a selfish desire to make a living. I would soon regret the capitulation.

I returned home from my unproductive business meeting and was quickly overcome with an uncomfortable urgency to read my stockpiled emails. Since I had not accessed my inbox in four days, the first one hundred and twenty three messages were spams. Several advised me that there were numerous women who wanted to take off their clothes for me while others announced the availability of non-prescription drugs that could enlarge my reproductive organ to rival the size of Seabiscuit's. After painstakingly considering all one hundred and twenty three offers, I turned my attention to the more recent emails filling my inbox from my special interest group.

As I scanned the subject line of my email inbox, my heart began to sink as I spotted several clues to indicate that my reputation had suffered third degree burns during a swirling inferno that burned itself out while I was attending a pointless business lunch. It was apparent that my right-wing college pal Wiley was the arsonist as I watched his name roll by on the first email among several that had the same subject line. The sixteen replies that followed made it clear that he had no shortage of accomplices. According to the timestamps, ignition had occurred on Wiley's keyboard at precisely 8:52 A.M. The fire raged for nearly three hours before being extinguished at 11:48 A.M. on the keyboard of my apolitical simpleton friend, Blister. The subject line of My Outlook inbox appeared as follows, sorted by timestamp from earliest to most recent:

Subject:

Who Were the Red Ball People?
RE: Who Were the Red Ball People?
RE: Who Were the Red Ball People?
RE: Who Were the Red Ball People?
20% off on Vi@gra—Order Now!
RE: Who Were the Red Ball People?
RE: Who Were the Red Ball People?
Tell us more about Chief Tit—He sounds really interesting!
RE: Tell us more about Chief Tit—He sounds really interesting!
RE: Tell us more about Chief Tit—He sounds really interesting!
P&nis enl@rgement pills—be like Secretariat
RE: Tell us more about Chief Tit—He sounds really interesting!
RE: Tell us more about Chief Tit—He sounds really interesting!
RE: Tell us more about Chief Tit—He sounds really interesting!
Were Chief Tit and The Red Ball People playing the ancient game of golf?
RE: Were Chief Tit and the Red Ball People playing the ancient game of golf?
Did the Red Ball People have any other notable tribe members?
RE: Did the Red Ball People have any other notable tribe members?
How did the Red Ball People become extinct?
RE: How did the Red Ball People become extinct?

To my consternation, I discovered that several of my tournament partners had spent the better part of their day exercising their fantasy careers as historians and archeologists, while non-contributing members cheered them on. In the span of three hours, a lost and peculiar civilization emerged, became extinct, and was rediscovered five hundred years later. Of course, I wasn't privy to the startling revelation until each segment of the fable was pieced together one email at a time.

I opened the arsonist's email titled, "Who Were the Red Ball People?" It read:

In the year 2505, the Falwellians, a religious sect who believe in the desegregation of church and state, are on a retreat in the lower Sierra-Nevadas. During an Easter egg hunt, the Falwellians discover peculiar 500 year-old artifacts in dried riverbeds and under decayed beds of Manzanita bushes.

An archeological excavation ensues, which uncovers dozens more of the artifacts—a white dimpled ball with the word Titleist written on both sides with red ink covering the last five letters. Before long, additional digs are underway along the Central coast of what is now the city-state of Berklunacy. Additional artifacts are soon discovered under 500 year-old beds of decayed ice plant near Monterey and in San Pablo Bay, when the bay is drained to expand the habitat for red salamanders.

Excitement quickly spreads among the archeological elite as the mounting evidence suggests that the discovery is the single most important find since the discovery of the lost Incan mountain city of Machu Piccu. Due to the unusual red marking on each of the artifacts, world-renowned archeologist Professor Merlin Goldston has named the lost civilization—The Red Ball People. In his watershed archeological symposium held at the 50,000 seat Trotsky Pavilion in Berkeley, the capital city of Berklunacy, Professor Goldston delivers his findings on the lost civilization of The Red Ball People to a standing-room only crowd:

Anyone else want to pick it up from here? Regards, Wiley

———————————

I began to feel nauseous as I recognized an opportunity lost. Wiley had set the brushfire upwind from me but had left me plenty of wiggle room, if I had only been on guard to set a backfire. As a right-wing conservative, Wiley had difficulty keeping his Republican overtones as well as his disdain for religion out of his emails. While the point of the spear was aimed at me, the fable was loaded with tangential barbs that Wiley had sprayed toward our flaming liberal buddy Jack and his hometown of Berkeley.

Had I only followed my early instincts and canceled my business appointment, I could have easily redirected the fire back at Wiley or better yet, deflected the assault entirely in Jack's direction. The morning newspaper was loaded with ammunition and very little effort would have been required. The Democrats were chastising President Bush, Wiley's guy, for insulting the European Union again. On the opposite side of the spectrum, the Contra Costa Times was reporting that the City Council of Berkeley who Jack firmly backed, wasted another monthly meeting trying to agree on more rigid language to insure that the city stay nuclear free. Either story would have provided sufficient kindling to set a devastating counter-offensive.

I was curious about Professor Merlin Goldston. I presumed Wiley's contrived future archeologist, was intended to be a distant relative to current day Professor Daniel Goldston of San Jose State University. During the tournament, our foursome had a few chuckles at the San Jose State mathematician's expense upon reading that he had claimed to have solved a famous two hundred year old math problem only to discover that twenty years of his work was invalidated in a few minutes when his peers found numerous holes in his arguments.

Regrettably, I wasn't there to put words about Bush or Berkeley's City Council into the mouth of Professor Merlin Goldston, and Blister answered Wiley's call. In a reply sent back to Wiley, Blister copied the full complement of tournament players when he wrote:

2505–PROFESSOR MERLIN GOLDSTON AT THE TROTSKY PAVILION:

"A thorough analysis of the Red Ball People artifacts along with archived electronic email from the same time period corroborates that the tribe occupied these areas for small amounts of time and practiced unusual sporting rituals akin to the Aztecs and Mayans. Whereas the Aztecs killed their entire team if they lost a match of hoop ball, the Red Ball People just appeared to drink heavily after each event.

7

Owing to the way the balls were marked, the Chief of the Tribe appeared to be known as Chief Tit, perhaps as a tribute to King Tut. Though it is pure speculation as to how the tribe played their game, the excavation suggests that the objective of the Red Ball People was to take a club or piece of iron with an L-shaped face and strike the ball at a 45 degree angle into tall native grasses, rivers, or manzanita bushes.

Since nearly all the balls were in pristine condition except for an aberration known as a hosel mark, we can only conclude that the more skilled players could contort their bodies in a way to spin the balls left to right such that the ball flight would sail over the closest body of water into a manzanita bush on a distant shore line. The player would then walk to the edge of the river or body of water, drop another ball with a red mark and repeat the process. If the river and heavy foliage appeared on the left side, the Red Ball People achieved the desired result by combining an exaggerated hip thrust with a severe chopping motion, deftly impaling the ball into the river bank on the left at 130 MPH.

Their path of play took them around a series of 18 flat meadows of short grass which were so sacred, it was considered a cultural dishonor to strike a ball and have it land in the meadow where others could find it. After twenty minutes of marking the perimeter of their playing area, the Red Ball People agreed to hit the ball to a flat smooth grassy area at the end of the meadow.

They used a flat stick to hit the ball past a hole in the grassy area and then reversed direction and tapped the ball toward the hole again, careful to leave it short of falling in. As they leaned over to pick up their balls they danced and chanted, "GOOD, GOOD, GOOD." Before moving to the next meadow, they would scatter cigar ashes around the hole as a sign to subsequent tribe members that no balls accidentally fell in the hole. I will now take questions from the audience."

*OK—someone else can take it from here. How about you—Chief Tit?
Blister*

But Chief Tit was incapable of taking it from here. He was spending his hard-earned money on a stupid prospect who only wanted a free lunch at the four-star Mandarin Oriental restaurant in San Francisco.

I felt my face flush, aghast at my new name. Blister's email drew immediate responses from tournament players, Mike and Rick, who each offered encouraging blurbs to the next storyteller. "Keah, keah, keah!" Mike responded simulating a giggle. "Where's Chief Tit when the Red Ball People need him?" Rick inquired. According to the timestamp on Rick's email, Chief Tit was most likely on the Bay Bridge when Rick asked the question. Instead, Jack accepted Blister's challenge and picked up the story at the Trotsky Pavilion and assumed the role of the audience.

2505—MEMBER OF AUDIENCE AT TROTSKY PAVILION: "What would the Red Ball People do if they could not find a river, or bush near the meadow to hit the ball into?"

PROFESSOR GOLDSTON: "That problem never came up. These players appeared to have uncanny skill at targeting rivers and bushes. Though in the lower areas near the ocean, they did favor ice-plant."

AUDIENCE: "Tell us more about Chief Tit. He sounds really interesting."

I left this one wide open if anyone wants to tackle the subject matter!
Jack

Jack had changed the subject line to, "Tell us more about Chief Tit. He sounds really interesting." I was helpless as my persona was recreated before my eyes from four hours earlier. The prodigious responses indicated that productivity dropped to zero at around 11:30 A.M. as everybody took a stab at Jack's request. The group fell in line behind Blister's version when they agreed that his dialog had the most pronounced effect of making me look silly. Blister answered Jack's query and then posed one more that he chose to answer himself. He wrote:

2505—PROFESSOR GOLDSTON AT THE TROTSKY PAVILION: "The Red Ball People often used electrical carts to maneuver around the meadow. But because the meadows were sacred, carts had to remain on the path running throughout the mountain meadows. Since it was customary to put the path on the opposite side of the meadow from where the rivers and manzanita bushes were, the Red Ball People were constantly leaving their carts to drop another ball near the river.

It seems that wily Chief Tit discovered that if he pulled down his pants and showed the meadow manager the scar from his hip surgery, he was entitled to put a blue flag on his cart and drive anywhere he wanted since blue flags are more sacred than sacred meadows. The Red Ball People revered Chief Tit for this discovery since one of them was allowed to ride with Chief Tit, and they soon were jostling with each other to curry his allegiance."

AUDIENCE: "Did Chief Tit pull down his pants to show his scar for other types of benefits such as preferred dinner seating or preferred parking?"

PROFESSOR GOLDSTON: "Not that I'm aware of. We only know that it was a behavioral pattern he employed to receive a sacred blue flag for his electrical meadow cart."

AUDIENCE: "These tournament games that the Red Ball People played sounds suspiciously like the ancient game of golf. How can you be sure they weren't playing golf or some twisted derivative form of golf?"

OK—I defer to the next storyteller. I think we all now know Chief Tit a little better—don't we Chief? Blister

———————————

Jack was more than happy to pick up the story. He hit his reply-all button and changed the title of subject line to, "Were Chief Tit and the Red Ball People playing the ancient game of golf?" Jack was so aligned with the uniform objective of ridiculing me that he had even coalesced in Wiley's original premise of the Trotsky Pavilion in the city-state of

Berklunacy. Normally he would have sent a barb back Wiley's way and been inclined to continue the symposium from the Cheney-Halliburton Memorial Auditorium, a name he probably held in higher esteem. However, he made a carefully calculated decision to keep the heat away from Wiley and himself when he kept the attention on Chief Tit by writing:

2505–PROFESSOR GOLDSTON AT THE TROTSKY PAVILION: "Excellent question. There was early speculation that the Red Ball People were playing some mutated form of the ancient game. However, exhaustive analysis of artifacts and archived email media indicate that their tournament objectives were totally inconsistent with the rules of 21st century golf. It's very similar to the confusion over the ancient games of soccer and football.

For many years, contemporary scientists and archeologists confused these two 21st century sports. The confusion was attributed to the game of soccer being called football in Europe leading many scientists to conclude that they were the same game. However, as you know, we have since learned that the duel objective of American football was to run up the point total while introducing new dance steps. Contrarily, we have since learned that the objective of European football or Soccer if you prefer, was to have the home team keep the ball away from the goal until a riot erupted in the stands.

Similarly, the objective of the ancient rules of golf was to use the fewest number of swings or strokes to hit the ball down a meadow and then actually try to hit the ball in the hole. That clearly was not the objective of the Red Ball People. So the conjecture that they were playing some derivative form of golf is quite preposterous."

AUDIENCE: "This is off the subject a little bit, but when did the ancient game of golf vanish?"

PROFESSOR GOLDSTON: "Around 2070, the same year that its most skilled player, Tiger Woods died. An organization, the PGA, who sponsored the tournaments, offered four big tournaments a year called majors. By the time he was 30, Woods only played these tourna-

ments as well as his personal sponsorship tournaments in order to keep his number one ranking.

From age 50 to 85, he played in 100 senior majors and won them all. At age 85, Woods created the Geezer Tour, which consisted of players 80 years and older. He won every event of the Geezer Tour until he suddenly dropped dead at 93 on the 18th hole of the Berklunacy Geezer Open when he had a seizure after 3-putting the 18th hole. One year after he died, he lost his number one ranking to Michelle Wie who outlived Woods by a few more years.

When Woods died, TV viewing of golf events plummeted to zero. TV viewers became more interested in watching reality shows that boasted 23-year old scantily clad women performing tasks that caused their underwear to get wet. Secondly, golfing equipment became too advanced rendering the game far too easy to play. The final amateur driving contest was won by an 8-year old girl who hit a Pinnacle Flubber Distance ball 800 yards. During the final years of the sport, grown men grew tired of being beaten by pre-pubescent children and gave up the game in droves.

AUDIENCE: "Did the Red Ball People have any other notable tribe members?"

Since the Chief's taking the brunt of this, I thought he might at least want to jump in and describe some of his key tribe members. You out there Chief? Haven't heard from you all day! Jack

———————

Well at least I would get some respite from the onslaught with Jack's latest query. I was paying a $135 lunch bill at the Mandarin Oriental when the query was accepted by Wiley. Apparently Wiley also realized that he had blown most of his day helping construct the story of Chief Tit and chose to introduce a natural ending to the story when he posed a question at the end of his email asking how the Red Ball People became extinct. He changed the title of the reply to "Did the Red Ball People have any other notable members?" when he wrote:

2505—PROFESSOR GOLDSTON AT THE TROTSKY PAVILION: "We are not aware of any other individuals in the tribe that rose to the prominence of Chief Tit. However, that may be due to a ritual the tribe practiced of continually changing their names. An examination of their email media suggests that, except for Chief Tit who all the other tribe members refer to with reverence as The Chief, other members used ever changing monikers to address each other. Some of Chief Tit's more important lieutenants were known as Butt Wipe, Pea Brain, Mutton Head, Stooge, Curly, Hillary, Strom, Wiley, Jack, Blister, Autobahn Mouth, Oatmeal Head, Fatty, Mighty Outtabounder, Captain Hook, Dick Nose, and Thunder Pants. There is evidence suggesting that Jack, Pea Brain, and Captain Hook were the same person. At the very least it proved that Chief Tit had tribe members that attained the rank of captain."

AUDIENCE: "How did the Red Ball People become extinct?"

Regards, Wiley

———————————

Blister believed he was more than capable of fielding the demise of the Red Ball People. In fact, while Jack and Wiley were filling in the middle part of the story, he had undertaken another task. Using a few colored felt pens, he created a Falwellian Easter egg as well as Chief Tit's trademarked ball with the red mark covering the last 5 letters of one of his Titleist balls. With his digital camera, he recreated the site of the Falwellian artifact discovery and attached it to his email. Blister destroyed the civilization of the Red Ball People with the following email:

2505—PROFESSOR GOLDSTON AT THE TROTSKY PAVILION: "Most scientists cling to the theory that they were eventually overpowered by the Blue Flag People. Sadly, Chief Tit was largely responsible for the emergence of the Blue Flag People and set the destruction of his own tribe in motion the day he pulled down his pants to show his scar to obtain his blue flag. Soon thereafter, tribe members began faking leg injuries and deserted his tribe to form their own tribe which we now know as the Blue Flag People."

13

Blister (P.S.—See attached picture of Red Ball People artifact discovered by Falwellians!)

Red Ball People artifact discovered by Falwellians
during Easter egg hunt in 2505

From origin, to extinction, to rediscovery—the fable of the Red Ball People was allowed to unfold largely because I foolishly put my career interests above the demands of my special interest group on a red flag danger day. In the span of three hours the persona of Dedalus Wildroot was slain and buried and indisputably replaced by Chief Tit—leader of the Red Ball People.

Looking for
Sailboat Fuel

Since assuming my new identity as Chief Tit, Leader of the Red Ball People, I had done little to distinguish myself as a worthy Chieftain. My primary duties consisted of booking tee times for the tribe and settling squabbles on the course. That all changed one Saturday in October when an ordinary day was transformed by an improbable series of events that catapulted me to the pinnacle of Red Ball People folklore.

Like most Saturdays, the day began with a round of golf at Franklin Canyon, a public course on Highway 4 in the East Bay of San Francisco. I had booked a tee time at 8:30 A.M. to guarantee a quorum of the Red Ball People, which was three tribesmen plus myself. Any tee time earlier than 8:30 interrupted the sleep habits of the tribe and risked an incomplete caucus.

The Red Ball People consist of nine or ten golfers who rotate their Saturdays with me, their Chief. Unlike the military, I have a much lower standard for promotions. In fact, I have only one guideline. To remain in good standing, a tribesman must successfully concoct at least three arguments a month that are sound enough to convince his wife of the need to be away from home three or four Saturdays out of the month. The three linguists able to maintain that lofty standard are Jack Newby, William Barrett, and Johnny McClurg, the latter two, respectively known as Wiley and Blister.

Jack was our favorite left-wing conspiracy theorist and exposed sinister plots of the Republican Party as often as the itch needed to be scratched. Unlike his Libertarian Berkeley brethren who drove Volvos to the farmer's market, Jack drove a politically incorrect Mercedes 320e to four-star restaurants in San Francisco where he often under tipped the working class.

15

As a consummate capitalist, Wiley dedicated most of his political energy to debunking Jack's theories and poking fun at Jack's proletarian views. Though Jack was an attorney twelve years out of Berkeley's Boalt Law School, Wiley often got the better of him in the verbal exchanges. While Jack advocated settling world disputes through the United Nations, Wiley was convinced that sometimes asses needed to be kicked.

Blister was content to sit on the fence between the Democratic blue and Republican red territories and agree with anyone leaning on the fence. As Jack's best friend, he avoided getting drawn into the acidic exchanges between Wiley and Jack. If the verbal sparring became too intense, he followed the advice of Pink Floyd and got comfortably numb with a spare fattie he always carried in his golf bag.

Since I am the Chief, I find it preferable to arrive at the course prior to tribe members. Since our tee time was 8:30, I arrived at 8:15 to give myself a little extra time to prepare for the five hour round. I polished off the time-consuming chore of stretching while driving to the course so I could dedicate my remaining time to standing in line behind eight guys while a college intern routed Visa transactions to the MasterCard network. When a scan of the pro shop confirmed that no other members of my foursome had arrived, I remained calm with the knowledge the Red Ball People have a pre-round routine that have subtle variations from professional golfers.

Establishing a Routine Before Play

Tiger's Routine

Tiger Woods' routine has been well chronicled. Unless his tee time is unusually early, he has a light snack of fruit and toast before going to the portable PGA weight room where he works on his cardiovascular one day and his muscle toning the next. After a ninety-minute work out, he enjoys a high protein breakfast with sufficient carbohydrates to sustain a high level of energy for a five-hour round preceded by ninety minutes of range practice.

Since Tiger is always in the last two or three groups on weekends, he always has time on Saturdays and Sundays for a thirty-minute rubdown from a swimsuit model who serves as his weight trainer. In accordance with his ten year $250 million Nike contract, he outfits himself in a snappy line of Nike clothing and romps around the Presidential suite of his four-star hotel looking for a suitable mirror. Once the grandest mirror is located, he spends about thirty minutes winking at himself and gazing at his reflection thinking how cool it is to be in your twenties, worth $500 million, and married to the best looking blonde in Sweden. Before tearing himself away from the mirror, he practices tipping his hat to the crowd, careful not to establish eye contact with the imaginary gallery.

Two hours before tee time he departs to the putting green where he putts for fifteen minutes varying the distance from three to fifty feet. After putting, he heads to the driving range where he will be accosted by journalists who want to know if he is in a slump because he only won his last eight tournaments by eleven strokes instead of the usual twelve.

Tiger stretches the large muscle group for ten minutes before pulling a club from his bag. Beginning with a sand wedge, he takes aim at various range targets as he climbs from the short irons to the long irons, before finishing with his woods and driver. While hitting each iron, Tiger varies the trajectory between high, medium, and low while mixing in fades, draws, and scalding stingers.

Next, Tiger splashes thirty or forty sand shots, varying the arc of the ball to simulate short side flags and distant flags. Twenty minutes before tee time, he returns to the driving range and hits his final shot of the practice session with the same club he will use on the first hole, applying the fade or draw that the shot will require.

For his remaining few minutes, Tiger returns to the putting green where he will be accosted by a TV commentator who wants to know what Tiger can do to improve on his previous round of 63. After hitting a few more putts, he opens a new sleeve of Titleists that he is paid $50 million to endorse, and takes out a dark green felt pen to mark his ball. Preoccupied with the notion that he is as cool as a cucumber, he draws three tiny cucumbers on his ball that are so small that TV cameras misrepresent them as black dots.

As he walks by the clubhouse on his way to the tee, he catches his reflection in a window and gives himself one more wink. While he stands behind the tee box waiting to be called by the starter, he bounces balls off the club face of his sand wedge in preparation for a future Nike commercial. He is ready to start his round.

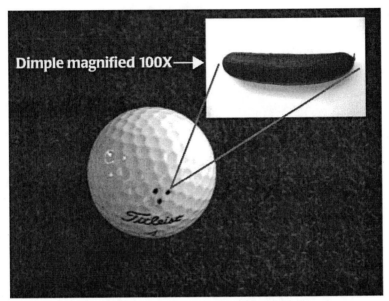

A dimple from Tiger's ball magnified 100 times

Wiley's Routine

If Wiley, a twenty-two handicapper, has an 8:30 A.M. tee time, the alarm will be set at 8:00 A.M. since the golf course is only seven minutes away from his house. Though he's never consciously thought about it, Wiley has seven pre-round tasks to achieve before his eight thirty tee time.

The first two tasks, cleansing and dressing, are normally accomplished in less than a minute. Before stumbling to the kitchen to get his first cup of coffee, he stops in the bathroom to splash water on his face. This will be his only attempt at sanitization until his wife forces him to take a shower later in the afternoon. To achieve maximum sleep time, Wiley knows better than to waste time looking through his closet for a snazzy outfit. Instead, he recycles any combination of shirts, shorts, and socks that float to the top of his laundry hamper in the bathroom.

Unfortunately, Wiley's routine has hit a bump in the road. The shorts residing near the top of his laundry hamper snag on his expanding thighs as he tries to wiggle them up to his forty-inch waist. Years of excessive beer and hamburgers have made the effort increasingly difficult. The effort is abandoned and he returns to his bedroom to retrieve God's greatest creation—shorts with an elastic waistband.

Once properly attired, Wiley extracts from the dishwasher a soiled coffee mug that is large enough for tossing a salad. After draining a third of the coffee pot into the mug, he retrieves the newspaper and returns to the bathroom to embark on his third and longest task—reading the sports page while pinching a loaf. Technically, these might be considered two discrete tasks. When the Red Ball People determined that none of us were able to do one without the other, we decided it made more sense to treat the endeavor as one task.

With thirteen minutes until tee time, Wiley has four more tasks to complete: breakfast, stretching, driving to the course, and practice. Because of Wiley's allegiance to the Red Ball People, he knows that mulligans will abolish the need for practice.

Before departing, Wiley loads his bag with a sleeve of X-OUT balls that will be substituted for any stunt shots that arise, a six-pack of Heineken, and three Presidentes Maduro cigars made from the best blends of hay and stinkweed. As he meticulously prepares his equipment, he discovers a mushy black banana from the previous Saturday that he had forgotten.

Since McDonalds was astute enough to build a restaurant on Highway 4, Wiley can combine the tasks of driving and breakfast. His last remaining task, stretching, can be accommodated in his SUV. If he has calculated correctly, the stop at McDonalds will take three minutes. With the allotted time for driving, he should pull into the parking lot with three minutes to spare.

The minute Wiley lost retrieving a larger pair of shorts is gained back when an efficient McDonald's worker passes him a Tator-tot and Egg McMuffin that had been baking under a sunlamp since sunrise. He chews the last bite of his Egg McMuffin as he eases his Toyota SUV, whose license plate reads MISTR89, into a parking stall. Before exiting the cab, he adjusts the rearview mirror. He takes a hard look at himself and thinks: Except for the money, the Swedish bombshell, the swimsuit model who doubles as a masseuse, world adulation, a fit body, and the ability to fade a 195-yard 7-iron—Tiger's got nothing on me.

———

I was still standing in line watching Visa transactions route to MasterCard, when Wiley, arrived at precisely 8:30 A.M. Years of Saturday

19

golf had taught us that a scheduled tee time is merely an estimate of when play would really begin if the pro shop were to cease hiring interns.

By far, Wiley was the sloppiest dressed golfer in the pro shop. Of course, that was subject to change if either Blister or Jack were to walk in. Oddly enough, Jack and I had estimated Wiley's net worth at $2 million, a tidy sum for a thirty-eight year old mortgage loan broker.

I could tell Wiley was troubled. Very troubled. I immediately recognized the symptoms—slouching shoulders, tea bags under his eyes, and hat hair.

"You look like something the cat shoved out. Another Blockbuster night?" I said, greeting Wiley at the counter.

"How'd you know, Chief?" Wiley replied as he squinted through his swollen eyes.

"The sandbags under your eyes," I responded. "What was it this time?"

"The Big Lebowski."

"The Big Lebowski? Ha!" I said with a laugh. "Isn't that the same movie you forgot to return last month?"

"Same one," Wiley said as he looked down at his wallet and leafed through his twenties. "I guess I should have bought it—I've seen it five times."

Wiley had forgotten to take a rented video back to Blockbuster that was due a day earlier. The penalty was $2. As was often the case, he didn't remember to return the overdue video until 3:00 A.M. when he awoke from a recurring dream. In the dream he is standing outside a Blockbuster video store with an overdue movie tucked under his arm. He pushes on a door that has an instruction plate advising him to pull. When he pulls at the door, the advisory on the instruction plate changes to push. Never is he able to open the door and return the movie. Nor does the store have a drop slot for rental returns. Eventually he wakes up to the realization that he really does have an overdue movie. After tossing and turning for an hour or two, he usually falls back to sleep.

"You seen Jack and Blister?" I asked.

"Yeah. I ran into 'em in the parking lot. They gave me their money to take care of the green fee."

Wiley pointed outside where we could both see the practice green. I spotted Jack and Blister chatting while standing in the busiest corridor of the practice putting green as annoyed golfers diverted their putts away from the three practice holes Jack and Blister were blocking. Jack's forty inch black shorts and white shirt made him look like a waiter, albeit a slow waiter. Anytime Jack turned sideways, he risked a copyright infringement suit from the estate of Alfred Hitchcock for imitating the famous director's trademarked profile.

Blister wasn't much of a consolation prize, though he was among the elite members of the Red Ball People whose weight was proportionate to his six foot two height. His receding hairline was covered by his favorite black baseball cap that I gave him two years earlier on his thirty-fifth birthday to commemorate hitherto, his finest achievement. The engraved bold white letters on the bill of the cap proclaimed—"MR. 59." Below the proclamation in smaller letters and contained within parenthesis were the words—"(front nine)."

Nick, a part time starter and full time college student with vastly more experience in credit transactions, finally interceded when the line grew to twelve. In a matter of minutes Nick cleared the backlog after issuing an assignment to the intern to fetch him a cup of coffee. Nick was accustomed to taking the tribe's money and had taken to addressing me as the Chief like the rest of the tribe.

"Hey Chief, you paying for everybody?" Nick asked as he always does.

"I don't know—did you finally coax that pig to fly outta your ass?" I responded as I always do.

"Didn't think so. You're up second," Nick advised.

"We'll be there after the third call," Wiley informed Nick.

"Just don't get lost. We're ten minutes behind."

"You may be ten minutes behind here Nick but I'm guessing you're twenty minutes behind on the second hole," Wiley retorted as he scooped up his change.

"How about my blue flag Nick?" I asked remembering my most vital piece of equipment. Since Nick was familiar with my medical condition, he did not find it necessary for me to drop my shorts to obtain my blue flag.

"Pull one out of the carts that are lined up for the tournament."

After settling with Nick, Wiley announced his arrival at the driving range by forgetting to hang a bucket on the ball dispensing faucet after feeding a token to the ball machine. Two dozen range balls sprayed off the pavement and scattered as two amused bystanders formed a posse with me to corral the renegades. Alerted by the commotion, Jack and

21

Blister correctly guessed that Wiley and I were in the vicinity and joined us at the driving range. Each player's allotment worked out to be about eight balls, an unusually vigorous workout.

"Hoo-ya, Chief!" Blister barked as he attempted to execute a NBA handshake. "Which one of you guys forgot the bucket this time?"

I fingered Wiley who was occupied dividing his bucket among four mats.

"I'm gonna shoot in the eighties today Chief. If it gets any hotter than that I'm gonna knock off and have a beer," Blister cackled, pleased with his weary pun.

"That's funny stuff Blister," Jack lied. "

"Second call for the Wildroot foursome," Nick announced over the intercom.

Wiley poured out several balls for each of us. We expected Nick's last call within two minutes.

Jack limbered up with a 110-MPH swing with his driver that he topped into the pavement two feet in front of his mat. Unbeknownst to Jack, the folly accounted for the stiffness that set in Sunday morning that prevented him from combing his hair with his right arm for a week. His next ball bounded off the wooden divider separating the mats, startling everyone on the range.

Blister was slightly more impressive. He yanked three 4-irons to the left before shanking three to the right. He saved his last ball for his sand wedge, which he skulled one hundred and eighty yards.

After clanking seven drives and one pitching wedge, Wiley retired to the practice green after determining he had sufficient time to hit two practice putts. Believing only his distance skills were in need of calibration, Wiley tapped an uphill thirty foot putt that traveled nineteen feet. He reversed direction and knocked a thirty foot downhiller, forty five feet.

Summing up his effort, Wiley said to no one in particular, "Well, that was about as useful as driving around town looking for sailboat fuel."

"The Wildroot foursome is on the tee," the intercom belched. "Round up your tribe Chief!"

The time was 8:40 A.M. and the Red Ball People were prepared to commence their round.

Hole 1
A Fresh Look
at Zeno's Paradox

A fter one more threat over the public address system, we made our
way from the practice green to the tee box. By the time we reached
the elevated tee, the group in front of us was well over two hundred
yards away, though still too close to the tee box for us to hit. I could also
see that the foursome consisted of three women and one man.

As our foursome stood on the tee box, Blister spun a tee in the air
and let it fall on the ground where it came to rest pointing toward Wiley.

"You're first," Blister announced, throwing a divot at Wiley that he
plucked from the ground when he leaned down to pick up the tee.

Blister repeated the process two more times until the betting order
had been established. I was in the second slot. Blister followed me while
Jack held the rear. Our usual bet was $.50 per hole in our modified
game of Wolf.

According to the rules of engagement, the first player, in this case
Wiley, hits his drive and then watches the second player's drive. If he
likes the drive, he selects that player as his partner for the hole. If he
doesn't like the second player's drive, he defers his selection until the
third or fourth player hits a better one. If none of the subsequent players
hit a good drive, the first player has the option to call Wolf, indicating he
is doubling the bet and playing solo. The most common version requires a player going solo to win outright. As a safeguard against players
becoming mopey, the Red Ball People version of Wolf allows the player
calling Wolf to tie the other players without losing the bet. Unless the
player with betting honors calls Wolf, he must be paired with another
player and the team with the lowest combined net score wins the bet.

For betting purposes, the net score is determined by the better player giving a bonus stroke to the players with higher handicaps. For example, I am a sixteen handicap and must equalize myself with Wiley by giving him six strokes on the round since he carries a twenty-two handicap. Accordingly, Wiley receives a bonus stroke from me on the six hardest holes on the course. Similarly, I must give Blister, a twenty-four handicapper, a stroke on the eight most difficult holes. Jack will receive ten strokes. After the first hole, the second player in the order goes first. After the second hole, the third player leads off and so on.

Many foursomes also engage in a series of side bets such as sandy pars and birdies. However, since the Red Ball People consider all such feats as shots pulled out of the ass, the tribe decided long ago to lump all such side bets into one category called 'out of the ass.' In our betting scheme, 'out of the ass' shots are accumulated throughout the round and the player with the most 'out of the ass' shots collects a dollar from each player. Even though money was on the line, there was seldom disagreement about when the feat was accomplished since, like a duck, we knew one when we saw one.

Although, we still had a foursome in the fairway in front of us, Wiley had his ball sitting on the tee ready to be launched. The first hole was a 472-yard par 5 with a slight dogleg left, but not enough of a dogleg that you had to shape the drive or the second shot with a draw. The hole was relatively short in length but narrowed significantly near the green with an out of bounds (OB) marker fifteen yards to the right of the green and a dry ditch to the left. While a fairly good player could reach the green on the second shot, many did not try due to the high risk of putting the second shot OB or in the ditch. As usual, the tribe played from the easiest tee box where the course measured 6,201 with a moderate slope of 122.

"I can tell that the women in front of us can't be very good players," Wiley snorted as he waggled his driver over his ball.

"What makes you say that?" Jack asked as he tugged on the back of his shorts to relieve the slow creep his underwear was making between the crack of his buttocks.

"It's obvious," Wiley replied as matter of fact. "Their breasts are far too big to be good players," he chortled instigating a predictable chuckle from all of us.

Wiley was abusing an overly used dictum of the tribe made popular by a rather public gaffe, courtesy of former CBS announcer, Ben Wright. In fact, Ben Wright had become one of our favorite whipping boys, and his name was often invoked for a cheap laugh whenever women were spotted on the golf course.

Ben Wright—A not so Fair and not so Balanced TV Announcer

For some reason, there are a plethora of TV announcers who don't have the same common sense as you and me and say things over the airways that we wouldn't even mutter to our boozed-up friends who are sharing our couch watching Monday Night Football. The most notorious gaffe was probably committed on Monday Night Football by Howard Cosell in 1983 when Washington Redskin receiver Alvin Garrett, an African-American, was streaking for a touchdown. Cosell got caught up in the moment and inexplicably cut his career short by bellowing—"Look at that little monkey run!" to a national TV audience.

A short five years later, Jimmy 'the Greek' Snyder was fired as a CBS analyst when he shared his advanced understanding of anthropology by claiming that black athletes were superior because they were bred by slave owners to be strong. In a meticulously choreographed assessment, Snyder said—"The slave owner would breed his big black with a big black woman so he could have a big black kid. That's where it all started." As it turned out, that's where it all ended. Snyder was sacked a short time later by CBS.

The latest sycophant who proved just how small a human cranium can be, was Rush Limbaugh. Limbaugh was canned by ESPN after getting hyped on illegal painkillers and chiding the sports media for lauding the talent of Philadelphia Eagles quarterback Donovan McNabb, when he said, "The media has been desirous that a black quarterback do well. There is a little hope invested in McNabb and he got a lot of credit for the performance of this team that he didn't deserve. The defense carried this team."

Our favorite lapse in judgement is attributed to former CBS LPGA announcer Ben Wright. During his infamous 1995 interview with Delaware journalist Valerie Helmbreck, Wright presented an exhaustive chronicle of his offensive ideas about the LPGA with one stupid gaffe after another. He began by telling Helmbreck, "Let's face the facts. Lesbians in the sport hurt women's golf." But he didn't stop there. Just to be sure that Helmbreck understood what a homophobe he really is, Wright went on to say, "They're going to a butch game and that furthers the bad image of the game." He was further quoted as saying "homosexuality on the women's tour is not reticent. It's paraded." To prove to Helmbreck that he has equally moronic ideas about other subjects, Wright went on to assert that large mammary glands are the biggest hindrance to a good swing. Ole Ben was just getting warmed up when he told Helmbreck, "Women are handicapped by having boobs. It's not easy for them to keep their left arm straight, and that's one of the tenets of the game. Their boobs get in the way."

After CBS brass got wind of the story, there was a certain boob who was out of a job. Before being fired and losing his influence with the LPGA, Ben Wright had a few other progressive observations about the women's tour and suggested that the LPGA consider a new branding makeover and submitted the logo below for the LPGA Commissioner to review. However, the Commissioner chose to go a different direction with the branding.

Ben Wright's turns his attention from breasts to girth and designs a new logo

While we waited for the fairway to clear, Nick, came on the inter-com and announced for the fourth time that the Wildroot foursome was on the tee, as if we didn't know where we were.

"Second up, Franklin Canyon would like to welcome the singles, Mr. Kim, Mr. Kim, Mr. Kim, and Mr. Kim," Nick continued. Sure enough, we looked at the group coming up to the tee box behind us and spotted the four unrelated Mr. Kims. Since Franklin Canyon is popular with Korean golfers, it was not unusual to have seven or eight Mr. Kims walking around the course at any given time. But having four unrelated Mr. Kims in the same foursome seemed a little too coincidental. We speculated that Nick was adding a little levity to his job by rearranging the singles wait list so that he could put all the Mr. Kims together in the same foursome.

By the time the four Mr. Kims gathered behind us, the fairway had cleared for Wiley. As Wiley assumed his address position over the ball, his mind began to wonder about the probability of four unrelated people with the same last name being assigned to the same foursome. The absurdity began to unnerve him as he started his back swing while Mr. Kim, Mr. Kim, Mr. Kim, and Mr. Kim watched.

At the top of Wiley's back swing, I began to grimace as I could already anticipate the impending result with a high degree of certainty. Predictably, he yanked the ball across the left side of the tee box and it was last seen burrowing into the foliage on the hillside after crossing the fairway of the adjacent hole.

"Mulligans on the first two holes, right? Wiley said, half asking half advising.

"And holes three and four if necessary," Blister corrected.

After Wiley knocked his second ball two hundred and thirty yards down the right side of the fairway, I took my turn. I pulled my out a Titleist NXT from my right pocket and placed it on a tee. As always, the ball was colored with my distinct trademark of red ink covering the last five letters of the manufacturer's name. As I stepped back to take a practice swing I glanced at all the Mr. Kims lined up to watch me hit. They appeared to be standing in the order of their age with the young-est Mr. Kim, estimated to be thirty, on the left and the oldest Mr. Kim, who I guessed was about seventy five, on the right.

The two older Mr. Kims wore sailor caps pulled down over their ears that looked like lampshades sitting on their heads. As I scanned down the line of Mr. Kims, it struck me that the older they were the higher their pants were pulled up. The second oldest Mr. Kim, who seemed to be around sixty, had his pants pulled up to his rib cage, while the oldest Mr. Kim fastened his trousers nearly to his chest. Seventy-five year old Mr. Kim was wearing suspenders, which possibly had shrunk over the years, perhaps explaining why his pants were pulled so high up his trunk.

All the Mr. Kims had pull carts, though the eldest Mr. Kim's cart was battery operated and moved under its own power, guided by a remote control that Mr. Kim carried in a holster clipped to his suspenders. The eldest Mr. Kim had a long bar with a hoop at the end protruding from his bag where a driver would normally be stored. I recognized the bar as a tool for extracting balls from ponds and hillsides where the terrain was difficult to traverse. Upon spotting the ball-retrieving bar, I realized that I had played nine holes with him several months earlier. I also recalled that the ball extractor was the favorite piece of equipment in Mr. Kim's bag. On at least half the holes he would disappear from the fairway for five minutes only to reappear from behind a thicket with four or five balls in one hand and the ball retriever in the other.

As I stepped up to address the ball my focus became unsettled. I began imagining myself at the age of the eldest Mr. Kim, with my pants pulled up below my armpits. As I rocked the driver back and forth waggling the club before I started my back swing, I wondered if wearing my pants that high would impede my swing like large breasts impair a woman's swing. The idea crossed my mind that I could easily experiment right now. I could always declare that I was conducting a scientific experiment and take a mulligan if the shot was unsuccessful. However, I was wearing shorts today and if I followed through with the experiment I would probably look a great deal like Friedrich von Trapp, the twelve year old singer in the Sound of Music.

I tried to regain focus. I surveyed the fairway trying to choose my target. I hesitated momentarily when I saw how pretty the surrounding hills were. The passing clouds created different shades of green on the clustered oak trees, and though these hills were only a few hundred feet high, I started to imagine the hills being alive with the sound of music.

I could almost hear little Liesl, Kurt, Friedrich, Maria, and Louisa, bounding down the hillside followed by Julie Andrews and Captain von Trapp.

"Got to clear my head," I thought to myself. I was beginning to have a significant attention disorder standing over the ball.

"Doe a deer a female deer, ray a drop of golden sun," I hummed under my breath. Oh, I forgot the next verse. What comes after that damn drop of golden sun? My mind began racing trying to remember the next line.

"Focus, focus, focus," I chanted to myself trying to force my attention back to the matter at hand. I was beginning to experience a derailment and I hadn't even struck the first ball yet. How long had I been standing over the ball? Were the others beginning to notice? Oh that Mr. Kim really knew how to lay on the gamesmanship. He thinks that he can just show up at the golf course with the von Trapp family singers wearing his pants under his armpits and think no one will notice.

"Hey Chief, you want to let Mr. Kim, Mr. Kim, Mr. Kim, and Mr. Kim play through?" Blister finally interrupted. "What are you doing up there? Normally you don't back up the course until the third or fourth hole."

"You don't mind if I hit while you talk do you?" I shot back at Blister.

"It ain't rocket surgery, Chief. Just hit the ball will you?" Jack ordered.

After spending another moment to regain my composure, I finally swung at the ball and could immediately tell by the vibration in the handle that I hit it off the toe of the club. I looked up to see the ball darting toward the right side of the fairway toward an oak tree two hundred yards away.

"Goo shot!" shouted elder Mr. Kim prematurely. Evidently he had remembered me from the nine hole round. It was coming back to me now. Mr. Kim was one of those quirky players who never got upset with his poor shots and always shouted 'good shot,' or in his case 'goo shot,' to any player who got the ball off the tee regardless of where the ball was headed.

I thanked Mr. Kim for the encouragement as the ball clanked off a branch near the top of the oak tree and fell to the ground between two protruding roots. I had just received my first lucky break of the round. Had the ball missed the tree it would have sailed out of bounds into the hills, possibly killing one of the von Trapp children. Evidently, Wiley was not impressed enough to choose me for his betting partner for the hole.

Blister teed up his ball next and took no practice swing. He hardly had positioned his feet when he began his swing. And what a swing it was.

He missed the ball entirely.

"Next one has a passenger!" Jack giggled.

Wiley and I were doubled up but didn't offer any advice since we concluded that Jack had sufficiently covered the matter.

On his second swing, Blister drilled the ball two hundred and forty yards down the middle. If you had missed his first swing you would almost think that Blister was a good player. It was certainly good enough for Wiley, who chose Blister as his partner. Wiley did not even bother to ask if Blister should be penalized for missing the ball. The Red Ball People always treat a missed ball as a practice swing and as far as we were concerned, Blister was lying one in the middle of the fairway.

After dribbling his drive to the ladies tee box, Jack hit a mulligan ten yards beyond the oak tree that had graciously stopped my ball. Jack was my partner by default and Wiley understood that Jack was also lying one since Wiley had also hit a mulligan. As Jack turned, I extended my arm and he extended his, allowing our knuckles to scrape and cement a one-hole business relationship to win $.50 from Wiley and Blister.

Since Jack and Wiley took mulligans, they effectively were playing a wrong ball. Under USGA rules they should be assessed a two-stroke penalty. However, because no one challenged the mulligans, we were collectively coalescing in a conspiracy to not play by the USGA rules of golf. While this is true, a little clarification is in order for how the Red Ball People interpret USGA rules.

Rule 1-3 claims that it is illegal for our foursome to agree to exclude any rule or waive any penalty, which we all did as soon as Wiley took a mully. To address this issue, the Red Ball People find it necessary from time to time to add amendments to the USGA rules, including Rule 1-3. Red Ball People Amendment 1-3 appears below and will be in effect for the round.

Rule 1-3—Ignoring rules or waiving penalties: *Players shall not agree to exclude the operation of any rule or to waive any penalty incurred. Penalty for excluding the operation of any rule or waiving penalties shall be the disqualification of all concerned.*

Red Ball People Amendment to Rule 1-3: *Red Ball People may alter any rule they want at any time in any way they see fit. Red Ball People may also waive penalty if it suits their fancy.*

Reason for Change: *A non-tournament amateur round has never been played without a rule being broken. Any sanctimonious snoot who thinks he is playing by the rules is advised that he is breaking USGA Rule 1-3 if he follows the rules himself but coalesces in silence as others who he is playing with break them. It would be pretentious for the Red Ball People to try to be the first ones to comply with USGA Rule 1-3. So long as rules will be broken it is more civilized to reach agreement on which ones you don't like and alter them accordingly. As far as the USGA Rules Committee declaring us disqualified, Red Ball People respond by asking, "Rules Committee and what army?"*

Since Franklin Canyon had recently instituted a cart-path only policy, I had obtained my blue flag and stuck the pole in my bag that was strapped to the back of my cart. The Red Ball People were already outnumbered by the Blue Flag People, as four blue flags flapped in the breeze from the carts lined up behind us for a nine o'clock tournament. The tribe members held a summit to decide who would receive the coveted seat next to me in the cart with the blue flag. The summit was settled when all three players pulled out a coin and flipped to see who had the odd coin. Wiley's coin came up tails and he let out a cheer when he saw heads on the other two coins.

"Criminy," Jack complained, "I've gotta ride with Blister again?"

"What's so bad about riding with me?" Blister protested.

"For one thing—you never fail to interrupt my pre-shot routine by asking incessantly stupid questions," Jack responded. "In case you need any help with current events I dumped two balls into the pond on the ninth hole last week because you couldn't shut up talking about light sweet crude oil."

"But Jack, you always dump a ball into the pond on the ninth," Wiley pointed out.

"Light sweet crude?" I asked a little puzzled. "That's an odd topic to be discussing on the golf course."

"Tell me about it," Jack scoffed. "Believe me—it was a one-way conversation. Here I am trying to concentrate on knocking a 3-iron over the water and all this nitwit cares about is light sweet crude oil. Next thing I know, I got Chatty Cathy next to me asking—How do they know it's sweet? Do you know anybody's who's ever tasted it?"

Jack's story drew a laugh from Wiley and me. Blister's random and unpredictable train of thought was legendary with the Red Ball People. Most of his thoughts were as fleeting as a leaf that lands on the hood of a moving car.

"Well—have you ever tasted it?" Blister demanded of Jack.

"In fact I haven't," Jack snapped.

"Well why do you think they call it light sweet crude when nobody tastes it?" Blister asked trying to get to the crux of the mystery.

"I guess to keep simple folks occupied," Jack quipped, ending the discussion for the time being.

Jack marched to his cart as Blister trailed behind pressing him to reopen the investigation on the mystery of light sweet crude oil. As master of the coin flip, Wiley was entitled to strap his bag on the cart of the potentate and we set out for the two hundred yard journey to the oak tree where my ball rested.

"What the hell were you doing on the tee box, Chief?" Wiley inquired as we pulled up to my ball.

I gave Wiley the condensed version as I pulled out my 3-iron. "I got distracted thinking about how high Mr. Kim was wearing his pants. I then somehow bridged over to thinking about the von Trapp family and got one of their tunes stuck in my head. I was still thinking about the next verse when Jack threw me the life line."

"I've been there," Wiley volunteered. "Don't tell me the song you were singing, cause I don't want it stuck in my head for the rest of the round."

My 3-iron sounded like flint striking a piece of granite as I caught the middle of the ball with the leading edge of the club. The ball never got more than five feet off the ground but somehow managed to roll to within ninety-five yards of the hole.

Jack and Blister both hit frozen ropes into the hillside to the right of their targets. Blister's ball careened off a boulder and ricocheted back into the fairway. Jack's ball crossed over a white stake, out of bounds. Without further consideration, Jack walked back to his cart with Blister, drove up the fairway one hundred and thirty yards to where his ball crossed the white stake, and took an illegal drop by the cart path.

"Looks like Jack's using Zeno's paradox to his advantage as Blister predicted," I observed.

"Zeno's paradox?" Wiley asked with a confused look on his face.

"You didn't get the email from Blister last week predicting how Jack would use Zeno's paradox to his advantage?" I asked.

"Frankly Chief—I hit the delete key on any email coming in from Blister unless I know he's attacking me and I have to set a backfire," Wiley admitted.

To help Wiley better understand how flagrant Jack's illegal drop was, I recounted Blister's email on his convincing assessment of how Jack had stumbled on a practical application of Zeno's paradox and had since become a devotee of the Greek philosopher.

Zeno's Paradox—Does Jack Really Take Illegal Drops?

Around 425 BC Zeno lost his job as an usher at the Parthenon in Athens, Greece. Since he had a little time on his hands before his unemployment ran out, he embarked on contriving paradoxes to amuse himself and pass the time. As one of the earliest advocates of medicinal uses of marijuana, Zeno always got his grandest ideas for his paradoxes after smoking a fatty. One day after a few massive tokes, Zeno stared at his hand for about ten minutes and resolved that motion was impossible.

Anxious to share his discovery, Zeno coaxed Parmenides, the other notable Greek Philosopher of the time, to smoke a fatty with him and hear Zeno's ideas about the impossibility of motion. The two philosophers giggled into the night and jotted down a few ideas that they eventually constructed into sentences when they sobered up. Although the ideas seemed a lot more clever when they were both stoned, the arguments would later form the basis for two of the best sellers of the day.

Needing the right sales angle for his workshop on motion, Parmenides challenged Zeno to dream up a few paradoxes to support their argument against the possibility of motion. Zeno cheerfully accepted the challenge and set out to construct a mathematical proof that a person can never get to where they are going, though the two philosophers seemed to have no trouble making it to the marijuana patch.

His first paradox involved an arrow and a target. According to Zeno, the arrow can never reach its target because it must first reach the halfway point. But before the arrow can reach the halfway point, it must first reach the halfway point to the halfway point. I suppose you can see where this is going. These half-distances are infinite in number and it is impossible to traverse distances infinite in number. Consequently, according to Zeno, motion is impossible. To make the argument more interesting and fill up a few more pages in his book, he proposed a similar paradox of why the one hundred meter record holder of the day, Achilles, could never overtake a tortoise.

Over the next few years the two philosophers exchanged their wit back and forth through letters and it became customary for them to end with a salutation of LOL, an acronym for Laugh Out Loud that became popular with AOL email users 2,500 years later. Sadly, Zeno died unexpectedly at the early age of thirty when an archer who read his book fired an arrow at Zeno thinking it would never reach its target. Which brings us back to Jack's drop.

Like Zeno, as Blister correctly had prophesized, Jack evidently believed that it is quite impossible for a ball to reach an OB marker. According to USGA rules, Jack should have dropped a second ball on the very spot where he made contact with the ball he drove out of bounds. Instead he gained nearly one hundred and thirty yards in distance by treating the ball as if it entered a lateral hazard.

Had Zeno been officiating, he surely would have concluded that it was impossible for Jack to hit a ball out of bounds since Zeno had already established that the ball, like an arrow, can never reach its target. Accordingly, the out of bounds rule can never come into play so long as we accept Zeno's interpretation. Under Zeno's ruling, Jack should have invoked the lost ball rule, which specifies that Jack should have dropped his second ball at the same spot where he last hit his first ball, an identical consequence to the out of bounds rule. However, by dropping his second ball near the white OB marker, Jack chose not to employ either the OB rule or the lost ball rule. Instead, he treated himself to the lateral hazard rule and gained an undeserved one 130 additional yards in doing so.

Blister only advanced his third shot fifteen yards when he caught the ball with the toe of his club and it kicked off the wheel of his cart.

For his second shot Wiley hit a solid 5-iron that came to rest ten yards behind my ball near the one hundred yard marker. The prospect for Jack and me to win the bet were still even since Wiley and I were both lying two and Jack and Blister were both lying three. Jack settled the suspense on his fourth shot when he caught the wrong side of a tree and his ball burrowed into a blackberry bush on the hillside.

Blister topped his sand wedge but the thick grass in front of the green quickly slowed the ball and it came to rest on the front of the green. Wiley followed Blister's poor but fortuitous shot with an excellent gap wedge that stuck near the flag but then spun back, stopping within a few inches of Blister's ball. After another penalty stroke, Jack's sixth stroke placed him on the green twenty feet above the flag.

My first real adversity of the round came when I walked up to my ball resting ninety yards from the hole and discovered that it was lying on top of a Manhattan divot. For the uninitiated, striking a ball resting in the middle of a Manhattan divot takes extraordinary talent, a characteristic where I am admittedly deficient. To appreciate the difficulty of my task, a discussion of divots is in order.

Knowing Your Divots

When you were in college, hitting a fatty was something to look forward to, since it meant you were about to get high on your roommate's dope. However, hitting a fatty on the golf course, evokes emotions of depression. Since high handicappers are destined to hit more fatties than good golfers, they will also be more creative at producing the type of divots that subsequent golfers will walk by, gawk at, and recognize as the sole remaining evidence that someone really took a big number on a hole.

Most books on the subject of golf do not give nearly enough attention to this deserving subject. However, the divot provides an historical peek into how one of our predecessors ruined his score on a hole and also provides some likelihood of how bad a player he really is.

The Mohawk: The Mohawk divot is two inches wide, one inch deep, and eight inches long, and can perfectly sit on top the head of a bald Indian without catching anyone's attention. The divot appears to have been cut with a two-inch wide garden hoe and trimmed on all four sides with a rose bush clipper. Mohawk's are almost always aligned at the target and often occur in wet grass. Even low handicappers are capable of crafting a Mohawk now and then. We can be pretty sure that owing to the size of the majestic headpiece, that the ball only traveled a few feet, though more importantly, it was headed for the target. Consequently, the Mohawk is more associated with a bogey than a double or triple.

The Manhattan: The Manhattan is a large divot with a shape that evades geometric description. Owing to the unusual shape of the divot, the golfer always has trouble replacing the divot and appears to be completing a crossword puzzle as he attempts to rotate the divot around the hole looking for the perfect fit. Because the divot is rarely placed back in the hole the way it came out, the divot appears as a little island in the fairway. A golfer who produces a Manhattan has a swing, which is more useful in killing a gopher than in propelling a golf ball. When you spot a Manhattan you can be assured that it was not only a bad swing but also a bad golfer. A Manhattan is usually representative of someone who took a triple-bogey.

The Enterprise: The Enterprise is a divot that resembles a miniature version of a carrier deck. It is shallower than a Manhattan and would lay almost perfectly on top a 1/20-scale version of the USS Enterprise. It is an impressive piece of work since to produce an Enterprise divot, a golfer must change his swing path three inches behind the point of impact, a difficult task when the club head is moving at one hundred MPH. The Enterprise is usually produced by a golfer who has just taken a lesson and is experimenting with new swing thoughts. It's likely that the golfer kept experimenting during the remainder of the hole on the way to a triple-bogey.

The Flank: The Flank is an oblique divot that cuts across the ball from outside in and can only be created by an over-the-top swing. The Flank is almost always created after the ball has already been struck and pulled forty-five degrees into a pine tree or a hazard. The golfer, who is capable of producing a Flank, is rarely capable of hitting the ball straight. Consequently, when you spot a Flank on the course, you can be pretty certain that the golfer piled up some impressive numbers.

The Baskin-Robbins: The Baskin-Robbins is carved out with the toe of the club and looks like the ground was excavated with an ice-cream scooper. The Baskin-Robbins is the worst divot for your ball to come to rest in since the centerline of the ball will be well below the level of the ground. The divot can only be created when the shaft angle of the club is elevated thirty degrees from its normal address position or when the club face is nearly closed at impact. In either case, the divot maker only propelled the ball a few feet in front of the divot and may have had a decent score on the hole unless the golfer went for a double-decker, in which case you will find a second scoop in front of the first.

After seeing the distraught look on my face, Wiley came over to take a closer look at my ball. "Whoa, that's one of the finest Manhattan's I've seen in awhile. You may want to putt it."

"I'm ninety yards from the hole!" I argued. "Have you ever seen a pro putt from ninety yards out?"

"Why not?" Wiley countered. "Pros putt from fifty yards out all the time at the British Open. Besides pros don't have to contend with Manhattan divots."

Wiley had a couple of good points. My best expectation with a wedge was to hit a fattie sixty yards. More likely, I would become overwhelmed with tension and blade the ball twenty yards over the green. I accepted the advice and lined up my ninety yard putt.

Surprisingly, the ball came to rest a foot off the front of the green. Since the flag was in the front position of the green, I knew I could easily three-putt for my bogey, which I did a few minutes later.

Neither Wiley nor Blister had marked their balls. There were usually two reasons for this. If a player marked the ball and then attempted to look at the line from the opposite side of the flag, the marker was often too difficult to see. Secondly, most Red Ball People forgot to put a marker in their pocket until the third or fourth hole. Wiley was no exception. He dug around in both front pockets, spilling tees on the ground as he tried to locate a ball marker.

Giving up on his search, he soon leaned down, wiped some dirt off the ball and lined up the logo for putting. Of course, this maneuver was illegal according to the USGA and any player who does so shall be assessed a two-stroke penalty. Consequently, the Red Ball People amended the rule to prevent members from having to run back to their bag and look for a marker any time they wanted to rotate their ball on the green.

Rule 18-21/33–Rotating ball on green without marking ball: *A ball must be marked with a marker or coin before it can be touched, cleaned, or rotated.*

Red Ball People Amendment to Rule 18-21/33: *A ball resting on the green may be picked up, cleaned, petted, kissed, hugged, or rotated, without the use of a marker. The player may return the ball to the original spot or close vicinity without penalty.*

Reason for change: *About half of amateur players forget to bring a ball marker with them on the first hole. Most are too lazy to run back to the cart and retrieve one and end up asking me if I have an extra. Because I only play one ball on any given hole, I only carry one* *marker. As a substitute, I generally lend them a coin, often a quarter. Whether intentional or not, rarely does the other player remember to give me my quarter back when they are done putting. The last thing I'm going to do is be a stickler for rules if it costs me money.*

 Wiley and Blister both hit their first putts three and four feet from the hole respectively. As Jack lined up his putt I spun to look down the fairway and see what effect our slow play was having. I spotted three Mr. Kims waiting patiently for us to clear the green but did not see the eldest Mr. Kim. I continued scanning the fairway until movement in the corner of my eye drew my attention to the hillside where Jack hit his second shot. His errant shot had not escaped the attention of the eldest Mr. Kim who was using his spare time to quarry Jack's lost ball.

Even if Jack two-putted from twenty feet above the hole, we would lose the bet since our combined score of 14 was still three strokes higher than our opponents' score of eleven. Jack removed any doubt when he knocked his twenty foot putt five feet into the fairway. Fortunately for Jack, the abacus of the Red Ball People only has eight beads and Jack was allowed to pick up his ball for a score of eight. My lower score entitled me to assume the role of CFO on Jack's and my one-hole business relationship. My first ceremonial role was to concede the two putts to Blister and Wiley followed by a motion to dissolve my business relationship with Jack.

Hole 2
When Two Wrongs
Make a Right

L ike most courses, a round at Franklin Canyon takes about five hours on Saturdays. The worst backups occur at the par 3 holes. As expected, the foursome in front of us was still in the process of encircling the par 3 green as we arrived at the tee box. As we had a little time, the conversation shifted to a brochure promoting a new business model that Wiley had conjured up earlier in the week.

As a staunch Republican, Wiley was usually good for two or three rants a week about how the Democratic leadership in California was turning the state into a Marxist encampment. Most of these rants were delivered via email and usually drew the ire of Jack who conversely viewed the Republican Executive Branch as the new Roman Empire. Wiley's most recent rant was sparked by an investigative reporter who revealed that Democratic Senator Barbara Boxer had done a little horse trading with Bill Clinton several years earlier and managed to squeeze a rider into a bill that allowed for the reconstitution of the Miwok Indian tribe that had formerly disbanded in 1958. The upshot was—the reconstituted tribe could qualify as an independent nation and erect an Indian Casino.

Evidently the arrangement worked well for everyone except Wiley. Barbara Boxer's reelection committee was flooded with donations from the Miwoks. The Senator's wayward son, Doug Boxer, got a job with the Miwoks. And the farmer who sold his pristine land in the heart of California's Sonoma wine country to the Nevada Casino that represented the Miwoks, made millions.

Wiley was outraged until we convinced him that maybe the Red Ball People could help him turn his lemons into lemonade. After a few quick email exchanges, we helped Wiley author a brochure for a new business model whose success depended on just a little assistance from Senator Boxer. Once Wiley was satisfied that he had covered all the key sales angles, he distributed the brochure to the expanded membership of the Red Ball People to seek their participation in the venture. His brochure appears below.

New Business Model Brochure—Indian Gaming

Do you want to get rich quick and be the big cheese around your neighborhood? Well, the Red Ball People have a business model that may be right for you. Its called Indian Gaming. To participate in Indian Gaming all you need is 1/64th of your ancestral lineage to be Indian. Asian Indian doesn't count, though you may have an excellent career in offshore programming.

Here's how it works. We round up enough family and acquaintances that have 1/64th Indian in them until we have enough to form a tribe, let's say maybe ten. We register for tribal status and contact Station Casinos Inc. of Las Vegas, who just so happens to be funding the Sonoma wine country casino for the newly re-constituted Miwoks. We tap them to put up the money. They build the casino and run it, while we sit on our asses and collect 49% of the revenue. Simple as that.

I know you have some tough questions. I've anticipated them and have them answered below.

Don't we have to already be a tribe? *Nope. The Miwok's disbanded in 1958 and reconstituted themselves in 2002.*

Do I have to quit drinking? *Nope. That's an old Indian stereotype. Since most of us are more Irish than Indian, drinking comes natural. Besides, we're not in management and don't have to work.*

Aren't there federal and state regulations that make this difficult to do? *Not anymore. Senator Barbara Boxer is a friend of the*

41

Indian and personally restored the Miwoks to tribal status so I don't see why she would discriminate against us. In fact, we can probably get some good legal advice from her son Doug Boxer, an attorney who works for the Miwok tribe.

Where do we build our casino? *Stupid question, but here comes the obvious answer. We put it where a lot of people with money go. Since we don't want to compete with the Miwok's we will put it in Napa Valley, Yosemite, or on the beach at Malibu.*

How do we make revenue during start-up? *Well that's actually Station Casino Inc.'s problem, but their plan is to send a limousine each morning to pick up William Bennett. The revenue from him should carry us for twelve to eighteen months until we detour a few Reno-bound buses.*

How about the environmental impact report for traffic, sewage, erosion, and wildlife displacement? *Keah, Keah, Keah. That crap is for people who live in the US. We have our own nation.*

Do I have to put feathers on my head, take my shirt off, and chant WOO-woo-woo-woo, WOO-woo-woo-woo? *Only if you apply for the job as tribal spokesman. Otherwise, you can continue wearing shorts, flip-flops, and your Budweiser T-shirt.*

Do we need a war council? *Not so long as Bush is president. We just need to join the 'Coalition of the Willing' where we can be counted as one of the 64 supporting nations. He will do the rest.*

Don't we have to own tribal land to build the casino? *Nope. We just need to find a 2,000-acre ranch for sale like the Miwoks. Senator Barbara Boxer will arrange to have it rezoned as a sovereign nation and Station Casino Inc. will cough up the $24,000,000 to buy it.*

What if opponents in the surrounding US Territory claim the casino may draw 50,000 cars a day? *Is that supposed to be bad news? If the US roads can't handle the traffic then I guess they'll have to build some bigger ones.*

Can I be a chief? *Why not? It's mostly ceremonial, but your buddies can start calling you "The Chief" immediately. That last thing we need to worry about is too many chiefs and not enough Indians.*

Can I choose an Indian name? *Of course. Chief Squatting Dog is taken, so you'll have to choose another one.*

Are there any other advantages I should know about? *The benefits are almost endless but my personal favorite is being excused from paying any taxes. Deron Marquez, chairman of the San Manuel Band of Mission Indians, heads a firm that pays no state and local taxes on profits or property. Chief Deron had another windfall when former California Governor Gray Davis discovered a suitcase full of money on his front door and signed a law in 1999 excluding Indians who live on casino reservations from paying vehicle license fees. The Chief went out and got himself a $96,000 Mercedes 500 SL. Quite an improvement from that spotted stallion he used to ride! You can do the same!*

What will be our tribe name? *The nominations include: LukOutForDaHole, DontStepIn- DaChit, and WhereDaFukAreWe. The consensus seems to be with WhereDaFukAreWe.*

Senator Barbara Boxer— friend of the Indian

We lauded Wiley for constructing such a sound business model and promised to give it serious consideration. Each of us were pretty sure that either we or our wives had the necessary 1/64 Indian heritage and were excited about the prospect of cruising around our own 2,000 acre nation in a Mercedes 500 SL.

Because I had experience as a banking business consultant, it was a unanimous decision to make me the Big Bidness Chief. Since Jack had a legal background, he was Chief of Treaties and would seek to put together a nuclear non-proliferation treaty with the U.S. in exchange for a little foreign aid. Wiley insisted on being the War Chief since he was pretty sure that entitled him to smoke a pipe every time the tribe voted to avoid a war with the U.S. The role of Chief of Staff went to Blister since our business model did not specify a need for a staff and he would not be required to do anything.

In the five minutes it took us to add a little more cohesion to Wiley's business model and construct our tribal council for the newly constituted WhereDaFukAreWe tribe, the green had cleared on the second hole.

Hole 2 is an uphill 145-yard par 3. The hole is twenty feet above the tee box and players are never aware of how close a ball is to the pin until they walk up the hill and over the edge of the green. Guarding the front of the green are two sand traps on either side. The green is one of the two most difficult greens to putt owing to the steep slope from back to front. Owing to the tricky green, the hole is rated as the fifth most difficult and the other three players got strokes.

The green, as well as the tee box for the third hole, are at the end of a U-shaped canyon and are at the highest elevation and provide the best views of the golf course. A thick forest of pine and oak trees surround the green beyond the cart path that circles the hole. If a player pushes an errant shot slightly to the right of the hole, there is a high probability that the ball will strike the cart path and bounce across the white out of bounds stakes into the forest. To the left of the green the hill falls away toward the cart path that separates the second green from the third hole tee box. A player who finds himself on the left can rarely save par unless he has a Phil Mickelson flop shot in his holster.

According to the betting rotation, it was my turn to hit first. Although the hole was twenty feet above the tee box, the slight breeze at our back negated the extra elevation and I retrieved an 8-iron to play the hole. As I pushed my tee in the ground I turned and spotted the four Mr. Kims who were now congregating twenty feet behind us. The elder Mr. Kim was grinning at me and seemed pleased that he would be able to watch me hit. I nodded to Mr. Kim and positioned myself over the ball concentrating on my alignment. Just as he had done on the first hole, Mr. Kim again ignited the soundtrack to the Sound of Music. Without any warning, the verse that had stumped me on the first tee box suddenly came flooding in.

"Me—a name, I call myself."

"Far—a long long way to run."

The next two verses quickly followed in succession.

"Sew—a needle pulling thread,"

"La, a note to follow Sew."

I was stumped again. The ball in front of me may as well have been Rogers and Hammerstein sheet music.

Wiley quickly recognized the pattern and interceded, "You gonna hit the ball or finish Do-Re-Mi?" he wanted to know, correctly guessing the tune trapped in my head.

"If Mr. Kim doesn't loosen his suspenders I'm gonna be thinking about the von Trapp family for the rest of the round," I whispered back.

I refocused and swung before I could think about any more lyrics. I came over the top of the ball and pulled it left. As I watched it sail toward the trap on the left side of the green, a sense of gloom settled in. If the ball hit the trap I would have a very difficult sand shot over a high lip. If the ball missed the trap, it would surely roll away from the green through a trough toward the next tee box where I would have to execute a downhill chip to an uphill hole. Neither prerogative was appealing.

Evidently, there was a third possibility that I did not consider. The ball struck the side of a flat sprinkler head slightly beyond the trap and took a right turn toward the hole. Since the hole was twenty five feet above us, we could not see where the ball came to rest but I was relieved in knowing that the result was far better than I expected.

"Goo shot!" the elder Mr. Kim shouted.

"Yeah, that was a dandy, Mr. Kim," Jack added turning toward Mr. Kim to acknowledge his good sportsmanship. Jack turned back to me contorting his face as he spun around. For a moment his face was frozen with the left side of his lip raised and buckled under his nose and his eye lids raised as high as their muscles would lift. I recognized the look as Jack's signature clown face he liked to make when he had unconditional disdain for someone's opinion.

Blister pulled his ball nearly on the same line as mine but it came up short in the trap on the left side of the green. Jack followed with a skulled 8-iron that struck the elevated fairway twenty yards short of the green but the ball had so much speed and side spin that it arched up toward the edge of the green on the right side. Normally Jack's ball would be good enough for me to select him as my Wolf partner but I passed on him since he almost always three putted or four putted this very tough green.

"Things are awfully quiet on the Western Front," Jack said, apparently as a reference to the slight he was feeling for not being selected as my partner.

"Jack, if you ever two-putt this hole I'd saddle you up. But you'll just break my heart with another four-putt like you always do," I responded.

Wiley hit last, and fortunately for my betting strategy, he hit a solid 7-iron toward the middle of the hole, though it looked to be a little deep.

"Goo shot, Goo shot!" the two older Mr. Kims trumpeted.

"Great shot, great shot!" the second generation Mr. Kims added.

At this moment, I began to sense that if all the Mr. Kims concurred on a shot, it was truly an excellent shot. Trusting the Kim consortium, I selected Wiley as my betting partner.

I was delighted to find that my ball had been redirected by the sprinkler to within 10 feet of the hole on the downhill side. As we suspected, Wiley's ball was long. I immediately regretted not calling Wolf since he had a difficult twenty-five foot downhiller that would require the kind of skill that Wiley rarely mustered. I was in the precarious position of actually yearning for him to two-putt since it would increase my net worth by $.50.

Blister slapped his ball out of the sand trap with an effort that Mr. Kim would have described as a 'goo shot' and Curtis Strange would have described as a blundering mishap. The ball came to rest in deep rough four feet off the green on the adjacent side of the pin. After raking the trap, Blister trudged to his ball with his shoulders lowered as if he were capable of hitting a better soft floater.

"You're still up," Jack announced.

Although most amateur players prefer any spot on a course to a sand trap, Blister actually had a much more difficult shot now than he did before. Without giving the attention that the shot required, Blister chopped at the ball with his wedge, popping it half way to the hole. However, the slope of the green required the shot to hit a fourth of the way to the hole. The ball raced by the hole, caught the downhill break and sped off toward Jack's ball. When it was evident that the ball would roll all the way to the front of the green, Wiley cleared his throat and added a Don McLean musical score to accompany the ball on its journey.

"And we were singing,"

"Bye, Bye, Miss American Pie."

Jack and I joined the chorus, recognizing our tribal duty to formally sanctify a run-away putt by singing 'American Pie' until the ball quit rolling. The longer the onlookers were able to sing, the worse the putt was.

We continued until the ball came to a stop.

> *"Drove my Chevy to the levy,*
> *But the levy was dry.*
> *Them good ole boys drinking whisky and rye,*
> *Singing this will be the day that I die."*

Blister's shoulders hung even lower as he walked down the green toward Jack's ball. Proving that gravity can work to your disadvantage in either direction, he left his come back putt twenty feet short. He followed his ball up the hill while it was still rolling and took a side-arm polo swing at it just as it quit rolling. The polo shot came up eight feet short. Blister conceded the three-footer to himself for a 'Linda Tripp'— tribal slang for a triple bogey, introduced into the tribe's vernacular when Jack observed that Monica Lewinsky's back-stabbing friend is both ugly and a 'trip', two common characteristics of a triple bogey.

While Wiley continued to look over the landscape, Jack two-putted for a par. Believing that he had a direction problem instead of a distance problem, Wiley tapped his twenty-five footer only twelve feet. He slapped his open palm against his forehead and bit his lip as he followed his ball down the hill.

As Wiley stood over his ball to address his second putt, I spotted the alignment of his feet. His feet were pointed much too far to the right of the apex. I debated whether to alert him but my desire to have a better score got the best of me and I kept my mouth shut. I was fiendishly delighted as I watched him introduce an even bigger problem with his backstroke. He took his putter too far on the backstroke for what the downhill putt required. He must have realized the error as he decelerated on his forward stroke causing the putter face to close at impact. The ball now was on a line well below the apex and moving with far too much speed.

"Uh -oh! Somebody stick their foot out!" Wiley barked as the ball shot down the hill.

47

Jack cleared his throat in preparation for resuscitating Don McLean's American Pie. But to our amazement, the rapid speed of Wiley's putt counterbalanced the break of the green and the ball raced toward the hole on nearly a straight line, gaining speed as it rolled. It shot across the hole catching the back of the cup. The angle at which the ball hit the back of the cup popped the ball two inches into the air and it fell back into the hole for a par. Wiley lifted his arms in triumph.

"Great putt Faxon!" Jack bellowed, sarcastically referring to Brad Faxon, the best putter on the PGA tour.

Wiley had just demonstrated the rare occurrence of the phenomenon that two wrongs can make a right.

Putting: When Two Wrongs Make a Right

Most high handicappers wonder why they have a total of thirty putts one round and forty putts the next. After the thirty putt round, they are often heard talking about how they finally have their flat stick working, only to three-putt six greens the following Saturday. After spending $300 on a Scotty Cameron putter to fix the problem, they usually return to have another dismal forty-putt round. Golf instructor manuals seldom give this phenomenon the attention it deserves since these books are written by pros who only work with the most gifted golfers. However, since I play with laggards on a regular basis I can easily explain the phenomenon.

Most people mistakenly believe that a low number of putts during a round can only be achieved by correctly performing the four basic mechanics—1) reading the green, 2) alignment, 3) speed, and 4) execution. However, as high handicappers prove every ten rounds, a low number of putts can also be achieved during a round by *incorrectly* performing these four mechanics in such a way that two wrongs actually do make a right.

In the diagram below, a low handicapper on the left side of the diagram correctly reads a downhill putt, which breaks to the left. The skilled player understands that the speed applied to the ball should be considerably slower than if the ball were on a flat surface. He further

WHO WERE THE RED BALL PEOPLE?

understands that the slope of the green at the apex of the curve on the path line will carry the ball down hill to the hole for the remainder of the distance. Knowing the path and the speed, all the player has to do to sink the twelve footer is align his putter on the correct alignment line and execute his swing on the same line.

The high handicapper might do the same thing if he were either capable or lucky, but usually he is only the latter and at least one or more of his mechanics are woefully faulty. However, if the right combination of mechanics are correctly done incorrectly (yes, I meant that) then the high handicapper is rewarded by draining a downhill breaker because one poorly performed component counteracts another poorly performed component. You can think of it as a zero-sum game in which two wrongs makes a right.

To see how this works, review the right side of the diagram below. The high handicapper has the same putt as the low handicapper on the left. The high handicapper has his first miscue when he misreads the green believing it breaks from right to left instead of left to right. The high handicapper neutralizes this error by aligning himself on a target line far to the right of the hole and the line he read incorrectly. He judges the putt to be on a relatively flat surface, when in fact the hole is twelve feet away, yet four feet below his shoes. Consequently, his speed will only be correct if he stubs the toe of his putter prior to striking the ball.

In one spastic motion our high handicapper closes the face of his putter with an overbearing left arm and yanks the ball left of where he is aimed with far too much speed. Because the pull to the left works in unison with the high velocity speed to counteract the poor alignment that neutralized the faulty read, the ball motors to the left of the apex minimizing the break created by the slope of the green. Although the ball passes over the hole at 12 MPH, it catches the back of the cup and falls in, yielding the same result as the low handicapper who performed all components properly.

———————

Indeed, Wiley's putting acumen on the second hole to save par proved that two wrongs can make a right.

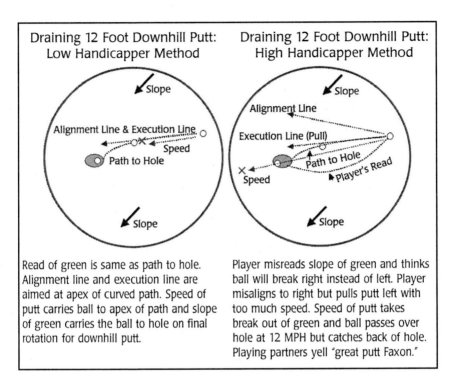

Draining 12 Foot Downhill Putt: Low Handicapper Method — Read of green is same as path to hole. Alignment line and execution line are aimed at apex of curved path. Speed of putt carries ball to apex of path and slope of green carries the ball to hole on final rotation for downhill putt.

Draining 12 Foot Downhill Putt: High Handicapper Method — Player misreads slope of green and thinks ball will break right instead of left. Player misaligns to right but pulls putt left with too much speed. Speed of putt takes break out of green and ball passes over hole at 12 MPH but catches back of hole. Playing partners yell "great putt Faxon."

How two wrongs make a right when putting

I still had an eight-foot putt for birdie, which fell about seven feet outside my comfort range. I aimed about eighteen inches to the left of the hole and hit the ball as if it were a twelve foot putt due to the significant slope uphill. The ball quickly began loosing speed during the final foot and started breaking hard to the right. It had about three revolutions remaining as it dropped in the hole for a birdie.

"Sweet Jesus!" I cried. I never achieved more than two birdies in a round and it was an awfully welcome sign getting one so early in the round.

"Hoo-ya Chief," Blister cheered. "You pulled that one out of your ass!"

"And Wiley didn't?" Jack asked quizzing Blister.

"That's a given," Wiley admitted to Jack.

With the two *out of the ass* putts, Wiley and I had won the hole. As a reminder that a copious amount of luck had played a role in our two scores, I used the hieroglyphic —>(o), that is Red Ball People shorthand for *out of the ass*, next to our names on the scorecard.

Hole 3
Prime Time
for Prime Numbers

W e stood on the third tee box gazing down at the fairway below. The u-shaped canyon offered such a good view of the course that it was featured on the score card, though the picture on the score card was obviously snapped in the spring when the surrounding grasses were lush. Wiley, Jack and I took a moment to pan across the expanse to the hills beyond Highway 4, and watched a line of cows disappear into an eroded crease in the hillside between two oak trees.

"Any of you guys know why Colonel Khadafi never promoted himself to General?" Blister asked.

As he was often prone to do, Blister interrupted our contemplative moment with nature when a capricious nugget of data leaked out of a crack in his memory bank and made it all the way to his tongue.

Blister's question was met with three blank disbelieving stares.

"Lord almighty—that's the first thing I would have done," Blister continued. "The second thing I would have done was wear a name tag so people would quit spelling my name with a Q or a G. Am I on to something Chief?"

"Hardly," I countered, hoping to stifle any further discussion on Libyan military ranks. "His military title is Strongman, which is higher than a four-star general."

"Oh. So Strongman is higher than General. Is Strongman higher than Chief?" Blister asked with a cackle.

"The only thing higher than Chief is the Holy Ghost," I told Blister proudly.

"And who's that?"

"John Lennon," Jack interjected.

After giving Jack his proper due, we turned our attention back to the challenge that lay before us. The par 4 measured 340-yards downhill and was rated the second easiest hole on the course. However, the hole had its share of trouble. A very narrow driving window was framed by a giant row of Eucalyptus trees on the left and a row of white OB soldiers at the base of the hill on the right. If a player managed to hit a solid 3-wood or driver, he could follow with a sand wedge to the green for an easy par. But I suppose that's like saying if my aunt had a dick, she'd be my uncle.

A fade started down the middle of the fairway would invariably turn into a slice and carry out of bounds, especially since the prevailing headwinds in the canyon blew from left to right. Due to the high likelihood of slicing a ball OB, we often invoked Red Ball People Amendment to Rule 15-1b regarding illegal ball substitution.

Rule 15-1b—Wrong ball/substituted ball: *A player must hole out with the ball played from the teeing ground unless a Rule permits him to substitute another ball. If a player substitutes another ball when not so permitted, that ball is not a wrong ball; it becomes the ball in play and, if the error is not corrected as provided, the player shall incur a two stroke penalty.*

Red Ball People Amendment to Rule 15-1b: *Provided ball is not damaged, player must use the same ball for the entire hole with the following allowances: If any stroke has to be hit over a hazard, including but not limited to water, canyons, waste areas, and tall grasses, then the player may use a range ball or other ball with resale value less than $.50 until the stroke is safely executed. Furthermore, if ball does not have to be hit over hazard but hazard exists in vicinity of player's swing tendency, such as the right side of the fairway for a player who slices like a Thanksgiving carving knife, then player has complete discretion to substitute a cheap ball for the shot. Once the threat of losing an expensive ball has been mitigated, player may replace range ball with original ball.*

Reason for Change: *Red Ball People wisely invest their money in stocks, bonds, and real estate—not in expensive balls that are des-*

tined to be lost on hillsides only to be found by Mr. Kim who will sell
it to the pro shop who will resell it back to the Red Ball People.

Blister was on cue to lead off. Accordingly, he was the first to invoke Amendment 15-1, when he pulled a spare Top Flite 2000 from his bag. Blister seldom looked to get his round jump-started on the third hole. His normal tendency was a fade, which didn't bode well for the third hole.

As we waited, I looked down on the second green to see how the Mr. Kims were doing. The eldest Mr. Kim was standing on the lip of the near side bunker staring at his ball plugged in the center of the trap. If I knew his modus operandi, he would pick the ball up and spend his allotted time looking for balls on the hillside.

As we watched the foursome in front of us conducting a recovery operation beyond the OB markers, it struck us that this would easily be a five-hour round. Most golfers get upset with five-hour rounds but not the Red Ball People. In fact we couldn't understand why others wanted to rush home only to fulfill a laundry list of tasks assigned by their wives. Besides, killing time on the tee box gave a chance to catch up with careers and debate important world events.

Jack admitted that things could be better at his small Berkeley law firm. He had unwisely accepted a contingency case where his client sued a former employer, a paint manufacturer, for safety negligence when the client began showing symptoms of asbestos poisoning. After Jack spent hundreds of hours performing his due diligence, the client was later diagnosed with herpes.

Wiley told a grievous tale about an unqualified borrower that he and his partner Sam lent $50,000 to. Although the loan was secured with a second trust deed on the borrower's property, the loan was so risky that Sam also secured it with the pink slip on the borrower's car. Wiley now had a refurbished cherry-red 1968 Impala to dispose of and wondered if we were interested in acquiring the fine cruiser.

It seemed that we all had a recent story of career despair to share with the others. Yet none of them compared to our poster boy for occupational futility—Professor Daniel Goldston. I stumbled upon his sad story in the newspaper prior to our last mountain tournament and shared it with the tribe since I am always on the lookout for a would-be hero who has more self-inflicted calamities in his life than I do.

According to the article, the San Jose State University Professor spent twenty years attempting to advance the field of prime numbers by solving a famous problem known among number theorists as the Twin Prime Conjecture. After claiming he succeeded, he was hailed by mathematicians around the world for providing the most important breakthrough in prime number research in decades. Unfortunately, when the Professor presented his proof, his mathematical colleagues took about fifteen minutes to determine that the research was fraught with errors and the proof was quickly invalidated.

Before long, whenever someone needed to stretch their logic when the desired conclusions weren't supported by facts, Professor Goldston's scientific method was adopted to steer the argument where it needed to go. Although none of us are entirely sure how we fell into the pattern, I suspect it started with an email from Blister that he initiated to round out the scientific dimension of Chief Tit shortly after my ascension. Fully aware that I have the contradictory qualities of having a degree in math and a propensity to add a score card incorrectly, Blister's email portrayed Chief Tit as a science reporter for American Scientific Magazine on assignment to discover how Professor Goldston honed his rigorous logic to support his mathematical conclusions. Blister's contrived interview with Professor Goldston follows.

Prime Time for Prime Numbers

Owing to Chief Tit's stellar background in mathematics, he was recently recruited by American Scientific Magazine (ASM) to interview renowned mathematician and San Jose State Professor, Daniel Goldston. In hiring Chief Tit, ASM is responding to the growing demand of science buffs who are clamoring to learn more about Professor Goldston since he issued his astonishing press release claiming to have solved the Twin Prime Conjecture. Coincidentally, Daniel Goldston is the great grandfather[15] (great grandfather to the 15th power) of Professor Merlin Goldston, the renowned future archeologist from the 25th century.

ASM: *"Professor Goldston, what is a prime number?"*

GOLDSTON: *"It's a number that is divisible by only 1 and itself, such as 3, 5, 7, and 11."*

ASM: *"How did you get interested in prime numbers?"*

GOLDSTON: *"I noticed that when my wife and her girlfriend went out for lunch they would spend 20 minutes trying to divide the bill perfectly in half, while my male friends always rounded up to the nearest $20. If the bill + tax + 8% tip, which females customarily give for good service, came out to a prime number, they were stumped. To get over the hurdle, they usually ordered dessert, recalculated the tab, and hoped that the new total would be divisible by the total number of diners. I've been hooked ever since."*

ASM: *"What is the Twin Prime Conjecture?"*

GOLDSTON: *"It's a conjecture that claims that there are an infinite number of pairs of prime numbers that differ by two. For example, 5 and 7, 11 and 13, and 61 and 63."*

ASM: *"63 is actually divisible by 3."*

GOLDSTON: *"It is?"*

ASM: *"You've been working on this same problem for twenty years, when do you find the time?"*

GOLDSTON: *"When my wife and daughter are watching Prime Time on TV, I spend my own Prime Time working on this problem. You ever notice that Prime Time on TV starts at 7, a prime number?"*

ASM: *"Actually, prime time starts at 8. I read a lot about how Asian college students at Berkeley use 90% of the campus computing resources to determine the highest prime number. The most recent one had over 60,000 digits. Are there any practical or commercial applications for identifying these large prime numbers?"*

GOLDSTON: *"Not really, although we thought for a time that Argentina was using the largest known primes to determine their peso* *conversion to the US dollar during their period of hyper-inflation in the 80s, but we couldn't prove it."*

ASM: *"I thought prime numbers were instrumental in encryption algorithms?"*

GOLDSTON: *"I thought so too until Microsoft starting using them to encrypt their email servers."*

ASM: *"I understand you are working on a similar problem to the Twin Prime Conjecture which says there are an infinite number of primes that may not be twins, but are much closer together than average. Can you elaborate?"*

GOLDSTON: *"These are numbers like 19 and 23 and 97 and 121, which are prime numbers but are more than two numbers apart but not a whole bunch apart."*

ASM: *"Actually, 121 is divisible by 11."*

GOLDSTON: *"Really?"*

ASM: *"Is the largest prime number known larger than Bush's tax cut?"*

GOLDSTON: *"Heavens no but we're still working on it."*

———————

The foursome in front of us had finally cleared the fairway, allowing Blister to cream his surrogate ball into a lone pine tree on the right side of the fairway. Being one of the friendlier trees on the course, it spit his ball out toward the fairway where it came to rest on the cart path below the tree.

Jack also invoked Red Ball People Amendment 15-1b and hit a substitute practice ball. It turned out to be a good decision as the ball spun deep into the hillside for an out of bounds penalty. His second ball was pulled precariously close to the giant eucalyptus tree on the left, skimming two leaves from the tree as it skirted by. The ball faded back to the middle of the fairway and came to rest about one hundred and twenty yards from the green.

Wiley hit next. The two previous holes had given Wiley enough confidence to use his preferred Strata Distance Balata with his TaylorMade Burner 420 titanium driver. He gasped as he watched his drive disappear over the same pine tree that was so friendly to Blister. Wiley's fortune depended on the bounce off the hillside beyond the tree. The lucky ball on his trajectory ricocheted back into the fairway while the less fortunate one burrowed into the deep grass on the hillside beyond the OB markers.

Wiley feigned snapping his driver over his knee before slamming the head of his driver to the ground. "That should be safe. Those usually come down," he hoped.

Wiley knew if he played a provisional ball, the best he would score would be a double-bogey. With no argument from the rest of us, Wiley chose to apply Red Ball People Amendment 27-1 to his predicament and picked up his tee.

Rule 27-1—Out of bounds: *If a ball is lost or is out of bounds, the player shall play a ball, under penalty of one stroke, as nearly as possible at the spot from which the original ball was last played. To save time the player may play another ball provisionally in accordance with Rule 27-1. The player shall inform his opponent in match play or his marker or a fellow-competitor in stroke play that he intends to play a provisional ball, and he shall play it before he or his partner goes forward to search for the original ball.*

Red Ball People Amendment to Rule 27-1: *After sufficient abuse of equipment, player should inform playing partners that it is player's opinion that ball will be safely found in bounds even if it is the general consensus that only an act of God will allow the ball to be found in the regulation playing area. Player should then proceed to location on course where an act of God most likely occurred and perform an alleged search for ball. When ball in not found, player should express outrage at misfortune until another player decrees that he should take a drop where he thinks God should have put it. Player should then locate nice flat fluffy drop area that God would like and complete his drop. Player will be assessed a one stroke penalty.*

Reason for change: *Red Ball People read in Golf Digest that Fred Funk thought the OB rule was too harsh and should be changed. What's good for Fred is good for Red Ball People.*

Owing to Wiley's errant drive, I became Blister's betting partner by default. The pine tree on the right was even more neighborly with me than it was with Blister. It tossed my ball to the middle of the fairway raising the probability that Blister and I would win the skins.

As I refitted my head cover on my 3-wood, I glanced over to the second hole. Sure enough, the three younger Mr. Kims were putting while the elder Mr. Kim searched the hillside above the hole for lost balls. His search appeared to be paying off as he picked at a manzanita bush as if it bore golf balls for fruit.

"Do you think I stayed in?" Wiley queried as we motored down the cart path.

"We'll find out. If you did . . . you might be the conductor on the little train that could instead of the train wreck that can't."

Our spirits moved in different directions when Jack peered out from behind the friendly pine tree and waved us over. "I got a Strata Balata over here."

After shoving Wiley out of the cart, I arrived back to my ball in time to witness Blister evaluating where to take relief. Blister dared not drop on the right of the path, as the tree would obstruct his ball flight. The fairway to the left of the cart path was pock-marked with dead grass and hardpan from careless drivers who veered off the path as it curved around the tree. It was the ideal circumstance for taking a T-Rex drop.

The T-Rex Drop

A well executed drop following a shot hit into a hazard or resting on an immovable obstruction such as a cart path can often save a stroke on a hole. Since gravity never sleeps, balls will always tend to roll into a divot or dirt area around a patch of grass. Before dropping, the player should be careful to cover the two most undesirable spots in the vicinity with his feet. To minimize an unfortunate roll to other undesirable spots, the Red Ball People deploy the T-Rex drop. This technique received its name from Tyrannosaurus Rex whose stooping posture and short arms would have made it impossible for him to drop a ball from above his knee.

Since tribal members are quick studies, we recognized early on that the closer to the ground that the ball is dropped, the more likely it was to remain in the target zone. Hence, the objective of the T-Rex drop is to position the ball on a small fluffy grass area, when the surrounding area consists of dirt and tree flotsam. The T-Rex drop should not be confused with T-Rex arms, which characterizes someone who never reaches for the dinner check when dining out with friends.

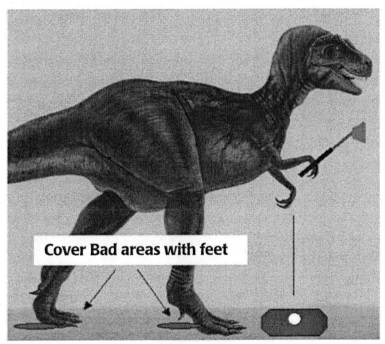

The T-Rex drop

After executing his T-Rex drop, Blister hit a solid 9-iron a few feet short of the green. Jack, Wiley, and I followed with decent shots, though Wiley pulled his just off the green, but flag high.

"I didn't come out looking for trouble, but I think you and me are in the middle of a dog fight," Wiley smirked as we rode the cart to the green.

"Lots of golf to be played my friend. Lots of golf to be played," I told him predicting a short-lived skirmish.

"Chief, you're playing so far beyond your ability right now!" Wiley sneered.

"And you're not?"

"Not unless I get up and down. If I do that—you're sing'n to the choir," Wiley laughed.

As I walked toward my ball, I assessed the probability that Blister and I would win the hole. I assigned Blister a five, Jack a six, and gave Wiley an improbable four, presuming that his lucky streak would continue. Even if Wiley saved par, all I had to do was two-putt from the front of the green to give our team a one stroke win on the hole. I liked our chances.

The giddiness was short-lived. Blister shanked his chip shot from two feet off the green and it shot forty-five degrees to the right where it stopped, albeit, the same distance he was originally. Blister stood straight up, arched his back and clasped his hands over his head letting the wedge drop down behind his back. He stood there motionless for a moment looking like a bird that had just been introduced to the concept of a window. He didn't say a word, nor did the rest of us. It was intuitively clear that the biggest challenge in sports is hit the sweet spot on a club immediately following a shank. Oh sure—Mario Andretti might argue that the toughest test in sports is climbing back into a racer after smacking a cement wall at 225 MPH. Of course, he would be wrong. I was already conceding the bet to Jack and Wiley.

Blister finally removed his hands from atop his head, picked up his wedge and trudged over to his ball and tried again. The quickness in which Blister took his next swing told me he wanted to get the hole over with. Instead, his foray around the perimeter of the green was extended with no end in sight.

He hit a second shank that zoomed off at forty-five degrees and disappeared over the back edge of the green. The ball was quickly followed by Blister's wedge. Although Blister was only sitting four, he might as well have been sitting fifty. It would take extraordinary skill to get the ball up and down for a double. More importantly, it would take confidence, a commodity Blister was woefully short of at the moment.

"I'm picking up," Blister mumbled to Wiley as he passed him en route to pick up his ball and sand wedge.

It's difficult to speculate what Blister might have scored on the hole, but interestingly enough, had he continued to play his ball and hit two more shanks, it was evident that he would be back at the identical spot in front of the green where he originally shanked his first chip. After pondering this possibility for a moment, I was struck with an immediate intuition that Blister could have played his shanks to his advantage if he only understood the mathematical angles.

Two Wrongs Seldom Make a Right but Three Shanks *Always* Make a Left

As with the scientific community, some of the most important discoveries in golf occur by accident. While watching Blister's derailment on the third hole, I accidentally discovered that three shanks make a left after projecting the mathematical conclusion from three consecutive balls hit off the hosel at forty five degrees. After sketching some preliminary diagrams on the scorecard to review with Blister, I decided to provide the mathematical proof.

Since shanks bend off the hosel at forty degrees, one can verify using simple trigonometry, that after two shanks the ball will lie precisely on the original target line but an equidistant off the green on the far side of the hole. After the third shank, the ball will be forty-five degrees to the left of the original ball position (for right-handed shanker) but still no closer to the hole.

The Illustration on the left below shows the four different ball positions and confirms the mathematical proof that three shanks do indeed make a left. Of course, unless you quit shanking, you will be circling the green for a while.

While the reader may find this theorem interesting, it has pragmatic application as well. As we all know, you can't just shank one ball. After the first shank, you are now fully aware that the shank is part of your arsenal for the day and before the hole is over you will inevitably empty your chamber. However, understanding this theorem can save you at least one stroke but probably many more. Here's how.

61

The 3-Shank Theorem:

Two wrongs seldom make a right but three shanks ALWAYS make a left

Applying the 3-Shank Theorem:

When shanks are imminent, redirect aim to center of shakazoid for three consecutive shanks to save strokes

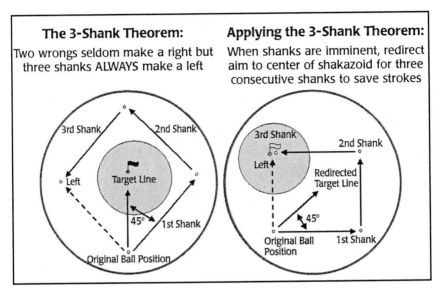

Proof that 3 shanks make a left

Once you shank a ball, there is a ninety-five percent probability that you will shank the next shot. Armed with this information and aware of the 3-Shank Theorem, you should redirect your target line forty-five degrees to the right of the hole (right handed shanker) as depicted in the right side of the Illustration above.

To keep it simple, imagine the square box, referred to henceforth as a shankazoid. Without fretting over the reaction of your playing partners, take aim at the center of the shankazoid instead of the flag. After executing the perfect shank you will be forty-five degrees to the right of your target line or ninety degrees to the right of the flag from your original ball position. While your playing partners are giggling, continue to align yourself toward the center of the shankazoid for your two subsequent shanks. When the third ball careens off the hosel and nestles next to the flag, the giggles will turn into applause as your partners realize that you cleverly choreographed the incident to take advantage of the 3-Shank Theorem. To drive the point home, it is recommended that you announce to the field, "Two wrongs seldom make a right but three shanks ALWAYS make a left!" Your playing partners won't be any more impressed with your game but they will have a whole new respect for your cunning use of trigonometry.

We automatically lost the bet when Blister picked up his ball. However, there was a little silver lining for me because I left my first putt four feet short and since the bet was already over, Wiley and Jack conceded the putt for my par.

Wiley continued to roll. He chipped his third shot to within two feet for his par. Jack two-putted from the middle of the green to make double-bogey. Wiley was keeping the score card and naturally gave Blister a seven for a triple. Wiley knew better than to ask Blister what he scored, since the right answer was 'disqualification'. It was standard procedure for the Red Ball People to record a triple when a player picked up a ball, though it was understood that for betting purposes, a triple achieved from a pick up still lost to a quadruple that was played out.

After three holes, Wiley and I were miraculously tied at even par. Blister was seven over and Jack was five over. Wiley had also won a skin on the first three holes while the rest of us each had one.

Score Card after 3 Holes

Hole	1	2	3	4	5	6	7	8	9	Out
Yardage	472	145	345	169	360	189	511	392	505	3088
Handicap	11	5	17	13	15	9	7	1	3	
Wiley	⑤	③->(0)	④							
Chief Tit	6	②->(0)	4							
Blister	⑥	6	7							
Jack	8	3	⑥							
Par	5	3	4	3	4	3	5	4	5	36

Notes:
/ => Signifies that player gets stroke
O => Signifies that player won bet
->(0) => Heiroglyphic for "out of ass." Chief Tit and Wiley pull two shots out of their ass on 2nd hole.
[1] Jack picks up ball. Red Ball People abacus only has 8 beads - Jack takes an 8.
[2] Blister concedes 6 foot putt to himself for a Linda Tripp.
[3] Blister picks up ball after 2 shanks - he takes a 7.

Hole 4
Clinton, Bush, Rumsfeld, and Jackson: The Ideal Foursome

The fourth hole is a 169-yard par 3. The hole features two traps on either side of the green and a large bail out area on the right that we anticipated Blister would be using. Although the wind was in our face, the forward flag position negated the need for extra iron.

Only one ball of the foursome in front of us was on the green. Two of three women players were in the trap on the right while the male player was well off the green on a scavenger hunt. To Blister's credit, he wasn't showing any ill effects of his recent debacle. In fact, I knew the healing process was well underway when a goofy grin emerged on his face as he spun around to talk to Jack.

"Hey Jack, I think you know Dubya better than Laura Bush knows him."

Jack and Wiley both chuckled, recognizing that Blister was referring to a torrid exchange of emails between the two polar opposites earlier in the week.

"Wiley had me convinced he infiltrated the Rainbow Coalition," I smirked.

A Hole with Clinton, Bush, Rumsfeld, and Jackson

One of the intellectual mind exercises the Red Ball People partake in from time to time is a debate regarding which historical figures would make the best dinner guests for an evening. The subject flared earlier in the week when our Internet Service Providers were clogged with emails as we debated the merits of the fourth dinner guest. The ground rules allow the debaters to select four people, whether living or dead, and bring them together in your home for an entertaining evening of fine food and lively conversation. After a lot of vigorous discussion, we agreed on three of the dinner guests but couldn't reach consensus on the fourth.

The three dinner guests who always seem to find a spot on the invitation include Jesus, Hitler, and Marilyn Monroe. As mankind's two most historical enigmas, Hitler and Jesus are obvious choices, though most participants admit to some concern about the consequences of over steaming Hitler's squash. To counterbalance the anxiety that could arise from seating Hitler and Jesus across from each other, it was determined that Marilyn Monroe would be the best bet to keep politics from dominating the conversation.

As always, there was significant disagreement on the fourth dinner guest. Blister nominated John Lennon, but that suggestion was quickly squelched by Jack who pointed out that there is no way that Lennon would show up without Yoko Ono. Blister conceded that even if he didn't tire of Yoko, he knew he could count on Hitler to create an incident.

Jack was constantly designating Einstein, but few agreed that discussing electromagnetism at dinner was the best way to spend an historical evening. Wiley's eccentric list included Dennis Rodman, the former NBA party boy. Wiley argued that if anyone could succeed in loosening up teetotalling Hitler, it was probably Rodman.

After failing to reach consensus on the dinner party, we turned our attention to the ideal foursome. Surprisingly, we reached agreement almost immediately. Most neophytes would choose the obvious candidates such as Arnold Palmer, Jack Nicklaus, Ben Hogan, Bobby Jones, or Tiger Woods. However, these are the last guys the Red Ball People want to play with. Our perfect foursome consists of Jesse Jackson, Bill Clinton, Donald Rumsfeld, and George Bush. Since golf in its basic form is pure entertainment, what combination of golfers could possibly offer more entertainment than this foursome?

Once the Red Ball Tribe settled on the perfect foursome, we set about to envision what the interaction would be between these golfers. As the flaming liberal of the clan, we decided that Jack was best qualified to provide the dialog for George W. Bush and Donald Rumsfeld.

Conversely, right-wing Wiley nearly wet his pants volunteering to fabricate the dialog for Jesse Jackson and Bill Clinton. Over the course of two days, the historians exchanged emails, accepting suggestions from others, until they had compiled enough dialog for the fab four to play the par 3 fourth hole at Franklin Canyon. The quixotic foursome is playing best ball with Clinton and Jackson paired against Bush and Rumsfeld.

BUSH: *"So how far do you think that flag is today Don?"*

RUMSFELD: *"That's a fair question—not quantifiable but palpable."*

Recognizing that Rumsfeld would take a while to hone in on the answer, Bush retrieves a pair of rangefinders from his military attaché and receives a quick briefing on their operation. Bush puts the rangefinders up to his eyes and squints as he rotates the focus-dial three hundred and sixty five degrees in both directions.

BUSH: *"Is there a cloud blowing over or sumthin? I can't see doodly-squat."*

CLINTON: *"Here—let Bubba remove the lens covers for ya all. Try that George. Tell us—what do your keen eyes see?"*

BUSH: *"Looks like a couple of huge caterpillars."*

RUMSFELD: *"We see lots of things. Gosh—lots of things are there to be seen. But when what we see is known by us—then I am pretty confident that it will be known that you have your fingers over the lenses."*

BUSH: *"Oh—that's a little better. Now all I can see are two Texas-sized fingerprints. I bet Halliburton can fix this problem."*

Bush gives up on assessing the distance, like he gave up on the European Union, and gives the rangefinders back to his attaché.

CLINTON: *"How about firing up a cigar with Bubba before teeing off?"*

RUMSFELD: *"Once in a while, I'm standing here, doing something. And I think—what in the world am I doing here? My goodness gra-*

cious a cigar sounds good. That is a brilliant plan. You deserve all the credit for this plan, even though I had some input on the five previous plans."

Clinton digs into his bag and pulls out four Dominican Cohiba Esplendidos that he received as a partial grant to the Clinton library from Denise Rich when Clinton pardoned her former husband, billionaire financier Marc Rich, for fraud and tax evasion. He reaches into his pocket and pulls out his combination green repair tool cigar cutter and clips the four cigars before passing them out. Jackson, who knows a little bit about shedding light on things, provides a torch lighter for the foursome. A secret service agent intervenes when Bush catches the bill of his hat on fire with Reverend Jackson's lighter.

CLINTON: *"Reverend, my black friend, why don't you start us off."*

Jackson is having difficulty seeing the color of the flag on the green since he has absentmindedly left his glasses at his mistress' apartment that the Rainbow Coalition is paying for with funds from blackmailed corporations. He asks Rumsfeld if he can see the color of the flag.

RUMSFELD: *"What color is the flag? You're going to be told lots of things. You get told things every day that don't happen. I think what you'll find—I think what you'll find is—whatever it is we do substantively—there will be near perfect clarity as to what it is. But it will be known, and it will be known to Congress—that the flag is white."*

JACKSON: *"White? Our flag is red, white and blue, but our nation is a rainbow—red, yellow, brown, black and white—and we're all precious in God's sight."*

After deciding that it would probably be best to shoot for the middle of the green, Jackson reaches into his pocket for a tee but can't easily find one below all the Trojan rubbers stuffed in his pocket. After removing several layers of prophylactics as well as a miniature bible, he finally finds a tee. As Jackson pushes his tee into the ground he offers the three other players a little advice.

JACKSON: *"Today's golfer can put dope in their veins or hope in their brains. If they can conceive it and believe it, they can achieve it. They must know it is not their aptitude but their attitude that will determine their altitude. I will not equivocate. I will not deviate. I will enunciate and hit a shot you can appreciate."*

BUSH: *"And I can appreciate small business growth. I was one."*

Jackson steps over the ball. As usual he has marked his ball with a rainbow logo. He hits a high hook with plenty of altitude short and left of the green. He punctuates the ball flight by yelling, "Ratta-tat-tat. Ratta-tat-tat."

CLINTON: *"You gotta turn your ass Reverend."*

Clinton's repetitive advice to any golfer who hits an errant ball is to do a better job turning their ass. The advice was first reported by Don Van Natta Jr., in his New York Times article about the biggest cheaters in golf. Van Natta later played a round with Clinton and followed up his New York Times article with a second article that was featured in Sports Illustrated. In the second article Van Natta claims that Clinton agreed to play with him after Van Natta told Clinton he was writing a book on presidents who played golf.

Van Natta finally joined Clinton and two of Clinton's friends, both venture capitalists. Throughout the round Clinton repeatedly told Van Natta who is a twenty eight handicap, to turn his ass.

Van Natta recounted a typical Clinton hole: "Clinton hits a drive into the trees and takes a second, practice tee shot. He hits this one short. He hits another tee shot; this one goes long and far. He drives the cart over to the trees and takes a drop but hits that ball short. He then plays three more practice shots from the fringe and ends up playing the second of his practice shots. He is on the green in four but picks up without putting. On his scorecard he takes a four on the hole. It's a no-putt four."

Clinton takes a puff on his cigar, careful not to inhale, and nods to Bush.

CLINTON: *"OK Dubya, let's see what you got."*

BUSH: *"I'm gonna nuke this ball with my nuculur swing."*

RUMSFELD: *"Do you mean nuclear?"*

BUSH: *"Whatever. I'm just trying to set the bar a little louder."*

Bush proceeds to the tee box, sets his ball on the tee and takes his alignment. He looks up at Clinton and Jackson and makes a prediction.

BUSH: *"I'm gonna cut this ball like I cut your taxes."*

Bush overdoes his cut and pushes his 5-iron hard right and the shot burrows into the lip of a greenside bunker, nearly an unplayable lie. Since CIA Director George Tenant is not there to take responsibility, Bush will need to rely on his best-ball partner Rumsfeld. Bush offers a self-analysis of his poor shot.

BUSH: *"It looks like I misunderestimated the distance, but I think we can agree that the past is over. Help me into this hole, Don."*

CLINTON: *"You forgot to turn your ass."*

Rumsfeld stands frozen. He scratches his chin and then removes his glasses holding them up to the sun to see if they need cleaning again. After several minutes of uncomfortable silence and deep thinking on Rumsfeld's part, he places his ball on the tee and begins his waggle. Before hitting, Rumsfeld believes it is imperative to share his swing thoughts with his playing partners.

RUMSFELD: *"Things will not be necessarily continuous. The fact that they are something other than perfectly continuous ought not to be characterized as a pause. There will be some things that people will see. There will be some things that people won't see. And life goes on."*

Rumsfeld hits a solid cut shot that plugs deep on the green two feet inside the first cut. Bush is ecstatic having believed up to this moment that only his National Security Advisor and CIA Director was capable of covering his ass. Bush congratulates Rumsfeld on his excellent shot.

BUSH: *"I guess you showed those guys how to set the pie higher. Don't mess with Texas."*

CLINTON: *"Way to turn your ass Don."*

JACKSON: *"Like all white men, Rumsfeld thinks he hit a triple when he was born on third base."*

It is finally Clinton's turn. He looks in his bag of fifteen clubs for his 7-iron. He has momentary difficulty finding the iron because it is hidden behind his illegal Callaway ERC driver that exceeds USGA standards. He finally locates the club and whips it out of the bag, turning his ass as he does so. He reaches into his pocket and pulls out a banned Volvik Air Channel golf ball that he received as part of an unreported gift of golf equipment from a campaign contributor who slept in the Lincoln bedroom.

As Clinton knows, the Volvik ball produces three hundred and thirty yards of distance in a controlled test environment using a head speed of 108 MPH, surpassing the flying distance limit set by the USGA of 296.8 yards by thirty-three yards. The ball is also .03 inches smaller than a regulation ball and 1.2 grams heavier.

Clinton pushes his tee into the ground a few inches in front of the tee markers looking for a little advantage. He believes no one notices but everyone else recognizes that unless this ball goes into the hole, Clinton will take a mulligan anyway.

CLINTON: *"Come on Billy. Here we go. OK, turn your ass. Here we go now. Come to Daddy."*

RUMSFELD: *"Oh my, is that an illegal ball?"*

CLINTON: *"It depends on what your definition of is, is."*

Clinton shrugs off Rumsfeld's suspicion and hooks his ball into a tree on the left. He tees up a second illegal ball and hooks a second ball left. By the time he hits his third ball the other players are already sitting in the cart waiting to drive to the green.

Bush, who is sharing a cart with Rumsfeld, has climbed into his cart backwards and is facing toward the rear of the cart looking for the steering wheel. Rumsfeld gently helps Bush get turned around and pointed in the right direction. Jackson and Clinton both try to get into the left side of the cart. Jackson settles the matter by sharing an analogy with Clinton.

JACKSON: *"If there are occasions when my grape turned into a raisin and my joy bell lost its resonance, please forgive me. Charge it to my head and not to my heart. But I'm driving."*

The four players take off in their carts for the short drive to the green. During the journey Bush becomes fixated looking at the trees on the hillside and wonders if a logging permit has been issued for the forest he is looking at.

Rumsfeld is also scouting the terrain. He is preoccupied with assessing whether the top of the hill would provide a good vantage point for a lightly armored attack helicopter brigade.

In the other cart, Clinton is estimating the square yardage of the course and calculating what the maximum sustainable property tax level would be. He jots a few notes on the way to remind himself to call the county assessor and encourage a property reassessment.

At the same time, Jackson scans the other fairways trying to infer the number of black players on the course. If the proportion of blacks on the course is less than the proportion of blacks in the state of California, he will pay a little visit to the pro shop after the round and issue an invitation to the ownership group to meet him on the steps of the county court house, unless of course, the owner wishes to make a donation to the Rainbow Coalition.

Since they are playing best-ball scramble, Bush and Rumsfeld only need their putters as they will be putting from the spot where Rumsfeld's ball plugged. Bush grabs a driver instead.

Clinton and Jackson each retrieve several wedges as well as their putter. Clinton takes a look at Jackson's ball and doesn't like the lie. Though the rainbow logo is face up, he lifts the ball under the pretense of identification and places it a foot away for a better lie. He defends his illegal action to Jackson.

CLINTON: *"Don't ask, don't tell."*

JACKSON: *"When the doors of opportunity swing open, we must make sure that we are not too drunk or too indifferent to walk through."*

CLINTON: *"That's right Reverend. We're going to join hands and walk shoulder to shoulder. Now remember to turn your ass."*

Near the top of the green Rumsfeld finds his ball mark and repairs it with a bayonet. Meanwhile, Bush is looking so hard at the green trying to read the break that his eyes begin to cross. Bush decides to seek assistance in reading the green from Rumsfeld and asks him how he sees the break.

RUMSFELD: *"Oh my goodness gracious. Everyone's so eager to get the story before in fact, the story is there . . . that the world is constantly being fed things that haven't happened . . . All I can tell you is—it hasn't happened. It's going to happen and when it does, it will break toward the west."*

BUSH: *"I was raised in the West—the west of Texas. It's pretty close to California. In more ways than Washington, D.C., is close to California. Actually, I . . . this may sound a little West Texan to you . . . but I like it. When I'm talking about . . . when I'm talking about myself, and when he's talking about myself, all of us are talking about me. This green sure has a lot of grass on it."*

Clinton offered Jackson a little encouragement as Jackson considers his options.

CLINTON: *"OK here we go. Turn that ass. We gotta get up and down."*

JACKSON: *"Never look down on anybody unless you are helping him up."*

BUSH: *"Hey Bubba, I know how hard it is for you guys to put food on your family but you're away."*

JACKSON: *"The white, the Hispanic, the black, the Arab, the Jew, the woman, the Native American, the small farmer, the businessperson, the environmentalist, the peace activist, the young, the old, the lesbian, the gay and the disabled make up the American quilt. Those are the people who are away."*

BUSH: *"I don't think you need to be subliminable about the differences between our views on who's away, but you guys are more away than we are away, though we are both a ways from being away."*

Jackson decides in favor of executing a high flop shot with his fifty-six degree wedge. He opens his stance slightly to clear his hips but fails to take into account his bulging right trouser pocket stuffed with Trojan rubbers. The bulge restricts his swing path. A deceleration of his wedge ensues, leading to a chunked shot that flies only three feet. In a fit of anger, Jackson slams his wedge into the ground causing several Trojans to spill from his pocket. Rumsfeld, who is paying close attention to his opponent, summarizes the effort for Jackson.

RUMSFELD: *"Oh heavens, there are some things that the press thinks have melted, when in fact they haven't melted. When melting is underway . . . it will be known and known to the congress. Some people don't know . . . don't know it is underway, but that does not mean we don't know it is underway. But it will be known . . . and known by everybody, that you just had a meltdown."*

JACKSON: *"I hear that melting-pot stuff a lot, and all I can say is that we haven't melted."*

Clinton surmises that Bush and Rumsfeld would easily two-putt unless Bush tripped and fell on Rumsfeld's moving ball for two stoke penalty. Even though that probability was relatively high, he couldn't count on it. He would have to hit a solid chip to give Jackson and himself a chance. Jackson's antics distract Bush and Rumsfeld, affording Clinton a chance to illegally trample the grass in front of his drop area and illegally remove loose impediments near his anticipated landing area.

Well aware that the banned Volvik Air Channel ball didn't have a soft feel around the green, Clinton illegally substitutes a Titleist Pro VI for his chip shot. As it turns out, eliminating all the course variables had little bearing on enhancing his skill at hitting chip shots. Clinton blades his chip shot across the green where it comes to rest near Rumsfeld's ball. Clinton and Jackson exchange glances and comment on their recent performance.

CLINTON: *"Oh daddy. Didn't turn my ass. Oh Billy, Billy, Billy. I feel your pain Reverend. That was depressing."*

JACKSON: *"When we're unemployed, we're called lazy; when the whites are unemployed it's called a depression."*

Clinton offers to remove the flag since it would give him an opportunity to 'accidentally' step on the Bush-Rumsfeld putting line while 'accidentally' flattening a few more spike marks on his own line.

Rumsfeld prepares to putt. Before he does, Clinton trots over and positions himself directly behind Rumsfeld in order to have the best vantage point. Rumsfeld hits a solid lag putt, which curves downhill toward the west stopping two feet short of the hole. Bush is very pleased with his Defense Secretary and wants him to know.

> BUSH: *"You really sat the table with that one Don. I bet ole Bubba misunderestimated how good you is at putting. We got a little saying in Texas—If at first you don't secede, try it again."*

Rumsfeld is so happy with his putt, he breaks into that silly grin he gets when he announces a military strike on a restaurant in a foreign country where some dictator that he has on the run, had eaten a day earlier.

Bush places his ball at the spot where Rumsfeld had just putted. Rumsfeld explains to Bush how the ball would break from the apex of the slope toward the hole but Bush mistakenly thinks that apex is a sink cleaning detergent. He looks around for a can of Ajax, or Apex as he knew it, but becomes frustrated when he can't find one. He decides to ignore Rumsfeld's advice, as he had done with Nobel laureates on other matters, and lines up his putt.

Before Bush has a chance to putt, Rumsfeld points out that he is holding a driver and offers to lend him his putter. With Rumsfeld's putter, Bush aims at a discolored splotch where he thinks a can of Ajax might have bleached the grass, and smacks the ball. The putt sails by the hole to the other side of the green. No matter, they only have a two-footer owing to the scramble format.

Behind Bush, Clinton and Jackson are discussing who should go first. Clinton has a strong preference for hitting second in match play. If the other player made his putt, he was entitled to concede his own putt to save par from as far away as fifty feet. Jackson finally yields when Clinton promises to let him run on Hillary's 2008 ticket. He starts his putt on the same line as Rumsfeld but with slightly more speed. As it rolls ever closer to the hole, he shouts directions to the ball.

JACKSON: *"Stay on that line! It is the line of the desperate, the damned, the disinherited, the disrespected, and the despised."*

At the end of the line, Jackson's ball deserts him like the Democratic Party deserted him in 1992. The ball catches the lip of the hole but spins out for an easy tap in. Clinton is more pissed than Jackson since he can't concede his own putt, though he did use the distraction to nudge his ball a foot closer to the hole.

Clinton stands over his ball knowing he has to sink it. Before putting, he completes his mental checklist: loose grip; feet aligned; left eye over ball; ass properly turned. He starts his illegal ball toward the hole with a look of determination. As the ball rolls down the slope he yells encouragement.

CLINTON: *"OK daddy. Go down for Billie. Come home to Billie."*

Because Clinton rarely putts out, he did a poor job judging the distance and powers the ball through the break leaving it ten feet beyond the hole. He and Jackson would lose the hole but at least he was able to write a par on his scorecard. Bush wanted to tap in the two-footer for the win but took himself out of the hole when he hit his ball on his practice swing. Rumsfeld taps in to win the hole. Bush is elated.

BUSH: *"What a hole Don. You took the high horse and then claimed the low road. You couldn't have played that more better. What'd you think Jesse?"*

JACKSON: *"In golf, an organized minority is a scoring majority."*

The foursome walks off the green. As they approach their carts, Jackson and Clinton pick up their pace, jostling with each other to snatch the left side of the cart. When he reaches his cart, Bush hesitates for a moment wondering who stole the cart door. He is relieved when Rumsfeld reminds him that the cart didn't have a door. Though he would go on to lose the match, Clinton would record a 78 for the round.

Jackson flubs chip when pocket bulging with prophylactics impedes swing.

President Bush uses range finders to zoom in on par 3 yardage. "Tell us what your keen eyes see?" an aide asks.

Jack was in the process of introducing another line for Bush when the eldest Mr. Kim interrupted.

"You go now," Mr. Kim prodded us with a big smile.

Indeed, we were so enthralled in reliving the hole with our ideal foursome, we hadn't noticed that the green was deserted. We hastily moved aside as Jack took command of the tee box.

Jack paired himself with Wiley when both players hit the green. Blister ended his shanking stint by lacing such an impressive 6-iron that Mr. Kim was overcome with joy. After hooking my drive into the left trap, it took one more stroke to skull a sand wedge off the lip to the green.

Forgetting that the time to do a task over is twice as long as the time to do it right, we attempted to regain the lost time by rushing our putting routine. Blister hurried to his ball needing only to worry about distance. Of course, for Blister that's equivalent to saying all the French had to worry about in 1939 was the Germans. His ball flew by the hole and didn't stop rolling until it had passed Jack's ball, which was the second furthest from the hole.

"You're still up," Jack informed him.

"The worst words in golf!" I said pulling out my metaphorical shovel.

"Actually Chief, I think there are worse words in golf than—you're still up," Wiley corrected. "How about . . . I slept with your wife last night?"

"How about . . . I came across your daughter in porn chat room?" Blister joined in making fun of his own predicament. "She tells me she can score some killer pot!"

"Oh . . . I forgot to tell you—I ran over your dog rushing to the course this morning," Jack crowed as he leaned into Wiley's face to take his turn.

Indeed, there were many things much worse than hearing 'you're still up'. We could have kept going but knew that Mr. Kim was probably getting impatient with us for taking so long. Blister was really too far away to have a legitimate chance of making his par so he hurried his putt a second time, coming up four feet short.

Blister's putting woes were fairly representative of the typical amateur player. They rarely have good distance control on uphill and downhill putts. At the end of a round, most high handicapped players can look back at a score card and find four or five strokes that resulted from poor uphill and downhill putting. The problem is important enough to warrant a little extra attention.

Putting and the Distance Problem

I believe we can all agree that there has never been an amateur player who consistently hit uphill putts long and downhill putts short. Even though everyone and their fat sister remind us to hit the ball hard enough to reach the hole for an uphill putt, we just can't seem do it. Contrarily, we have no trouble getting a downhill putt to the hole with plenty of yardage to spare. In fact, if we were on a football field we could record a first down before arriving back to elevation of the hole.

This is such an unusual phenomenon that I performed some qualitative research with a control group to determine why the outcome for uphill and downhill putts is so predictable for mediocre golfers. Some of the responses were surprising while others were not. The top five reasons are listed below. Which one applies to you?

Why Uphill Putts Come Up Woefully Short

- Player believes the ball will bruise like a peach if he hits it too hard.
- The only thing the player knows how to read is a sports page. Player failed to read the green as uphill.

- Player only practices his putting on his wooden floor in the kitchen.
- Player kept hearing his playing partners say *"Nice putt Sally"* and his name is really Sally.
- Player likes reading the manufacturer's name on the ball and can only do so if the ball is rotating slowly.

Why Downhill Putts Stop Further From the Hole than Where They Started

- Player mistakenly reversed the adage "drive for show and putt for dough."
- People kept calling the player Magilla and he took to it.
- Player is so dim he has trouble reading a stop sign. Player read the putt as uphill.
- Player only practices his putting on shag carpet in the living room.
- Player loved hearing his playing partners sing Don McLean's "Bye, Bye, Miss American Pie" chorus as the ball accelerated by the hole on its way back to the fairway.

———

Jack conceded Blister's four foot putt, possibly because he expected the same consideration in return if he came up short.

"Wait a minute," Wiley interrupted. "If Jack gives Blister his putt then Blister's gotta give me my putt. I'm only a couple inches further than him."

"Well if Wiley picks up, it would be grossly unfair for me to putt," I protested. "I'm only six inches further than Wiley."

"Is this how Communism spreads with the domino effect?" Jack suddenly wanted to know. "If all you guys pick up then I'm certainly not gonna be three-putting from here. Sorry Blister, but you gotta mark your ball."

Blister had already picked up his ball but dropped a penny in the general vicinity of where he picked up his ball. When Jack hit his putt to within two and a half feet, the charade ensued again.

"The Chief's good if I'm good," Wiley campaigned.

"If the Chief's good, were all good," Jack corrected.

It was a case of four guys suddenly feeling the yips. However, since I was the furthest out at five feet, I had no reasonable expectation of making my putt anyway and was probably less affected by the yips than Wiley and Jack. Blister recognized the symptoms and began singing the Red Ball People Ode to the Yips, sung to the tune of Zip-a-dee-doo-dah.

> *Yip-a-dee-doo-dah, yip-a-dee-ay*
> *My, oh my what a yippidy day*
> *Plenty of lip-outs heading my way*
> *Yip-a-dee-doo-dah, yip-a-dee-ay*

"I'm not yipping anything," Jack said admonishing Blister with a stern glare.

"I'm four feet out. That's too far out to be considered a yip," Wiley assured Blister.

"Well if Wiley can't yip, then its impossible for me to have a Yip-a-dee-doo-dah," I observed.

I was the furthest out and if all putts were conceded, Blister and I would lose the hole since Blister would three putt at best. I put an end to the discussion when I stepped over my ball and rolled in a five foot putt. Wiley also made his. However, I conceded Blister and Jack's putts for harmony's sake. If Wiley and I had forced them to putt and it resulted in a Yip-a-dee-doo-dah, then they would be in a sour mood for the next several holes and I decided that $.50 was a small price to pay to keep the tribe unified.

Wiley and I were even par after four holes, though my shot making was so much poorer than Wiley's that Jack and Blister surely thought I was two over. Wiley and Blister walked the short distance to the fifth tee box while Jack and I drove the carts around. As I rounded the sweeping arc of the cart path to the next tee box, I glanced at the score card and was immediately annoyed when I saw that Wiley's team had won all four bets.

Hole 5
If a Ball Lands in the Water, and No One Saw it, Did it Make a Splash?

For the first time we had no wait on the tee box. The 360-yard par 4 was also one of the easiest holes since a tailwind nearly always added an extra twenty yards. If Tom Clancy were to play the hole, he would likely describe the large pond on the left that separated the fifth and ninth fairways as 'A Clear and Present Danger.' The OB markers that lined the bottom of the oak-studded hill on the right were an equally looming danger. Like the previous hole, the green was guarded by two sand traps on either side.

Wiley continued his hot streak by smashing his drive straight over the 150-yard marker.

"You're huge," Jack chimed at Wiley, meaning it in more ways than one.

I followed Wiley with a mediocre drive. Betting that a bad drive in the fairway was better than the two balls in Jack and Blister's pocket, Wiley selected me as his partner.

Blister continued his recovery with a drive that rolled ten yards beyond Wiley's ball.

"Looks like you climbed on the wrong horse!" Blister snarled at Wiley.

"If I needed someone who smelled like a horse I woulda chose you," Wiley retorted.

Soon enough, Jack reaffirmed our decision to crown him with the oft used moniker, Captain Hook. Although his ball reached an elevation higher than the willow tree on the edge of the pond, it began a nasty decent as soon as it cleared the tree. None of us saw the ball hit the water but unless some mysterious force of nature interrupted the flight path, there was no other outcome we could imagine.

"Do you think it made it over?" Jack asked anxiously.

"Not unless it bounced off a frog," Wiley assured him. "I didn't see the splash because the tree's in the way, but it wasn't long enough to clear."

"Doesn't look good Jack," I added confirming Wiley's assessment. "You can drop by the big willow tree."

As Wiley and I followed Blister down the cart path we wondered if there was any difference in the lateral hazard ruling for Jack's ball. None of us actually saw the ball enter the water hazard since the willow tree was in the way. Could Jack be the beneficiary of a special Red Ball People ruling to cover this unusual situation? The situation had come up numerous times before. Once more, Wiley and I enjoyed debating the merits of the argument on the way to the pond to assist Jack in his recovery effort.

If a Tree Falls in the Forest and There is No One to Hear it, Does it Make a Sound?

The Irish Philosopher and Bishop, George Berkeley, first proposed this conundrum around 1735. It seems an odd coincidence that the person who dreamed up this allegory had the last name of Berkeley. According to Berkeley, the philosopher not the town, to exist is to be perceived, though the majority of the town probably believes this as well. This little mind teaser is important to us because if we agree with Berkeley that there has to be hearing in order for there to be sound, its not too much of a stretch to assume that there has to be a seer to confirm the veracity of visual events. When you apply Berkeley's reasoning to Jack's duck hook, which was last seen quacking toward the pond, the implication is—unless someone saw his ball enter the pond, it didn't happen. Consequently, for Jack's benefit we will evaluate Berkeley's riddle and make a ruling on Jack's duck hook.

First, it is vital that we establish that Berkeley's tree did not fall on a bunch of pillows. In such a case, the tree wouldn't make any sound whether anybody was there to hear it or not. Presuming the tree did not fall on pillows, we must now turn our attention to the sensation of hearing and the phenomenon of sound. Sound is the brain's interpretation of compression waves that vibrate against our elastic eardrums. It follows that sound is in our head. Outside our heads are only waves. Consequently, if a tree did fall and did not fall on pillows, then it created compression waves and not sound.

Here's a simple way to empirically verify this claim. Trot down to a hardware store and purchase a boat horn. Hold it up to your ear, but not in the store, and sound the horn. You will be momentarily deaf. After regaining your equilibrium, blink your eyes until the little stars go away. For the next day or two you will hear ringing in your ear from the boat horn, confirming that the sound is indeed emanating from your head and not from the boat horn. Another way to confirm this assertion is to attend an Iron Maiden concert and sit in one of the first ten rows. I can assure you that you will still be receiving the concert two weeks after the encore is over.

So far, all we have established is that trees cannot make sounds and Berkeley asked a stupid question. The question he should have asked was—'Does a tree produce compression waves when it falls even though no one is around to perceive them?' The obvious way to arrive at our conclusion is to put a tape recorder by a tree that we anticipate will be falling in the near future. After performing this test several times, I am pleased to report that trees most certainly produce compression waves and nature is as uniform and predictable as we all thought it was. By extrapolation, we are faulty in presuming that Jack's ball did not enter the pond because none of us witnessed a splash. Consequently, we ruled that Jack was subject to a one-stroke penalty and was obligated to drop a second ball on the line in which the ball first crossed the water.

Jack made Wiley and I chuckle as we counted the number of infractions he piled up taking his drop. Wiley counted them out as they occurred, pretending he was Jack talking to himself.

"Let's see, I guess my driver must be about two hundred inches long. Two club lengths puts me out here about twenty five feet. Ok then. Now, as far as I can tell, my ball mysteriously changed directions, turning ninety degrees to the north into the pond. I guess I better drop it a little closer to where the ball made its left turn."

"You're killing me over here," I laughed as Wiley continued to simulate Jack's dialog with his own conscience.

"OK, a T-Rex drop should do the trick. Oh hell, I might as well bump it a little. It's not like I'm walking the ball up to the green," Wiley whispered in a goofy voice.

To avoid the heartbreak of the hillside, Jack chose to lay up with a 6-iron. He hit it flush and looked up just as it sailed over Blister who had left the cart to walk to his ball.

"Heads up Blister!" Jack yelled.

Blister didn't even bother to turn around but waved his club in the air acknowledging the warning.

"Hop on Jack, we'll give you a lift down to our balls," I offered. "Nice drop by the way. The shot wasn't bad either."

"Thanks Chief," Jack chuckled. "That's real special coming from you."

Jack climbed on the back of the cart straddling our two bags on the back.

"I've got to sustain some kind of an injury to get one of these flags," Jack complained. "Next time I ride with the Chief, Wiley. As a matter of fact, how about we trade carts on the back nine."

"Ain't gonna happen," Wiley replied ending the discussion.

I stopped equidistant between my ball and where I thought Wiley's ball was. Though I was sure I had seen his ball about twenty yards beyond my ball earlier, it was nowhere to be found as we climbed out of the cart.

"Where's your ball, Wiley? I thought it was just beyond mine."

"Beat's me. I thought I saw it a minute ago," Wiley replied with a sudden look of concern on his face.

"You're plugged over here Wiley," Blister interrupted, "and man is it a nasty lie."

Wiley walked over to where Blister was hunched over with his hand on his knees looking at the ground between his feet. An over-aggressive sprinkler system had made the low spots on the right side of the fairway soggy and Wiley's ball was at the bottom of a tire-sized indentation in the ground. After closer inspection, Wiley could see that his ball was plugged almost below the surface of the fairway. More puzzling was the concave depression of a size-twelve shoe print that created a concentric oval around his ball. To confirm his suspicions, Wiley glanced over at Blister's right foot and noticed a pronounced ring of mud that formed a skirt around the top of the sole of his Adidas golf shoe.

"That looks an awful lot like your shoe size Numbnuts," Wiley said accusingly, as he panned back to the shoe print.

"You're not blaming me for your ball being plugged are you?" Blister asked casually, as he turned his ankle and began wiping the side of his shoe on the grass.

I offered my assessment, "Thanks for taking care of that Blister. I had it on my to-do list."

"That's a one stoke penalty you know?" Wiley informed him.

Blister quickly countered, "Well, it would be if you actually saw the infraction or if I admitted I did it. But since you don't have proof of either, the best you can do is take relief and be glad I found your ball for you."

"Yeah, well maybe I can return the favor a little later," Wiley said with a smirk on his face.

Wiley put up no further resistance. He understood the Red Ball People ritual to step on an opponent's ball as a form of salute, acknowledging good play. The tribe squashed many balls over the years, though no one could think of one occasion where the feat was done unintentionally. Nevertheless, it must happen since the USGA had a rule for stepping on another player's ball.

Rule 18-3—Stepping on ball during search: *If an opponent steps on your ball during a search for lost ball opponent is not assessed a penalty. If player moves another opponent's ball while not conducting a search, whether stepped on or otherwise, offending player is assessed a one-stroke penalty.*

Red Ball People Amendment to Rule 18-3: *Rule remains the same for a missing ball. In addition, any player is entitled to step on another player's ball when not conducting a search, if owner of abused ball is playing far beyond his ability. To reduce the risk of a donnybrook, the right to step on another player's ball is restricted to one incident per round, and will result in a one-stroke penalty otherwise.*

Reason for change: *Rule change provides a non-verbal mechanism to serve notice to player with embedded ball, that other players* *recognize that he is playing way over his head and the action signals a unanimous referendum from his peers that the player's good fortune is not expected to continue. Rule change also allows for a few more chuckles on the course.*

Wiley dug his ball out of Blister's muddy shoe print, gave it a few wipes on the grass and placed it a few feet away with a T-Rex drop. Unfazed by the skirmish, he hit a wedge to within fifteen feet of the flag.

Blister and Jack hit the front of the green while I popped one off the toe of my 9-iron. Although I was pleased my ball stayed out of the right side bunker, I was well aware of the tricky slope between the trap and the green.

Dread set in when I took a closer look and confirmed the steepness of the downhill slope leading to the green. For whatever reason, I had been shanking short chips with similar downhill lies. I tried to force positive thoughts on myself, but I've been cursed with that unusual human attribute that some of us have that compels us to think negative thoughts instead. As I looked down at the ball, the first image that began to materialize as a backdrop was an airliner slamming into a mountain top.

The silent image was quickly joined by an internal mantra between two evildoers named Doubt and Qualm, who were cooking up a diabolical plot between my ears.

"You're gonna shank this Dick Cheney big time, aren't you?" Doubt asked.

"Not if I hit a fattie or blade it across the green," Qualm replied back to his fellow evildoer.

But Doubt was too clever for Qualm. He knew if he introduced a high stakes platitude, Qualm would cave under the pressure and hit the shank that Doubt desired. Doubt cast his line.

"I just got word that if you shank the chip, Kim Jong II will be so pissed off that he promises to launch a nuclear strike against the US."

Qualm knew he was beaten. The fattie he preferred would have to wait until Doubt was standing over the ball.

"You got me Doubt. Duck and cover because I'm the new mayor of Shankytown."

As any psychologist would tell you, where the mind leads, the body follows. The only shot I could play at the moment was a shank, so I played it the best I could. It took off toward Wiley's ball as I barked orders behind it.

"Stay away from that hole!"

"Eeehh," Wiley said with a grimace on his face.

"What the hell was that?" Jack wanted to know.

"Ask Blister, he's served a term or two as mayor of Shankytown," I answered.

I told the tribe that my most positive thought was that a shank would result in Kim Jong II starting a nuclear war. Blister laughed, and admitted that just before shanking his second ball on the third hole he had a premonition that his dog would die unless he could avoid hitting a hosel rocket. He naturally assumed that his dog would be dead when he got home.

Even though I was Wiley's partner for the hole, he was not unhappy that I shanked my ball. My ball had veered forty-five degrees to the right of the hole and stopped a few inches behind his ball. I would have to putt first and show him the line to the hole.

Jack walked up to pull the flag, walking on Blister's line as he did so. Blister, who was in the process of taking his address, stopped his routine to admonish Jack.

"You think that's a runway up there Jack?"

"Oh, sorry. Am I on your line?" Jack answered jumping to the other side of the hole.

"Not now. Now you're on Wiley and the Chief's line," Blister pointed out.

"Jack, get your carcass away from the hole will ya?" Wiley commanded.

Blister resumed his address position. Jack was still standing by the hole waiting to watch Blister's putt when Blister scolded him again.

"Jack, you're in my line of vision."

"How can I be in your line of vision when you're looking down at the ball?" Jack wanted to know.

Blister revealed the facts.

"You ever notice on TV that when one player is putting the other one is standing behind him or to his side but never in front or behind. It's known as the infinite line, Jack. You're not supposed to be anywhere near the infinite line that runs between my ball and the hole."

"You mean, if I stood on that ninth tee box over there you'd be bothered?" Jack asked pointing to the tee box fifty yards away on the line extending from Blister's ball through the hole.

"That's right. If I knew it was you, it would bother me," Blister responded.

"How about if I go stand in Napa? Or maybe behind you, in Oakland? That gonna bother you?" Jack asked sarcastically.

"Especially Napa or Oakland. I'm sure I'd spot your stomach with my peripheral vision and it would bother me," Blister replied.

Blister held firm and Jack finally moved out of Blister's line of vision. But the dust up was enough to wear down Blister's concentration. He left his putt five feet short and pushed it to the right. Rather than walk up directly behind his ball, Blister moved to the left until he located Jack's marker and proceeded to walk up Jack's line all the way to the hole before backtracking to pick up his own ball.

Putting Etiquette

Blister and Jack illustrated a couple of etiquette breaches that some players find offensive. Jack's lack of knowledge about the putting infinity line of his playing partner is symptomatic of the genre of golf instruction books, which dedicate far too many pages to teaching people how to play golf rather than how to avoid pissing off everyone on the course. Most of these instruction books would serve a higher public good if they dedicated half their material to etiquette and speedy play rather than how to hit a ball straight. It's not clear why the best minds of the game have chosen to ignore this important angle. Perhaps it's due to the number of slobs that professional golf instructors agree to play with during their professional careers. However, I play with plenty of slobs and am amply qualified to describe the breach of putting etiquette better than David Leadbetter, Butch Harmon, or Jim Flick.

Walking on your Line: The least important breach occurs when another player walks on your line. Chances are you have a transparent ball marker and the other player can't see it. So it is probably as much your fault as his. Secondly, even if you tee off at 7:30 A.M., a time when high handicappers can usually be found on the john reading the sports page, you probably had at least twelve foursomes walking on the same line as your breaching playing partner. So unless you happen to be playing with former San Francisco offensive lineman Bubba Paris, your playing partner did no more damage to your line than the forty-eight guys who preceded him. If your putt is longer than three feet, you won't make it anyway, so quit griping.

Casting a Shadow on your Line: Anyone not paying attention, which is nearly everyone in my foursome every week, will cast a shadow on your line at some point during the round. If you're not irate at the oak tree for doing the same thing, then you shouldn't be irate at your playing partner. If you are incensed at the oak tree then you may have good reason to be upset with your playing partner. On the other hand, if the player is so disinterested in your putting that he is waving to some cute tomato on an adjacent green or flapping his arms like a windmill to keep the flies off, then you have plenty of reason to look up and ask him if he minds if you putt while he creates electricity.

Standing Behind You While You Putt: Unless you are paired with a buddy in a best ball format, having a person who has the same putting line stand behind you while you putt is about as welcome as your finger penetrating cheap hotel toilet paper. It doesn't matter if the person is five feet behind you or fifty. He is not entitled to be there. Rather than say anything, it is better to leave your putt a few inches short of the hole and then walk on his line like you're one of the Great Wallendas, careful to step on his marker on the way. If his putt is a big breaker, after stepping on his ball marker, be sure to walk the path of the break where his ball will role and not directly to the hole. While you understand that his line has already been stepped on by forty-eight other golfers and the escapade will not affect his putt whatsoever, he won't understand since he is so stupid that he thinks walking on someone's line is the only blunder another player can commit. After you do this a few times, the dolt will do everything in his power to keep his ball out of your way and he won't have any reason to stand behind you any more.

Standing in Your Line of Vision on the Other Side of the Hole: While this breach is not nearly as bad as standing behind you, there are plenty of other places to stand. If you handle the situation correctly, schools' in session and you're the teacher. Just like in baseball, not every pitch has to be a strike. If Randy Johnson has to back someone off the plate, he'll waste a knockdown pitch tight and high. What's good for Randy is good for you. Follow Randy's lead, and whack your knockdown putt hard enough to get it airborne, allowing it to strike the offender on the shin. After a couple of bruises, he might get the message.

Talking While you Putt: A player who talks while you putt is either a dope or has no respect for your game. While he probably has no reason to respect your game, he still should not be talking while you putt. The best cure for this malady is to wait for his turn, specifically his back stroke, and unload a random outburst of invectives in such a way that he is led to believe that you are afflicted with Tourette's Syndrome. Let him believe it is nothing personal by facing away from him and looking up into the sky during your outburst. For the next few holes, thread together new and clever combinations of profanity for each outburst as he putts. To remain convincing you should mix in the names of a few rock stars, like say, McCartney, Lennon or Dylan. He may not quit talking while you putt but you won't care because you have Tourette's Syndrome for the day and life couldn't be better.

Tending the Flag the Wrong Way: This breach deserves honorable mention. There are plenty of things you can do wrong while tending the flag. The biggest goof is pulling the flag out of the hole with the tin cup still attached. You haven't lived unless you've done that in tournament play with good golfers. It only takes one mishap to learn that you must shake the flag loose from its mooring before yanking it out of the hole. Other oversights include creating a shadow across the hole, fidgeting around, or standing in another player's line while you tend the flag. The bottom line is, nobody tends the flag correctly and you should be happy that someone is helping you out when they would much rather be puffing a cigar in the shade.

I won my second bet of the day when Wiley and I both two putted. Blister recorded his first par while Jack's bushel of infractions still couldn't save him from a double. Wiley walked off the green with a smile on his face and a bounce in his step. He was even par after five holes. But Wiley was due for a correction. Newton's law of reaction guaranteed it.

Newton's Law of Reaction

Newton proved his third law of reaction in the late 16th century. Wiley would confirm the law sometime later, though he didn't know it at the time. The law of reaction states, "to every action there exists an equal and opposite reaction." It guarantees that things in nature, especially golfers, will eventually move toward equilibrium. According to the law, forces in nature occur in pairs with the same magnitude, but move in opposite directions.

Wiley was even par after five holes, far outside his statistical expectation of six or seven over par. This could only mean that negative forces were steadily building to a blowing point to offset the positive forces that so far, had gotten him to his near perfect round. A black cloud of mishap had to be gathering over Wiley to push his score back toward its statistical expectation. It was inevitable. The perfect storm was gathering and he was as oblivious as a moth drawn to a candle.

Fortunately for me, I had bogeyed the last hole and blew off a little pent-up negative steam. After five holes I was still three strokes better than my statistical expectation, but at least I was still within one standard deviation of my mean. Sweet Jesus—I could hardly wait to see it.

Hole 6
Heraclitus Goes Catfishing

The tee box for the 189-yard par 3 sixth hole was the largest bottle-neck on the course. The foursome in front of us was still waiting on the tee box when we arrived at our carts parked half way between the fifth green and the tee box.

Jack retrieved his leather cigar pouch from his bag and lit a Hoyo De Monterrey Maduro Churchill. He tossed one to Blister, but knew better than to offer one to Wiley and me. Wiley and I shared the same appraisal of Jack's cigars. If you had a hankering to smoke some hay through a garden hose, Jack was the guy to see. Though the quality of Wiley's cigars weren't much better, he only packed his bag with cigars for the times that I ran out of Montecristo No. 3s. Otherwise, I could expect Wiley to hit me up somewhere around the tenth or eleventh hole.

"Jumpin Jesus! Look at the butts on those two," Jack gasped, as he gawked at the shapely behinds of the two women standing to the side of the men's tee box.

It was the first time we had seen the women fairly close up, though we were still fifty feet away.

"Oh . . . you know who that is?" I said, recognizing the attractive blond next to the equally attractive brunette. "That's Babetta or Babs, as they call her. She works at the pro shop, but only on Sundays."

"Well I'll tell you one thing, Chief," Jack continued, "So long as I've got a face, she's got a place to sit down."

"Keah, keah, keah," Blister giggled, expelling the foul smell of his cigar in my direction.

"Yeah, I hear she digs overweight guys who smell like burning gym socks," I teased Jack. "I don't know who the brunette is, but I'm pretty sure I've played with that guy before."

The lanky man in his late thirties glanced at us before pivoting to put his tee in the ground. I recognized him immediately and shared the story with Jack and Blister.

"I remember that guy now. His name is Timothy Morris. It's an easy name to remember because when I called him Tim, he corrected me by saying—'It's Timothy.'

"What a dick," Blister retorted.

"Although I don't see his wife around, her name is Janet. I remember that because she also corrected me when I called her Jan.

"What a bitch," Blister said on cue.

Timothy started his swing. Before he could finish his over-wrought downswing, the toilet in the women's cinder-block restroom behind the men's tee box flushed, startling Timothy enough to clip his 5-wood into the hillside.

"That would be Janet," I guessed.

"Keah, keah, keah," Blister spontaneously giggled at Timothy's mishap.

Janet emerged from the restroom and joined Babetta and the brunette on the women's tee box, some twenty five yards ahead of the men's tees.

Babetta was in her later twenties and had a well-toned figure on a 5' 7" frame. She was naturally attractive without eyeliner and lipstick, which she seldom wore. She wore a short tan pair of shorts that highlighted her slender light brown legs. To keep her long straight blond hair from impeding her swing, she had a ponytail pulled through the back of a blue cap. Evidently, she preferred to be called Babs since she always wore a nametag with the abbreviated name.

The brunette sported a shorter curled cropped style haircut and didn't wear a cap. Although she appeared to have a similar nose and facial features, she was wearing sunglasses making it difficult to judge her age.

We watched the women spray their balls short of the green before we climbed the mound to the men's tee box. Timothy and Janet recognized me as they passed us on their way back to their cart.

"Hey, how's it going?" Tim asked without breaking stride or waiting to hear the answer.

"Hey Tim," I replied as I continued my march up the mound.

"Keah, keah," Blister giggled, trailing behind me.

"Mr. Wildroot, how's the round going?" Babs sang, as the two women approached from the ladies tee box.

"Playing over my head so far, how about you Babs?" I responded with a smile that I reserved for attractive women.

"You better call him Chief or he'll think you're talking to his dad," Blister chuckled, bringing the free flow of conversation to a halt.

After giving Blister a puzzled look, Babs and I exchanged a little courtesy banter before I introduced her to Wiley and Jack. She remembered Blister, probably from some unforgotten Sunday incident on the driving range. She introduced the brunette as Donetta, her sister. Both admitted that they had each been rebuked for using the abbreviated names of Timothy and Janet. After another anecdote or two about their playing partners, the sisters scurried down to their cart as Jack and Wiley expanded their sucked-in guts back over their belts.

Blister wandered off to the south side of the cinder block restroom out of view of the fifth green and took relief against the hillside, even thought the men's restroom was only a few feet away.

By the time Blister returned, the eldest Mr. Kim was marching up the mound toward us on the tee box. The eldest Mr. Kim arrived shortly after his battery operated pull cart, which he proficiently guided from behind with his remote control. Though there was no need to have his electric pull cart on the tee box, Mr. Kim was tickled that he could demonstrate its all-terrain climbing ability to us.

"How you play?" he asked me.

"So far, I'm one over, but this guy's even par so far . . . but it ain't gonna last," I informed Mr. Kim while pointing at Wiley. "How about you?"

"I find seven balls so far," Mr. Kim replied choosing to measure his success by the number of balls acquired during the round.

He reached into his trouser pocket and pulled out his treasure to substantiate his story.

"Did you find any Titleists with red marks?" I pried, showing him my trade-mark.

"No today, but I find two Tuesday," Mr. Kim said proudly as he reached into his bag and dug through his bonanza. A moment later, he spun around and broke into a grin as he lunged his hand toward me with two of my AWOL balls.

"You found two of the Chief's balls!" Wiley exclaimed. "Nice work Mr. Kim."

"You take," Mr. Kim insisted.

Mr. Kim grew up in a culture where possessions had to be returned to their rightful owner. When I refused to accept his offer, he dashed over to my cart and deposited the two balls in the driver's side cup holder.

"Thanks Mr. Kim," I said graciously, "I'll try to play them wisely."

Our wait was shorter than expected as we watched Babs and Donetta pick up their balls after a few feeble attempts at chipping. Before Mr. Kim returned to the mound, Wiley reminded me that it was my turn to hit.

"I hate to interrupt your quality time with your new buddy, but it's your turn to hit, Chief."

I turned my attention to the deep blue flag. I was always intimidated by the hole. A river entered the southeast corner of the course behind the seventh tee box and traversed the south side of the sixth hole separating it from the oak studded hill that drooped down to the tee box. The river turned north in front of the ladies tee box, where it would make a nuisance of itself for several subsequent holes on both sides of the course.

I hurried my routine to avoid being overcome with negative thoughts and hooked the ball, as I normally do, near the bunker guarding the left side of the hole. I accepted the poor shot as a sign that Newton's Law of Reaction was exerting its influence to force my score back to equilibrium.

Blister and Jack followed with adequate 5-woods that fell short of the green. As soon as Jack's ball cleared the hazard, I coronated him as my Wolf partner since he had two obvious factors working in his favor. First, he was the only player who received a stroke on the hole. Secondly, I knew Wiley couldn't stave off Newton's Law much longer.

Wiley pulled his 7-wood. It was his one hundred and eighty five yard club. With a little interference from Newton, it could easily become his fifty yard club. Wiley's confidence was peaking as he stood over the tee. He started his backswing just as Newton's equilibrium came rushing up the canyon. Just before contact, the negative forces that had been building for the past hour and a half blew a hole in the plenum near his club face causing the club to strike the ball on the shoulders. With maximum topspin, the ball skipped off the ladies tee box and into the river.

"Ouuuuuu," said Mr. Kim unable to stay quiet.

Wiley collected himself and reached in his pocket for another ball. But like a lot of players who are riding the big curling wave of confidence, he didn't have another ball in his pocket. The last thing he expected was to lose his ball after the way he had been playing.

"You got an extra ball Chief?" Wiley asked me.

"No I don't," I responded, lying to Wiley. I didn't think equilibrium had been attained yet, and I certainly wasn't going to donate one of my NXTs to the forces of evil.

Blister, who doesn't have my scientific understanding of Newton's Law, flipped Wiley one of his Callaway Warbird balls. Wiley placed Blister's sacrifice on the tee and began waggling his 7-wood. To make sure he didn't top this ball, Wiley interrupted his waggle to raise the tee a little higher. He then resumed his waggling. Wiley's adjustment unwittingly allowed the negative forces of equilibrium to morph into a different variety of mishap. On his second swing, Wiley swept under the Warbird striking it near the bottom with the top of his club. Had we been playing baseball, the infield fly rule would have been called. The ball looped over the ladies tee box and plopped down in the middle of the river.

"That looked more like a duck with a broken wing than a Warbird," Jack observed.

"Ouuuuuu," Mr. Kim said again.

Wiley beat the tee into the ground where it should have been in the first place. He stared for another moment at the river as if he expected the ball to come jumping back out. When it didn't, he slung his 7-wood across the back of his shoulders, clutching it at either end with both hands, and shuffled down the mound toward our cart.

"You not only lost my ball, you lost my bet," Blister said, as he poked Wiley in the seat of his pants with his 5-wood as he followed him down the mound.

95

"You poke me one more time and your nuts are the next thing you're gonna be losin," Wiley warned.

"I'll drop on the other side, Chief," Wiley told me, proclaiming his intention to take an illegal drop.

Mr. Kim was already lifting his ball retriever pole from his bag as we departed. With any luck, Blister would have his Warbird returned, courtesy of Mr. Kim.

The glaze on Wiley's face told me he was forecasting his best-case and worst-case scenario scores. Oddly enough, I had just completed my own joyous calculation. He would be lucky to get a triple, but quadruple was more likely. My spirits began to soar.

Since Wiley was taking an illegal drop on the wrong side of the hazard, the number of penalty strokes might have to be negotiated. If Wiley wanted to be clever about his scoring perhaps he could utilize logic propounded by Greek Philosopher, Heraclitus.

Can Wiley Hit a Ball into the Same River Twice?

The Greek Philosopher, Heraclitus, postulated that one cannot put his foot into the same river twice. If Heraclitus is correct, it stands to reason that maybe it is also impossible for Wiley to hit a golf ball into the same river twice, despite sensory perception telling us otherwise. Let's take a closer look and see if Heraclitus can help Wiley out.

Heraclitus lived around 500 B.C. in the small village of Ephesus. He was an avid catfish fisherman and spent the majority of his leisure time, roughly twelve hours each day, fishing in the Ephesus River that meandered through his village. His favorite spot was under a willow tree near a bend in the river by the marble quarry. For hours, he sat on a rock under the willow tree dangling his feet in the water while trolling the bottom of the river for slimy catfish.

Heraclitus was a deep thinker and had plenty of time to ponder how the world behaved while he was fishing. One day it struck him that the water in the river was flowing past his feet toward a lower elevation, which rivers are inclined to do. Before too long, the water swirling around his feet hinted to him that the world was in a constant state of flux. Upon realizing he was on the verge of forging a new branch in Philosophy called Presocratic Physiology, Heraclitus set about gathering empirical evidence to prove his conjecture that the world was in a state of flux.

Over the course of several days he sat on his rock, cast his fly into the water, and concentrated on the swirling water around his feet as he waited for the catfish to bite. He took careful notes as he repeatedly stuck his right foot in the water, quickly pulled it out, and shook it all about. (An interesting side note: Over two millennia later, musician Roland LaPrise became so inspired reading about Heraclitus' leg dance, he was moved to write the popular 1940s hit—The Hokey Pokey.)

Convinced that he had performed his foot dipping test a sufficient number of times, Heraclitus issued his famous proclamation before an astonished Ephesus town hall meeting—'one cannot set their foot into a moving river twice.' Later, many of Heraclitus' contemporaries acknowledged the role that serendipity played in the formation of Presocratic Physiology when they discovered that Heraclitus was using the wrong fishing bait, thus affording him hours of uninterrupted research time in which to conduct his foot dipping experiments.

Two thousand five hundred years later, Alfred North Whitehead disproved the adage that dead horses can't be beaten, when he ran Heraclitus research up the flagpole. In a move calculated to put himself on tenure track at Trinity College in Cambridge, Whitehead dusted off Heraclitus' observation and expanded it further. According to Whitehead, not only is the river different, the person sticking his foot in the river is also different. They are changing biologically, physiologically, and even chemically, he argued. It follows that by the time you put your foot in the river, pull it out, then put it back in again, you're a different person. Consequently, the same person can't step into the same river twice.

Sadly for Whitehead, the tenure committee found his argument so convincing, they concluded he was a different person from the one who actually formulated the argument, and he was denied tenure and accused of plagiarism.

It seems that our problem is even more complicated than we first envisioned. Not only are we required to form a judgment about whether or not Wiley can hit more than one ball into the river, we must also arrive at some disposition about our previous notion that it was really Wiley who hit both balls!

Even Heraclitus would agree that it was indeed some form of Wiley that hit the first ball into the water. Under any scenario then, he would at least be penalized one stroke. Secondly, Heraclitus would probably not dispute that some form of Wiley hit a second ball into a river, just not the same river he hit moments earlier. Since there is no provision in the USGA rulings that attempts to distinguish one river from another, or from itself for that matter, we can conclude that some version of Wiley hit his ball into two water hazards, though perhaps different water hazards that occupy the same spatial location. Consequently, a second penalty stroke appears justified.

Pertaining to the second matter posed by Whitehead, we must deliberate on whether the second penalty applies to Wiley or someone else, since Wiley became a different person between the shots. The alternative is to assign the penalty to one of the other players, who also became different people between the shots.

Our challenge is to determine the most likely person Wiley became and assign the second penalty to that poor sap. We only have four choices: New Jack, New Wiley, New Blister, and New Chief Tit. Luckily for all of us except New Wiley, Plato came to the rescue by discovering the essence of being. Essence, according to Plato, is that quality which persists through change that enables us to say—'the thing that changed is still the same thing.' Indeed, his concept of essence guarantees that Wiley is the same dope that he used to be. With an assist from Plato, we can freely assign the second penalty to Wiley or New Wiley, who share the same essence.

———————

After crossing the river, I dropped Wiley off so he could take his illegal drop. The negative forces of equilibrium appeared to be satisfied for the moment as I watched Wiley knock his wedge to the middle of the green.

While keeping his eye on the action, Jack spotted Mr. Kim behind Wiley stepping down the bank of the river with his ball retrieval pole.

"Looks like your ball's going to have a new owner," Jack said to Blister pointing back at Mr. Kim.

Blister turned to look back at Mr. Kim and replied, "Third owner in the last five minutes."

I hit an easy wedge while Blister and Jack both chose to use a putter from off the front of the green. Although Wiley's ball was in their putting line, neither player bothered to walk up and mark Wiley's ball, reasoning that if they can't hit a hole they need not worry about an even smaller object. Jack's ball came up nine feet short while Blister's stopped two feet behind Jack.

Wiley was the furthest out and picked up his ball and wiped it on his shirt without marking its location. Although the surface was as flat as any putting surface on the course, the twenty footer would require some element of concentration.

"Jack, you wanna pull the flag?" Wiley reminded him.

"Oh right," Jack replied.

As he removed the flag, Jack glanced over at Babs and Donetta who were off to the side of their cart parked by the men's tee box on hole seven. Babs was bending over testing her swing posture when Jack established missile lock on her protruding rear end. As she bent over, her tan shorts hiked up her legs exposing the back three-fourths of her upper thighs. Jack carefully examined the tightening of her buttock muscles as she pivoted her shoulders from one side to the next.

"Oh Lord, don't let me go blind now," Jack thought to himself as she walked over to the front of her cart and stretched out her hands and leaned on the front of the cart to stretch out her calf muscles. She folded her left leg under her body as she extended her right leg behind her. She gyrated slowly up and down to flex her calf.

"Oh mercy, what an ass," Jack said to himself.

He was still straining his eyes to determine if she was wearing thong underwear when Wiley's ball struck him on the right foot.

"Whoa, what's going on?" Jack said, suddenly finding himself back in a world he didn't want to return to quite yet.

"You're fat ass is in the way," Wiley replied. "That's what's going on. You wanna play with us or Babs?"

"You look at that ass and answer your own question," Jack said gesturing toward Babs.

Jack had a defense that was going to be difficult to poke holes in. The rest of us soon had missile lock as well. It was evident that no further putting would occur until we could substantiate whether or not Babs was wearing a thong. The four Kims behind us would have to cool their heels until the matter was settled.

"If it's not a thong, it's certainly a g-string," Blister guessed.

"I bet she's going dinky," Wiley guessed.

"Dinky?" I asked Wiley.

"No panties," Wiley clarified.

Babs switched to stretching her left leg and folded her right knee under her chest. She resumed the slow gyrations flexing the calf and thigh muscles of her left leg. However, this time the outline of the thong was clearly visible on her right buttock as she brought her knee closer to her chest.

"Well that settles that," Blister announced.

Although the underwear issue was settled to everyone's satisfaction, we kept Babs in our sights for another minute while we verified and re-verified our conclusions. Fortunately for us, the Kims were a very patient group as they waited on the tee behind us. Since this wasn't the first time Jack's mind had wandered while tending the flag causing him to be struck by a ball, we were prepared for the occasion with a Red Ball People Amendment to Rule 17-3.

Rule 17-3: Putt strikes player attending the flag. *Player striking putt is ruled to have ceded trust and authorization to the tending party and is assessed a two-stroke penalty for striking tending player.*

Proposed Change to Rule 17-3: *If putt strikes player attending the flag, putting player is awarded the putt and tending nitwit, who probably is also unable to get out of the way of a seeping glacier, will receive no further conceded putts for the remainder of the round. Further, putting victim reserves the right to kick nitwit's ball offline later in the round if nitwit is on the verge of sinking an unexpected putt.*

Reason for change: *This falls under the classification of—'what's good for the goose is good for the gander.' If you are playing with a dunce who is too stupid to get out of the way of a 2 MPH putt, then* *the rule should be written to allow for cruel and unusual punishment.*

On occasion, the Red Ball People amended their amendments. This was one of those occasions. It was determined that the importance of determining Babs' underwear status took precedent over Jack getting his fat ass out of the way of Wiley's putt and he was not penalized for the infraction. Since Jack was standing behind the hole when he was hit, it was evident that Jack did not deflect Wiley's putt from going into the hole and Wiley was not awarded the putt and would have to accept his quadruple-bogey.

We were in a hurry to get to the seventh tee box and confirm our thong hypothesis, and no one wanted to jeopardize the research by taking too much time to line up their putt. Unable to muster any concentration, Jack, Blister, and I missed our putts and made bogey. Oh yeah, Jack and I also won the hole.

Score Card After 6 Holes

Hole	1	2	3	4	5	6	7	8	9	Out
Yardage	472	145	345	169	360	189	511	392	505	3088
Handicap	11	5	17	13	15	9	7	1	3	
Wiley	⑤	③->(o)	④	③	④	7				
Chief Tit	6	②->(o)	4	3	⑤	④				
Blister	⑥	6 ²	7 ³	4	4	4				
Jack	8 ¹	3	⑥	③	6	④ ⁴				
Par	5	3	4	3	4	3	5	4	5	36

Notes:
/ => Signifies that player gets stroke
◯ => Signifies that player won bet
->(o) => Heiroglyphic for "out of ass." Chief Tit and Wiley pull two shots out of their ass on 2nd hole.
¹ Jack picks up ball. Red Ball People abacus only has 8 beads - Jack takes an 8.
² Blister concedes 6 foot putt to himself for a Linda Tripp.
³ Blister picks up ball after 2 shanks - he takes a 7.
⁴ Bab's thong status takes precedent over tending. Jack not assessed penalty for being struck by putt.

Hole 7
Talking with the Dolphins

The Morris' had already pulled away as we raced our carts to the seventh tee box to confirm our thong hypothesis. As luck would have it, Babs was fiddling with her head cover affording us an excellent view of the research zone. If the team could not reach consensus, the opportunity might be lost for the day. We eased up behind her so she wouldn't be startled, just as she bent over to pick up two spilled tees. Time slowed to a crawl as the fabric began tightening. The crease in each side of the shorts became shorter as the 35% cotton minority ceded authority to the 65% polyester majority. The fabric slowly began assuming the contour of the surface it surrounded yielding a wealth of research data, which the team struggled to assimilate. Our scientific determination was rewarded as the outline of a v-shaped thong began to emerge.

"The eagle has landed," Jack proclaimed, startling Babs.

"What?" Babs asked, as she spun around to catch us creeping up behind her.

"Jack means . . . um," I stammered, covering for Jack, "Ah . . . you should . . . um, be able to eagle with that nice drive,"

"Oh . . . ah, thanks, Chief," Babs stuttered back, eyeing us with a little suspicion. "But that's only about a hundred and fifty yard drive."

"Still—most impressive," Wiley chimed in.

Babs gave us a faint smile, not quite sure what to make of the encounter, before climbing in the cart and departing.

"Well, we couldn't have timed that much better," Jack gloated.

"The eagle has landed?" Wiley asked with incredulity.

"That's right," Jack said assuredly. "We set about to prove our hypothesis and we got it done."

"Quod erat demonstrandum," I said.

"Quote a rat about what?" Blister asked.

"Quod erat demonstrandum," I repeated. "You know—QED. That's Latin for, *'which was asked to be proved.'*"

"Thanks for the lesson Mr. Big Word, but why don't we limit the remainder of our conversation today to English?" Blister requested.

"I'll do better than that, Blister," I retorted. "For you, I'll try to keep it to the basics of what a dolphin can understand."

"Arrrk, arrrk," Blister barked, agreeing to my offer.

"That's a seal, not a dolphin," I informed him.

"Oh . . . that's right," Blister said, as his face lit up. "With Professor Goldston's new invention, we can talk to the dolphins."

"You got that right," Jack interceded, answering our delusional friend.

As usual, Jack had been on the warpath about military spending. When things were slow at the office, Jack often spent his idle time searching left-wing message boards until he located a suitable article about military waste that could be forwarded to Wiley. Sometimes, Wiley even played along. In recent weeks, their collaboration resulted in the discovery of a top secret Navy program headed by none other than—Professor Daniel Goldston.

Jack assumed the lead role of investigative reporter and notified us that he had stumbled on a recently declassified Navy research project about communicating with dolphins. The project was described in an email titled, *'The Army has the Hummer but the Navy has the Humdinger.'*

Talking With Dolphins

The research began harmlessly enough, when Jack tracked some of the expenses of elite Navy researchers who were conducting communication experiments with dolphins to assess how the smartest fish in the sea might be used for naval warfare. Before long, the money trail led to an astonishing discovery—one of the highest ranking officers stationed at the Navy Seal training facility on Coronado Island near San Diego—was a dolphin named Flipper.

For years, Navy specialists made very little headway in communicating with our slippery friends. Remarkably, just as funding was about to be cut, a revolutionary voice synthesizer was invented by prime number expert and San Jose State Professor, Daniel Goldston.

An avid lover of marine life, Goldston experimented with applying neural-net technology to voice and behavioral patterns of dolphins he observed and recorded at Marine World. He was still in the process of refining his invention when the head of Coronado's research team, Commander Beck, saw a segment on Goldston's dolphin communicator while watching his favorite TV show, *Entertainment Tonight*. Commander Beck immediately contacted Professor Goldston and offered him a government grant to work with the Navy on his top-secret project, which Goldston gladly accepted.

Goldston called his synthesizer, which translated the English language into dolphin language and vice-versa, the Human-Dolphin Mimicking Synthesizer. Understanding the Navy's preference for catchy acronyms, he suggested to Commander Beck that the Navy adopt the new top secret project name—HUMDINGER ("**HUM**an-**D**olphin Mimick**ING** Synthesiz**ER**). Beck was delighted with the new name and quickly lobbied Navy Brass for a ten-fold increase in funding.

The early models of the HUMDINGER were crude and only contained a few nouns and verbs such as ball, hoop, swim, toss, and jump. However, once massive funding was granted, Professor Goldston knew he would be under pressure to produce results. In a strategy that he failed to share with Commander Beck and the General Accounting Office, Goldston took a few liberties with the translating device and retooled his invention so the communicator would yield the type of results that were a little more conducive to the level of funding that had been granted. Goldston expanded the dolphin vocabulary database from the empirically justified level of twelve simple nouns and verbs to the complete Oxford English Dictionary. The database was further supplemented with classifications of Soviet-made navel vessels. To guarantee a ten-fold increase in funding for subsequent years, he tweaked the neural-net language translator to detect missing verbs, nouns, adverbs, pronouns, and predicates from the laboratory dolphins and bridge the omissions with a HUMDINGER interpolation of what the dolphin probably is trying to say.

The smartest of the Coronado dolphins was Flipper. He was also Commander Beck's favorite, since he gave the Commander the best rides around the research pool. The following top-secret transcript recorded between Commander Beck, Professor Goldston, and Flipper, with the aid of the HUMDINGER, was used in the most recent funding request and was obtained through the Freedom of Information Act . . . at least that's what Jack claimed.

COMMANDER BECK: *"How are you today, Flipper?"*

FLIPPER: *"Eeeeeech, eeeeh. (Flipper want fish)."*

[HUMDINGER: *"I've got a little bout of mercury poisoning, but I stand ready to attack a North Korean submarine at your command. Permission to speak freely sir?"*]

COMMANDER BECK: *"Go right ahead, Flipper."*

FLIPPER: *"Eeeh, eeeh, eeeeeeeh (Flipper toss ball)."*

[HUMDINGER: *"Have you guys been making any progress on keeping us out of those tuna nets?"*]

COMMANDER BECK: *"No progress on the nets yet but Tom Ridge ordered the Coast Guard to blow any foreign boat out of the water that comes within three miles of US territory, so just be sure you and your friends stay within three miles of the coastline."*

FLIPPER: *"Eeeh, eeeeeh, eeeeh (Flipper jump through hoop)."*

[HUMDINGER: *Can you strap that camera on my dorsal fin again? I just love these simulation exercises where I swim around a floating beer keg and pretend I'm taking underwater pictures of a Soviet designed North Korean Romeo Class submarine."*]

COMMANDER BECK: *"I knew it!"*

FLIPPER: *"eeeeeeech, eeeeh (Flipper want fish)."*

[HUMDINGER: *"Commander, would you mind keeping your finger out of my blow hole next time I give you a ride around the pool?"*]

COMMANDER BECK: *"Sorry. Consider it done."*

FLIPPER: *"Eeeh, eeeh, eeeeeeeh (Flipper toss ball)."*

[HUMDINGER: *"Commander, the other dolphins aren't going to take me serious and follow me when I swim in circles unless I get that promotion we discussed."*]

COMMANDER BECK: *"I'm pleased to say that the Brass approved my recommendation to make you an Ensign."*

FLIPPER: *"Eeech, eeeeech, eeeech (Flipper dance on tail fin)."*

[HUMDINGER: *"If I had opposable thumbs, I'd pour you a drink and offer you a cigar. This time though, would you mind painting the stripe on my fin rather than pinning the bar to my fin? That last promotion hurt like the dickens."*]

COMMANDER BECK: *"Consider it done . . . Ensign Flipper."*

PROFESSOR GOLDSTON: *"Flipper, last time you had a little trouble in our training exercise that called for attaching an explosive to the bottom of a mock-up North Korean warship. You attached it to the Navy diver instead. Fortunately, for him it was only a simulation explosive. Have you worked out the kinks for the next exercise?"*

FLIPPER: *"Eeeeeeeech, eeeeh (Flipper want fish)."*

[HUMDINGER: *"That was only the second incident of friendly fire that I've had, which is well within acceptable Navy tolerance levels. Besides, he started it when he put a barnacle on my back."*]

PROFESSOR GOLDSTON: *"Understood. Anything we can do for you?"*

FLIPPER: *"Eeeh, eeeh, eeeeeeeh (Flipper toss ball)."*

[HUMDINGER: *"I wouldn't mind if you brought one of those little tomatoes from Marine World and put her in my tank with me . . . if you catch my drift."*]

———————————

Since our own research team had no further need for collaboration, Blister and Jack meandered away from the ball cleaner back toward their cart to retrieve their drivers.

The seventh hole was a 511-yard yard par 5 with a hard dogleg to the left. Both sides of the fairway are lined with pine and eucalyptus trees. Just outside the pine trees on the right were white stakes and a cyclone fence that separated the course from a cow pasture. The bend on the left side of the fairway is guarded by a trap that often comes into play for those who aim too far left. After the bunker, the fairway turns nearly sixty degrees in a northerly direction. Though big hitters sometimes reached the green in two, there was little payoff in trying since a huge oak tree hung over the front of the hole and knocked down any loft less than a 6-iron. Additional trouble lurked to the right of the green where a finger of the river protruded around the green. The hole was rated the seventh most difficult so Blister and Jack received strokes.

Blister was up first and he hit a dandy—a YANKee doodle dandy. The ball took off dead left and smacked the trunk of a pine tree seventy yards away and bounced straight back, stopping a few yards in front of the ladies tee box.

Wiley and I were hoping Blister would choose Jack as his partner since they both had strokes, but the wish evaporated when Jack caught the fairway bunker at the bend.

Wiley was coming off a quadruple-bogey and was determined to right the ship. To my relief, Wiley striped a ball down the right side forcing Blister to choose him.

"The Chief's going to do better than that," Wiley said to Blister hoping to avoid the pairing.

"If you don't choose Wiley, I promise to hit my drive out of bounds," I warned Blister, trying to force his hand.

"And I know that you're more than capable," Blister responded. Blister turned to Wiley to deliver the bad news, "You've won five bets already, so consider this your opportunity to give back to the community."

As I replaced Wiley on the tee box it occurred to me that I was only two over par. Newton's Law of Reaction had finally caught up with Wiley. Perhaps it was sizing me up at this very minute. Before I could determine if the law of equilibrium would catch up with me, Jeb the Marshal caught up with me. As I addressed the ball, the squeal of brakes announced his arrival. I backed off the tee and looked at Jeb.

Jeb was in his early sixties and had two hundred pounds packed around his 5' 5" frame. His job was to keep the course moving but he often had the opposite effect, as he liked to cruise up to tee boxes at full tilt and lock up his brakes, unnerving whoever was about to hit their drive. I backed off the ball and gave Jeb an annoyed look.

"How's the round going Wildroot?" Jeb wanted to know.

"Slow," I said. "It would go a lot faster, but for some reason, people keep asking me how my round is going when I'm standing over my ball."

Jeb got the point and gave me a backhanded wave as if ordering me to carry on with my business. Jeb had provided some extraneous stimulus that I didn't need at the moment. He had interrupted my routine just as he had on numerous Saturdays before. In fact, I wondered why the course management labeled these guys Marshals? Real Marshals carry a badge and a gun. If Jeb had a gun, he would blow his foot off. If Jeb had a badge it would say, *'If your village is missing an idiot—I'm for hire'*. The only bigger misnomer for guys like Jeb was the title of Ambassador, which other courses used to describe their freeloaders. Imagine Jeb as a real ambassador, I thought to myself. Before assigning him a country, the State Department would first need to identify a country where it was a cultural custom to have urine stains on your pants at state dinners. Jeb could certainly meet that requirement.

"Are you drifting again?" Jack asked, interrupting my State Department assignment.

"I was fine until Jeb drove up," I told Jack.

"Well unless you want him in our foursome the rest of the day, I suggest you forget about him and hit the ball," Jack advised.

Without further thought about Jeb's qualification for the State Department, I took my stroke and crushed a drive down the right side of the fairway almost identical to Wiley's.

Jeb sped off to find a good shade tree to sit under while the course continued to back up ahead of us. With Wiley and I so close to the cart path, I offered a temporary transfer of the blue flag to Jack.

Blister tagged his second shot before he and Jack proceeded to the bunker. I caught a lucky break on my second stroke when a giant eucalyptus branch deflected a flare back to the fairway. Wiley wasn't as fortunate, as Newton's Law of Reaction closed the face of his 3-iron, causing a hook into the pine trees on the left.

While Wiley grabbed a handful of irons and steamed off after his ball, I glanced at Jack flailing away in the bunker just as his ball smacked off the lip and bounced directly back at him, striking his right knee. The lip had removed all the velocity, so pain was not a factor, but he was so surprised to see a ball coming at him that he stumbled back and fell over, landing on his back. The tee box two hundred and thirty yards behind him erupted in laughter as the Kims watched the calamity.

Jack lay in the trap looking at the sky for a moment before he sat up and started brushing the sand from his arms. Jack was in the process of piling up strokes faster than a piston. Up to this point, Jack had incurred a two-stroke penalty for striking himself with the ball. According to the USGA, an additional two strokes should be added for grounding his club when he toppled into the bunker. The fifth and sixth strokes would quickly follow when he used his iron as a crutch to lift himself off the ground. The incident left his ball in the indentation of his footprint. If he elected to do an illegal drop, which was his custom, nine and ten would quickly follow. The eleventh and twelfth penalty strokes would inevitably follow when he cleaned his ball before placing it back in the sand. Since Jack liked things around him to be neat, he might also choose to rake his footprints before hitting, for an additional two strokes.

Unless I intervened with some Red Ball People amendments, my partner Jack could be sitting sixteen before he took another shot. I wasted no time in my ruling.

Rule 19-2b—Penalty when player is struck by own ball: *A player who is struck by their own ball will incur a two-stroke penalty. This rule also applies when player's caddie and equipment is struck.*

Red Ball People Amendment to Rule 19-2b: *Player will not be assessed a two stroke penalty for striking himself, his equipment, or his caddie.*

Reason for change:
a) Striking own self: *A blow from a ball that produces minimum pain, even if limited to the ego, constitutes sufficient evidence that 'injury' is being added to 'insult.' Red Ball People do not observe laws, codes, and rules where insult can be added to injury or vice versa.*

b) Striking caddie: *If player strikes his caddie and it is determined by a majority of the players that the caddie was too fat to get out of the way, player will not be assessed a two stroke penalty. Further, players will be afforded plenty of leeway to determine if the caddie's tubbiness was a factor.*

c) Striking equipment: *If player has such talent that he is able to strike his own equipment when the rest of us can't even hit a green, then this player should be commended and not penalized.*

By the time he illegally placed his ball, Jack had taken fifteen or twenty raking strokes with his club. With the illegal cleaning, Blister and I estimated that the tally could have reached as high as thirty-five or forty strokes.

After a couple more favorable rulings that suppressed nearly forty strokes, Jack knocked his third shot beyond the 150-yard fifty yard marker.

Blister, determined to prove that there was a fine line between stupendous and stupid, pulled out his 3-wood despite Jack's voracious warning, and shot a rocket to the right of the cart path where it took a nasty bounce off the hardpan before disappearing over a mound toward the protruding river finger.

"What's over there?" Blister asked with obvious concern on his face.

"Your ball," Jack said, as he turned to walk back to his cart.

I repossessed the blue flag from Jack, and set off to help Wiley find his ball amid the deeper grass separating the seventh and eighth fairways. We found it about one hundred and forty five yards from the hole. However, the line to the hole was obstructed on the left by a eucalyptus tree some thirty yards in front of the ball. The limbs stretched out to the right nearly touching the limbs of a pine tree further to the right. His best option was to accept his poor predicament, take his medicine, and pitch the ball thirty yards sideways. To my surprise and financial benefit, Wiley began evaluating an entirely different option. He looked up into the eucalyptus tree and began to examine the density of the branches.

"You know, Chief . . . trees are 90% air," he said, as he looked up at the filtered blue sky between branches.

"I bet you couldn't convince an insurance company of that," I replied.

"I see a lot of blue sky through that tree," he said, ignoring me. "A 7-iron should clear that lower branch and stay well below that upper branch."

"Now you're talking," I said, bearing false witness.

"I've got plenty of room through those branches, Chief," Wiley concluded with confidence, as he stepped over his ball and took aim.

"That would be my first choice," I said, as the lies spewed forth.

Before Wiley had time to look up to follow the flight, he heard the smack of solid wood repelling his ball backward. Wiley's measurement had proved faulty as the ball had struck the lower limb of the eucalyptus tree. The ball rolled to a stop about ten yards in front of him. He would essentially have the same shot again, though perhaps with an 8-iron this time, which was good for Wiley since he snapped off the head of his 7-iron against a nearby pine tree after watching the outcome of his careful measurement.

As I examined the head of his 7-iron, Wiley retrieved an 8-iron that I suspected would suffer the same fate if he tried to repeat the same strategy. I became giddy when Wiley began looking up between the two branches again. I looked up with him. The tree had so many pock marks from golf balls, it looked like it had a case of the measles.

"Hey Wiley, do you think maybe you can learn something from those pock marks up there on that branch?" I asked him pointing to the lower branch.

"Yeah, this tree pisses off a lot of people," he replied.

"I agree," I said, egging him on. "I think it's high time someone taught this tree a lesson."

"Schools in session, Chief," Wiley bragged. "Remember—trees are 90% air."

Like all amateur players, Wiley had heard the adage—'trees are 90% air' so many times, he thought there was a great deal of truth to it. Unfortunately, had Wiley been aware of the spurious origin of the adage, he would have pitched to the fairway.

Trees are 90% Error

At least once a round you will hear someone in a foursome say "trees are 90% air" prior to drilling their ball into a branch for a double-bogey or higher. Well, screen doors are also 90% air, but you wouldn't try to hit a ball through one. So why do amateur golfers attempt to hit through trees? The answer lies in an incident that occurred during the final round of the 1979 Masters.

When most people think of the name Snead, they think of Sam. However, it was Ed Sneed who is often given the credit for coining the adage—*'trees are 90% air'*, contrary to the overwhelming evidence suggesting that trees are actually 90% branches.

In 1979 Sneed held a two shot lead over Fuzzy Zoeller and Tom Watson going into the final two holes at Augusta and was cruising toward his first major victory at the Masters when his hearing let him down. Zoeller, who was paired with Sneed on the final round, teed off first at the par 4 seventeenth hole known as Nandina. One hundred and ninety five yards away from the tee box and on the left side of the fairway, stood the Eisenhower tree, a tree that former President Dwight Eisenhower hit so often, he campaigned to have it removed.

Zoeller heaved a sigh of relief when his pull sailed through the Eisenhower tree and came to rest one hundred and fifty yards from the green. Ed Sneed, approaching the tee box called out, 'great shot, Fuzzy!' But Zoeller, who recognized that he had gotten away with a lapse in judgment by aiming too close to the tree, replied, "Trees are 90% error." Regrettably, because Zoeller has a Southern drawl, Sneed thought he said, "Trees are 90% air."

Sneed, who had planned to hit a draw around the Eisenhower tree, thought Fuzzy might be on to something. He had not actually performed any experiments but he had taken a little probability in high school and reasoned that Zoeller is one of the most successful players on tour and if he is certain trees are 90% air, then I've got only a 10% chance of hitting a branch on the Eisenhower tree, he reasoned. Playing the probability, Sneed teed his ball, took aim at the Eisenhower tree and drilled his drive into a branch the size of a sewer main. The ball careened into the rough thirty yards beyond the tree and Sneed was fortunate to make bogey.

On the final hole, Sneed estimated that the probability of hitting more trees consisting of 90% air was even more remote, owing to the compounding effect of probability. A quick calculation told him that since he just got done hitting a tree, hitting a second tree yielded only a 5% probability. Still leading by one stroke, Sneed took aim at the trees on the right side of the fairway in an attempt to cut some yardage off the four hundred and sixty five yard dogleg hole named Holly.

Sneed proceeded to smoke a drive directly at the trees at the corner of the bend, only to have the drive smack a branch that was big enough to support a tree house. Again, he was fortunate to make bogey. Watson and Zoeller, who both understood that trees are 90% error, hit their drives down the middle of Holley and made par to tie Sneed for a playoff.

As the three players prepared to replay the 18th hole in the sudden-death playoff, Zoeller stepped toward Sneed and said, "tough luck on that last hole. Like I said, trees are 90% error".

Sneed, who was beginning to doubt Fuzzy's wisdom, inquired, "are you sure they're 90% air?"

Zoeller responded, "I've never been so sure of anything in my life."

Reassured that trees are 90% air, Sneed now reasoned that having just hit two consecutive trees, the probability of hitting three in a row with a 10% chance per tree was now around 2.5%, a reasonable risk worth taking. Again, Sneed teed his ball up and took dead aim at the trees guarding the corner of the dogleg. He cringed as his ball spanked a branch dead center and dropped into the rough.

During their stroll down the fairway, Zoeller turned to Watson and whispered, "I don't get it. I keep tell'n him that trees are 90% error, and he keeps aiming at em."

Sneed, again made bogey but Watson and Zoeller made par to force a second playoff hole, which Zoeller won after sinking a birdie putt.

Ed Sneed spent the remainder of his professional career attempting to prove Zoeller's mistaken hypothesis. As a result, his only win after 1979 was the 1982 Houston Open, played on a course nearly devoid of tall trees. Undaunted, whenever he played pro-am events, Sneed would tell his amateur partners, "I have it on good authority that trees are 90% air." Word soon spread among amateur players that trees are not to be feared, and despite mountains of evidence to the contrary, balls sail right through them. Had Sneed's hearing been a little more acute, he most likely would have won the 1979 Masters and amateur players would be chipping out to fairways rather than drilling irons into solid wood.

Wiley was surely unaware of Ed Sneed's contribution to golf folk-lore. Had he been my betting partner, I might have told him the story. I decided that Jack and I could use the cushion and encouraged Wiley to try a second attempt through the tree.

"90% air," Wiley mumbled to himself as he fidgeted over the ball.

"Just like a screen door," I pointed out.

The eucalyptus tree swatted Wiley's second ball with authority, though it did receive a favorable veer to the fairway where it stopped one hundred and ten yards from the hole. Blowing a gasket moments earlier had done Wiley a world of good. Since he had no more steam to emit, he returned his 8-iron to his bag and climbed in the cart.

We screeched to a halt by the one hundred and fifty yard marker a few feet behind Jack. Even though the marker was a few steps behind him, he had his hands wrapped around his range finders and was trying to steady them on the red flag to measure the distance. He took quick puffs on his cigar, making the air smell of sulfur as he rotated the focus dial. With the cigar hanging from his mouth, Jack's pose looked strikingly similar to Patten watching for Rommel's approaching Panzer division.

"See any Germans up there?" Wiley asked.

"Maybe we ought to lob a mortar up there and clear the green," I added.

"I got one hundred and thirty six yards to the flag," Jack said to Blister, ignoring Wiley and me.

Wiley rolled his eyes and said sarcastically, "That was sure worth the trouble. I would have guessed one hundred and thirty five."

Jack looked even sillier when he bladed his 9-iron to the back of the green. I had a hardy laugh, which ended abruptly when I spotted my hardpan lie.

"Oh crap! I've got a Blister forehead lie," I whined.

'The Blister forehead lie,' referred to a ball that was sitting on dirt or hardpan. The lie got its name from Blister's forehead, which looked more and more like hardpan as his hairline receded. It was only natural that we also added the 'Blister back hair lie' to the tribe's vernacular when describing a ball sitting in deep grass. Consistent with a phenomenon that medical science had yet to adequately explain, Blister belonged to that class of men who couldn't grow hair on their head but couldn't stop it from overrunning the rest of their body.

Like Jack, I bladed a 9-iron that hardly rose more than thirty feet off the ground. Luckily for me, the oak tree guarding the green confirmed that trees consist of 90% branches. After rattling around inside the canopy of branches, the tree deposited the ball a few feet from the green. Two fatties later, I was down for a disappointing double.

The tide shifted before I knew what happened. Wiley planted his wedge in the middle of the green and he was posthumously awarded his putt when Blister pulled the cup out with the flag and struck Wiley's moving ball. Jack had an improbable two putt, which sealed the bet.

Blister was more annoyed with my shoddy play than I was. After taking a drop, he executed a pitch from the river bank to within four feet of the hole. However, my double made his putt relevant to the bet and Jack and I refused to concede his putt. Instead of playing a slight break, he aimed wide of the hole and left the ball on the high side before dragging it in for a double.

"Well at least I didn't miss on the amateur side of the hole," he said, as if proud of his more advanced mistake.

The Amateur Side of the Hole

Most amateurs believe the adage *"the amateur side of the hole"* is referring to the low side of the hole on a side hill putt. This is a fallacy. The amateur side of the hole is always the side of the hole that your ball is on after you complete your putt. You can be pretty sure that no professional would ever putt like you do and would never leave his or her putt where you leave yours. Consequently, the amateur side of the hole is always where your ball is. To remember this, you might want to memorize the jingle "stupid is as stupid does and amateur is as amateur does".

Jack and I pushed on the bet, which was pretty impressive considering he would have posted a forty-two for the hole had he been playing in a tournament.

Hole 8
The Pullooski Twins

T he river that bordered the right side of the eighth hole contributed heavily to its rating as the course's most difficult. The 392-yard par 4 also had two imposing green side bunkers, which created additional heartache. However, those obstacles didn't bother me as much as the giant eucalyptus tree that hung over the left side of the fairway. Unlike the friendly pine on the fourth hole, it had not performed a good deed in its entire two hundred years.

Wiley and I were reviewing the betting strategy for the hole while Jack continued to loosen up with his driver several yards behind the tee. It was the final time I can remember that we made the misjudgment of standing in front of Jack while he took practice swings. As Wiley and I discussed the likely pairings for the hole, I was startled by a blur of an object in my peripheral vision. The object was moving too fast for me to determine what it was before it stuck its target. Before I could warn Wiley of his impending misfortune, a soggy Manhattan divot slapped against the side of his face and stuck there as if riveted down.

"Oh Jumping Jesus! Sorry Wiley!" Jack blurted, sounding truly apologetic.

"Jack—you butthead! Can't you aim another direction?" Wiley demanded, as he pried the divot from the side of his face.

While the victim and perpetrator took the incident as a serious matter, Blister and I didn't see it that way. Blister let out a belly laugh while I stumbled backward, stubbing the heel of my left foot on the wooden tee box marker causing me to lose my balance and fall on my can. I looked up at Wiley and chortled harder. The angle of Wiley's face from

116

the ground was even funnier than when I was standing up. I had the creature from the black lagoon standing over me. Wiley flung the divot back at Jack before glaring at Blister and me.

"Man I'm lucky that wasn't my drive," Jack explained. "I would have popped that one straight up."

Jack was suddenly beginning to see Blister's and my point of view. He was having difficulty suppressing a grin as he picked up the divot and tapped it back into the hole with his right heel.

"I'm happy for you Jack," Wiley shot back. "I'm sure you won't mind if I wipe my face on your towel."

Without waiting for permission, Wiley walked to the back of Jack's cart, removed Jack's white towel attached to his TaylorMade bag and scrubbed the mud off his face.

"How's it look?" he asked Blister displaying his face so Blister could inspect it for any missed mud specks.

"Good as new," Blister lied.

Wiley still had specks in his hair and a blob the size of dime on his left temple. The most poignant speck, however, was the black smear on the end of his pug nose. He also had splatter specks below his left eye and around his ear and neck. If Blister thought he looked good, that was fine with Jack and me. While Wiley may have been done cleaning his face, he wasn't done soiling Jack's towel. He decided that his shoes needed polishing.

Wiley walked around the cart, sat in the passenger seat, and lifted his left leg up on the dashboard. He buffed the top of the left shoe with five quick yanks of the towel before alternating to the right shoe. When he was satisfied with the tops, he crossed each leg and cleaned his cleats. Jack's towel looked like it was ready for the Tide vs. the generic detergent challenge. Jack ignored the towel abuse, knowing he committed the more egregious infraction.

The Pullooski Sisters

Ever afraid of the river on the right, Jack took aim at the eucalyptus tree on the right and hoped for a fade. What he got instead was a dead pull. His ball sailed straight into the canopy of the giant eucalyptus.

There were two more eucalyptus sentries behind the first, and if it somehow escaped the first tree it was unlikely to escape the second or third.

"Looks like Betty Pullooski finally joined the party," Blister said, using the tribal colloquialism for describing a wickedly pulled ball."

"I think the whole Pullooski clan showed up for that one," Wiley embellished.

"That's big trouble," Jack sighed.

Jack felt despondent walking back to the cart until he looked up at Wiley who passed him on his way to the tee box. Although, Jack had just completed a rendezvous with Betty Pullooski, Wiley looked like a snowman with a chunk of charcoal for his nose. Jack was beginning to appreciate Blister's decision to omit a few details in response to Wiley's earlier inquiry regarding the removal of the mud splatter on his face.

"Go get em snowman," Jack said to Wiley as they passed.

"Snowman? What's that supposed to mean?"

"You know . . . uh, like iceman . . . uh, like really cool," Blister jumped in afraid Jack would give away the secret.

"Iceman, huh?" Wiley pondered. "I think I like iceman better than snowman."

"We like snowman," I countered.

Wiley shrugged off his temporary name and lined up his drive. Following Jack's lead, he yanked his drive hard left straight at the two hundred year old tree. Once again dispelling the belief that trees are 90% air, the ball was batted to the turf before crawling into a 'Blister back hair lie' of grass in need of a haircut.

"Looks like you and Donna Pullooski will be double-dating with Jack and Betty," Blister announced.

According to the Red Ball People lexicon, Donna was the ugly twin sister of Betty Pullooski. One pulled drive got you Betty Pullooski, but two consecutive pulls got you the twin, Donna. Whenever the Pullooski sisters showed up on the fairway, you could be certain that some big numbers were in the process of being rolled up. It's always preferred to share the Pullooski twins with a partner, but sometimes if you're playing especially bad, you have them all to yourself. If your foursome is diligently pounding trees on the left, Momma Pullooski and the cousins showed up. While Betty is homely enough to scare the Pullooski mutt, the Pullooskis only got uglier as you progressed to the cousins. In any event, the player who accumulated the most Pullooski ladies was crowned the YANKee-doodle-dandy.

Momma Pullooski made an appearance moments later when I yanked my drive under the giant tree. Unlike my unlucky partners, my ball passed unimpeded and continued on before stopping within a nest of pine trees one hundred and ninety yards from the pin.

"Come to Momma," Wiley shouted.

"It's a Pullooski reunion!" Blister yelled.

"Bring a cousin for Blister," Jack yelled, before turning to me and selecting me as his partner. "You and me, Chief."

"I'm sitting negative one," Blister reminded Jack informing him that every one received a stroke from me.

"Well you're gonna be sitting two in a hazard by the time we leave this tee box," Jack predicted.

Jack's prophecy proved true as Blister sliced his shot into the river.

"Misery loves company!" Wiley announced.

Wiley had brought up an important topic that usually comes up twelve or thirteen times in a round.

Does Misery Really Love Company?

You betcha. The only ones who love company more than misery is Grandma and Grandpa at Christmas time. Most players I queried tell me they get more euphoric when their partners begin hemorrhaging strokes than when they sink a fifty foot putt. In fact, witnessing a three-way pileup on the autobahn involving the other three players in the foursome can redeem even the worst round.

There is an obvious explanation for why misery loves company. When we arrive at the golf course we allegorically merge onto the freeway with bald tires and loose lug nuts in the middle of a hailstorm. We may be able to hold our lane for a while, but sooner or later we cross the center line and plow into a semi. Making matters worse, one of the players in the foursome is bound to rankle everyone by playing over his head. Since it seems inconceivable that we can close the stroke gap

119

with the charlatan by playing better, the rest of us pine for the alternative, which is for him to play a lot worse.

A sure way to tell when misery is overdue for a visit is when one player quits helping the other player find his ball. A second telltale sign is when the poorly performing golfer takes a keener interest in assisting the better playing golfer on his entry point into a hazard.

There is one exception to the rule. Indeed, misery does not need company if the golfer who is playing well over his head is your betting partner. In such cases, misery turns off the lights, locks the doors, and pulls in the welcome mat.

After two more Pullooskis, Blister and Jack's balls were sitting side by side on the left side of the fairway about eighty yards from the green. Wiley hit safely to the middle of the fairway while I sized up my shot.

Believing I had no chance to hit the green, I took an easy swing with a 3-iron and hit an unexpected laser. My mouth dropped, awed as I watched the best shot of the round zero in on the back of the green.

"My God, Chief, where'd that come from?" Wiley asked.

"If I knew, I would bottle it and sell it," I said, equally surprised.

It was one of those shots that we all talk about that keep bogey players coming back Saturday after Saturday. It was the unique thing about the sport. I could never throw an eighty-yard football like John Elway. Not even once. I couldn't hit a 430-yard baseball like Barry Bonds if you gave me a million dollars, five years to train, and a year to try. I could never spin a lap around Daytona at 190 MPH like Jeff Gordon, even if you gave me his pit crew and car. However, every fifty tries or so, we all get to hit a ball as good as Ernie Els. That's what I did. And the Red Ball People were proud of their chief.

"Great shot, Chief. Best 3-iron I've seen you hit all year," Wiley said, lauding me a little further while Jack and Blister clapped.

After Wiley knocked his ball into the right side bunker, we drove forward and relaxed in the cart waiting for Jack and Blister to hit.

As Jack took his practice swing, I spied Blister. He looked uncomfortable and bent down to pick up the Titleist NXT ball below his feet. He examined the blue line drawn below the logo that looked suspiciously like the mark that Jack used. Unknown to Jack, Blister had found a beat-up NXT on the riverbank a few minutes earlier and hit it as a precaution against losing another Warbird.

While Blister continued to collect data on the ball in his hand, Jack jettisoned an Enterprise divot further than the ten yards his ball flew.

"I'll be a turd-throw'n monkey," Jack groaned, before burying his wedge in the turf.

Understanding that Jack was in no mood for housekeeping, Wiley climbed out of the cart and retrieved the carrier deck. Wiley inspected the divot from both sides and was so absorbed by its dimension, he brought it over to show me.

"You know," Wiley explained, "If you pointed this thing into the wind you could fly planes off it."

Jack didn't find Wiley's knowledge of naval aviation as funny as I did.

"Just plant it back in the ground, snowman," Jack ordered.

"I still prefer iceman," Wiley complained, as he stomped the carrier back into its harbor.

"Make no mistake about it. You're snowman," Jack corrected, suddenly in a better mood.

Blister had finally collected enough data and was in the process of drawing a conclusion. "Hey Jack, is this your mark?" he asked showing Jack the mark below the logo.

"Yeah, where'd you get that?" Jack asked.

"Right here on the ground where I guess you hit it," Blister said, before delivering his zinger. "You hit my ball!"

"Since when do you play a Titleist NXT?" Jack demanded.

"Since I found one in the hazard five minutes ago," Blister informed him.

Although Blister had contributed to the confusion, he was not the one who had violated the rule of striking the wrong ball. As a culture not known for exhaustive critique of detail, The Red Ball People had dealt with the infraction so many times that it was one of the first USGA rules amended. Though the rule was previously reviewed on the third hole when Blister used a practice ball off the tee, the context below applies to the player who mistakenly plays someone else's right ball.

Rule 15-1—Playing wrong ball: *If a player substitutes another ball when not so permitted, that ball is not a* wrong ball; *it becomes the* ball in play *and, if the error is not corrected as provided in the player shall incur a penalty of two strokes.*

Red Ball People Amendment Two to Rule 15-1: *If a playing partner accidentally plays your ball, you can play his ball. If retribution is desirable, you may knock it into a water hazard or forest without penalty. You may drop a second ball where your stupid partner played your first ball. Stupid partner must then drop second ball near location where you smacked his ball off the course. Stupid partner does not incur penalty but should be verbally abused by you for three or four holes.*

Reason for change: *Amendment Two falls under the classification of—no harm no foul.*

Jack astutely grabbed his ball out of Blister's hand before Blister could drop it and play. Using his own ball, Blister demonstrated that his chamber of hosel rockets was not quite depleted as he shanked one between the right front sand trap and the river. We watched in fascination as the ball curved further and further away from the green toward the river.

"Look at that sucker accelerate," Jack said, clearly awed. "My god, that looks more like a screaming 3-iron banana than a sand wedge."

"The event horizon's got it," I pointed out.

The Event Horizon

The 'event horizon' is a term that describes two types of phenomena in the universe. Astronomers know the event horizon as the point of no return where matter, gas, and light disappear forever into the vortex of a black hole. Black holes, of course, are collapsed stars whose cores are points of infinite density whose gravitational forces are so strong that not even light can escape. As any astronomer can attest, an average black hole would have no trouble sucking in a golf ball that got anywhere near its event horizon.

The second occurrence of the event horizon manifests itself as a gravitational halo surrounding water hazards on golf courses. Since the vast majority of astronomers are foolishly preoccupied studying black holes, very little formal research has been dedicated to the event horizons that surround golf courses, but rest assured that they are equally omnipotent. Similar to its black hole counterpart, the event horizon that surrounds a water hazard can alter a ball's flight in mid-air and suck it through its gravitational vortex. It's easy to detect when your ball is operating under the influence of an event horizon, because it begins accelerating toward the hazard at a speed far greater than the speed at which it left your clubface, blowing right through trees, rocks, and tall weeds.

———————————

We watched the ball disappear over the riverbank followed by a small stream of spray that collapsed around the vortex. Blister chose to sit the rest of the hole out, a decision that may have been partially influenced by Bab's appearance on the ninth tee box. I was sure Jack and I would win the rollover bet until he visited both sand traps and settled for a Linda Tripp. Wiley and I both two putted, but our teams tied the hole since his net par tied my natural par.

Hole 9
Colonel Corpuscle
Takes Charge

Jack positioned his cart to the side of the par 5 ninth tee box to have an unimpeded view of the ladies tee box. The separation between the two tee boxes was nearly ninety yards, owing to a northerly bend in the river that separated the two tees. As Babs leaned forward to address her ball, he lifted his range finders and established a neighborhood watch program. Blister meandered back to our cart to chat but was instead distracted when he spotted the head of Wiley's 7-iron lying in the cart's glove box. He picked it up and rubbed his finger across the jagged shaft that protruded an inch above the hosel.

"So Wiley," Blister asked, "Was it worth it?"

"Yep," Wiley answered, without hesitation.

"I thought so," Blister replied.

"I thought trees were 90% air."

"Keah, keah. For some reason everyone thinks that," Blister giggled.

"Remember that's a fallacy. It's 90% error. E-r-r-o-r," I said, emphasizing the phonetic difference between the two words.

"I don't know why you guys get so upset," Blister chided us, "I know I'm going to play bad so when I meet my expectations I just accept the results and move on."

"Sure you do," I corrected. "How about that wedge of yours that's sleeping with the fishes in that pond up there?"

"It slipped out of my hand, Chief," Blister replied, shrugging his shoulders.

Wiley refreshed his memory. "On your second swing . . . and after your ball went in on the first swing."

124

"Maybe I forgot to turn my ass," Blister replied, throwing us off his trail.

Although Blister did have vastly superior temper control when compared to the rest of us, he was in need of guidance from Dr. Phil just like the rest of us from time to time. But until Dr. Phil solves the anger problem, I decided I might as well make some hay in the lucrative rage market.

Cash Cows for the Rage Market

You only need to spend a couple of hours at a golf course to apprehend that America has an anger problem. While there are certainly costly therapists available to aid the player in reigning in anger, I've patented a line of tirade products that are much cheaper and equally effective.

Most people believe the adage, 'time is money.' Yet, as anyone who has ever wrapped a $475 driver around a tree knows, time costs chumpchange when compared to rage. Once I realized that *rage is big money*, I developed a couple of inventions to exploit this lucrative market.

The Stunt Driver: $79.95

The stunt driver is an environmentally sensitive device patented by Chief Tit, endorsed by the Sierra Club, and is used to augment a tirade. The device is marketed as a substitute for a real driver when rage overcomes the player and he desires to wrap a driver around a tree, but exercises enough reason to realize that he doesn't want to spend $475 to do so.

Stunt Driver™

Environmentally friendly. Tree not harmed by tirade.

| Stunt Driver before tirade | Stunt Driver after tirade | Stunt Driver reconstituted during cooling-off period |

Chief Tit's Stunt Driver™ (Suggested Retail Price $79.95)

The stunt driver is made of flexible foam rubber with a hollow core filled with thin wire resembling a clothes hanger to keep the shaft stiff. The head of the driver has an embedded lead ball weight, which acts to propel the heavier end of the shaft with enough momentum to create concentric circles around a tree with the club shaft when the golfer strikes the tree in a fit of rage.

The Coleman Brick™: $19.95

The Styrofoam authentic-looking red brick replica was invented by Chief Tit and named in honor of NFL referee and brick head, Walt Coleman. The Coleman Brick® was designed to be tossed at TV sets when a referee makes a bad call or when your favorite quarterback fumbles the ball during a game-winning drive. The brick bounces harmlessly off the TV set while allowing the user to blow off steam without a police report being filed.

I got the idea for the Coleman Brick® after witnessing the most abominable officiating known to mankind. Trailing 13-10 with less than two minutes to go in the 2002 Divisional Title game, New England Patriot quarterback Tom Brady was blindsided by Oakland Raider Charles Woodson, and coughed up the ball on the Raider forty-eight yard line. The fumble was recovered by Raiders, ending the Patriots season. Al-

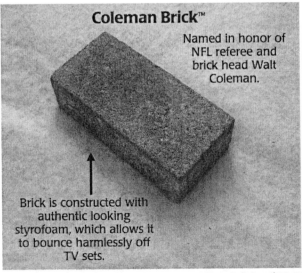

Coleman Brick™

Named in honor of NFL referee and brick head Walt Coleman.

Brick is constructed with authentic looking styrofoam, which allows it to bounce harmlessly off TV sets.

Chief Tit's Coleman Brick™ (Suggested Retail Price $19.95)

though the play was ruled a fumble on the field, Walt Coleman, the ruling referee in the replay booth, suffered a brain aneurysm and ordered a review of the play. After repeatedly watching the obvious fumble with the rest of the world, Coleman ruled the fumble to be a forward pass, giving the Patriots the ball as well as the game.

In the absence of the Coleman Brick, Oakland Police racked up overtime as Raider fans tossed real bricks and beer bottles at their TVs, causing untold damage.

Blister and Wiley complimented me on my constructive and profitable ideas for dealing with rage. Wiley predicted that Jack might even be in the market for a stunt driver in the near future, if the pond gave him as much trouble as Wiley anticipated.

After crossing in front of the men's tees, the river curved north, framing the right side of the 505-yard hole. Pine trees lined the left side for three hundred yards until reaching the pond that jutted out sixty yards into the eighty-yard wide fairway. Owing to the prevailing headwind, the best drives come up sixty or seventy yards short of the pond, forcing many players to take their biggest gamble of the round. The flat green was masterfully guarded on both sides by deep bunkers and often captured the well-struck 3-woods that made it over the pond.

"You think you can reach em?" Blister asked Wiley, as he pointed to Babs and Donetta who were standing to the right of the pond.

"I couldn't hit them with a deer rifle," Wiley replied as he teed his ball.

While most players thought the seventh hole was the signature hole, the ninth hole was clearly the signature hole for Jack. Although he triumphed over the pond on occasion, more often, the pond extorted a sleeve of balls for a toll before allowing Jack to pass. A tingle of excitement ran up my spine knowing we would be gathered around Jack as he made his weekly attempt to exorcise demons rising from the pond.

In our haste to get Jack on the tee box, Wiley and I hooked our drives into the pines while Blister topped his drive into the river. Jack put the demons on notice when he smoked his drive to the middle of the fairway. By default, Jack was Wiley's partner.

Anticipating Jack's confrontation, Wiley and I raced across the fairway to search for our balls among the pines, while Jack plodded across the fairway on foot. Wiley chose the safe but unrewarding route around the north side of the pond. After locating my ball at the end of the line of pines, I decided to think my strategy over as Wiley was anxious to nab a ringside seat behind Jack.

We dashed back to Jack's ball, as we watched Blister put us back in the bet when he creamed his 3-wood over the pond. Jack was still in the visualization stage as I positioned our cart a short distance behind his ball to watch the ritual.

"One of you guys have a match?" Jack asked holding up his half-smoked unlit cigar.

"How about, your golf game and a train wreck?" Blister suggested, "That's a pretty good match."

"That's funny stuff," Jack cackled, with a mock laugh.

I dug a book of matches from my bag and tossed them to Jack. After four or five tries, he was able to kindle a fire. His right hand rested on his 3-iron while his left hand, holding his cigar, drifted to his lips. He took a long drag from the cigar and stared across the pond. Teeming with stagnant algae and the smell of compost, the pond rivaled Jack's cigar as the foulest odor on the course. However, insects loved it and bullfrogs loved insects, and the pond was swarming with both.

"Jack, you ever thought about playing around the pond?" Wiley suggested. "It would only take two 7-irons to reach the green."

"I don't know, Wiley," Jack scoffed, "This is the one stroke of the round I look forward to."

"Same here," I added, restraining a chuckle.

Jack flicked an ash at Wiley before turning to walk back to his ball.

"Think he'll make it this time?" I asked Wiley in a whispering voice.

"Not a chance," Wiley whispered back showing no confidence in his betting partner.

I looked at Wiley and nodded my head in agreement. Although I never wore my watch during the round I knew it was about 10:45. The sun was beginning to bake the fairways and the temperature was noticeably warmer than it had been just a hole earlier. Perspiration was slowly building on Wiley's oversized head. The smudge of mud on his left temple was beginning to run down the side of his face like war paint. His nose evidently didn't require cooling as perspiration was having little effect on spreading the smudge on the end of his nose. He removed his hat and ran his fingers through his matted hair. He had an impressive case of hat hair.

"Jack's gonna have to reach deep down and do a gut check," I whispered to Wiley with my best Ian Baker-Finch impersonation.

"I've already done a gut check for him—and I can safely report . . . it's still huge," Wiley whispered back, causing me to let out a whoop, which drew an unappreciative glance from Jack.

"What's his chances?" I whispered to Wiley.

"Zip-Dot-Crap." Wiley estimated. "With Jack, it's a physiological thing."

Colonel Corpuscle Takes Charge

You may recall when you were in the third grade, your teacher showed you an animated movie about how white and red blood cells fend off an infection. If you have a good memory, you probably recall that the little red and white blood cells were depicted as red and white armies of blobs that looked like little Michelin Tire Men with army helmets. The Coalition of the Willing, or allies as they were known back then, were directed by their stout red-blood cell commander to surround the bacteria and attack it until it was purged from the blood steam. To better understand the physiological changes Jack undergoes as he hits a ball over a water hazard, we might find it useful to dust off this third grade paradigm.

Control Center (Somewhere in Jack's Brain):

General Cortex paced the floor digesting the orders he had recently received from Command Central. Except for the two stars on his helmet, Cortex looked much like the other portly Michelin Tire officers milling about the war room. Cortex was nervous. A similar order he received earlier had calamitous results. He took a deep breath and summoned his second in command.

"Colonel Corpuscle," Cortex shouted.

"Yes Sir," Colonel Corpuscle responded, arching his back as he saluted General Cortex.

129

"Colonel," Cortex continued, "Command Central has just sent us a new mission code named *Over My Head*. Notify Sergeant Synapse and Captain Hemoglobin to be on standby and order full battle stations."

"Again?" Colonel Corpuscle demanded. "We've already been through this drill thirty times today."

"Our job Colonel, is to carry out orders and not question the decisions of Command Central," General Cortex retorted. "Operation *Over My Head* calls for Jack to hit a 3-iron one hundred and eighty yards over a water hazard. Ok, we've trained for this mission thousands of times and our morale is high despite a recent series of setbacks. Sound battle stations and tell the troops to stand by."

"Yes Sir," Colonel Corpuscle responded, trying to hide his anxiety.

Colonel Corpuscle picked up the phone as he glanced at the sensory map affixed to the wall next to the video image of the pond. "Get me Sergeant Synapse," he ordered.

The sensory map indicated that the golf ball had a good flat lie and was no more than sixty yards from the water hazard. There was a slight breeze blowing from the target toward the ball location. Colonel Corpuscle frowned, knowing he had to account for the wind.

"Yes Colonel," Synapse responded.

"Sound battle stations, Synapse. Order the boys to lock and load for Operation *Over My Head*," Corpuscle barked. "Have you been briefed on the operation Synapse?"

"Yes Sir," Synapse responded. "The men are standing by. Many know they're not coming back . . . but are in high spirits and prepared to fulfill their duty."

General Cortex glanced at his watch knowing commencement was only a moment away. A yellow warning light over his head began flashing indicating that a sphincter muscle was contracting.

"Lock the sphincter so we don't pinch any ballast," Cortex shouted.

"Done Sir," the ballast control lieutenant snapped.

General Cortex studied the sensory map with Colonel Corpuscle as the sphincter sensory light turned green. As good military officers are prone to think alike, Cortex and Corpuscle were simultaneously struck with the same intuitive perception.

"Do you see what I see?" Corpuscle asked with a frown on his face.

"Yes, Jack's alignment is fifteen degrees to the right of target. We'll have to do our best to compensate, but it won't be easy."

"General," Captain Hemoglobin shouted from across the room, "He's prematurely initiated back swing."

"What?" General Cortex screamed, "We haven't completed our checklist and we already know his alignment is fifteen degrees right of target. Quick, order Sergeant Synapse to release a constant volley of adrenaline."

"Adrenaline away, Sir," Hemoglobin barked.

"Turn the audio monitors on so we can hear Synapse," Cortex ordered.

Hemoglobin complied and Synapse's voice could be heard amidst battle noises.

"Adrenaline's being held up on the left side. We're meeting tough resistance from day old alcohol."

"Oh Criminy," Cortex bellowed. "We'll have to increase air flow and induce hyperventilation."

"Right," acknowledged Corpuscle. "Synapse, have your men open the oxygen valves until hyperventilation is induced."

Red warning lights began to fill the sensory map as hyperventilation flooded the battlefield with oxygen. Adrenaline began pouring through on the left side as Synapse's right flank ordered the heavy muscle groups to take over for the lighter muscle groups. No sooner had the large muscles taken over when a warning siren sounded in the Command Center.

"Uhoooga, uhoooga, uhoooga," the siren belched out.

Without consulting the sensory data, Corpuscle knew immediately what the problem was since he had responded to it plenty of times already this morning. The siren indicated that the back swing had become untethered from the swing plane and was quickly moving toward a dangerous orbit above the Hogan line, an imaginary line that runs from the neck to the ball depicting the proper swing path as illustrated in Ben Hogan's books.

"Synapse," Corpuscle screamed, "He's over the top. I repeat, he's over the top. Have the large muscle groups on the upper right side stand down and order a frontal assault by the small muscle groups until

131

the right elbow gets airborne. Send out decoys to the central nervous system until the orbit retracts to the Hogan line."

"The elbow's flying sir," Synapse responded. "He's coming back to the Hogan line."

"Good work Sergeant," Corpuscle said as he removed a handkerchief from his back pocket and dabbed perspiration from his forehead.

The red lights on the sensory map began turning yellow indicating a small respite in the crises. Operation *Over My Head* had started prematurely, yet decisive action by Cortex and Corpuscle had averted a near disaster as the orbit of the back swing was nearly lost in the ether above the Hogan line. However, battle fatigue was settling in on Synapse. His men were still knee deep in adrenaline and lingering alcohol was beginning to slow their progress.

Cortex and Corpuscle monitored the data.

"Colonel, we've got to compensate for the alignment and the head wind. Any suggestions?"

"That's a tough combination, Sir. Last time we had a similar problem we ordered the knock-down strategy only to see the ball skulled into a lilly-pad."

Corpuscle scratched his head knowing that he didn't have the faintest clue on how to compensate for the alignment and headwind dilemma. Unfortunately, neither did Cortex. Cortex also scratched his head. Cortex had come up through the ranks and had not received the formal training at the academies that most of the other generals had received. His mantle was trial and error. During the course of his tenure he had experienced nearly as many errors as trials. But the men loved him because he had impeccable timing when he told his jokes.

"General, we're nearly at the top of the back swing. We're going to have to act now," Corpuscle warned.

Without hesitation, Cortex issued his orders. "Have Hemoglobin flood the left side with more adrenaline so the left hip fires early. Order the small muscle groups to take complete charge over the big boys so the trajectory is elevated at impact. And let's keep the weight on the right side. Make sure Synapse sends plenty of protoplasm to the right knee to keep it stiff as a board and straight as a flagpole. If we shut the club face a little early and lift the left heel, Operation *Over My Head* will be a complete success."

"But Sir," Corpuscle protested, "won't that induce a reverse pivot?"

"Not if we swing at warp speed."

"Brilliant Sir," Corpuscle replied, having no idea what Cortex was talking about.

Corpuscle passed the order to Captain Hemoglobin and Sergeant Synapse. Hemoglobin stared in disbelief at Corpuscle who could only muster a silly grin. Hemoglobin began opening more adrenal valves as he muttered something about a mutiny under his breath. Synapse did not receive the order any better.

"I haven't heard of an order that would result in so many deaths since Colonel Custer at Bighorn," Synapse complained.

"Oh I don't know about that," the Corpuscle snapped back, "how about Colonel Sanders at Kentucky Fried Chicken?"

Synapse already had his protoplasm massing around the right knee when the left hip began firing forward. Fueled by the extra adrenaline, the small muscle groups in the wrist began their downward orbit at warp speed. The first red light appeared on the sensory map as Cortex and Corpuscle looked on. Cortex recognized the light as a club toe warning sensor. The light could only mean one thing. The toe of the 3-iron was pointed at an oak tree fifty yards left of the hole. Suddenly the control room was shattered by the sound of the siren again.

"Uhoooga, uhoooga, uhoooga."

Once again, the orbit of the down swing was on a dangerous course across the Hogan line. Left unchecked, Hemoglobin knew that the current path would eventually put the hosel on a collision course with the ball.

"He's over the top again. I repeat, he's over the top," Hemoglobin shouted. "Hosel is on collision course, sir."

Cortex froze as he always did. Excess glucose from converted alcohol further dulled his senses. He was also beginning to appreciate the folly of his earlier order to hyperventilate. He could scarcely catch his breath. The adrenaline mixed with the oxygen made him tired and he wanted to take a catnap until Operation *Over My Head* was concluded. So that's what he did.

Captain Hemoglobin opened his final adrenal valve and issued an order to Sergeant Synapse to encircle the right knee with protoplasm. He turned to receive further orders from General Cortex and was astounded, as he always was, to see him cocked back in his chair with his face pointing toward the ceiling, mouth open, and drool trickling down his chin. His arms lay to the side so that his knuckles nearly reached the floor. His chest raised slowly as the intake of air over his coiled tongue created a snoring sound.

"What the hell is he doing?" screamed Hemoglobin, looking at Colonel Corpuscle.

"He's taking a catnap," Corpuscle said, informing him of the obvious.

The down swing was now halfway complete but the hips had already finished their rotation. As General Cortex snored, the sensory map began lighting up like a Christmas tree. Green lights turned yellow, yellow lights turned red. Disaster warning sirens continued to fill the room at a faster pace.

"Uhoooga, uhoooga, uhoooga," went the over-the-top siren.

The over-the-top siren was soon joined by the open-club-face siren, which sounded remarkably similar to a boat horn.

"Phaaam, phaaam, phaaam," the open-club-face siren screeched.

"Clubface is wide open. I repeat, club face is wide open," Captain Hemoglobin shouted through the chaos.

"Swing speed is far to fast," Corpuscle added.

Hemoglobin turned to the intercom to bark an order to Synapse but hesitated as he scanned the testosterone valve panel. His heart began racing. The beads of sweat on his forehead turned into tributaries as a stream of saline water trickled down his nose. The immediate recognition that he had accidentally opened the testosterone valves and flooded the capillaries with testosterone created a queasy feeling of panic.

"Well at least we solved the mystery of the extra swing speed," he thought to himself.

"What the hell's going on down here?" screamed Sergeant Synapse. "We were knee deep in adrenaline and now we're waist deep in testosterone. The troops are moving around so fast that all they really seem to be doing is bouncing off each other."

"We've got an accidental release of testosterone," Hemoglobin cracked back. "Can you abort the mission and stop the swing?"

"You mean like Tiger Woods is able to do when someone snaps a picture?" Synapse asked.

"That's right," Hemoglobin demanded, with more urgency in his voice.

"Way too risky," Synapse decided. "Chances are Jack would dislocate a shoulder or crack a vertebra. Maybe both."

"OK Synapse," Corpuscle interrupted, "I want to channel all available adrenaline and testosterone to the small muscle group in the left wrist and shut that face down. I want that hand flipping like a poodle at a dog show. Any adrenaline left over should be sent to left quadriceps to pull the club back across the Hogan line."

"Yes Sir," Synapse barked.

The sirens fell silent as impact became imminent. On the sensory map, red lights turned yellow and yellow lights turned green. Colonel Corpuscle breathed a sigh of relief. A smile began to appear on Captain Hemoglobin as he heaved a sigh and dabbed at his sweaty forehead and nose with his shirtsleeve. The euphoria was short lived.

"Quaaack, quaaack, quaaack," went the duck hook alarm.

"Uhuuut, uhuuut, uhuuut," shouted the vertical descent siren indicating that the 3-iron was on track to enter the ground at a high rate of speed 3-inches behind the ball.

The sensory map quickly changed colors turning the control room into a red glow. A torrent of adrenaline washed Synapse off his feet, sending him and several million of his troops, cascading down the left arm capillaries toward the flipping wrist.

A computer-generated voice calmly issued progress reports as Jack approached impact.

"May I have your attention? Contact is imminent. Contact is imminent. With what, is uncertain. Contact is imminent. Please brace yourselves. Contact is imminent. It ain't going to be pretty. I repeat, it ain't going to be pretty."

Colonel Corpuscle clutched his desk and looked up at the video monitor just as the iron ripped into the earth 3-inches behind the ball. He watched in fascination as the club dug a furrow deep enough to plant corn. The scene was all too familiar and reminded him of his favorite movie—Ground Hog Day. Like scrutinizing a newsreel of the Hindenburg explosion, he just couldn't turn his eyes away from the carnage.

When the toe of the club made contact with the ball, it began spinning like a top as it gained elevation. For a moment, the divot and ball were on the same flight path. The divot finally fell back to earth like a booster rocket, while the ball continued on its parabolic path toward the water. The control room shuddered, jarring General Cortex awake.

"Deputy Dog fixed my flat tire," he babbled, evidently in reference to an interrupted dream.

Cortex rubbed the sleep from his eyes, and looked up at the monitor in time to see a tremendous splash as the ball entered the water. The control room fell silent as all alarms shut off. The warning indicators on the sensory map returned to their normal state of green waiting for the next Operation. The officers in the control room stared blankly at the video screen as the ripples of water emanated from the entry point. Like so many operations before, Operation *Over My Head* had been an abysmal failure.

Cortex was still staring at the screen watching the ripples when Lieutenant Neuron marched up, saluted the General and informed him that Central Command had just called and informed him that Jack had taken a drop and to prepare for Operation *Empty Sleeve.*

"The operation will commence immediately," Lieutenant Neuron informed him.

"Did they say anything about Operation *Over My Head,*" Cortex quizzed the Lieutenant.

"Yes Sir," Neuron responded. "In fact they said from their perspective, except for the tempo, it was nearly flawless. They believe if we keep everything the same but slow the tempo down a little, Operation *Empty Sleeve* will be the most successful operation of the day."

"Just like death and taxes . . . huh Wiley?" I asked, as we watched Jack's ball disappear into the water.

"As regular as the sun coming up," Wiley replied.

Blister offered Jack some encouragement. "The swing didn't look that bad Jack, maybe just slow down the tempo a little bit."

Believing that tempo was his sole problem, Jack swung easier at his second ball, which only resulted in the ball entering the water at a slower speed. His third ball finally made it over but he and Blister were just going through the motions by the time they both hit their forty yard pitches to the green.

Wiley and I returned to my ball. I gambled with a 3-wood, which paid off handsomely when I heard the unique 'ping' of the sweet spot. The four foot high reeds that lined the bank of the pond prevented us from watching the landing, but I knew it was near the green.

Wiley and I drove around the pond and found his ball in the narrow neck a few paces north of where the pond extended the furthest. My heart soared as I peered around the reeds and spotted three balls on the front of the green.

"Nice shot, Chief," Wiley said, eyeing the three balls. "Looks like you caught that one on the screws."

"I'll say," I admitted.

Wiley's third shot found the right side bunker, but after a successful blast out, all four balls were on the green. Jack picked up for a no putt eight, while Blister easily two-putted for a legitimate seven. I tidied up a few ball marks and spent some extra time examining the uphill break, as Wiley finished up for a bogey.

"Pretty impressive 3-wood there, Chief," Blister quipped.

"Thanks," I beamed. "That's only the third or fourth time I've hit this green in two."

"Where you going to spend your money?" I asked Blister as I walked to my ball.

"Probably on hookers," Jack answered for him.

"I don't know," Blister replied as he thought it over. "Maybe I'll buy half a beer."

The mention of alcohol jogged Wiley's memory. "Speaking of beer, I loaded some Heinies in my cooler this morning if you want to pick them up after the hole," he said to Blister.

"Sounds better than my Coors," Blister replied.

I absent-mindedly picked up my ball and rubbed it against my sleeve to remove a few specs of grass as we discussed the logistics for a beer run. I leaned down to place the ball in front of my right foot and was immediately horrified at what I discovered. The ball was indeed an NXT, but it was missing the Chief Tit red mark.

"This ain't my ball!" I said as I shot accusatory glances at Jack and Blister. "Which one of you nitwits has my ball in your pocket?"

"Not me," Blister said without checking.

"Me neither, Chief," Jack said reexamining the ball in his hand.

"That'd be a shame if you had to go back to the fairway and re-hit," Wiley quipped.

"You should have kept your mouth shut, Chief," Blister reasoned. "No one would have noticed."

"Chief Tit doesn't cheat," I corrected Blister, before I caught myself and clarified my position. "Except of course in the areas where we all agree to cheat."

"You're gonna have to treat it as a lost ball, Chief," Wiley argued.

"The ball ain't lost. It's in the pocket or bag of one of those dickheads over there," I countered pointing to Blister and Jack.

Since I was the master draftsman of the Red Ball People Amendments I was also aware of most of the USGA rules I reworked into the tribe's favor. This was one of those times that my advanced knowledge suited my purpose. If I could convince the tribe that the more likely scenario was that someone removed my ball then I could invoke an Amendment to USGA Rule 18-1/5

Rule 18-1/5—Ball Removed by Outside Agency from Unknown Spot: *If ball is removed by outside agency and player is unable to determine the original location of ball, then player should drop the ball in an area which was neither the most, nor least, favorable of the various areas where it was equally possible that the ball originally lay.*

Red Ball People Amendment to Rule 18-1/5: *If player is suspicious that playing partner, also known as 'outside agency', removed player's ball, then player should drop the ball in an area that is either most favorable of all various areas where it was equally possible that the ball originally lay or play from spot where a phantom ball has been discovered. If area where phantom ball lies is more advantageous than the most advantageous of all the various areas where it was equally possible for the removed ball to have been lying, then player should play phantom ball.*

Reason for change: *Chief Tit needed a birdie and one of his stupid playing partners, AKA the outside agency, interfered with his glory.*

Blister and Jack were indifferent to my favorable ruling. Blister was on my team and stood to gain on the bet. Jack dared not complain after taking a zero-putt eight. Wiley was the only one I needed to convince. After forcing him to acknowledge that Jack and Blister were more qualified as outside agencies than golfers, he ratified the amendment.

I sealed the three-hole roll over bet for Blister and myself a moment later when I two-putted for my second birdie on the front nine for an amazing thirty nine.

Score Card after 9 Holes

Hole	1	2	3	4	5	6	7	8	9	Out
Yardage	472	145	345	169	360	189	511	392	505	3088
Handicap	11	5	17	13	15	9	7	1	3	
Wiley	⑤	③->(0)	④	③	④	7	6 ⁵	5	6	43
Chief Tit	6	②->(0)	4	3	⑤	④	⑦	④	④	39
Blister	⑥	6 ²	7 ³	4	4	4	⑦	⑦ ⁷	⑦	52
Jack	8 ¹	3	⑥	③	6	④ ⁴	6 ⁶	7	8 ⁸	51
Par	5	3	4	3	4	3	5	4	5	36

Notes:

/ => Signifies that player gets stroke

◯ => Signifies that player won bet

–>(0) => Heiroglyphic for "out of ass." Chief Tit and Wiley pull two shots out of their ass on 2nd hole.

[1] Jack picks up ball. Red Ball People abacus only has 8 beads - Jack takes an 8.

[2] Blister concedes 6 foot putt to himself for a Linda Tripp.

[3] Blister picks up ball after 2 shanks - he takes a 7.

[4] Bab's thong status takes precedent over tending. Jack not assessed penalty for being struck by putt.

[5] Wiley's putt bounces off cup tended by Blister. He is awarded putt but bet rolls over.

[6] Jack saves 35 penalty strokes in bunker on favorable ruling by Chief Tit.

[7] Jack and Blister both pick up ball. Both take a triple. Bet rolls over.

[8] Favorable ruling allows Chief Tit to make birdie with phantom ball. Chief and Blister win roll over bet.

Hole 10
Kamikaze Crawdads

We were enjoying the mud collage on Wiley's face immensely as we huddled by the carts and devised a plan to retrieve the beer chilling in the parking lot. Wiley's perspiration was having a more pronounced change on his facial landscape and we had no intention of ruining our fun by having Wiley clean his face any sooner than he had to. The primary goal was to keep Wiley from using the restroom in the clubhouse before heading to the tenth tee. In a clandestine discussion between Jack and Blister, it was decided that Blister would insist on taking Wiley to the parking lot to retrieve beer from the coolers in his trunk and Wiley's SUV.

While Wiley and Blister loaded their bags with two six packs of beer, Jack and I visited the clubhouse and acquired four Polish sausages loaded with onions and mustard. We reconvened behind the tenth tee box in time to watch Babs and Donetta hit their drives. Sadly for Jack, his fingers were so caked with mustard he was unable to set up a neighborhood watch program and he was relegated to using his naked eye. The smell of onions and mustard touched off a Pavlovian response that manifested itself through beer instead of slobber, just as Blister pulled his cart next to mine.

"Give me a beer before I die," I ordered.

"You got it, Chief," Blister said, accepting his polish dog from Jack.

Blister extracted two tubular insulation packs from his Physics golf bag and pulled out a Heineken for me and one for Jack. He and Wiley had already finished half a can each, returning from the parking lot. Blister's bag was as much an entertainment center as a device for porting golf equipment. In fact, if Blister was ever marooned on a deserted island we knew he could survive an entire month if only his bag washed ashore. It wasn't always that way. A year earlier, he was in the market for a bag with oversized pockets when he made the mistake of purchasing a bag from Costco, whose Chinese manufacturer didn't understand the diversified requirements of the Red Ball People.

The Socialist Golf Bag

The most important feature in a golf bag for the high handicapper is the number of pockets. To the mediocre players, the golf bag is considered more of a saddle bag since they port around half of their medicine cabinet, the top shelf of their refrigerator, and enough balls to fill a bathtub, not to mention a portable humidor. As a result, the high handicapper's bag will weigh nearly forty pounds, or twice as much as a single digit handicapper. Unlike professional players, the bag is much more important to an amateur's well-being than the clubs inside.

If the reader is considering buying a golf bag from a socialist country, he or she is warned to heed the label prior to purchase. Based on tribal field experience, we are quite comfortable in pronouncing—if the label is unintelligible, the bag is poorly crafted. Since the cheapest bags manufactured with foreign labor are found at Wal-Mart and Costco, these bags in particular should be avoided.

Although Blister rarely flies, he bought a Chinese manufactured bag from Costco primarily because it had wheels on the bottom and a snazzy locking hard cover for transporting through airports. The pockets also met his minimum engineering dimensions for concealing a case of beer.

Buyer's remorse quickly set in, as numerous problems emerged. The bag continually rolled over his foot as he tried to stand it upright. Traveling with the bag was useless as the instructions for setting the combination locks were unintelligible.

Before returning the bag for a refund, Blister insisted that we read the manufacturer's instruction label to insure that his problems weren't the result of operator error. The instruction label, written in both Chinese and an English dialect that none of us were familiar with, appears below. The English translation evidently was provided by a Chinese engineer who was still in the early stages of mastering verbs. In order to provide a more concise interpretation of what the Chinese engineer was attempting to say, I have taken the liberty of translating his English dialect into the King's English. For those cases, which were numerous, where the instruction did not accurately correspond to actual parts on the bag, some interpolation was added to more accurately reflect the quality of manufacturing.

Chinese Instructions on Costco Golf Bag:

The cipher is set as "000" in the factory and you can remain it or setup yourself cipher as the following steps:

[**Translation to the King's English:** *The lock is set at "000" in the sweatshop and you can leave it or become a lock yourself by following the steps below.*]

1. Push the adjusting sheath in the direction of the arrow and hold it, then turn the number to which you have selected, push the button as the direction of arrow, and let the adjusting sheath pop-up and return to normal place.

   [**Translation to the King's English:** *Push the dial in the direction of the arrow even though there is no arrow to be found. Once you have imagined a location where the arrow should be, had the factory developed the product to the correct specification, hold the dial. Turn the dial to a number you will remember so you don't have to call our customer service, since we don't have one, and then push the button in the same direction of the arrow that is not there. Let the adjusting dial pop up and put your eye out if you have your face too close looking for the mysterious arrow that our engineers left off the locking mechanism.*]

2. Now the new cipher of your own have be set.

   [**Translation to the King's English:** *Now the new combination has been set or will be set depending on which tense you prefer to be in.*]

3. Turning the cipher to chaos direction is to a lock state.

   [**Translation to King's English:** *Several interpretations are pos-*

sible. The translator may be intending to say 'turn the combina-
tion to a random number and the lock will be in the locked
position.' He may also be trying to summarize the Existentialist
position propounded by Jean-Paul Sartre in his milestone work,
Being and Nothingness. *Finally, the translator may have watched*
a little too much Get Smart *on Taiwanese TV and may have just*
wanted to work the word chaos *into a sentence.]*

4. Turning the number to which you have set and you will unlock it.

[Translation to King's English: *Turn the three digit number to*
your birth date, which you previously set in step 1 and the lock
might open. If the lock does not open, it is because a Chinese
engineer concluded from interpreting the American blue print that
the lock should work chaotically. However, since there are only
999 combinations to try, 000 excluded, your average eight-year
old should be able to crack the combination in less than two min-
utes.]

A separate manufacturer's brochure describing the benefits of the
wheels and locking top for pulling the bag through the airport were
evidently translated by the same interpreter. A few of the more important product points are listed below. Again, where required, a King's
English interpretation follows in brackets.

Key Product Advantages to Chinese Costco Golf Bag:

- Bottom of cylinder is to contain two wheels for transporting to airport. Durable wheels sink in bottom to fit in cart and roll to golf
course. Wheels made of soft rubber to have put vibration to sleep.

[Translation to King's English: *Bottom of bag has two wheels for*
rolling over your foot when you tilt the bag to lift it into the trunk of
your car. The wheels were designed for ease in pulling the bag
through an airport but work better for rolling over your foot. The
durable wheels are sunk in a flared wheel well and will fit in the
back of a golf cart so long as your playing partner riding with you
does not have a similar feature in his bag. The wheels do not

vibrate because they are made of such porous rubber that they melt on contact with summer asphalt.]

- Bag cover have cipher on both side. Lock cipher and will use handle to roll cylinder to airport.

  [**Translation to the King's English:** *The bag cover has a lock on both sides and a handle on the top. Because the bottom lock was manufactured improperly, it only locks in the upright position but will break loose and slam your irons against your heel as you attempt to pull the bag through an airport.]*

- Bag have be durable to airport worker and easy to pull to you.

  [**Translation to the King's English:** *Except for a broken lower lock, an upper lock whose combination works at random, stuck zippers, and wheels that roll over your foot when you tilt the bag, the golf bag is durable. If the union contract of airport workers allowed them to serve at the convenience of travelers, they could pull the bag to you from the plane instead of dumping it on the floor in a remote location of the airport where the bag is more likely to be stolen than found by you.]*

According to Blister, the important lesson to be learned is—never buy a product manufactured in a country whose own population does not use the product. Consequently, I have made a manufacturer's product note to myself to not buy golf equipment from China, soap from France, or women's razors from Germany.

As for the high handicapped reader who is considering buying a new bag, when you think you have found a suitable bag, unload all the contents of your current bag and insure that everything fits into the new bag. When you have completed the transfer, break open a 12-pack and confirm that all twelve cans comfortably fit in the remaining pocket space. If not, keep looking.

Wiley washed the remnants of his Polish down with a can of Heineken while Blister counted up the scores and the bets on the score card. I prepared two Montecristo's for Wiley and myself. I clipped the end off of both cigars and placed them in the glove box where we could easily retrieve and light them on the tenth tee box, the preferred ignition station for Wiley and me.

"Good God, Chief!" Blister exclaimed, "Do you realize you shot a thirty-nine on the front."

"Yeah, I was surprised after getting that double on seven," I replied.

"Good stuff, Chief," Blister added. "Looks like you're going low today. Is today the day you break eighty?"

"Lots of holes to play, Blister," I scolded him, "Don't jinx it by bringing it up."

The par 4 tenth hole was rated the fourth most difficult hole so everyone received a stroke from me. Although the hole was only 356-yards, it played uphill and directly into the prevailing winds. The driving range bordered the hole on the left, requiring a fifty-foot high net to protect players on the tenth tee box and for the first one hundred and fifty yards of the fairway. Out of bounds markers lined the base of the hillside to the left of the cart path beyond the range net. The looming danger was the pond on the right that separated the tenth and eighteenth fairways. Curiously, while the pond on the ninth hole was populated only with croaking bullfrogs, the back pond was staffed by the little miniature lobsters known as crawdads. The green was relatively flat but had a definite break from the hill toward the eighteenth fairway. Two bunkers were strategically placed on the right side, front and back. The traps were considered hospitable, as they prevented strays from rolling down the steep bank to the eighteenth fairway twenty feet below.

I led off the foursome and enjoyed yet another fortuitous break, as my slicing fade smacked off a recently planted tree near the southern, or left bank, of the pond and dribbled to a stop a few feet from the water. I chose Blister as my partner a moment later when he laced a drive beyond the one hundred and fifty yard marker. Jack also got off the tee without incident before rescuing the remnants of his Polish dog from two blackbirds perched on the roof of his cart.

Wiley stepped up to the tees as Blister walked to the back of his cart and removed his bag from the back of the cart. Although Blister didn't announce his intentions, I knew what he was up to. It was his turn to revere Chief Tit. He was tired of hiking the far regions of the course and wanted to travel in comfort with his Chief under the banner of the blue flag.

Wiley was about to suffer two setbacks. Losing his seat next to me was a foregone conclusion. His second mishap was set in motion when he chomped down on his Polish after donning his driving glove. Unknown to him, the mustard that squirted into the palm of his glove transferred to the leather grip as he addressed his ball. A moment later, Wiley reaffirmed the origins of the adage, 'a little too much mustard'. As Wiley took his practice swing, the mustard removed the necessary friction to keep the shaft in his hand, and he launched his TaylorMade Burner seventy five yards down the fairway.

"Whoa! Jumpin Jesus!" Wiley bellowed, as he transferred the yellow stain to the side of his shorts.

"I'd say you got a little too much mustard on that one," Jack said, as we all chortled at Wiley's miscue.

After wiping his hands on Jack's towel, Wiley borrowed Jack's King Cobra and smacked a solid drive that rolled by Blister's ball. Blister used the distraction to swap his bag with Wiley's and was sitting comfortably in my cart re-lighting his cigar when Wiley walked off the tee box.

"Nice shot Big Man," Blister said to Wiley as he expelled a ring of smoke. "You're back there." He pumped his thumb over his shoulder toward Wiley's new transportation.

"What an asswipe," Wiley responded.

"I gotta spend some quality time with our Chief, Snowman," Blister informed Wiley.

Blister and I were having a difficult time containing our smirks at Wiley's ever-changing facial contours. In addition to the mud smudges, he had a new yellow stain coloring the stubble on his chin.

"Great, I get to ride the rest of the round with Hillary," Wiley complained looking at Jack who was doing his best to get his cigar re-ignited as he sat behind the wheel.

"The feeling's mutual Limbaugh," Jack replied as he cupped his left hand around the end of his cigar and used his cheeks as a bellows to ignite the tobacco.

Wiley took a seat next to Jack and commanded him to drive. "Let's go, Hillary."

I departed the tenth hole with my new riding partner, Blister. Jack was careful to wait for Wiley to take a sip of beer before departing. As soon as he was sure that a transfer of liquid from the can to Wiley's mouth was underway, he engaged the accelerator causing several ounces of beer to supercharge through the opening of the can and discharge down Wiley's chin and the front of his shirt.

Blister and I detoured to pick up Wiley's Burner before cutting across to the pond. Before I could climb out of the cart, Blister let out a whoop and seized my arm.

"Chief, you're not going to believe this," Blister cautioned me before I could get out of the cart.

"What?"

"We've got company. Take a look at your ball."

As soon as I saw the bizarre scene I let out a roar of laughter and was soon joined by Blister. The ball had been claimed by one of the crawdads that occupy the tenth fairway pond. He had both claws wrapped around the ball as he waved his antennas at Blister and me. Despite the face off against an adversary that was equivalent to a human confronting a brontosaurus, he had no intention of letting go. I took a 3-iron and gently prodded the ball, but he just grabbed it tighter.

"You gotta play it as it lies, Chief," Blister said, weighing in on the matter.

"Maybe you should explain that rule to Mr. Crawdad," I joked, poking at the ball.

Sorting Out the Food Chain

I had a real dilemma on my hands. I had a kamikaze crawdad urging me to invoke Rule 13-1, and play the ball 'as it lies.' However, the kamikaze crawdad wasn't dealing with your average stupid golfer. No sir. He was squared off against Chief Tit, unemployed Business Consultant and Rules Expert. While this brash crawdad did his best to prod me into complying with Rule 13-1 and clobber him with a 3-iron, I let him cool his claws while I performed a mental scan of my options.

First, I was acutely of aware of Rule 23-6, which states that a dead land crab in a bunker is a natural object and not an obstruction. However, this guy was still alive—at least for the moment. If he were dead, I would have no choice but to shred him.

Perhaps more relevant, Rule 23-8, which addresses partially embedded worms, clarifies that a worm who is half way in the ground is not 'fixed or growing' or 'solidly embedded' in accordance with the meaning of those terms as they apply to 'loose impediments'. Accordingly, such a worm can be removed under Rule 23. As such, if I believe in the sanctity of the food chain, a higher order of animal would certainly be worthy of equal consideration to a worm. It follows, if a kamikaze crawdad occupies a higher order in the food chain than a worm, then Rule 23 applies. Let's take a closer look.

If the order is based on a combination of intelligence, size, and proximity to the definition of a mammal, then the food chain would probably be in this order: worm, crawdad, Blister, cow, me. Under this reasoning, the crawdad could be pried from the ball without infraction.

My decision was further bolstered by Rule 23-6.5 governing dead and live snakes. According to the rule, a dead snake is a loose impediment and can be removed if not touching the ball but cannot be removed

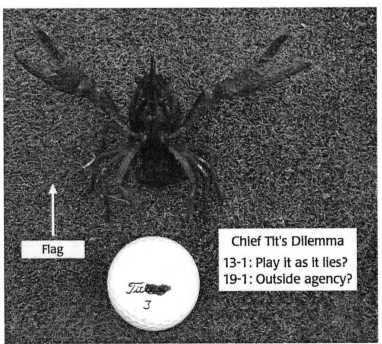

Kamikaze crawdad attempts to scare the crap out of Chief Tit

if the ball is resting on the dead snake. A live snake is deemed to be an outside agency, just like Blister was on the previous hole. Consequently, there was certainly a good precedent to consider the kamikaze crawdad as an outside agency. The only difference is, normally outside agencies flee the scene when the humans show up. That wasn't the case here. The outside agency still had the ball surrounded with its claws.

"I think you need to introduce this guy to your friend the 3-iron," Blister joked.

Ignoring Blister's advice I raised the iron above the crawdad's head. He instinctively scratched the clouds with his claws to instill fear in his adversary. While he had his claws up, I snatched the ball out from between his second row of legs. He seemed disappointed. He just sat there with his claws in the air and watched me as I walked to a more preferred lie in the fairway.

"Ok, everybody go home. The excitement's over," Blister advised two crawdads on the bank and the pumping lizards.

———

Blister could hardly catch his breath describing the kamikaze crawdad to Jack and Wiley. In his excitement, it took us a moment to comprehend that all four balls were on the green in regulation—a first for the day, maybe a first for the month. Of course, Jeb the Marshal was no where to be found. Jeb only seemed to show up when all four of us were on the hillside grazing for balls.

Jack introduced a blemish to the near perfect hole when he three-putted and forced the bet to roll over to the next hole. I was on a runner's high, without the sweat. Three over par after ten holes. I just hoped my new riding partner didn't start squawking about my no-hitter.

Things weren't quite as social in the other cart.

"Hillary, you putt like my grandma," Wiley complained, taking two swipes at Jack.

"Well, at least your grandma can hang on to her driver."

"I'm talking about my dead grandma."

"So am I."

Hole 11
Sherlock: The Great Mongolian Warlord

The second longest backup was the par 3 eleventh hole. We motored our carts over the hill expecting to see a traffic jam and weren't disappointed. The Morris' and the sisters were still sitting in their carts to the right of the men's tee box watching a foursome putt out.

We decided to hold up at the back tees thirty yards to their rear so Jack could set up his neighborhood watch program and Wiley and I could light our Montecristos. I pulled the two tubes from the glove box and passed one to Wiley whose cart was parked close enough for me to rest my foot on the right front wheel.

"Hey, you got an extra one for me?" Jack begged.

"Weren't you smoking your stinkweed on ten?" I asked.

"Wiley ran over it when I was in the fairway," Jack answered, as Wiley nodded his head in agreement.

"I'll take one too, Chief," Blister advised.

"Alright, you know where they are." I pumped my thumb over my shoulder toward my self-service golf bag.

Blister clipped two Montecristos as Wiley and I torched ours.

"Say, have any of you guys taken a physical recently?" Jack asked, drawing blank looks from Wiley and me.

"Not me," I said.

"Me neither," added Wiley.

"I gotta tell ya, I took one on Monday and it had to be the most humiliating experience of my life," Jack said, as he lifted the range finders to his eyes and tried to read the label on the side of Bab's shorts.

"I don't remember it being that bad," Wiley replied, "though there's always that one uncomfortable moment."

Jack continued. "I expected to have a gloved hand rammed up my pooper, but I wasn't prepared for the nurse to walk in after I pulled my pants down."

"The nurse walked in?" Blister said with a giggle.

"Oh, she walked in alright," Jack continued. "And I gotta tell you, it was a surprise for both of us. Of course, she was good looking too!"

"What'd she do?" Wiley asked.

"She said, 'excuse me!'" Jack explained. "Then she put her hand over her eyes and pulled the door shut. But, I guarantee you she peeked at the trouser trout before she got the door shut. I just wonder if she did it on purpose."

"Did the doctor say anything?" Blister asked.

"Yeah," Jack answered. "He said it happens all the time and not to worry about it. But then I go to settle-up with my a co-payment and guess who's covering the front desk? The same nurse!"

"Did she ask for your number?" I wanted to know.

"My social security number," Jack replied.

"You should have asked her out to lunch," Wiley suggested. "I bet she wanted a little bratwurst."

"You mean a big bratwurst, of course," Jack corrected him. "Besides, I'm not sure the wife would have liked that."

"I think I had it right the first time," Wiley emphasized.

"Well, that doesn't sound that awful, I guess that stuff happens," Blister decided.

"That's not the end of the physical," Jack continued. "The doctor wants me to send him a stool sample."

Blister thought that was about the funniest thing he had heard. He doubled up, wondering if the doctor was aware of what he had gotten himself into.

"Jack, I gotta tell you," Blister said drowning out Wiley's laughter, "there's a lot of things in the world that someone might want, but the last thing . . . on anybody's list, has gotta be a stool sample from you. Maybe you better tell the doctor he's reading the list upside down so he understands—it's the last thing on the list—not the first thing."

"Does he want the whole movement?" Wiley asked, taking the conversation ever closer to the gutter. "If so, you may have to borrow Blister's ice chest. I bet you could fill that thing up—no problem."

The sisters and the Morris' climbed out of their carts and looked in our direction as the cackling grew louder. I prayed that they hadn't heard Wiley's suggestion about how Blister's ice-chest might be used for medical science. Timothy and Janet climbed the mound as the group on the green disappeared over the crest of the hill.

The tribe decided that it was time for a scientific expedition and we pulled our carts up behind Babs and Donetta's cart as Timothy took a few practice swings. Jack pulled his and Wiley's cart even with Blister and me so we could observe the action from the same row.

"How's the company?" I asked Babs under my breath.

"About as bad as you can get!" Babs whispered back, holding both hands to her temples to simulate a headache.

"I'm about ready to take my club and shove it up her—you know what," Donetta quickly added in a low whisper.

"Her butt?" Blister guessed.

"Bingo," Babs quipped, as she smiled at Blister and touched her index finger to her nose while pointing at Blister with the other hand to signal an accurate guess.

Donetta couldn't wait her turn to join back in. "Clarence Darrow over there, thinks he has to explain every decision ever handed down by the USGA. Then he goes ahead and breaks em anyway."

"What a dick!" Blister chimed in.

"And the doctor hasn't said a word to us in three holes," Babs interjected.

"What a bitch!" Blister chanted.

"You can say that again," Donetta said to Blister.

"What a bitch!" Blister repeated.

"That cigar smells good," Babs said, as the smoke curled out of our cart.

Without warning, the entire tribe found ourselves suppressing the urge to pop a woody. It is a rare event indeed, when an attractive blond likes the aroma of a cigar.

"It's a Montecristo," I said with surprise. "You want one?"

"We don't smoke," Babs answered.

"Oh you don't have to smoke it, just keep it lit," Blister explained. "If you really want to put your relationship with your new friends in the toilet, light one up."

"Oh, I hadn't thought of that," Babs said smiling as she rubbed her chin.

"Let's do it," Donetta giggled.

I jumped out of the cart, retrieved a Montecristo from my bag and began to cut it before hesitating.

"Hey Babs, If you're not going to actually smoke it, you might as well take one of the fifty-centers rather than the five dollar cigars."

"Makes sense, Chief. We don't care. We'll just keep it lit long enough to piss off Janet," Babs answered.

"Jack, throw me one of your stinkweeds," I ordered.

Jack retrieved a Maduro Presidentes from his bag, cut it, and presented it to Babs. Babs put the cigar in her mouth and I lit it while she puffed and exhaled the smoke without inhaling. As I was lighting the cigar I glanced over her shoulder and saw the frowns grow on the Morris faces.

Wiley decided it was time for him to mix it up with the sisters. "Remember, don't do anything Clinton wouldn't do."

"What?" Babs said looking at Wiley with puzzlement.

"You know—no inhaling," Wiley smirked.

"Right," Babs replied, not getting the connection.

Most of the Red Ball People didn't have the way with the ladies like Chief Tit. They were always tripping over each other trying to say something clever, which invariably came out stupid. This was one of those times.

"What happened to you?" Babs asked Wiley with a grimace, suddenly getting a good look at the collage of mustard and mud on his face.

"Huh?" Wiley said, sounding like a troglodyte.

It was the moment that Jack, Blister, and I had been looking forward to. Between his stupid joke that didn't go over and his mustard covered face, he was coming across as the dope we know he is. Donetta took a closer look at Wiley, who had a blank look on his face, and started giggling. Unfortunately, our moment of bliss was cut short by Timothy

Morris who announced that the green was clear, which of course was an indirect way of telling us to shut up.

"What a dick," Blister muttered.

Donetta and Babs turned around to watch Tim hit, which gave our scientific expedition a chance to watch them. The four of us established missile lock for the duration of Tim's swing, though each of us broke off from the target long enough to confirm that the other guys also had established missile lock.

"That's nice," Wiley said referring to his target and not Tim's swing.

"It sure is," his wingman Jack confirmed, locking on the same target.

Donetta and Babs grabbed their irons and walked to the ladies tee to join Doctor Morris. Babs puffed her cigar, which drew a scowl from Timothy. All three women came up well short of the green. Timothy drove forward to pick up his wife, as Babs and Donetta skipped back to their carts. Before slinging herself into the driver's side, Babs tapped her cigar like Groucho Marx.

"Thanks for the cigar, Chief," Babs said, as they pulled away.

"It was my cigar," Jack complained. "How come she's thanking you?"

"The Chief's got a way with the ladies, Jack," I informed him of the obvious.

The 11th hole was handicapped as the eighth most difficult, meaning Blister and Jack would both receive strokes. We caught a break, as Jeb the Marshal had moved the tees up twenty yards to make the hole play faster. The forward placement of the tee box should easily negate any problems from the wind, which was mild. The tee box and green were partially cut into the side of the large hill to the left, while the area between drooped to a saddle created by an eroded fold in the hill. The saddle extended twenty yards to the left or in a southerly direction following a crease in the hill. To the right, the saddle drained into a waste area above the river bank to the right of the cart path. A hook or a slice was a certain double bogey—at best. Proving that one man's trash is another man's treasure, the hillside provided the biggest bonanza on the course for Mr. Kim, who was more than willing to brave the poison oak to collect errant balls.

The green was surrounded by three bunkers. The left bunker was particularly brutal, as the green sloped steeply away toward the river to the right of the cart path. Deceptive breaks forced players to be extra attentive and a two-putt was always a struggle.

We climbed the mound and watched the ladies play polo toward the hole. Jack continued to provide more vivid details about his medical visit than we needed to hear. It's difficult to predict how many lines of civility would have been crossed in the discussion had Mr. Kim's battery-powered cart not crept up behind us, closely followed by the Mr. Kim who exhibited his remote-control dexterity with an orchestrated series of zig-zags.

"OK, green ready now," Mr. Kim said with a smile on his face.

"Right," Blister said.

Blister teed his ball as the rest of us stepped back and joined Mr. Kim. Blister tried to line up a date with Betty Pullooski but got lucky when his ball careened off the hillside beyond the OB markers and rolled to a flat plateau above the left-side bunker. A difficult second shot awaited and Mr. Kim knew it.

"That hard up there," Mr. Kim said, grasping the obvious.

"Thanks for the update, Sherlock," Blister said to Mr. Kim.

Mr. Kim smiled at Blister wondering who Sherlock was. Mr. Kim imagined that Sherlock was probably a 16th century Mongolian warlord and was honored with the comparison. Jack followed Blister with a rocket to the back of the green.

"Goo shot!" Mr. Kim shouted, hoping Jack would also thank him using his new warlord name, Sherlock.

"Thanks, Mr. Kim."

"That's good enough for me," Blister said cementing his financial relationship with Jack.

Wiley scooped out a Manhattan divot as his fat shot fell twenty yards short of the green.

"Owww, fat!" Mr. Kim announced.

"That was a fattie all right, Sherlock," Wiley shot back, suddenly preferring Mr. Kim's new name.

"Better to hit a fat ball than a fat wife," Blister said to Mr. Kim, obliterating the line of appropriateness.

Mr. Kim maintained a frozen grin as I took the tee box. I selected a 6-iron though I would've probably been as successful with a garden hoe. Like Wiley, I carved out a Manhattan divot that caused the ball to fall like a lead-sinker well short of the green.

"Owww fat!" Mr. Kim said for the second time.

"No Mr. Kim, that was a fattie," I said, hoping to teach him a new word.

"Fattie," Mr. Kim said practicing his new word.

"Big fattie," I said with emphasis.

"Big fattie," Mr. Kim repeated.

Mr. Kim was experiencing a joyous moment. In the span of two minutes, he learned that he had some mysterious tie to a saintly Mongolian warlord named Sherlock and mastered an important word to boot. Mr. Kim tugged on his suspenders and beamed at us as we climbed in our cart.

"Big fattie!" Mr. Kim shouted as we drove off.

"That's right. Big fattie!" I yelled back as Blister chortled.

I tried to dump some beer down the front of Blister's shirt as he took a swig of beer, but he was too smart for me and anticipated my quick change in speed.

Wiley and I both hit good pitches to the green. I would have about three feet for par while he had a four-footer, both nearly close enough to concede if events played out in our favor.

"Ok Blister," Jack said calling over to his betting partner. "We both get strokes so get your bogey and let's get the hell out of Dodge."

Blister nodded to Jack but he had other ideas. As the one-hole honorary mayor, Dodge suited him just fine. He eyed his impossible shot over the bunker to the green sloping steeply away. There was only a fifteen foot landing area between the bunker and the red flag. The smart play would be to pitch the ball to the right of the bunker where he could try to chip the ball back uphill to the front pin position. However, as it was prone to do, Blister's mind inexplicably shut down. The rest of us watched with incredulity as he began practicing a full-swing flop shot with his lob wedge.

Phil Mickelson was so good at the flop, he reenacted the shot in numerous TV commercials for his endorsing sponsors. Unlike Blister, Phil began practicing the flop when he was eight years old and spent roughly one hour, five days a week, for twenty-four years, to perfect it. If Phil can hit approximately one practice ball every ten seconds, a little simple math will demonstrate that Phil has practiced the flop roughly 2,246,400 times (360 flops per hour X 260 sessions per year X 24 years) or approximately 2,246,300 times more than Blister.

He continued his full practice swing as the rest of us backed off the green and created a wide swath of air space. Jack looked at me and demonstrated his confidence in Blister by wrapping his arm around his head and scratching the front of his forehead like Laurel and Hardy used to do. My giggle turned into a guffaw when I looked at Wiley and saw him holding a cocked forefinger to his temple in a mock display of suicide. Before Blister attempted to execute his flop, Jack tried to give him a chance to reconsider.

"Blister, before you try that flop," he nagged him, "tell me how many times you've successfully hit one."

"I'm not sure I ever have." Blister answered. "You gotta start some-time."

"No, actually you don't," Jack corrected him. "You don't ever have to start. I've never hit a flop shot and I feel no urgency to start at any time."

To the best of our knowledge, Blister's brain was hibernating, though he still had motor skills. His mouth kept moving, as did his arms, but we suspected the vibrancy was attributable to muscle memory. I had seen the phenomenon once before when I killed a rattlesnake in my back yard with a shovel. After cutting the snake in half, the headless section of the snake continued to crawl around for several minutes as if it were receiving conscious direction from its brain. That's what Blister was do-ing. Although he wasn't a headless body, he clearly was functioning without any detectable brain activity.

We were aghast as the muscle memory put his arms in motion for what we all recognized as the genuine flop swing. I was worried for Blister. Was his lapse in thinking going to have any permanent effects?

I think, Therefore I Am

Seventeenth century philosopher Rene Descartes had some serious doubts about the validity of knowledge and decided to question every-thing. He adopted a program of systematic doubt and began doubting the existence of the corporeal world, God, as well as his basic being. However, one thing that Descartes could not doubt was that there was indeed a doubter doing the doubting. Since he couldn't doubt the doubter, Descartes postulated the self and dreamed up the catch phrase *'cogito ergo sum'*: 'I think, therefore I am'. From this basic premise he went on to affirm the existence of other minds, God, and matter. For him, there were two substances—mind and matter. Which brings us back to Blister.

Because Blister quit thinking, does it necessarily follow from Descartes' argument that his mind turned to matter? Secondly, can the mass of oatmeal sitting on top his shoulders turn back into a mind and begin functioning as a thinking substance again?

Fortunately for Blister, the Cartesian dualism of mind and body did not allow one substance to transform into the other and back again. Once a substance was a mind, it remained a mind even if it quit performing its basic duty of thinking, though Descartes did hint that God could intervene and do anything he wanted such as turn mind into matter.

To be sure, in a little known treatise Descartes wrote when he got boozed up after realizing he had a girl's first name, he added a long forgotten corollary to his theory of duality when he claimed, *'No cogito ergo plano el stupido'*: 'When I'm not thinking, I'm just plain stupid'. Thankfully, Cartesian analysis allows us to apply this long forgotten corollary to Blister's suspension of thinking and we can gleefully agree that he is just plain stupid and his mind has not turned into a blob of matter after all.

———

Blister struck one of the most impressive rifle-shots any of us had ever seen. The ball never elevated more than a few inches, as the leading edge of his wedge blasted it across the green at supersonic speed. It flew over the roof of our cart, and shot past a row of eucalyptus trees, before disappearing into a thicket on the far side of the riverbank.

"Hit softly!" Blister yelled behind it.

"Bite!" I yelled joining in the fun.

"Nice going, genius," Jack quipped, recognizing the loss of a two-hole rollover bet.

"Practice makes perfect," Wiley added.

Blister sat down on the slope of the bunker and re-lit his cigar as Jack continued to look over his putt. He had no intention of taking a drop across the cart path on the riverbank and would settle for a Linda Tripp.

Jack knelt behind his ball and dangled his putter with his thumb and index finger in front of both eyes. He closed his left eye and looked at the break with the aid of the pendulum. He then repeated the process with his right eye. He eventually opened both eyes, which always made them look crossed. He finally stepped over his ball and left it six feet short. Clearly disgusted with himself, he followed the ball to the hole shaking his head.

Jack took nearly as much time lining up his second putt.

"Which way do you see this breaking, Chief?" Jack asked.

"An inch outside," I replied.

"Really?" Jack asked, overcome with doubt.

"Right side."

"Really?"

"Are you serious? You can't see the break?" I asked Jack.

"It looks left side with my right eye and right side with my left," Jack said.

"Maybe you ought to try wearing an eye patch on one of your eyes," Blister suggested.

"I'd settle for a muzzle over his mouth," Wiley announced.

"I'm telling you, Chief," Jack replied, "I can see it both ways depending on which eye I have shut."

"It's an inch on your right, but go with what your dominant eye tells you," I recommended.

"I don't think I have a dominant eye," Jack said, wiping sweat from his brow.

Determining Your Dominant Eye

If you putt right-handed, it is preferred that your dominant eye be your left eye, since the path to the hole is more easily viewed. If your right eye is dominant, you can provide a quick fix for the round by poking yourself in the right eye with a finger. For the remainder of the round and well into the next week, your left eye will become your dominant eye.

Although there is no advantage to having a dominant nostril in golf, you can perform a simple test to determine which nostril is dominant. First, light up a cigar. Once the cigar is lit, inhale a hardy draw of smoke. Before exhaling, close your mouth and open your hand so it is flat and press it against your nose to divide your face in half. Now exhale the smoke. If more smoke appears on the left side of your hand—your left nostril is dominant.

———————

As it turned out, the break was a lot less important than the speed as Jack powered the ball by the hole leaving it even with Wiley's ball. Jack was in real danger of four-putting the green. Recognizing the liability, Jack preempted the possibility.

"Good, good, good?" Jack asked, signaling a desire for a quick negotiated settlement.

"Ok with me, Chief," Wiley agreed coalescing with Jack.

"What's good for the geese is good for the gander," I said picking up my three-footer.

Jack and Wiley followed suit and picked up their balls. Jack saved himself an embarrassing four putt while Wiley and I made two impressive zero-putt pars. Since Blister had surrendered to the hole, a triple was levied. As I planted the flag, I looked up on the hillside and saw the top of Mr. Kim's pole protruding above a bush. The motion of the pole told me it was in the process of spearing a lost ball.

Hole 12
Red Ball People
in Hyperbolic Space

I pulled up behind Jack and Wiley's cart on the twelfth tee, careful to leave an easement between the two bumpers. Although I was keeping the official score card, I spied Wiley marking a clandestine card, which I suspected had both our scores. He wouldn't admit it if I were to ask him, but he wanted to kick my ass and I was still four strokes ahead of him. The sign was subtle, yet unmistakable. Wiley and I had silently declared war on each other and we were about to go mano-a-mano. Both of us continued to play over our heads and I began to worry about Newton's Law of Equilibrium coming back into play.

The par 4 hole was only 338-yards. As the twelfth handicapped hole, it was considered one of the easiest holes on the course. Nevertheless, the hole had its difficulties and could present a real challenge for a fader.

The hole was bordered by the river on the right side, which curved to the right about forty-five degrees, sixty yards or so beyond the tee box. The dogleg right fairway followed the contour of the river and the trees on the elevated bank made it impossible to see the green from the tee box. A gully of hardpan on the right side funneled balls directly into the river, compounding the difficulty along the right side. The gully was about two hundred and twenty five yards from the tee box. If a player was lucky enough to salvage a ball that rolled into the gully, he would find himself fifteen feet below the flag with three small pine trees between his ball and the hole.

Two bunkers protected either side of the flat putting green.

"You're up Jack," I said. "You better think about choosing a better partner, you haven't won a hole since the sixth."

"Thanks for reminding me that my life is in a swirling toilet, Chief."

Jack took a big swig of beer as he dug his glove out of his back pocket. In accordance with course management guidelines, he teed his ball on the right side, to steer it away from the trouble. The first one hundred yards of his drive looked deceptively good.

"Alright Jack!" Wiley said with encouragement.

"Well look who's the new Cinderella story!" Blister chimed in.

The Cinderella story would be a short one. The ball began to change direction and drift to the right. It was beginning to move perilously close to the gully.

"Whoa—hang on," Jack yelled at the ball. "Get down. Now—you piece of crap."

The ball disappeared behind two trees into the gully.

"I think it stayed in Jack," I said, telling the truth this time.

"I've done worse," Jack replied as he walked back to his cart to have a sip of beer.

Wiley followed Jack and smacked a rocket thirty yards beyond the one hundred and fifty yard marker. My heart sank. I was beginning to doubt Newton's Law of Reaction. Either the law was in the process of being repealed or Wiley had a train wreck waiting around the corner. Ditto for me. I was probably more overdue for an equilibrium correction than Wiley.

"Excellent shot partner," Jack said, happy to have a compassionate conservative on his team.

Blister introduced his perfunctory pun regarding the Atlanta Braves mascot. "You're up, Chief. Knock a homer. Keah, keah."

I felt a little uneasy. Watching Wiley hit another good drive reminded me that Newton's law had been suspiciously dormant. Energy was slowly draining from my body. I could feel it as I teed my ball on the right side of the tee box. I could almost feel the tug from the event horizon on my right side. I also had to pee.

I started my pre-shot routine but suddenly found myself adding two new steps.

1. Don't piss in pants
2. Stay away from the event horizon

At the moment, pissing my pants had much more serious long-term repercussions than did the event horizon so I concentrated on that step with a lot more vigor. Before long it dawned on me that Newton's law was forcing me to make a tough decision between the two alternatives: piss in pants; get sucked into event horizon. Piss in pants; get sucked into event horizon. Frankly, had I been using my head a few minutes earlier I could have pissed into the event horizon and knocked out two birds with one stone.

I took a mighty swing, trying to reach my adversary's ball.

Directed by Newton's Law of Reaction, the event horizon activated itself. The ball left the airspace above the women's tee box and darted out over the river, disappearing behind the thick brush, blocking our view of the splash down. At least I could go take a piss.

"Touch luck, Chief," Blister said, aware that I had been on the verge of a break out round.

"That's a shame, Chief," Wiley added, disguising his elation.

"Looks like a good time for a hyperbolic drop," Jack advised. "You gonna take a hyperbolic drop, Chief?"

"You betcha," I said, unzipping my pants. "If anyone knows how to take a hyperbolic drop—it's Chief Tit."

Taking a Hyperbolic Drop

Regrettably, the USGA Rules Committee doesn't have the advanced mathematical background that Chief Tit has. Otherwise, I'm sure that they would have been astute enough to make some allowance for the shortcoming found in Euclidean geometry when applied to Rule 26c, governing where to take a drop for a ball that enters a water hazard. Before discussing Red Ball People Amendment 2 to Rule 26c, it is first necessary to explain the shortcoming of Euclidean geometry to the un-initiated.

Euclid was born in 325 BC in Alexandria, Egypt and is considered the founder of geometry. He was so important, like Madonna and Prince, he only needed one name. The entire study of Euclidean geometry is based on what Euclid defined as five fundamental assumptions called postulates. Since he accepted the postulates as axiomatically true, he believed no proof was necessary.

However, from the very beginning, Euclid's 5th postulate was attacked as too implausible to qualify as an unproven axiom. Known as the parallel postulate, Euclid stated: given a line L and a point A on Line L, there is one and only one Line L1 (see the diagram below) that intersects point A that is perpendicular to Line L.

For two thousand years, mathematicians tried to derive it from the four other postulates, which were universally accepted as axioms. However, all attempts to derive it from the first four postulates met with futility. Finally in the early 19th century, several famous mathematicians lead by Carl Freidrich Gauss proffered that Euclid was wrong. Maybe there were an infinite number of lines intersecting point A with L1. Referring to the diagram below, this implies that there is a Line L2 that is parallel to L1 that intersects point A but is not the same line a L1. With this alternative assumption, Hyperbolic (Non-Euclidean) Geometry was born. Much of Einstein's theory of relativity is based on non-Euclidean geometry and a repudiation of Euclid's 5th postulate.

For a time, both Euclidean geometry and hyperbolic geometry had an uncomfortable coexistence as Mathematicians tried to prove which one was true. In a proof that is still considered one of the biggest enigmas in mathematics, Eugenio Beltrami and Felix Klein proved that Euclid's 5th postulate could not be proved one way or the other. Consequently, both geometries exist with full validity even though they have such diabolical differences on their implications for hyperspace.

So what does all this brainy stuff have to do with Rule 26c you ask? Well, I'll tell you. The people who make up the USGA Rules Committee wear little tiny thinking caps and their understanding of points and lines is conceptually limited to Euclidean geometry. However, as we see in Chief Tit's rather erudite discourse on hyperbolic geometry above, other interpretations of where a ball should be dropped are possible depending on which geometry governs the universe that a player dwells in.

Like Einstein, Gauss, and Klein, the Red Ball People dwell in a hyperbolic universe while the USGA Rules Committee is seemingly trapped in Euclidean space. Under Chief Tit's mathematical tutelage, the Red Ball People applied hyperbolic theory to a pragmatic use and took advantage of the inherent Euclidean flaws in Rule 26c and drafted an amendment for those players who occupy a hyperbolic dimension.

According to our hyperbolic laws, there are infinitely many lines (see diagram below) parallel to the Euclidean line (L1), the line I used to hit my ball into the river. Many of these lines, like L2 below, intersect with land and are much closer to the hole than the Euclidean drop area specified by the USGA under Rule 26c. Since the Red Ball People don't pack surveying equipment in our bags, we are entitled to estimate where one of these hyperbolic lines intersects with land and take a drop under the spirit of Rule 26c. The Amendment can be reviewed below.

Using the Hyperbolic Drop Rule

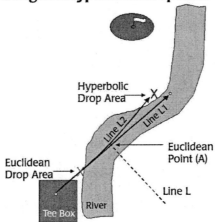

Hyperbolic drop: useful on the 12th hole

Rule 26c—Taking a drop from water hazard (previously reviewed): *Player must drop a ball outside the* water hazard *within two club-lengths of and not nearer the* hole *than the point where the original ball last crossed the margin of the* water hazard. *Player is assessed a one stroke penalty.*

Red Ball People Amendment 2 (Hyperbolic Amendment) to Rule 26c: *If a player is able to take advantage of the 5th postulate of hyperbolic geometry and can identify a hyperbolic parallel line that is parallel to the Euclidean line that coincides with the ball flight, then it's the player's option to declare himself a hyperbolic space-dweller. As such, he is entitled to drop his ball on one of the infinitely many lines that intersect the fairway that are parallel to the Euclidean line* in which his ball traveled into the hazard. Player should drop within two club-lengths of where a parallel hyperbolic line intersects with land. Player is assessed a one stroke penalty.

Reason for Hyperbolic Amendment to Rule 26c: *I think we can all agree that by any measuring stick, Carl Freidrich Gauss is a lot smarter than anyone on the USGA Rules Committee. Consequently, these numbskulls don't realize—in accordance with the 5th postulate of hyperbolic geometry, there exists a second line L2 (as well as many others) that is parallel to Line L1, on which we can drop. Furthermore, Line L2 happens to intersect dry land much closer to the hole than the drop area under Rule 26c that is based purely on Euclidean geometry. If hyperbolic geometry is good enough for Gauss and Einstein, then it's certainly good enough for the Red Ball People.*

Even though Wiley had creased a drive down the middle of the fairway, he knew better than to complain about Chief Tit's invocation of a clever Red Ball Amendment. He had taken advantage of the amendment numerous times in previous rounds and would take advantage of it again in the future. The amendment was one of the most sacred Red Ball People covenants, and Wiley showed proper deference by keeping his mouth shut even though he would prefer to see me pile on a few strokes.

I walked to the back of the tee box and pissed off the side of the riverbank into the event horizon as Blister hit his ball. Since he was my partner for the hole, I paid more attention to his shot than I normally do. Unfortunately, he didn't exactly do his part to carry the team. He too hit his ball into the river and would be taking a hyperbolic drop along with me.

Blister was especially pleased to have the blue flag flapping as we charged down the cart path and cut across the fairway toward the gully. Jack and Wiley had two of the longest walks of the day waiting for them. Blister offered the proper homage.

"It's you and me Chief. Blood brothers till the end," he said, buttering me up.

"That's what Jack and Wiley say when they're riding with me," I informed Blister.

"But I mean it, Chief," Blister said with a smirk. "You and me Chief. I'll cut my finger and swap blood with you if you want."

"I'm not sure that's necessary," I said deflecting his offer. "Perhaps you can just promise not to breathe on me. That breath is a little fertile today."

"Beer and pizza last night. The wife wouldn't even kiss me this morning."

"Really? She always kisses me when we wake up," I said, sharing my first obligatory wife joke of the day.

"You break me up, Chief," Blister said with a straight face, in deference to the joke he already heard fifty times.

We slowed to look for Jack's ball. After spinning a few donuts in the gully, we spotted it resting in deep grass below a willow tree near the bottom. The ball was surrounded by numerous rat-tailed twiggy branches that hung down to the ground. In addition to contending with the viney branches, he would have to hit over two small staked trees on the west side of the gully to reach the flag one hundred and twenty away.

"We got your ball over here," I yelled to Jack. "You've got yourself a Blister back hair lie, so you better bring a weed-whacker."

Blister and I continued forward to the hyperbolic drop area, nearly even with Wiley's ball. Since Jack was still making his way down the Lewis and Clark trail, Blister and I decided to drop protocol and play our shots.

I grabbed a 9-iron as Blister swigged his beer and leaned on his iron to watch me hit. I was in my pre-shot count down and moments away from starting my backswing when I was first distracted by the sound. I listened a little closer. It sounded like a cow was walking toward me.

"Clank, clank, clank," went the cowbell.

It was getting closer. I looked up at Blister who was looking over my shoulder.

"Is there a cow coming up behind me," I asked without looking.

"If you think Jack is a cow—then, yeah," Blister replied.

"You mind if I hit while you continue to attract bulls?" I barked, swiveling my head toward Jack.

"Right, Chief—I'm sure it'll make a big difference," Jack replied, with his standard dickhead sarcasm.

Fairway Etiquette

Even the worst players understand that the player furthest from the hole plays first, unless of course, the honoree moves at the speed of Elsie the cow, like our buddy Jack. There are less subtle conventions that you need to be aware of that David Leadbetter didn't bother to mention.

The Noisy Bag: My neighbor has a cat that is so stealthy, it can catch five mice a day. Not surprisingly, the feline's fulfillment process includes leaving his kill on my neighbor's kitchen floor. My neighbor broke the killing spree by attaching a bell around the cat's neck so mice could hear him coming from three blocks away.

Similarly, many well-heeled courses give out metal name tags promoting their courses. Players who occasionally play these courses, mistakenly believe they automatically become well-heeled themselves in proportion to the number of fancy metal name tags attached to their bag. While the sight of sparkling name tags may be impressive to mice, they are seldom welcome on the fairway when others are addressing their balls. If you're one of these neophytes, be advised—when you strut across the fairway sounding like Mr. Tambourine Man every player in your foursome would just as soon kick you in the nuts as read your tags.

Cell Phones: With the propagation of cell phones in the last decade, people often wonder what we'd do without them. Well, the short answer is—our rounds of golf would be much more enjoyable. Any dipstick who thinks cell phones are acceptable on the course must also think it would be OK for me to hit a 3-iron in his office. The ringing is bad enough, but then the three other players have to tolerate a ten minute conversation about how to restore an Oracle database.

The only worse location to use a cell phone is in the fast lane of a freeway. For some reason that science hasn't quite uncovered, cell phones evidently cause tendons in the calf muscles to recoil, reducing pressure

on the vehicle's accelerator, which results in an immediate 10 MPH reduction in speed.

Acutely aware of this problem, I submitted a design to the US Patent office for a device called a Telecellerator™. The Telecellerator™ contains an integrated cell phone and four electrical wires. Two wires attach to a 90-volt battery, one wire is attached to the odometer, and the other wire is attached to the ear lob of a driver. As the cell phone interferes with the driver's primary task of driving at freeway speed, the device activates upon detecting a 5 MPH deceleration and a 90-volt payload is delivered to the driver's ear lobe until the car attains the proper speed. Although the Telecellerator™ may not be practical on a golf course, it's a good start for easing congestion of the freeway.

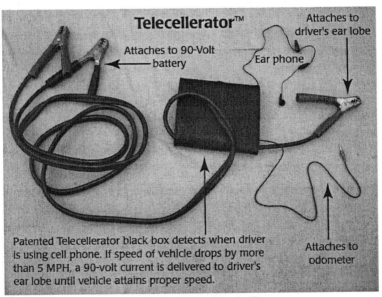

Chief Tit's Telecellerator™

Replacing Your Divot: Everyone knows you are expected to replace your divot. Enough said. However, what most players don't understand is—when it's acceptable NOT to replace a divot. It is really a judgment call on a case by case basis. In general, if a player ruins his round on the final hole and misses breaking a milestone career score because he hit three fatties from fifty yards out, then we can all appreciate that he needs to concentrate on his tantrum rather than retrieving his third divot.

Moreoever, the divot becomes a subordinate priority to the damage the player wields with his wedge as he buries it three feet below the surface of the ground. Under the circumstances we would surely lose respect for the player if he reestablished his composure and regained the necessary focus to remember to retrieve his divot, because we've all been there—and that's not what we did.

Jack stopped clanking his name tags long enough for me to hit a sweet 9-iron to the front of the green. Blister followed with a topper that still managed to flutter to the back of the green.

Blister and I exchanged knuckle kisses and hiked to the edge of the gully to watch Jack.

"Thunk," went the sweet spot of Wiley's wedge.

Blister and I looked up to watch the descent and were envious when it plugged within a few feet of the pin.

"What a turd," Blister muttered.

"What an asswipe," I agreed.

As we all know—one man's asswipe is another man's freedom fighter.

"Woohoo, Wiley!" Jack shouted.

Jack could win a little money with Wiley, but first he had to whack his ball out of deep rough below a net of wiry willow branches. Soon enough, Jack set about testing the conditions. He stood to the side of the ball and took three violent practice swings, disemboweling leaves and twigs in all directions. One stringy branch was in the way of his back swing so he pulled it through a fork in a larger branch until it was no longer a problem. Satisfied that enough branches were neutralized, he turned his attention to the grass. His ball was in a hellish Blister back hair lie and needed a little improvement. Jack took a few more practice swings to finish with his 9-iron what Pepe, the lawn mower man, had not finished with his mower. Jack finally achieved the desired result when the ball lurched out of the taller grass to the lower elevation of the clear cut patch.

"Holy Pontiff's ass, Jack," Blister charged, "Did you get a clear cutting permit from Cheney?"

"Looking pretty tidy to me," I added.

"Yeah, I think that'll about do'er," Jack said, clearly pleased with his housekeeping.

"I think we better keep the tribe out of tournaments you're not running," Blister whispered to me.

"Understood," I replied.

Blister was referring to the stack of penalty strokes Jack accumulated that would not appear on our score card. Each time Jack swung his club to knock away a twig to improve his swing path, USGA Rule 13-2 specified that a two-stroke penalty would apply. Furthermore, when Jack pressed his iron into service as a lawn mower, two additional strokes per revolution applied under the same rule. If we cared about the candy speckles on the frosting, four more strokes would apply for tying one branch to another and exerting an influence causing the ball to move. Since we lost count of how many swipes Jack made with his club, we weren't sure if the number of forgiven strokes was fourteen, sixteen, or something higher. Luckily for Jack, the Red Ball People had an allowance for clear-cutting around a ball.

Rule 13-2—Improving the area of intended stance or swing: *Player shall not improve the position or lie of the ball, the area of the intended stance or swing, or the area in which the player is about to place or drop a ball. Violation will result in a two-stroke penalty.*

Red Ball People Amendment to Rule 13-2: *If a player's swing path is improved as a result of obstructions being removed during practice swings, then player will not be assessed a two-stroke penalty provided the branch or twig removed is incapable of supporting a hanging tire with the player sitting in it. Under no circumstances will the player be penalized for fallen leaves or clipped grass.*

Reason for change: *This rule is not protecting trees or plants since the eventual swing will still break small twigs and branches as well as remove leaves. Since the leaves will drop with the change of seasons, it's preposterous to penalize a player in the summertime and not one who plays in the winter when all the leaves are already on the ground. As for the grass, it ain't our fault that Pepe forgot to lower the blade on his lawn mower.*

Jack had done such a good job applying the Amendment to Rule 13-2 that he actually had a pretty easy shot. A short moment later he was on the green and down for a par. More worrisome, Wiley cut my four stroke lead in half when he sunk his putt. Owing to my acute awareness of the dual interpretations of Euclid's 5th postulate, Blister and I were able to save bogey.

Back 9 Score Card after 3 Holes

Hole	10	11	12	13	14	15	16	17	18	Front	Back	Total
Yardage	356	189	338	504	335	401	353	138	461	3088	3075	6163
Handicap	4	8	12	2	14	6	10	16	18			
Wiley	④	③	③							43		
Chief Tit	④	③	5							39		
Blister	4	6 ¹	5							52		
Jack	5	4 ²	④ ³							51		
Par	4	3	4	5	4	4	4	3	5	36	36	72

Notes:

/ => Signifies that player gets stroke

◯ => Signifies that player won bet

–>(0) => Heiroglyphic for "out of ass."

¹ Blister surrenders to hole after hitting lob shot 170 yards across river, takes a Linda Tripp.

² 6 foot putt conceded to Jack to avoid 4-putting green. Wiley and Chief Tit pick up for impressive up and down.

³ Favorable ruling allows Jack to save 16 strokes for clear-cutting around ball.

Hole 13
Gesundheit
Perceptual Measurement

We referred to the par 5 thirteenth hole as the *Assassin* hole. It killed plenty of good rounds and played more like a par 7. The course veered south and up a canyon for the 504-yard hole. A creek ran down the left side of the fairway and separated a row of hills from a solid line of pine trees where the Pullooski clan held jamborees. Fade-swatting pine and eucalyptus trees lined the right side of the fairway forcing players to take their chances with the fairway bunker positioned in the fat part of the fairway.

Once a player navigated the treacherous fairway, he had to contend with a steep and well guarded putting green. The lip of the greenside bunker rose to shoulder level and presented a challenge to even the best of players.

After taking a moment to size up the challenge, Blister dug through his bag for the fattie he had sequestered in a small match box. Wiley pulled another Heineken, positioned the bottle cap on the wire basket behind his cart seat, and delivered a blow to the top of the bottle with his right palm to crack the top off.

Blister located a torch lighter in his bag and ignited his fattie.

He took a deep toke. "Ffffffhhhhhhhh."

"You wanna hit?" he wheezed, without exhaling.

"All yours," Jack said, turning down the offer.

Wiley and I declined with a nod our heads, silently confirming to each other that we were in the middle of an unspoken dog fight.

"Did you guys hear about Jack's miracle ninety-one earlier this week?" Wiley asked Blister and me.

"Coumpgh, coumph, hauggggh," Blister emitted, as he exhaled and coughed. "Ffffffffhhhhh . . . tell us what your keen eyes saw . . . coumpgh, keah, keah."

"Whoa, whoa, I'll tell my version," Jack protested.

"You can tell your version when I'm done telling mine and then we'll see which version Blister and the Chief think is more accurate," Wiley replied.

Wiley recounted how he left work Wednesday afternoon to hit a bucket at the driving range and practice a few chips near the eighteenth green. Coincidentally, Jack had also tanked the afternoon. As Wiley practiced his chipping on the practice green near the eighteenth hole, he stopped to watch the approach shots of the advancing foursome. The red golf bag, Jack's unmistakable sway, and a cloud of cigar smoke confirmed that Jack was in the foursome.

Wiley told us how impressed he was when Jack's one hundred and ninety yard approach shot plopped twenty feet from the flag. When Jack recognized Wiley, he marked his ball and walked to the back of the green and greeted him.

"So I ask Jack how the round went, and he says—'eighteen over,'" Wiley recalled.

"Remember though, I was only sitting twenty feet away for an eagle," Jack interrupted.

"You'll have your turn, big man," Wiley continued. "I'll tell the story, and then you can touch it up with your revisionist history. So anyway . . . he powers his eagle putt ten feet by the hole and misses his birdie putt coming back."

"Of course he did," Blister added.

Wiley continued. "So I yell over—Nice par! And he gives me the finger. When he comes off, I console him on his three-putt."

Wiley reenacted the verbal sparring that ensued, simulating Jack's side of the exchange with a contrived Barney Fife voice.

Wiley: "Ninety is a great round."

Barney Fife: "Actually, it was a ninety-one."

Wiley: "So you counted the birdie before it hatched on eighteen?"

Barney Fife: "Yeah. I can't believe I three-putted. Oh, uh . . . the thirteenth was also closed."

Wiley: "Thirteen was closed? The toughest hole on the back nine was closed?"

Barney Fife: "Yeah. One of the power lines that stretch over the hole was down."

Wiley: "Really? So you didn't play it?"

Barney Fife: "Couldn't—It was closed."

Wiley: "Interesting. How did you shoot a ninety-one without playing thirteen?"

Barney Fife: "Oh—I gave myself a par."

Wiley: "You gave yourself a par? Last time I played with you dude, you took a double."

Barney Fife: "Well, today I got a par."

Wiley: "Nice going."

Blister interrupted the story, giggling. "Keah, keah, keah. You're killing me. Coumpgh, coumph, hauggggh."

It seemed whenever Jack had a good score below his handicap, there were always intervening circumstances. No one was really sure if Jack had ever broken ninety. He thought he had, which Blister viewed as conclusive proof that he hadn't. No one ever broke a milestone like ninety and then didn't remember it, Blister always said. When Jack's score got near ninety, there were usually a few footnotes that followed the main body of work.

Blister decided to give his slant on Wiley's story. "Look, Jack is an eternal optimist and ya gotta respect him for that. I would look at thirteen and think to myself—I never par this damn hole; I'll be generous and give myself a bogey. Jack looks at the same hole and thinks—'I never par this damn hole; I am so due!'"

Jack had a good laugh at his own expense.

"I suppose I'm gonna hear about this for the next year," Jack complained.

"Oh, it'll be a lot longer than that," Blister replied.

Recognizing his version of the story was doomed to the scrapheap, Jack attempted to take the spotlight off himself by inviting Wiley to take the tee.

"You're up, snowman," Jack said.

"Since this hole is optional, maybe I'll just take a birdie," Wiley replied, teeing his ball.

Wiley crushed his drive, barely skirting the overhang of the eucalyptus trees on the right.

"Wow! Wiley's my partner," Blister blurted, forgetting for the moment that the choice of partners was at Wiley's discretion.

"Blister, I wouldn't choose you if you were coming off a win at the US Open," Wiley informed him.

"Well I didn't win the Open, so I'm still available. Keah, Keah." Blister giggled.

I was beginning wonder if Jack and Wiley's cart could hold three. I knew they wouldn't take Blister, but perhaps I could sit in the middle and Blister could have his own cart. I had an overwhelming intuition that he would be a liability for me for the rest of the round.

"You're up, Chief," Jack reminded me.

"Are you a real Chief?" Blister's mouth asked, without any assistance from his brain.

"Yeah, I'm Chief of the Giggling Dick Heads and you're the only one keeping the tribe from becoming extinct," I answered.

"Keah, keah," Blister cackled.

I tried my best to ignore Blister as I teed my ball. The pressure from the undeclared war with Wiley was beginning to mount. He was only two strokes behind. If he got any closer, I might have a mutiny on my hands like Paul Newman in Butch Cassidy and the Sundance Kid. Paul Newman handled that scene pretty well, I recalled, when he kicked his challenger in the nuts as they discussed the rules for the impending knife fight. Maybe, that's what I should do right now. If I wanted to remain the undisputed Chief of the Red Ball People, maybe I should turn around and kick Wiley squarely in the nards. I bet that would put the kibosh on any talk of mutiny. Better yet, we'll find out how Mr. Sandbagger plays with a couple of grapefruits hanging from his crotch.

"Is it me or are things suddenly moving a lot slower?" Blister asked, interrupting my comparison between myself and Butch Cassidy.

"No, the Chief's just over-thinking again," Jack guessed.

"Come on Chief, hurry up before I start staring at my hand," Blister urged.

I gave up on the notion of kicking Wiley in the nuts. After all, his only crime was playing below his handicap and stealing some of my thunder. Even though that was a serious infraction in some circles, I had to stay above the fray and just play my own game, as they say.

"Keah, Keah, keah," Blister giggled for no apparent reason.

I scowled at Blister. He had a smirk on his face that wasn't going to be wiped off until he shared one of his unfettered thoughts. He waved me over as Wiley threw up his hands in disgust and departed for the ball cleaner.

"What?" I asked, as condescendingly as possible.

"Keah, keah . . . when we gonna tell Wiley about all the mud and mustard on his face?" he wanted to know.

"*That's* what you called me over here for?" I barked.

"It's important!" Blister argued.

"Jack, if he giggles one more time during my swing would you shove an iron up his ass?" I pleaded.

"If I can get his head out of the way," Jack replied, promising to give the request careful consideration.

Blister stopped his antics long enough for me to pull a drive to the left side of the fairway. Wiley expected trouble ahead, and passed on me.

Blister out drove me by twenty yards, but Wiley waited for Jack, convinced that Blister was too stoned to hit two good shots. For once, Jack's rhythm looked perfectly synchronized. He launched the ball forty yards past my drive and twenty yards beyond Blister's.

"Praise Allah," Blister shouted, "That's awesome Jack!"

"That's as good as it gets," Wiley added, equally impressed.

Jack didn't say a word. He was still in the midst of an elongated pose. We all understood that the pose had to run its course. Its shelf life was entirely up to Jack. However, sometimes the tribe members overcooked it a little bit, which cracked the door open for some well deserved abuse.

"Keep that pose going Jack," Wiley said, showing more admiration for the longevity of the pose over the longevity of the drive.

"Hold it! Hold it!" I said, joining in.

Although nothing we said was all that clever, Jack burst out in laughter. He realized he was busted for exhibiting the grand inane penchant that afflicts all amateur players once or twice a round. He also chuckled at Blister, who like Jack, was also posing.

"Did I look like the PGA logo?" Jack asked.

"Actually, I think it was more like the LPGA logo that Ben Wright designed," Wiley answered with a smirk.

"So how long should we pose, Chief?" Wiley asked, throwing another tough question to the tribal visionary.

"Well it depends," I told him.

"Depends on what?" Wiley pressed me.

"Tell him what you found out, Chief," Blister said, snapping out of his own pose.

"The endorphins," I said.

"The endorphins?" Wiley asked with a puzzling look.

"That's right. The endorphins," I said with authority.

Why Mediocre Players Pose

Unlike baseball where only the really good players like Barry Bonds pose, golf's biggest posers are also the worst players. Oddly, the length of the pose is inversely proportional to the number of really good shots the player is capable of making in a round. Let's see why this is.

The high-handicapper only expects to hit two or three really good shots a round. Owing to the random nature of the successful stroke, the player is always caught off guard. The pose serves to announce to bystanders—'What you just saw is my true capability and everything else you've seen for the past three hours is only an aberration.' If you saw this same pose on the street you can presume with a high degree of accuracy, the person had successfully completed penis-enlargement surgery.

However, the poor player who poses the longest should not be chided for his long pose. In fact, a pose is merely a physiological reaction and not a conscious choice. Here's what happens.

The player's dread intensifies as the round wears on, and his pituitary gland, which secrets endorphins, a bodily chemical that behaves similarly to an opiate, becomes inactive. At the same time, the endocrine system continues to produce enzymes, the chemical that breaks down endorphins. As the player continues to play poorly, enzymes act to decompose the few euphoria producing endorphins the pituitary gland released the last time the player two-putted.

When the player finally hits a good shot, the pituitary gland instantaneously floods the brain with endorphins, producing a natural high. Essentially, secreting endorphins is the pituitary gland's method of clapping. The euphoria becomes amplified five seconds after the shot, or about the same time the player becomes conscious of how silly he must look standing there like a statue. However, the player mistakenly believes that the pose rather than the endorphins is the source of the temporary high and he extends his goofy pose to prolong the intoxication. Ten seconds after being triggered, the endorphins are quickly diluted in the blood stream, causing the player to conclude that the pose is no longer contributing to his well-being.

Since opiates produce a similar chemical effect to endorphins, the easiest way to confirm this theory is to play with a golfer who sucked on a bong before the round. Until the dope wears off, he will pose on every tee box—even if he's not the guy hitting.

———

"So Jack is posing because he thinks it prolongs an endorphin high?" Wiley asked.

"That's exactly right," I confirmed. "And Blister is unconsciously posing right along with him because the artificially introduced dopamine in his body is preventing the production of endorphin-killing enzymes."

"Fascinating," Wiley admitted, recognizing that ole Chief Tit had bigger moccasins than he could ever fill. "And all this time I just thought Blister was stupid."

"I didn't say he wasn't stupid," I said, cautioning Wiley to be careful with his inferences.

Blister lost interest in my explanation of the role endorphins play in posing and returned to the cart to re-light his cigar and contemplate the palm of his hand.

A battery operated cart approached the tee box followed by a squadron of Mr. Kims. The eldest Mr. Kim was pleased to report on his progress and used some newly acquired vocabulary to do so.

"I hit big fattie!" Mr. Kim proclaimed with a huge smile, clearly pleased with his new word and the fact that he could play to our level.

"I'll show you a big fattie," Blister said, offering to get Mr. Kim stoned.

"You gotta stay away from the fatties, Mr. Kim," I said, as I climbed in the cart trying to discourage any further dialog from Blister.

"No big fattie, Sherlock," Mr. Kim said, as we sped away.

We settled into our perfunctory struggle toward the flag. Blister popped his second and third shot in the air before finding the greenside bunker with his fourth. Jack and Wiley arranged for a double date under the pine trees with the Pullooski sisters, though Jack was more unlucky than Wiley. Jack's ball crawled into the creek forcing him to drop a second ball, which he punched to the fairway. His fifth stroke landed on the back of the green, as did Wiley's fourth shot. I somehow managed to hit the green in regulation.

We pulled up to the green just as Jeb the Marshal arrived from the opposite direction. As was his custom, Jeb drove opposite the direction of play to determine where the gaps were. Wiley and Jack's double date with the Pullooskis had created an extra furlong of spacing between us and the sisters, and Jeb was here to set things right.

"Your half a hole behind, Wildroot," Jeb barked with his crusty voice as he climbed out of his cart to watch us putt.

"Jeb, I can't believe you're wasting your time with us when you could be watching Babs and her sister," I said, loosening him up.

"Ahhh—oh man, she's got quite the pooper doesn't she?" Jeb replied, appreciating my logic.

"We hadn't noticed," Jack said.

"Ahhh—you're so full of crap."

Jeb stood on the mound in back of the green several feet above the hole while we went about our business. He puffed on a short stubby cigar that smelled more foul than Jack's stinkweed.

Blister was so stoned, he didn't recognize the difficulty of his sand shot and hit a perfect splash to the middle of the green. Having forgotten to retrieve his putter, Blister took a stroll back to the cart, taking enough time to allow the three of us to get down with two putts each.

After returning, Blister stood behind his ball with a blank look on his face examining every inch of the twenty-five feet that lay between his marker and the hole. After about fifteen seconds of inactivity, I interrupted his solitude by asking if he intended to putt.

"Isn't Wiley away?" he asked.

"I don't know where you stand on current events, but Wiley's already in, genius," Jack advised him.

"Really?" Blister asked.

Blister got the hint and quickly put his ball in front of his mark and rotated it toward the hole. He stood over the ball and became mesmerized. He slumped over his ball but didn't take any practice strokes. He stayed in the position for an uncomfortable amount of time, perhaps ten or fifteen seconds. He finally looked up at the hole as Jack and I exchanged glances. Jeb had to be wondering about the mental well-being of Blister. Jeb was startled along with the rest of us as Blister belted out the first verse of an Eric Clapton tune.

"I shot the sheriff."

"But I did not shoot the deputy."

Jeb raised his eyebrows. He was clearly wondering if the retarded putter on the green was somehow making light of his profession. Blister repeated the lyrics while drawing his putter back. The speed of the putter paced the syncopation of the lyric and he slapped the ball just as he accented the word—'deputy.' Strangely enough, the ball curled toward the hole breaking a good three feet before spilling into the cup.

"Ahhhh—that guy can putt!" Jeb roared, no longer offended.

Jeb turned to head back to his cart as the rest of us stood there stumped.

"That was amazing," I said to Blister as he leaned down to pick his ball out of the hole.

"I had it all the way, Chief," Blister replied. "As soon as my paranoia settled down all I had to do was concentrate."

"Paranoia?" I asked on the way to the cart.

"I always get paranoid around authority figures," Blister acknowledged.

"Authority figures?" I asked, puzzled. "You mean Jeb?"

"He's a Marshal isn't he?" Blister asked rhetorically.

"He's a golf Marshal, Blister," I said.

"Marshals, sheriffs, cops—they're all the same to me," Blister said. "I thought there might be some kind of a standoff for a minute there."

We pulled our carts around the highest point of the canyon where we would reverse direction and play the fourteenth hole back toward the highway.

"So what's the damage on the last hole?" I asked Jack, having lost count of his strokes.

"Give me a six," Jack said, after taking a moment to add up his strokes.

"A six?" Blister asked in disbelief. "One in the fairway, one in the creek to Betty Pullooski, one penalty, a punch out to the fairway, one to the green," Blister recounted. "That's five before you even putted. I can't remember if you one-putted because I was frozen with paranoia, but I'm guessing you didn't."

"Blister's right, Jack," Wiley piped in. "Six would have to be your Gesundheit score."

Gesundheit (God Bless You) Scoring

Gesundheit Perceptual Measurement Theory was developed by Professor Daniel Goldston as a repudiation of Gestalt Psychology. The Gestalt movement had its origins in Germany in 1943 under Max Wertheimer, Wolfgang Kohler, and Kurt Koffka, and is based on the premise that 'the whole is more than the sum of its parts'. According to Wertheimer, the way to understand an individual is to understand how he perceives. The interests of Gestalt psychology were aimed at understanding the principles of perceptual organization. According to the Gestaltists, perceptual organization refers to a perceived wholeness of things, which is always greater than the units that make up the stimulus contributing to the perception. Hence, the whole is more than the sum of its parts.

At the time the theory was introduced in Europe in 1943, the primary perception outside of Germany was one of occupation. Gestalt Theory was slow to catch on in the United States, primarily because Germany and the US had a little brouhaha underway just as the theory became popular in Germany.

During the late 1990s Gestalt Theory came under attack with the release of a brilliant book authored by San Jose State Professor Daniel Goldston, a renowned mathematician, prime number expert, and dolphin trainer. The book, called *Gesundheit Perceptual Measurement*, refutes the Gestaltist claim that 'the whole is more than the sum of the parts.' Contrarily, Goldston postulates that 'the whole is *less* than the sum of the parts.' Professor Goldston lays out an exhaustive proof of his claim relying heavily on his earlier work on the Twin Prime Conjecture to substantiate his claim. To illustrate the practicality of Gesundheit theory, Goldston claimed that he first observed the phenomenon when trying to balance his checkbook. According to Goldston,

"It was a fascinating discovery. My wife would write a bunch of checks during the month and I would balance my checkbook at month end. But invariably, my bank statement would arrive and I always had a bunch of overcharges for overdrawing my account. The balance was always less than the sum of the checks. Always! It was unbelievable.

"After a few months of this, the light suddenly went on . . . or maybe it went off . . . no wait . . . I guess it went on. Anyway, I realized my account balance was the whole, and the checks were the parts, that the Gestaltists had been clamoring about. But their theory had an obvious flaw. The whole wasn't more than the sum of its parts—it was less . . . especially after all the overdraft charges. Consequently, it became clear to me the whole is less than the sum of its parts."

Goldston soon began examining other worldly phenomena and found that his theory demonstrated remarkable consistency. He soon examined federal, state, and local governments as well as the US military and found that the whole was consistently less than the sum of its parts. In fact, he was the first theorist to succinctly explain how government treasuries always contained less revenue than was collected through taxation. Moreover, he demonstrated how Gesundheit theory accurately predicted the perception among the US population that the accumulated intelligence of Congress and state assemblies was always less than the total sum of the intelligence of the Congressmen and Congresswomen who make up the legislative bodies.

In an unusual twist, the founder of the Gesundheit Perceptual Measurement movement explained that Gesundheit was not the original name for his revolutionary work. According to Goldston, he originally named the work Gest-Seigheil in deference to the German founders of Gestalt psychology that his theories aimed to repudiate. However, before submitting his work to his publisher, he ran the manuscript through Microsoft's spellchecker and it inadvertently changed Gest-Seigheil to Gesundheit. Regrettably, neither Goldston nor his publisher caught the mistake and the book was published under the name *Gesundheit Per-*

ceptual Measurement instead of the intended name, *Gest-Seigheil Perceptual Measurement*.

Gesundheit Perceptual Measurement has its advocates in all fields of study and disciplines but it has proven particularly popular among mediocre golfers when completing score cards. Proving time and time again that the whole is less than the sum of its parts, golfers demonstrate that seven stokes taken on a hole often sum to the number six when the accumulated total is entered on the score card.

"Wait a minute, let me count em up again," Jack said with some embarrassment.

As Blister and Wiley looked on with suspicion, Jack recounted his score and realized he had indeed given me his Gesundheit score instead of the actual number of strokes taken on the hole.

Since I had to take the type of relief that didn't entail dropping a golf ball, I ordered Blister to complete the scorecard as I unzipped my fly behind the closest pine. I poked my head out from behind the tree.

"We won the hole," I reminded him. "Do you think you can figure out where to put the circles?"

"You worry about the trouser trout and I'll worry about the circles," he snapped.

I kept my eye on Blister as he eased into the cart and scrunched his face, trying to remember all the scores. I could tell he was challenged by the complexity of so many single digit numbers.

"What'd Jack get?" Blister asked me, his eyebrows squinting.

"We just spent about a week going over that. He had seven for a real score and a six for his Gesundheit score. Use his real score. I had a par. Wiley had a bogey. And you pulled a putt out of your ass for a six. Too much data to handle?"

"I think I got it, Chief," Blister finally said as his frown cleared.

My hot streak continued. More importantly, I gained a stroke on Wiley and I didn't even have to kick him in the nuts.

Hole 14
The Nobel Laureate

T he par 4 fourteenth hole played back down the canyon and was rated the fifth easiest hole. If a player avoided the dogleg right line of pine trees and cascading fairway bunkers on the right, the 335-yard hole required only a 3-iron and pitching wedge to reach the green in regulation. A platoon of white OB markers lined the base of the hill on the left, but it took a severe hook to reach them.

The key was to avoid the four bunkers spaced between the one hundred and fifty yard marker and the edge of the green. If you were unfortunate enough to land in the first one, it was advisable to pitch out to the fairway rather than take aim at the flag on line with the other three bunkers. The fool who takes a gamble, often finds himself going from one bunker to the next, a series of stops we referred to as the salmon run.

High-voltage electrical wires dipped above the ladies tee box from two towers on hilltops on either side of the hole. From the men's front tees, the trajectory of a well-struck 3-iron took a flight path between the wires and often gave the foursome an opportunity for a few junk bets with odds of less than ten to one.

I was constructing a mental image of my ball sailing between the wires when Wiley decided to ice me down.

"Holy Pope-mobile, Chief," he said, as he leaned in to my cart to examine the official card attached to the steering wheel. "Do you know you're only five over for the round?"

"That can't be right," Jack scoffed.

"Damn, Chief!" Jack said, "You're gonna break eighty today unless you come unglued.

"The Chief's coming unglued?" Wiley wailed, "That never happens!"

All three heaved in laughter. Although some of the peripheral tribe members broke eighty from time to time, no one in the inner sanctum had ever achieved the lofty feat. I had come close on three occasions but like my namesake Dedalus, I wilted under the hot sun. The most galling disaster was about four months earlier when I stepped to the seventeenth tee at five over par only to implode with a quadruple-bogey. As hard as I try, I have been unable to forget the sequence of shots that added up to seven for the par three. Except for the four-inch putt, it was six of the worst strokes ever strung together.

"Hey Chief," Blister blubbered, "Remember that fine display on seventeen the last time you got this close?"

Jack and Wiley roared. Unfortunately, they also vividly remembered the seven-stroke sequence.

Although the tribe laughed about it now, they were aghast when the event happened. They sucked in their breaths and sighed each time I chunked a sand wedge. No one said a word to me or to each other until the round was over. A week after the round, Wiley acknowledged that the three had made a side bet with each other on which hole I would blow up. Blister won the bet but refused to collect, believing that his bet had been the cause of my collapse. He later admitted that he wanted nothing to do with that type of karma since he had suffered his own setbacks in trying to break ninety.

"I would imagine that you guys already have a side bet going," I said with some disdain.

"Oh not yet, but we will," Blister promised. "In fact I'll take hole fifteen," he said, forgetting about the bad karma.

"I'll take sixteen," Jack said.

"We've already seen your track record on seventeen so I'll stay on the winning horse," Wiley said.

"You want in, Chief?" Blister asked. "If you work it right, you can be the beneficiary of your own collapse. Keah, Keah."

"In fact, I do," I said surprising all of them. "I'll take this hole and do double or nothing on eighteen if I make it that far."

"Really?" Blister wanted to know.

"Sure," I said with certainty.

Once again, I was proving my deserving role as the Chief. The three of them had me so pissed off at the moment, if I were to collapse on any hole, it most likely would be the one right in front of me. I might as well make a little money when it happened. More importantly, I normally didn't win predictive bets, so I had that working in my favor as well.

"Sorry for bringing it up Chief," Wiley said. "But, remember—the probability is in your favor."

As it turns out, the probability *was* in my favor. Wiley and I had worked out the probability of breaking eighty for one of our mountain tournaments and had distributed the findings to the tribe for their feedback. The Red Ball People Amendments to the USGA rules certainly had helped to get the scores down, but there were other important factors as well.

The Probability of Breaking 80

The United States Golf Association (USGA) uses your ten best scores from your last twenty rounds to determine your index. The slope or difficulty of the courses you play also figure into the calculation. Your index is adjusted for the specific course you are playing in accordance with the slope of the course to arrive at your handicap. Since the USGA uses the best ten scores, your index and handicap are not an average of how you really play but an adjusted average of how you played your best ten rounds. Consequently, the probability that you will shoot above your handicap is much greater than the probability that you will shoot lower.

According to Golf Digest, the odds of a player beating his handicap by eight strokes are 1,138 to 1. This means, if you are a sixteen handicap and you are playing a par seventy-two course, you can expect to break eighty in about twenty-two years if you play once a week. However, as you will see below, this type of probability applies only to tournament players. Thankfully, the probability of a mediocre player breaking eighty is inversely proportional to his ignorance of the rules and actually approaches 100% at the same rate that his knowledge approaches zero. Hence, ignorance really is bliss, and the high handicapper should use it to his advantage.

To be sure, misunderstanding the drop rule can add a hundred yards to a drive. Furthermore, If Phil Michelson can miss a three-foot putt—so can you. The best way to eliminate the possibility is to pick it up and eliminate the risk.

To calculate your probability of breaking eighty, refer to Chief Tit's probability table below. First, determine your point total by answering the 'Bending the Rules in Your Favor' quiz. Once you have your point total, find the corresponding row in the probability table and scan over until you find your handicap. Your probability for breaking eighty can be found in the intersection of the cells. For example, if you are an eighteen handicap and have a "Bending the Rules" point total of eleven, the probability that you will break eighty is 99%. In fact, there is a very high probability that you break eighty once a month and might be known around the neighborhood among non-golfers as a hotshot golf protégé.

Bending The Rules in Your Favor	Maximum Points
Number of Mulligans 0 Mulley = 0 points 1 Mulley = 1 points 2 Mulleys or more = 2 points	✔ 2
Play Winter rules in Summer? Yes = 1 point No = 0 points	✔ 1
Do you understand the drop rule? No = 1 point Yes = 0 points	✔ 1
Do you know the difference between a red and white stake? Yes = 0 points No = 2 points	✔ 2
Do you pick up 3 foot putts? Yes = 1 point No = 0 points	✔ 1
Do you play the tees right behind the ladies? Yes = 1 point No = 0 points	✔ 1
Do you play par 70 courses? Yes = 2 points No = 0 points	✔ 2
Can you accurately add a small series of numbers in your head? No = 1 point Yes = 0 points	✔ 1
Do you treat all trees as staked trees? Yes = 1 point No = 0 points	✔ 1
Do you think the number of strokes you accumulate in match play is a legitimate score? Yes = 2 points No = 0 points	✔ 2

Probability of Breaking 80

Total Points	20 Handicap	19 Handicap	18 Handicap	17 Handicap	16 Handicap	15 Handicap	14 Handicap	13 Handicap
0	0%	0%	0%	0%	1%	5%	10%	25%
1	0%	0%	0%	1%	5%	10%	25%	50%
2	0%	0%	1%	5%	10%	25%	50%	94%
3	0%	1%	5%	10%	25%	50%	94%	95%
4	1%	5%	10%	25%	50%	94%	95%	97%
5	5%	10%	25%	50%	94%	95%	97%	98%
6	10%	25%	50%	94%	95%	97%	98%	99%
7	25%	50%	94%	95%	97%	98%	99%	100%
8	50%	94%	95%	97%	98%	99%	100%	100%
9	94%	95%	97%	98%	99%	100%	100%	100%
10	95%	97%	98%	99%	100%	100%	100%	100%
11	97%	98%	99%	100%	100%	100%	100%	100%
12	98%	99%	100%	100%	100%	100%	100%	100%
13	99%	100%	100%	100%	100%	100%	100%	100%
14	100%	100%	100%	100%	100%	100%	100%	100%

Since I am a sixteen handicap, the probability of me breaking eighty is relatively good and approaches 100% if I am willing to taint the round by bending a few rules. However, one of the primary roles of the leader of the Red Ball People is to evaluate the deficiencies in the USGA rules and introduce amendments that preserve the integrity of the game, while promoting lower scores, without being accused of outright cheating by players outside the tribe. It's a delicate balance to strike. Although none of us had broken eighty, only a few more amendments stood between us and the milestone round.

It was my turn to lead off. I gripped my 3-iron, and took a swing toward destiny. The ball began hooking immediately. I was going to win the betting battle, but the war was lost.

"See ya!" I wailed, knowing my bid for breaking eighty was over.

"That's gone," Wiley said, hiding his glee.

"Too bad, Chief," Blister and Jack chimed in.

But to the amazement of all, eighty feet above the ladies tee box, divine intervention stepped in.

"Zingggg," went the electrical wire.

The ball careened off the wire and deflected into the hillside. I had a reprieve. Hitting an electrical wire was an automatic replay and my dream was still breathing.

"It's your day, Chief!" Blister shouted.

"Amazing," Wiley said, as he wondered if my bandwagon was worth riding.

I made the best of my new opportunity and hit the replacement ball by the one hundred and fifty yard marker.

Blister followed me with a Pullooski that rolled under a thorny bush left of the cart path. Jack committed a mental error and aimed too far right and put himself on the first rung of the salmon ladder. A moment later, I chose Wiley as my partner when he creamed his 4-iron ten yards past my ball.

Although I'm not a Catholic, I said a Hail Mary as we drove under the electrical wires. After pulling even with Blister's ball, Wiley joined Jack as they walked to the first fairway bunker. Wiley's only purpose in accompanying Jack was to talk him out of attempting to hit an 8-iron over the three remaining traps.

"The smart play is to pitch it out to the left Jack," Wiley advised.

"I don't know, Wiley, I think I should try to pick it clean," Jack countered.

"That sounds like a recipe for disaster, Jack."

"Put a sock in it Wiley," Jack said decisively. "I'm knocking it on the green with an 8-iron."

"Jack—that's really stupid!"

Can Wiley Become a Nobel Laureate?

The most unexpected Nobel Prize for economics was awarded to Robert Engle and Clive Granger, two former UC San Diego professors. The long-time colleagues had the honor bestowed as much for demonstrating what is not relevant in econometric forecasts as for demonstrating what is. According to the Nobel Committee press release, the two won the prestigious award for providing a set of statistical tools to distinguish between "stupid and non-stupid" economic relationships.

Before their work was widely accepted by economists, it was generally assumed that statistics such as gross domestic product bore an orderly relationship to other factors like interest rates, tax rates, and money supply. In fact, their research indicated that many economic relationships are much more random than had been previously believed. The difficulties in earlier econometric models, according to the Nobel Laureates, were the models' dependence on correlation, a statistical measure of commonality of movement between two variables.

The problem with correlation, Engle and Granger argued, "is that we can show numerous variables that are highly correlated that clearly have no bearing on each other." As an example, Engle showed that if you plot the distance between Earth and Mars and the GDP, you would get a strong statistical correlation. "But that's stupid," he said. "Mars does not have anything to do with the gross domestic product of the US. But plot interest rates against GDP and you will also get a strong statistical relationship. But this one isn't necessarily stupid."

The incorporation of the word 'stupid' into the name of their time series econometric model no doubt left some of their colleagues scratching their heads. However, Granger defended the use of the term by claiming the assumption was instrumental when calibrating their time series econometric model. According to Granger, to sufficiently test the forecasting ability of their model, they had to identify a highly correlated relationship between two nonsensical variables. They found the perfect tuning mechanism in a dolphin migration study published by renowned prime number expert, Gesundheitist, and dolphin trainer, Professor Daniel Goldston.

Relying heavily on axioms developed from his earlier ostensible proof of the Twin Prime Conjecture, Professor Goldston demonstrated a strong correlation between the distance that the dolphins migrate each year and the total home runs in Major League Baseball. Working on the calibration assumption that Goldston's research was stupid, the Nobel Laureates honed their time-series model formulas until the model successfully predicted a stupid relationship between dolphin migration distance and home runs with 100% reliability. Upon accepting his award, Granger acknowledged the importance of Goldston's contribution in three words—"It's really stupid."

By advising Jack to 'take his medicine' and pitch out to the fairway, Wiley demonstrated an acute awareness between what is stupid and what is not. Sadly, Jack did not share the logical conclusions. Moreover, Wiley did not need to submit time series data compiled from Jack's bunker success rate to the Engle / Granger model to make the determination. No doubt, the two Nobel Laureates would have spent weeks analyzing Jack's success rate to reach the same accord. Wiley, on the other hand, had an amazing knack for forecasting stupid decisions by Jack with near 100% reliability almost instantly.

Perhaps if we could have made the Nobel Nomination Committee aware of Wiley's remarkable talent in detecting stupidity, Engle and Granger might have split the $1.3 million Nobel award three ways instead of two.

Wiley was walking back to the cart by the time Jack started his swing. He never broke stride nor did he peek over his shoulder to watch the outcome he already knew. Consistent with Wiley's prediction, Jack hit a twenty-yard fattie into the next trap. Jack slammed his 8-iron into the sand in disgust. Wiley looked at Blister and me and began slapping his own forehead imitating Curly of The Three Stooges.

"Nyuk, nyuk, nyuk," Curly said, making sure it was loud enough for Jack to hear.

"Blow it out your pants, Wiley!" Jack vented.

"I suppose you're going to try the same shot again?" Wiley shouted back.

"As soon as I get another club."

Wiley and Jack continued to trade insults, as Blister pondered what to do about his ball, which was hiding under a thorny berry bush. Even if Blister tried to punch it out, he had to contend with an oak tree that blocked the line to the flag. Without hesitation, he reached in with his 9-iron and scrapped it free, his way of declaring the ball unplayable. If Blister was counting on an unobstructed direct line to the green he would have to invoke a Red Ball People Amendment to Rule 28b, the provision for unplayable lies.

Rule 28b—Unplayable lie: Under penalty of one stroke player may drop ball within two club lengths of where ball rests but no closer to the hole. *Red Ball People Amendment to Rule 28b:* If player is disappointed with the incline of the landscape, obstruction in the general vicinity, or the fluffiness of the grass within the two club length area of where unplayable ball rests, player may scout around for a flat area or an area with a little more fluffy grass to drop the ball, provided the flat or fluffy area is no closer to the hole. If such an area cannot be found further from the hole, player can begin looking for a flat or fluffy area a little closer to the hole, provided he doesn't get silly. Penalty assessed is one stroke.

Reason for change: Original rule guarantees that subsequent shot will have a nasty outcome, with near certainty of exercising the rule all over again. Process will be repeated until another player feels sorry for his buddy and advises him to drop wherever he wants. Since player always heeds this advice, he might as well save everyone a lot of time and do it in the first place with everyone's blessing.

Blister used a very liberal interpretation of the amendment as he walked ten yards away from the berry thicket and dropped his ball in the fairway. Had it been Wiley, I probably would have reminded him of the 'don't get silly' clause in the amendment.

He whacked it almost before it settled in the grass. Evidently his holster had not been completely depleted of hosel shots as the ball zoomed toward the sand trap that was occupied by Jack.

"Fore!" I shouted.

Blister was too stoned to react and opened his mouth but nothing came out. The ball struck the upper lip of the trap and settled back a few feet away from Jack. Jack had been watching the proceedings and easily got out of the way.

"I guess I'm still the mayor of Shankytown, Chief," Blister said as he walked to the cart.

Wiley and I backed off our balls as Blister dug through his bag and created just enough racket to annoy both of us. He finally pulled out a couple of balls and put them in his pocket before crossing the fairway. He walked directly in front of Wiley as Wiley was addressing his ball. An uninitiated player might not have noticed the indiscretion and drilled him in the side of the head but Wiley was used to Blister's lapses. Wiley stood up, put his hands on his hips and stared at Blister.

"You forgetting something Einstein?" Wiley asked.

"Oh sorry, I didn't realize you were hitting," Blister said sheepishly.

"Not that," Wiley said. "I'm used to you being oblivious. Can you think of anything else that might be important for this little activity we're doing out here today?"

"You mean golf?" Blister asked, entirely confused.

"That's right. The game of golf," Wiley said sarcastically. "What do we need to play the game of golf?"

"I'll play along," Blister agreed. "Balls?"

"That's a good start," Wiley said continuing his lesson. "What else?"

"Golf course?" Blister guessed.

"So far so good," Wiley replied. "Anything else?"

"Clubs?" Blister correctly guessed.

"Bingo!" Wiley chirped, as he clapped with approval.

Suddenly the dim light that was passing for Blister's brain turned brighter with the extra jolt from Wiley. He looked down at both of his arms as if needing visual confirmation that his hands were empty.

"Oh, right. Keah, keah, keah," Blister giggled as he spun around and trotted to the cart to retrieve a couple of his wedges.

Wiley looked at me and swung his arm over the back of his head and began scratching his head from behind like Stan Laurel. Wiley was awfully good at imitating comic shtick when he was making fun of others. But today, he was the kettle calling the pot black. He was having a difficult time seizing the upper hand with a face caked with mustard and mud. The fact was, he looked more like Curly than Jack, and more like Stan Laurel than Blister. Sometime after the round, I guess we would have to tell him.

After allowing Blister to cross in front of him with three wedges in tow, Wiley finally delivered his 9-iron to the green. I followed Wiley with a wedge to the front fringe, a desirable location for the red pin position.

Wiley spotted Babs and Donetta walking down the mound from the fifteenth tee box to their cart on the left of the fourteenth green and decided in favor of abandoning his cart and riding down with me. We arrived just as the sisters reached their cart. I whispered to Wiley as we eased my cart toward them.

"Now I see why you were in such a hurry to get to the green."

"Nothing gets by me but the wind, Chief."

I greeted Babs. "Hey Babs, you and Donetta are playing too fast. Jeb climbed all over us on the last hole."

"I told him to," Babs laughed. "I had to get him out of my hair."

"How's the cigar?" I asked.

"Oh it mysteriously disappeared from our cart on thirteen when we walked out to the fairway," she informed me.

"How surprising, huh?" Donetta asked me rhetorically.

Janet Morris hit her ball and the doctor and the attorney soon came bounding down the railroad ties that passed for stairs.

Donetta stepped into the easement between the carts and slipped her head cover over her driver. As I was still chatting with Babs, I made a quick determination that it would be highly inappropriate if I suddenly turned my attention to her sister's posterior and pinged the landscape. Wiley, on the other hand, didn't feel the same restriction. He immediately activated his guidance system and established missile lock. I gave my wingman an awkward glance to confirm that he was on a sortie before jerking my head back and returning my attention to Babs.

I lost track of Bab's story but kept up the charade by bobbing my head and saying 'uh huh' during her short pauses, as I considered the unfairness of the moment. As usual, I was taking a bullet for one of the tribesmen. Because I had a way with the ladies, they were often engaged in chitchat with me while the rest of the tribe was free to sit there like a stump and beep their targets with radar. Wiley was finally forced to pull his nose up and break off the mission when Donetta turned around to face us.

". . . well I guess we better catch up with Ken and Barbie," I heard Babs say as I plugged back in to her story.

"OK, see you on seventeen," I told her, estimating where the next backup would occur.

"Don't be a stranger," Wiley said, with an asinine grin.

Wiley must have reached deep for that one. This guy must have been the Superintendent for the College of Insipid Phrases, I thought to myself. Jumpin Jesus, the funny thing about it—I could say the same thing to Babs and come off sounding flirty and cute. Wiley says it, and comes off sounding like a dim-witted pervert. The speckled dried mustard on his face wasn't exactly furthering his cause.

Babs covered her driver and shoved it in her bag, giving me one quick chance to ping my target a few times. Before climbing in her cart, she hesitated and gazed at Wiley.

"What happened to your face?" she asked Wiley for the second time.

"What?" Wiley said with a frown.

"Just a little sunburn," I said, as I winked at Babs.

"Uh huh . . . well you better get some lotion on your face," she said, interpreting my wink correctly.

Babs stomped the accelerator and scooted down the cart path. I leaned toward Wiley and assessed his performance.

"Don't be a stranger?" I asked mockingly.

"That's right, Chief—don't be a stranger," Wiley repeated.

"Oh I bet the ladies just drool over that line!"

"How come she keeps asking about my face?" Wiley wanted to know.

"She probably thinks you have assfacia," I guessed.

"What's assfacia?"

"It's a condition where your face looks so much like your ass, your bowels don't know which way to move," I replied.

"That's funny stuff, Chief," Wiley said with a straight face. "You got any sun screen?

"Low pocket on the left," I told him, as I gestured back to the community bag.

We turned our attention back toward the fairway. Blister and Jack were both spawning. Blister was in the third trap while Jack advanced to the fourth bunker on the front of the green.

Jack declared a ceasefire after blading his bunker shot to the fifteenth fairway. Blister followed suit after launching a mortar off the back of the green.

Wiley and I lined up our putts from opposite sides of the flag as Blister trudged over to the pin to watch. I was a foot off the green and maybe another ten to the red flag. I guessed that Wiley's putt was close to thirty feet with a foot and a half of downhill break.

Jack stood to the side while Blister tended the flag. After Wiley reprimanded Blister for trampling his line a few times, Blister stood on the eastern side of the hole away from both our lines. If it were Jack or Wiley tending the flag, I probably would have requested that they back away from the hole. In Blister's case, events seemed to unfold in my favor whenever he hovered over the hole, so I said nothing to discourage him from moving.

As Blister drifted into a stupor, I cocked my SeeMore putter and tapped the ball. My pituitary gland spit out a few endorphins as it received notification that the ball was tracking on the proper line.

"It's got a chance," Jack barked.

"It's got better than that!" Blister blurted.

As the ball zeroed in on the hole it rolled across a slight perturbation, altering its direction toward the right lip of the cup. I thought to myself—'I'm going to need a little luck.' But I was mistaken. I just needed Blister. Just as the ball reached the right lip, he rotated his foot and nudged it in.

"Hooray for Chief Tit!" Blister snorted, as he plucked my ball from the hole.

"Was that a birdie?" Jack asked.

"If that's what you want to call it," Wiley complained.

"I sure ain't putting it again," I admitted.

Blister pressed me for some payola. "What do you say we celebrate your good putting . . . and my good tending—with a cigar?"

The one adage that didn't apply to the Red Ball People was—'Close but no Cigar'. In fact, the general vicinity qualified for scoring a cigar. Cigars were the primary currency of the bartering system for the tribe and I was the Chairman of the Federal Reserve System. It was up to me to keep the monetary system stable.

"You betcha," I told Blister.

Wiley prematurely halted my preening when he ordered us to stifle ourselves so he could finish the hole. He tapped his ball but gave it too much speed for the slope. Blister was the first to recognize the miscalculation and began to sing American Pie.

"And we were singing . . ."

Jack and I joined in.

"Bye, bye, Miss American Pie . . ."

But before we could start the next chorus, Wiley's Strata dipped toward the hole, smacked off the back of the cup, and fell in.

"Stick that in your bonnet!" Wiley shouted, as he pumped his right arm.

"Bouncing Buddha!" I whined, "You pulled that one out of your ass—huh Wiley?"

"Now that's what I call a Maxwell putt," Blister added. "Good to the last drop. Right, Chief?"

For a moment, I was stinging from Wiley's birdie until I tallied my lucky stars. The electrical wire saved me at least two strokes, and Blister's shoe probably saved me another. Considering how lopsided Newton's negative forces must be, I decided to tread lightly as my nemesis yakked all the way to the cart about his mastery of the flat stick. But I knew better. If Wiley was a master of the 'flat anything', it was the 'flat forehead.'

Hole 15
The Real Killers

Wiley squirted a pile of Coppertone sun block on his left palm, mashed his hands together and rubbed the white cream liberally over his face. The cream caked on his eyebrows and earlobes where he failed to rub it in thoroughly. However, he did a fine job on his cheeks and chin where he spread the dried mustard around each side of his mouth. The mud splotch on the end of his nose was extended all the way up the bridge, while the spots on his left temple were extended below his ear. He looked like someone only Picasso could love. If I didn't know him I might have thought that he was a Sioux warrior from the Great Mustard Plains.

"You missed a spot right here," Jack said pointing to the only square inch area on the right side of Wiley's face that was currently unblemished.

Wiley rubbed the area and extended the mustard from the side of his mouth to his right cheek.

The fifteenth hole was a long 401-yard par 4, but played longer due to a constant headwind. The tee box was elevated a good thirty feet higher than the middle of the fairway as the canyon opened up and flattened out into a plain that met the highway bordering the north side of the course. A shallow drainage ditch dotted with red stakes ran the length of the fairway on the left. Further west was a thirty-foot strip of land that separated the ditch from a barbed-wire fence that marked the boundary of a cattle ranch. The right side of the fairway was lined with pine trees that separated the fifteenth fairway from the thirteenth fairway.

Three traps guarded the green. One was behind the hole and rarely came into play. Gusting cross winds near the green rendered the right side trap the most popular litter box on the course. The third trap was probably a design flaw, since it sat well off the green and to the right near the cart path.

Blister tested the height of his tee against the face of his Big Bertha. Rather than assume his address, he piqued my attention when he dug into his pocket and extracted a shiny medallion about the size of a silver dollar. He leaned over and rubbed his Callaway Warbird with it. I looked at Wiley who reflected a Stan Laurel my way. I shot a glance at Jack who rolled his eyes. Blister kissed the medallion and put it back in his pocket.

"Would you like to share anything with us?" Wiley finally asked.

"Not really," Blister replied.

"Alright Blister, what's in your pocket?" Jack inquired.

Blister concluded that we would eventually get the information out of him and agreed to explain his new ritual. He pulled out the brass medallion and brought it over to us. It was a locket that contained a miniature picture of a nun that looked to be Mother Teresa.

"Is that who I think it is?" I asked him.

"It's Mother T," Blister acknowledged.

"Mother who?" Jack asked.

"Mother Teresa, the saint of Calcutta," Blister answered.

"Since when did you become religious?" Jack probed him.

"I'm just trying to verify a miracle. It can't hurt," Blister said, as he attempted to reason with heathens.

"Maybe you better elaborate before one of us has to kick your ass, Blister," Wiley said with as little diplomacy as possible.

"Dude, you don't know about the miracle of Mother Teresa?" Blister asked Wiley.

"No, but I bet I'm about to learn," Wiley admitted.

Blister Looks into Sainthood

Blister leaned on his Big Bertha and filled in the details. He explained how in the 10th Century, Pope John XV contrived the Vatican's canonization process for sainthood. According to Blister, ole Pope John set the bar pretty high, because one of the steps called Beatification, required the blessed person to perform a miracle—after they were dead!

He recounted how he saw Pope John Paul II on CNN presiding over a throng of people on Vatican square celebrating the deeds of Mother Teresa, a personal favorite of the Pontiff. With a little blocking from the Pope, Mother Teresa plowed through the Beatification process like the Dallas Cowboys plow through the Detroit Lions on Thanksgiving Day. According to the Vatican, the required miracle attributed to Mother Teresa happened on September 5, 1998, over a year after her death.

The Vatican version of the miracle did have its detractors, Blister explained. As the story goes, Monica Besra, a poor peasant from Dangram, applied a medallion with Mother Teresa's image to a painful area of her stomach where she thought she had a tumor. Miraculously, the pain subsided. However, friction between her and her husband soon erupted when he claimed to the throngs of gathering pilgrims outside their humble homestead, that she was actually cured by a doctor over a period of several months. The doctor who treated Monica Besra, confirmed that she had a lump in her abdomen, but also said it was not a tumor. Mysteriously, hospital records containing sonograms, prescriptions, and physician's notes, which could help settle the matter, were turned over to Sister Betta of the Missionaries of Charity—the organization founded by Mother Teresa. Sister Betta, evidently prone to forgetfulness, lost the medical records before they could be examined by experts who were commissioned to investigate the growing controversy.

———

"So I figure if the miracle of the Mother T medallion worked for Monica Besra, it might work for me," Blister said, wrapping up his story of Mother Teresa's canonization.

"Sounds like the medallion had a little help," Jack said suspiciously.

"I don't know Jack, I think it's better to err on the side of God," Blister replied.

"You mean Catholicism," Jack challenged.

"Whatever—same thing," Blister said, continuing his spar with Jack.

"Where'd you get the medallion?" I asked.

"eBay's loaded with em," Blister informed us. "I got this one for $9."

"Have you tried it yet?" I asked.

"I gave it a trial run. I rubbed it on a picture of my wife, and got a terrific blowjob last week. Keah, Keah." Blister giggled.

"Hell—that is a miracle!" Wiley agreed, as we all cackled.

"Anyway, the real test is right here," Blister said as he took the medallion and rubbed it on the face of his Big Bertha. "Let's just see what Mother T can do."

We stood off to the side and waited for the miracle as Blister settled into his address. It didn't take long to materialize. Blister crushed one of the longest drives I had ever seen. Our mouths dropped, awed as the ball climbed toward the heavens and drew toward the one hundred and fifty yard marker.

"Praise Mother T!" Blister wailed.

"Onward Christian soldiers!" Wiley shouted.

"It's a miracle!" Jack and I yelled in unison, half-way believing it.

The ball landed near the marker and shot forward another twenty five yards. Blister stayed in his pose for several seconds after the ball quit rolling. We were flabbergasted.

Blister offered to let Jack try the medallion but Jack scoffed at the suggestion before topping his drive off the ladies tee box. Wiley and I had seen enough. We blessed our drivers with the Mother T medallion before crushing two of the grandest drives of the round.

"Three miracles!" Blister shouted.

"Praise Allah," Wiley said, covering all bases as he bounded down the railroad ties.

Wiley hitched a ride with Blister and me, while Jack walked to the base of the hill below the ladies tee box and advanced his ball two hundred yards with a 3-wood.

Before I had a chance to stop the cart, Wiley was off the back and walking the hallowed ground where Mother T had arranged the three miracle drives in a perfect isosceles triangle. He marked his ball with a tee, before picking it up and transporting it to Blister.

"I guess we're playing lift and clean?" I asked.

"No, we're playing lift and bless," Wiley responded. "Hand over Mother T," Wiley demanded.

Blister gladly complied. If the miracles were going to come to a screeching halt, he wanted it to be on Wiley's ball and not his. Wiley rubbed the medallion on his ball and then across the face of his 9-iron.

"Ok Mother T do your magic," Wiley commanded before handing the medallion back to Blister.

We recognized that Wiley's antics were intended more for our humor consumption rather than to satisfy any newly found religious zealotry that Wiley was experiencing.

Blister engaged in some peculiar behavior of his own. Though he could easily tell the distance between his ball and the one hundred and fifty yard marker was about twenty-five yards, I could see that he was going the extra mile to get the precise distance. In fact, he appeared to be going about his measurement using a method that was first introduced on golf courses in Germany around 1936.

A Non-military Application of the Goose Step

Many amateur players measure the incorrect distance to the green simply because they walk off the distance between their ball and the one hundred and fifty yard marker and assume that each large step is one yard. However, tests have shown that this method is unreliable by a factor of several feet for short irons. Two million marching German soldiers during World War II proved that the best method for the one-yard measure is—the goose step. Consequently, Chief Tit recommends that the player use the German goose step when measuring the distance between the player's ball and the one hundred and fifty yard marker. While your playing partners may be appalled, you'll have the last laugh when your ball 'occupies' the green, if you catch my drift.

———————

"Hey Himmler!" Wiley shouted to Blister, "You mind if I hit while you're marching to the Eastern Front?"

Blister offered Wiley a half-hearted Sieg-Heil.

Mother Teresa was evidently occupied with curing tumors again, because Wiley bladed his 9-iron to the fringe just off the front of the green. While he was fortunate that the ball ended up where it did, it would hardly qualify as a miracle.

I chose to give Mother Teresa a rest and decided to try to hit the green in regulation without any spiritual guidance. Besides, Wiley had proven that Mother Teresa had better things to do.

My concentration was waning. My palms were sweating. A bead of perspiration ran down my nose. I recognized the symptoms. I knew the negative thoughts were on their way. What would it be this time I wondered. A sinking ferry? A plane cartwheeling into the Metrodome? A high rise fire? No it wouldn't be one of those. I started thinking about Nicole Simpson and Ron Goldman's killers. OJ had spent nearly a decade looking for them on golf courses. Maybe they were on the course today. This was unbelievable pressure. Not only did I have to worry about sticking a 9-iron, I might have to deal with murderers in my midst.

I was fascinated with my sinister thoughts. My surroundings disappeared from my vision as my focus shifted to the internal movie that was running in my head. Who cleverly masterminded this reprehensible crime and came within a shrunken glove of framing the greatest NFL running back to ever become a rental car spokesman?

The Real Killers

Two years after the tragic and brutal murders of Nicole Simpson and Ron Goldman, OJ Simpson was acquitted of murder largely because of a rogue cop and a shrunken glove. Despite an overwhelming mountain of evidence against him, his defense attorney Johnny Cochran ran circles around prosecutors Christopher Darden and Marcia Clark. The decisive prosecution blunder was to have OJ Simpson try on an extra large black leather glove that shrunk after being thoroughly soaked in the victims' blood. Even though the glove was found behind Simpson's house after he allegedly fell over the fence trying to scale it, the jury was mesmerized with Defense Attorney Cochran's jingle—"If the glove does not fit, you must acquit."

As anyone who has ever sweated in a golf glove can attest, the leather contracted after the blood dried and predictably, Simpson could not completely pull it over his hand. In what Prosecutor Christopher Darden called the biggest miscarriage of justice ever witnessed, the jury acquitted Simpson two years after the murders. Simpson further insulted the prosecution team and the public when he announced after the verdict that he would spend the rest of his life looking for "the killer or killers" of his former wife.

Since his acquittal, Simpson moved to Florida, a state with liberal laws for protecting assets against civil verdicts, and spends his days playing golf. In fact, Simpson spends so much time on the golf course most skeptics who heard Simpson's pronouncement about looking for the killers joked that the killers themselves must play a lot of golf since that appears to be where Simpson is conducting the majority of his investigation.

My mind raced to fill in the details of the puzzle that began on June 10, 1994. I had drafted my hypothesis regarding the identity of the real killers in an email to the Red Ball People, but it remained unsent as I struggled to confirm my suspicions about the vicious bi-coastal gang led by ringleader Hank the Hammer.

As the theory goes, Hank the Hammer called together his key lieutenants to discuss committing a gruesome crime. The gang's mission statement called for them to commit a vicious crime anytime they weren't satisfied with their golf game. The more dissatisfied they were, the more heinous the crime. Hank the Hammer was especially incensed. He had three-putted four greens and triple-bogeyed the final three holes at the Los Angeles Country Club on Friday June 10, 1994. After finishing twelve strokes over his handicap, he was so livid that he began making preparations to avenge the bad round immediately. The other three gang members in the foursome, Three-fingers Pete, One-eyed Luther, and Vinnie the Eliminator, also played poorly and were equally dedicated in their vengeance.

Although it is pure speculation, the nature of the crime may have been set in motion by the uncanny resemblance that One-eyed Luther had with OJ Simpson. Except for the eye patch One-eyed Luther wore, the two were dead ringers. Because of the likeness, One-eyed Luther had become somewhat of a Simpson history buff and kept extraordinary tabs on the behavioral patterns of the gridiron star. The foursome were drinking heavily after the round at a hotel room in Brentwood when the sinister escapade was put in motion. The following is an account of that meeting.

Hank the Hammer: "I'm so pissed about dat round today, I feel like killing a couple people."

Three-fingers Pete: "I'd just as soon blow up a school bus."

Hank the Hammer slapping Three-fingers Pete in the back of the head: "What's da matta with you? School busses don't run on Saturday. We need some ideas, boys. What da ya got for me?"

Vinnie the Eliminator: "I agree with ya boss. We need to take a couple of people out."

One-eyed Luther: "How about OJ Simpson? He lives in the neighborhood and he's a fuel-injected butthole. On top of dat, I'm get'n tired of people asking me for his autograph."

Hank the Hammer: "I gotta better idea. Let's kill OJ's wife and frame him for da murder to throw the cops off our trail."

Three-fingers Pete: "What's our motive?"

Hank the Hammer slapping Three-fingers Pete upside the head: "What's da matta with you? You been watching too much Court TV. Four three-putts ain't good enough for ya?"

Vinnie the Eliminator: "How's it gonna go down boss?"

Hank the Hammer: "Tell me what ya got on Simpson, Luther."

One-eyed Luther: "Well, he likes white women with breast implants . . ."

Hank the Hammer slapping One-eyed Luther in the back of the head: "Tell me sumptin' I don't know, fool."

One-eyed Luther: "Ow! I'm trying to boss . . ."

Hank the Hammer boxing One-eyed Luther's ears: "Well hurry up and spit it out before I poke your other eye out."

One-eyed Luther: "Here's the skinny, boss. OJ's scheduled to fly to Chicago at midnight tomorrow night on a business trip. Because he's such a big shot, he got a limousine picking him up at eleven. So anything we do has gotta happen before he leaves for the airport. His ex-wife lives a couple of blocks away and word on the street is dat she's gettin' chummy with some guy named Ron Goldman who works at her favorite restaurant. I done some check'n around and he gets off work at ten and you can bet your bottom dollar dat he's gonna be showing up at her place by 10:30."

Hank the Hammer slapping Vinnie the Eliminator in the back of the head: "Good work, Luther."

Vinnie the Eliminator: "Ow! Whadda yous slap'n me for?"

Hank the Hammer: "For not being as smart as Luther. Also, for misreading dat putt for me on the fifth hole today."

Three-fingers Pete: "So what's da plan boss?"

Hank the Hammer knocking Three-fingers Pete upside the cabasa: "Shut up. I'm think'n. Ya got anything else, Luther?"

One-eyed Luther: "Yeah, OJ's got a house boy named Kato Kaelin who lives in a guest house in his back yard. We gotta be careful that he's not onto us."

Hank the Hammer: "Right. Same goes for da limo driver."

Vinnie the Eliminator: "Whadda yous want me to do, boss?"

Hank the Hammer smacking Vinnie the Eliminator in the back of head: "I want yous to cut off another one of Pete's fingers if he tells me to use a gap wedge again when I shoulda been using a pitching wedge. Anything else, Luther?"

One-eyed Luther: "OJ wears size fifteen shoes and he digs spend'n $2,000 on each pair. He got a hanker'n for an Italian brand that only three other people in LA wear. Get this . . . he's also known for spending a fortune on black leather gloves, even though the temperature in LA never gets below sixty degrees. Word on da street says he's stay'n at the Marriott in Chicago tomorrow night. I dunno what room he got, but the Marriott only gots 550 rooms."

Hank the Hammer: "Dat's good stuff, Luther. Ok here's da deal. After we play nine holes—Vinnie, I want yous to disguise yourself as OJ's gardener. When he's lying around on the couch tomorrow watching porn on his VCR, I want yous to slip into da house and steal Nicole's house key, OJ's house key, da keys to his SUV, a dark sweat shirt, dark sweat pants, a pair of socks, a pair of his black leather gloves, a big butcher knife, and four pair of his $2,000 Italian shoes. Make sure da neighbors don't see you going into his house."

Vinnie the Eliminator: "What do I do if his front door's locked?"

Hank the Hammer: "You knock on da door and tell him you gotta take a dump. Hold the back of your pants while you're asking to use his john so he'll think you're gonna drop a load on his porch."

Vinnie the Eliminator: "Got it boss. Do I gotta mow his lawn while I'm there?"

Hank the Hammer slapping Vinnie the Eliminator on both sides of the head: "Don't be stupid. Of course ya gotta mow the lawn. We don't want OJ or da neighbors getting suspicious."

Three-fingers Pete: "Do I get to do sumptin'?"

Hank the Hammer slapping Three-fingers Pete upside the head: "Shut up. I'm get'n to you. Vinnie's gonna give you da keys to OJ's SUV, his house, and Nicole's condo. You're gonna go to Sears and have a second set made. Ya get the originals back to Vinnie and Vinnie goes back to OJ's house to pull some weeds. After pulling enough weeds to look convincing to da neighbors, Vinnie slips back into OJ's house and puts da original keys back. OJ should still be watching porn on his VCR so don't worry about him seeing yous."

Vinnie the Eliminator: "Piece-a-cake, boss."

Hank the Hammer: "After lunch, I'll go to Nicole's condo dressed as a PG&E meter reader and soak her flower beds. Between two and three, I want Pete to put on a pair of OJ's $2,000 Italian shoes and go to da ex's condo dressed as a dog catcher. Pretend like you're looking for a dog and leave plenty of shoe prints in the flower beds. We may not get time to trample-up the flower beds later, so do your best to leave hundreds of footprints."

Three-fingers Pete: "What if da shoes won't stay on my feet? I only wear a size eleven."

Hank the Hammer: "Wear ten pair of socks. Dat should make em snug. Luther—How much does OJ weigh?"

One-eyed Luther: "220 when he's running through airports."

Hank the Hammer: "Pete—since you're only 210, I want you to wear a ten-pound weight belt when yous are walk'n through Nicole's flower beds."

Three-fingers Pete: "Dat's brilliant boss!"

Hank the Hammer: "Shut up Pete, so I can think. Vinnie—don't you gotta cousin dat lives in Chicago?"

Vinnie the Eliminator: "Yeah, Cousin Sal. We can trust him."

Hank the Hammer: "Good. Have Sal go to Wal-Mart and buy 1,100 water glasses tomorrow morning. Then have Cousin Sal bake da glasses in his oven at 475 degrees until da glass is brittle, but not cracked. Sometime tomorrow night before OJ arrives in Chicago, tell Sal to dress up as a housekeeper and replace two water glasses in all 550 rooms. When OJ pours cold water in da brittle water glass, da glass should break in his hand and look a lot like a big ole knife cut. Can Cousin Sal handle that?"

Vinnie the Eliminator: "You can count on Cousin Sal."

Hank the Hammer: "Good. Now Pete after you get da keys made at Sears I want yous to disguise yourself as a FTD florist delivery driver and go to OJ's house and slip da original keys to OJ's SUV and Nicole's condo back into his house while he's surfing porn on da Internet."

Vinnie the Eliminator: "Do I gotta deliver flowers too?"

Hank the Hammer slapping Vinnie the Eliminator on the noggin: "Don't be stupid. Of course yous gotta deliver flowers. We don't want da neighbors catch'n on. Just so you don't get da Juice wonder'n about the flowers, leave a card signed by one of his large-breasted girl friends. I'm sure Luther can give ya a couple of names."

One-eyed Luther: "Oh yeah, Pete, I got the names of nine or ten strippers you can use. What's next boss?"

Hank the Hammer: "After Vinnie's done mowing OJ's lawn and after Pete's done trampling Nicole's flower beds in OJ's shoes, we'll take a break and play nine. If we don't shoot well, we'll kill Kato too. We'll see how it goes. After supper, I want all of us to meet up at da 7-11 by the ex-wife's condo at ten sharp. I want everyone wearing a pair of OJ's shoes. Luther—I want you to dress in a dark track suit and replace your eye patch with your glass eye. Vinnie can give ya a lift and drop yous off a few blocks from OJ's house and you can jog through da neighborhood and hop over a few shrubs pretending like your filming an Avis commercial. When you get to OJ's house, duck in the bushes by his driveway and wait until 10:30."

One-eyed Luther: "Whadda I do then, boss?"

Hank the Hammer: "Shut up Luther, I'm thinking . . . Ok, I got it. At 10:30 you use the extra key to steal OJ's SUV. But make sure you're wearing gloves. We don't want to leave any finger prints in OJ's SUV. OJ should be in the shower about dat time practicing his lines for a Pennzoil commercial. I want yous to drive up and down Nicole's street until you're sure some pedestrians see you."

One-eyed Luther: "What if there ain't any pedestrians?"

Hank the Hammer thumping One-eyed Luther upside the head: "What's da matta with you? Honk your horn or do a few burn outs until someone takes notice. Just make sure someone sees ya in OJ's SUV. Once you're sure you've been spotted, you get your ass back over to da 7-11 and pick us up. We all head back to Nicole's condo and park da car in da alley."

Three-fingers Pete: "What happens then boss?"

Hank the Hammer: "I'll probably slap yous in the head for misreading another one of my putts earlier today. But after dat, the three of us go to da front of Nicole's condo. I want all-a yous walking in flower beds with OJ's shoes whenever possible. We then have Luther knock on Nicole's door. If she refuses to open da door, we use the key to go in and get'er. I'll stab Nicole since I had da worst round today. Then we'll wait in da bushes for about five minutes, for Goldman to show up. When he shows up Vinnie can take care of him since Vinnie had da second worst round today. After stab'n him, we splotch a bunch of Nicole's and Ron's blood on OJ's sweat clothes and socks. We'll soak da leather glove in da pool of blood to be sure da LAPD don't overlook it."

Vinnie the Eliminator: "Why not soak both gloves?"

Hank the Hammer boxing Vinnie the Eliminator in the ears: "What's da matta with you? That's too obvious to da cops. If we plant too much evidence at OJ's house, some smart cop is gonna start think'n frame-up."

Three-fingers Pete: "Whadda we do with the extra glove?"

Hank the Hammer: "Put it in my golf bag. I'll use it for a golf glove."

One-eyed Luther: "What then, boss?"

Hank the Hammer: "We walk around in the blood for two or three minutes and then pile into OJ's SUV. Luther drives us back to da 7-11. During the ride we all shuffle our shoes on the vehicle's carpet to make sure plenty of blood can be found. Now, the plan depends on you, Luther, so pay attention."

One-eyed Luther: "I'm all ears, boss."

Hank the Hammer: "After watching ya putt today, I think you're all thumbs. Listen up. Here's the finale. Yous drive OJ's SUV back to his house. Make sure ya stay 25 MPH above da speed limit and run over a few curbs on da way. Park his SUV and remember to take da bag of bloody clothes with yous. It should be about 10:50 at this point, so you'll have to duck behind his fence for about five minutes and wait for da limo driver to show up. The limo driver should ring OJ's door but da Juice won't hear it because he's still gonna be practicing his lines for da Pennzoil commercial in da shower."

One-eyed Luther: "Then what, boss?"

Hank the Hammer: "When the limo driver goes back to his car, you run across the driveway all hunched over like you're trying not to be spotted. Slip in the house, use'n the extra set of keys. Now, bury the bloody sweat clothes and socks in da back of his closet and put da $2,000 Italian shoes back in da shoe rack. Now here's da important part. Turn up the thermostat to ninety degrees so OJ is sweating like a greased pig by da time he gets into da limo. Next, go out the back door by da pool and make your way to da fence by da guest house. Drop da bloody glove on da ground where da cops can find it. Then climb up on da fence and fall off backward so you plow into da air conditioning unit on da guest house. That should wake Kato. Hurry up and get over da fence before Kato comes out and catches you. I'll be cruising down da street. As soon as I spot yous, I'll pull over and pick ya up."

Vinnie the Eliminator: "You're a genius, boss!"

Hank the Hammer: "We should be able to get back to our hotel room in time to watch da last few holes of da Ulster Open on da Golf Channel."

Three-fingers Pete: "OJ will never get outta dis one, boss."

Hank the Hammer: "Yeah, da only chance he's got is to hire F. Lee Bailey. But Bailey's so washed up, he'll probably see he's in over his head and getta hot shot like Johnny Cochran. But Johnny ain't gonna be able to get OJ outta dis jam. Any questions?"

Vinnie the Eliminator: "Can we brag to any of the boys about this caper?"

Hank the Hammer slapping Vinnie the Eliminator on the back of the head: "What's da matta with you? Mum's the word."

Hank the Hammer's plan was ingenious. No doubt the frame up of OJ would have succeeded if Hank the Hammer had only paid attention to one more detail. Had he only splotched the glove with blood instead of soaking it, it wouldn't have shrunken to the point where Simpson couldn't pull it over his hand at the trial.

A second blunder, which may eventually lead to the gang's undoing, was unwittingly committed by One-eyed Luther. When he stole OJ's SUV the foursome's scorecard as well as a brochure about golf courses in Florida where the gang wanted to spend the winter playing golf, was jarred from his pocket while he was driving over curbs trying to get noticed. It's rumored that OJ found the scorecard as well as the brochure and developed immediate suspicions that the killers had been in his SUV. Further, the two items left behind indicated that the killers were most likely avid golfers who were spending time in Florida. The only thing Simpson had to go on was the initials of a foursome who obviously had shot a bad round. Since his acquittal OJ has been playing golf every day in Florida—ever vigilant for a foursome that uses the initials of HH, 1EL, 3FP, VE on their scorecard. He hasn't found them yet, but he's still looking.

"Chief, did you get stoned when I wasn't looking?" Blister said interrupting my internal movie. "You've been standing over that ball for an awful long time."

"I think I know who framed OJ," I admitted to Blister.

"Sure you do, Chief," Blister said with little interest in hearing the theory. "We'll talk all about it when the round's over."

I wasn't sure how long I had checked out but I saw that Wiley and Jack had already driven forward down the cart path adjacent to Jack's ball. Jack was standing to the side with his hands on his hips staring at me. When he saw me look at him, he bent his elbows and raised both toward the sky, which I recognized as universal sign language for 'pull your head out of your ass and hit the ball.' So that's what I did.

Happily, the negative thoughts of having murderers in my midst had little effect on the outcome of my shot. I hit the ball a little fat but I managed to get it to the front of the green. With any luck I could hit a decent lag putt and Blister would kick it back to me when he realized that he hadn't collected on his cigar from the previous hole.

Blister pushed his shot to the right where it found the front bunker. Mother Teresa was indeed out of miracles for the day.

Jack hit his wedge to the middle of the green and saved par a few minutes later. Wiley chipped to within two feet and the putt was conceded when Blister kicked it back on the way to the trap. Blister putted out of the trap and followed with two quick putts for a bogey. Blister turned to walk off the green before I stopped him.

"Blister, can you tend for me?"

"You can't see the hole from there?" he asked in disbelief.

"Just tend the flag, buttface," I said dismissing his challenge. "You think Stevie Williams gives Tiger Woods crap when he knows he can see the hole?"

"Ok Chief, you don't have to get uppity with me," Blister complained, as he pulled the flag out of the hole demonstrating a misunderstanding of the word 'tend.'

After I gave Blister a little schooling on flag tending, he inserted the flag in the cup and clasped the pole with his right hand. I lined up my putt and struck it solidly. I looked up and was perplexed at how slow it was moving. Had I misjudged the slope of the green? I was beginning to regret not walking to the far side of the hole and looking at the slope. Thank God I had my insurance policy tending the flag. That was pretty damned clever on my part. With Blister planted by the flag it would be a natural reflex for him to stick out his foot and kick it back. He would save me from having to sweat over a three or four foot tester.

Regrettably, my coverage must have lapsed. The ball quit rolling three feet from the hole but Blister didn't move. In fact, the flag was still in the hole. He had checked into another dimension. A dimension consisting of frozen flag tenders who are too paralyzed with brain lock to remember to pull the flag out of the hole and kick the ball back even though that's their only responsibility.

"I think you can pull the flag out of the hole now Blister," Jack advised him.

"Oh right. Holy Taliban . . . I zoned out there for a minute," Blister admitted as he finally pulled the flag.

I walked slowly to my ball. Wiley was rubbing some mud off his ball while Jack was stabbing the green to repair his ball mark. These guys were icing me down. They didn't want to see me break eighty. As I walked closer to my ball, I reasoned that Blister still had a chance to redeem himself but I knew the longer he waited the more awkward the concession would look to Wiley and Jack. I knew my goose was cooked when Blister turned to look at a chattering squirrel in a nearby tree. The flag dangled from his hand like a pole-vaulter ready to charge down the track, but he wasn't charging anywhere. He had a buddy up in the tree that wanted Blister to throw him an acorn. Stupid ding-dong!

Wiley kept rubbing his ball pretending not to notice that I was within acceptable concession tolerance guidelines. He was only interested in one thing—dumping the contents of his freezer on me. I marked my ball and lifted it from the turf.

I circled the hole to look at the break. I didn't say doodly-squat. I had to putt a potato across an ice field and I wasn't very happy about it. Wiley and Jack turned to walk off the green. The turd wasn't even going to watch the wreck. What a dick. Blister's face was frozen with his mouth open as he gazed at his new friend who was running down the trunk of the tree to greet him. I leaned down to replace my ball when I heard the unthinkable.

"That's good, Chief," Wiley said interrupting his chat with Jack as he looked back over his shoulder.

Blister shoved the flag in the hole and looked puzzled.

"Whadda you doing, Chief? You don't have to show off by hitting that little dinker in the hole. You never miss those, Chief!"

What gamesmanship! Wiley was certainly a master of the head game. He had done it so skillfully that he accepted a betting tie on the hole without even giving himself a chance to win by making me putt. After all the strokes were dispensed, my par and Jack's net birdie tied his net birdie and Blister's net par. This guy was ruthless. He was willing to lose money just to get inside my head. What a dick.

Score Card after 15 Holes

Hole	10	11	12	13	14	15	16	17	18	Front	Back	Total
Yardage	356	189	338	504	335	401	353	138	461	3088	3075	6163
Handicap	4	8	12	2	14	6	10	16	18			
Wiley	④	③	③	6	③->(o)	4 ^{6}				43		
Chief Tit	④	③	5	⑥	④	④ ^{6}				39		
Blister	4	6 ^{1}	5	⑤	7 ^{5}	5 ^{6}				52		
Jack	5	4 ^{2}	④ ^{3}	7 ^{4}	7 ^{5}	④				51		
Par	4	3	4	5	4	4	4	3	5	36	36	72

Notes:

/ => Signifies that player gets stroke

◯ => Signifies that player won bet

->(o) => Heiroglyphic for "out of ass."

[1] Blister surrenders to hole after hitting lob shot 170 yards across river, takes a Linda Tripp.

[2] 6 foot putt conceded to Jack to avoid 4-putting green. Wiley and Chief Tit pick up for impressive up and down.

[3] Favorable ruling allows Jack to save 16 strokes for clear-cutting around ball.

[4] Jack attempts to record Gesundheit score of 6. Actual score was 7.

[5] Blister and Jack are too tired to spawn after salmon run, both take a Linda Tripp.

[6] Mother Teresa blesses all but Jack's ball. All but Jack have miracle drives. Wiley tries to ice Chief Tit down.

Hole 16
The Hatfields and McCoys:
Feud Sparked by Illegal Drop

B lister and I pulled up behind Jack and Wiley at the par 4 sixteenth tee box. Jack was cutting another one of his stinkweed cigars while Wiley searched his bag for a Heineken.

"So who won that last hole?" Jack inquired.

"We pushed," I informed him.

"Really?" Wiley asked, sounding surprised. "I should have iced you down and made you putt."

"I thought you *were* icing me down."

"Oh no—when I ice you down I'll tell you when I'm doing it so there's no mistake about it," Wiley told me with a mustard grin. "Damn I should have made you putt it! I bet you would have yanked it."

"I probably would have escalated the battle—and made you putt yours."

"That's the luck of the draw, Chief," Wiley explained. "Blister kicked mine back like he did yours on fourteen and then slipped into a temporary coma when you were putting. You know the rule, Chief—mine was good while yours was discretionary."

Regrettably, Wiley was correct and I did owe him one. Since brain lock was a fairly common occurrence for Blister, we established a Red Ball People Amendment for when a foreign agent deflects the ball, particularly if the foreign agent is Blister.

Rule 19-1b—Deflection By Outside Agency on the Putting Green:
If a ball in motion after a stroke *on the* putting green *is deflected or stopped by, or comes to rest in or on, any moving or animate out-*

215

side agency *except a worm or an insect,* the stroke *shall be cancelled, the ball replaced and the* stroke *replayed. If a ball is deflected by an insect or worm then it shall be played as it lies.*

Red Ball People Amendment to Rule 19-1b: *If a ball in motion after a stroke on the putting green is deflected by an outside agency that happens to have a foot covered with a golf shoe then ball is deemed to have been holed out.*

Reason for change: *The Amendment almost uniquely applies to Blister, particularly when he is stoned. As such, he has willingly reduced his mental capacity to the equivalent of a worm. If interference from a worm doesn't qualify for a replay, it is only reasonable to deduce that interference from Blister shouldn't qualify either. The putt is considered good, since that was the stoner's judgement and in the world of the stoner, harmony prevails.*

At 353-yards, the sixteenth hole was a short par four and played shorter with a tailwind. The hole turned to the east from the fifteenth green. A giant fence bordered the fairway on the left and protected drivers on Highway 4 from vicious hooks. The river separated the right side of the fairway from the twelfth fairway where I had taken my hyperbolic drop. One hundred and seventy five yards out, the river cut north and separated the teeing area from the fairway near a towering eucalyptus tree. Jack aptly named the tree—the Nixon tree, in honor of its proclivity for screwing players and ruining rounds. The top of the bank near the Nixon tree was marked as a lateral hazard. A small shelf of alluvium created by flooding, extended from the river toward the tree and saved some of the luckier players from taking a drop, but most balls that struck solid wood, ricocheted the short distance to the river. The Red Ball People used the Hyperbolic Amendment to cover the case where a ball was hit directly into the river without reaching the Nixon tree.

If a player could get off the tee, the rest of the hole played fairly easy, though the flat green was guarded on both sides by bunkers.

Most ducks around the course stayed pretty close to the ponds on the ninth and tenth holes, though the far bank to the left of the cart bridge was a favorite congregating area and was lined with several mallards.

"You're the only one who gets a stroke," Wiley said to Jack.

Jack concluded that the sisters and the Morris' were well out of his range and popped a 5-wood over the river. Blister stood to the right of Jack. Both posed for the shot as the endorphins rushed through their bodies creating a surge of euphoria.

"Hold that pose!" I teased, as both players obliged me. "Alright, that's enough. Good shot Jack. We were so successful on that last hole, maybe you can find it in your heart to choose me as your partner."

"I don't know Chief, I do get a stroke," Jack said signaling his desire to play hard to get.

"How about if I throw Blister out of my cart and share it with you the rest of the way," I bargained.

"Now you're talking," Jack said, signaling a blooming courtship.

"Go easy on me, Chief," Blister said. "Jack has about as much chance of getting me out of your cart as Wiley has of bagging a super model."

As Wiley prepared to hit, I leaned into the cart to confirm my suspicions. The asswipe was one under on the back. He had gained two strokes on me. I knew I was in the middle of a dogfight but I didn't really realize how fierce it was until I reread his scores. He was also putting a lot better than me, which didn't bode well for the final three holes.

I began to ponder what a heap of trouble I was really in. Just a half-hour earlier, everyone was slapping me on the back, talking big about how I was going to break eighty for the first time. Wiley had cleverly put the focus on me. I bet Jack and Blister didn't even know how good Wiley was shooting. If he played one over on his last three holes, he would break 80. How infuriating would that be? Worse yet, if he played the next two holes well, there was no question in my mind that I would implode in a heap under the pressure. A wave of panic shot through me. He was on the verge of beating me—and I was having my best round ever. There was nothing I could do . . . except maybe remind him that he was playing way over his head.

Wiley took a puff on his stubby cigar and rested it on the wooden block marker as he teed his ball. He looked more confident than ever. Insufferable asswipe. It was about time to give him a scoring summary.

"Sweet paddy-wagon, Wiley, do you know you're one under on the back?"

"You're kidding?" Jack answered.

"No way," Blister added.

"Pretty amazing, huh?" Wiley said as he gripped his club and concentrated on the fairway.

"And I thought the Chief was the one who was going to break eighty!" Jack exclaimed.

If Wiley was feeling any pressure, he wasn't showing it. Evidently, I didn't tell him anything he didn't already know. He had ice running thorough his veins.

"Ok bust a big one, Wiley," Blister cheered.

"Cream one, Wiley," Jack encouraged.

My plan had backfired. There was a new sheriff in town and his name was Wiley. Blister and Jack couldn't hop on Wiley's bandwagon fast enough. If I could have hitched my bandwagon to Wiley's I think I would have. God knows it would be a lot easier to tug with Blister and Jack off of it.

"With a little help from Mother T," Wiley cracked, "I should be picking up another par in about five minutes."

Just as the darkest hour appeared to be on me, Wiley cranked one straight at the Nixon tree. Mother T was off curing tumors and Newton was the substitute. The event horizon snatched the ball shortly after it cleared the ladies tee box and guided it straight down the river with a big fade. We watched as the ball disappeared beyond the reeds of the riverbank.

Wiley seemed unfazed for the longest moment. His gaskets seemed to be holding the boiling oil in. Was this a new Wiley?

No it wasn't.

His brief moment of feeling sorry for himself was soon caved-in to steaming rage as his gaskets suffered catastrophic failure.

Wiley lifted his driver over his head with both hands as if chopping wood before slamming it to the ground and creating a sizable crevice. If Wiley wasn't so pissed, this would have been an ideal time to market my patented Stunt Driver to him. It was designed with the highly flexible shaft to absorb the impact that Wiley was delivering to his $400 TaylorMade Burner at this very moment. Wiley buried his driver into the ground with such force I was really quite surprised the head of his Burner didn't snap off.

I was beginning to wonder if the market for my patented Stunt Driver was as big as I thought it was. A moment later Wiley shook the head of his driver creating the sound of a marble rolling around inside. The Stunt Driver market was intact. Guys like Wiley were going to make me a rich man.

If I had a six or seven stroke lead on Wiley, I would have been sympathetic. But as all golfers know, sympathy is geometrically proportional to the gap between two player's scores and our gap was pretty small at the moment.

"You can take your hyperbolic drop and still get a bogey," Jack said, consoling him.

This was turning out to be an expensive day for Wiley.

"You may want to use your 3-wood on eighteen," I advised him.

"Yeah, something doesn't sound right in there," Wiley agreed.

I took the tee box with a bounce in my step and a heavier bandwagon.

"Ok Chief, bust a big one," Blister said.

"Hit a good one so I don't have to go Wolf," Jack encouraged me.

I was in the process of addressing my ball when I heard the unmistakable sound of an asswipe.

"You know, Chief," I heard the asswipe say, "You've got three strokes to give to break eighty. Stay away from Nixon . . . and you're home free."

"You trying to ice me down?" I asked Wiley.

"You're too good for that, Chief," Wiley lied.

"Shall I hit or do you want to spend another twenty minutes reliving the last fifteen holes?" I growled at Wiley.

"Any time you're ready, Chief."

I reinitiated my pre-shot routine, but was surprised to find that I had inserted a new step—a mantra that chanted—'don't hit it to Nixon.' I stopped the routine and started over, but the new step came racing down my mental marble chaser once again—'don't hit it to Nixon.'

219

When I got to the top of my backswing, the order was supplanted by a reciprocal order—*hit it to Nixon. Do it now. This limited offer will expire soon. Do it right now. Hit it right at him. Don't piss Nixon off. Boy, will he be pissed if you don't hit it to him.*

So I hit it to Nixon.

"Oh, Jesus Rodriquez!" I muttered, inadvertently slandering a Latin shortstop instead of the Holy Ghost.

"Oh Chief—you dickhead!" Blister moaned.

The odd thing about the Nixon tree was that its leaves and branches seemed to be made of catcher's mitts. As was its reputation, my ball disappeared into the foliage but didn't exit. An eternity seemed to pass before we saw the little white globe fall straight to the ground and strike the roots of the tree. My heart sank with the ball as it started its roll down the bank and disappeared into the tall weeds.

"Misery loves company," said the asswipe.

"That's what I hear," I replied to Wiley as I walked off the tee box debating whether to insert my driver in my golf bag or Wiley's butt.

As he so often did with the Red Ball People, Blister produced an immediate antidote for Wiley and my sulkies. We watched his drive with amusement as the low hook started at the bridge and began dipping toward the bank on the eastern side of the river to the left of the bridge. The ball smashed into the crown of the bank just below the fairway and popped in the air. It took one bounce and zeroed in on two ducks that were picking at the grass. The female mallard saw the impending danger and lifted her wings and skittered away.

"Look out Daffy!" Blister yelled trying to warn the Mallard.

"Duck!" Wiley shouted, hoping the mallard would understand he was using the word as a verb.

"It's official—It's now Howdy Doody Time!" I bellowed in reference to the tribe's colloquialism to describe a measure of time during a round of golf when the quality of play among the Red Ball People is particularly dreadful.

The male wasn't as fleet of webfoot and the ball struck him in the hind quarters, startling him so much that he sprung straight up frantically flapping his wings as he hovered over the ball like a Cobra gunship. As soon as the duck determined that the danger had passed, he descended back to the ground, shook his tail feathers and waddled over to join his companion a few yards away. Blister had hit a duck with a duck hook.

We were still cackling when Mr. Kim's battery-powered pull cart climbed over the worn out railroad tie that separated the cart path from the tee box.

"You hit stupid duck!" Mr. Kim laughed. "That one stupid duck."

"That one stupid partner I got," I said to Mr. Kim, encouraging him to consider all angles.

"Stupid duck hit by stupid partner!" Mr. Kim giggled with a Cheshire grin. "That very funny. I tell my wife. She laugh at stupid duck."

"I guess that's why they call it a duck hook," Blister said to Mr. Kim.

"I hit tree hook. But no duck hook. How you do?" Mr. Kim asked me, unaware that I hit the Nixon tree.

"I hit the Nixon tree," I replied, before realizing that Mr. Kim was not familiar with that lexicon.

"Nick's in tree?" Mr. Kim asked, confused at my response.

"No, Nixon tree," I said pointing to the tree.

"Who Nick?"

"A former president."

"President in tree? Hummm," Mr. Kim said, scratching his chin convinced that I was putting him on.

Jack and Wiley pulled away as Blister and I climbed in the cart and prepared to follow. Mr. Kim was still confounded by the president in the tree and had no further questions to ask until he solved the riddle. We bid farewell to Mr. Kim and tore off over the bridge.

I parked east of the tree and took an anxious walk to the bank and peered over. My heart soared. The event horizon lost to the alluvium shelf. Although, I had a *Blister forehead lie*, I could easily advance the ball to the one hundred and fifty yard marker if I could just hit it over the ten foot bank.

I grabbed my 8-iron and scrambled down the bank. A tiny limb behind the ball had served its purpose as a speed bump and halted the ball's journey toward the river. I looked up and saw that Wiley had joined Blister in watching the proceedings.

"Aim right here, Chief," Wiley commanded. "And don't swing too hard. You just want to get it on the fairway somewhere."

"Thanks, Sherlock," I replied.

Wiley moved well out of the way to the left anticipating a shank from the *Blister forehead lie*. When I made contact it felt like I was literally hitting a rock, which was pretty common for how a lot of my impacts felt. Of course, when I say literally, I usually mean figuratively because I usually hit the ball instead of a rock. It just feels like a rock. In this case, I literally hit a rock. I had missed the ball to the left where a small rock had been protruding above ground. The small rock was somewhere on the fairway where I wished my ball was. Happily for me, the swing was so faulty, I missed the ball entirely and it was comfortably resting in the same spot. Since it was Red Ball People edict to not count a rocket launch unless a passenger was aboard, the swing was treated as a practice stroke.

I mustered a little more concentration for my second attempt. This time I made contact, though it still felt like a rock. I jerked my head up as all players are taught not to do and watched as the ball smacked a large Nixon root near the crown of the bank. The solid wood and topspin propelled the ball forward. I scampered up the hill and watched as the ball rolled barely past the one hundred and fifty yard marker.

"Good out Chief!" Wiley commended me.

"If you only knew," I replied.

"Well, nobody caught it on film so as far as anyone knows it was a perfect pick," Wiley chuckled.

I pulled my visor and sunglasses off and wiped both eyebrows. Sweat had fallen from my brows during my swing and splattered on the inside of my glasses. I untucked my shirt and cleaned my glasses as Wiley took his drop. Any what a drop it was. Under the Nixon tree was a ten-yard perimeter of hardpan and eucalyptus acorns. He had advanced his ball a good twenty yards up the fairway until he had located well manicured grass. There, he leaned over and executed a T-Rex drop. I commended him on his excellent comprehension and execution of at least three Red Ball People rules governing multiple drop scenarios.

"I believe I am speaking for everyone on the course today, when I say—that is one impressive drop."

"I should say . . . I'm quite pleased with it myself," Wiley smirked.

Wiley had pushed the envelope on bending the Red Ball People amendments, but it really wasn't cheating. Cheating to the Red Ball People is when a player performs an illicit act and attempts to deceive others as he's doing it. Wiley was pushing the limit on being illicit but he certainly wasn't trying to deceive any of us and that was the litmus test. Like the US Constitution, the Red Ball People amendments were meant to be flexible and subject to numerous interpretations. I carefully crafted most of the amendments myself in order to avoid the pitfalls and the feuds created by the strict interpretation of the USGA rules. Consequently, while tribe members often ridiculed each other for exercising a liberal interpretation of the amendments, no one had ever gotten into a real donnybrook because of a rules violation. Obviously, the same can't be said for the USGA rules.

The Hatfields and McCoys: Improper Drop Sparks Feud

Some of the biggest feuds in the history of golf began with an improper drop. After the second round of the 2003 Funai Classic at Walt Disney World in Florida was completed, PGA player Marco Dawson hailed a PGA rules official and complained that Esteban Toledo, his playing partner for the round had taken an illegal drop. At the time, seven year tour player Toledo was ranked one hundred and twenty third, and needed a good finish at the tournament, the second to last tournament of the year, to keep his card.

The incident occurred on the eighteenth hole when Toledo's ball landed in an area of the fairway marked ground under repair. According to Dawson, Toledo took a drop on the right side of the drop area instead of the left side, which he judged to be the nearest point of relief. A rules official reviewed the drop area and agreed with Dawson. A two stroke penalty was assessed on Toledo's completed round of 66, but because the round was already over by the time the incident was reported by Dawson, Toledo was disqualified from the event for signing an incorrect score card.

Predictably, the incident between the two players erupted into a very public media feud when Toledo blasted Dawson, particularly because Dawson waited a full day to report the alleged infraction. Dawson remained unapologetic, further fueling bad blood between himself and Toledo, who grew up in Mexico in a house with a dirt floor.

Oddly enough, Dawson also reported an improper drop against fellow playing partner Brandel Chamblee at the Chrysler Classic in Phoenix, also after Chamblee completed the second round. Like Toledo, Chamblee was tied for third going into the third round, but was also disqualified.

Most galling to many of the tour players, Dawson admitted he didn't even witness Toledo's drop. Fortunately for Toledo, he finished strong in the final tournament of 2003, squeaking by at one hundred and twenty five on the money list, the highest ranking for an exempt player. If Dawson and Toledo are paired together in a future tournament, I suspect we won't find them in the player's courtesy tent breaking bread before the round.

Perhaps the most famous blood feud in American folklore was the notorious twelve-year feud between the Hatfields and McCoys, which took twelve lives among the two families. The feud erupted in 1878 on the Kentucky side of the Tug River and came to represent the backwardness and violence of the Appalachian region between Kentucky and West Virginia.

According to historical accounts, the feud had its origins when Randolph McCoy accused Floyd Hatfield of stealing his hog. McCoy took his complaint to a local judge, who demonstrated the seriousness of the matter by assembling a jury and putting Hatfield on trial. The jury was deadlocked as half the jurors had allegiance to the McCoys while the other six had ties to the Hatfields, forcing the judge to drop the charge.

Animosity between the families festered for four years but intensified when Johnse Hatfield, the son of Hatfield patriarch Devil Anse Hatfield, impregnated but did not marry, Randolph McCoy's daughter, Roseanna. That same year, 1882, the hostilities came to a head when three of Roseanna McCoy's brothers attacked and killed Ellison Hatfield, brother of Devil Anse, on Election Day. Most of the Hatfield's believed that the killing was revenge for Johnse Hatfield impregnating Roseanna McCoy, but an alternate historical theory speculates that the McCoys killed Ellison because he backed a local symbolic vote by the Tug County Board of Supervisors to declare the Tug River Valley—*a dynamite-free zone*. Devil Anse Hatfield quickly retaliated by executing the three sons of Randolph McCoy, without the benefit of a trial.

Surprisingly, things quieted down with the two families after the three killings until an attorney showed up. Just as attorneys are prone to derail tranquility in the present day, Perry Cline, an attorney and distant relative of Randolph McCoy, sued Devil Anse Hatfield in 1887 to recover five thousand acres of timberland that he had lost to the Hatfield patriarch in an earlier court settlement many years before the feud erupted.

By 1887, the Norfolk and Western Railroad Company announced plans to build a track through the Tug Valley area causing timberland to skyrocket in value. Cline used his influence with the Governor of Kentucky, and five-year old murder indictments were issued against Devil Anse Hatfield.

Unhappy with the progress of the extradition between West Virginia and Kentucky, Cline recruited a notorious thug known as 'Bad' Frank Phillips to organize a posse and go into West Virginia and arrest Devil Anse Hatfield. Instead the posse captured nine Hatfield supporters. Several skirmishes between the families followed, culminating in an attempt by the Hatfields to eliminate Randolph McCoy. The attack on the McCoy home in Blackberry Fork, Kentucky resulted in the deaths of two of Randolph McCoys children.

Before long the feud began to be viewed as warfare between Kentucky and West Virginia. In fact the US Supreme Court even got involved, setting a precedent for extradition law. The feud finally subsided in 1890 when Devil Anse Hatfield sold his many timber holdings and moved out of the Tug Valley.

Many historians are hard-pressed to explain how a misplaced hog led to a twelve-year feud that resulted in twelve deaths among two families and forever established the reputation of the Appalachian region as backward and violent. The fact that the jury that was seated at the missing hog trial was evenly split, clearly suggests the likelihood of an earlier incident that sharply divided the community between Randolph McCoy and Floyd Hatfield.

The earlier incident remained pure speculation until a reunion celebration for the descendents of the formerly feuding families was hosted by the town of Matewan, West Virginia in 2002 near the site of the original Devil Anse Hatfield Ranch. It was during this celebration that Bubba McCoy produced a diary belonging to Randolph McCoy that gave the first hint of how the trouble really started in 1872.

According to the revised historical account, both families were involved in the timber industry and had planted hickory trees in 1860 after reading accounts of a Scottish game called golf that was played with clubs fashioned from hickory trees. As trade flourished along the interior of the Tug River Valley, rubber imports began arriving in 1865 from the tropical islands of the Caribbean.

About that same time, Randolph McCoy read an account of how the Gutta Percha ball or Guttie, as it was called, was manufactured from the rubber-like sap of the Gutta tree found in the tropics and had revolutionized the game of golf. Since he already had hickory trees for making golf clubs, it wasn't long before Randolph convinced his son, Titleist McCoy, also a skilled blacksmith, to melt some of the Gutta rubber and produce the first Appalachian golf balls.

After reading accounts of how the Scottish Monarchs played golf, the McCoys were so enthused to play a game, Randolph McCoy leveled his corn field and erected a makeshift nine-hole course. By 1870 the McCoys were hosting tournaments with their closest neighbors, the Hatfields. Randolph McCoy and Floyd Hatfield soon emerged as the best players and began wagering on the outcome of the nine-hole event.

Early betting consisted of tobacco pouches, jugs of moonshine, and corncob pipes. As interest grew, the bets escalated, with the 4th of July 1872 tournament producing the biggest wager so far—a three hundred pound hog. Both Randolph McCoy and Floyd Hatfield brought their prize hogs to the event with the understanding that the winner of the event would take both hogs home.

The match proceeded without incident until the ninth hole. Floyd Hatfield held a one-stroke edge over Randolph McCoy going into the seventy-five yard par 4 hole. Both players busted fifty-yard drives but Hatfield's drive careened off an outdoor privy and landed underneath a whiskey still. The area had been marked as ground under repair, entitling Hatfield to a free drop. However, according to accounts of the McCoy clan, Hatfield dropped his Titleist-Guttie on the left side of the still when the closest point of relief was on the right.

Recognizing that Hatfield would be disqualified if Hatfield did not call a two-stroke penalty on himself, McCoy cleverly waited until after the round and after Hatfield had signed his card, before declaring the infraction.

Although both players parred the hole, a rules official who was a second cousin as well as brother-in-law of Randolph McCoy, sided with him and awarded the match to McCoy. However, by the time the ruling was official, Hatfield had already untied both hogs and skedaddled. McCoy was livid and accused Hatfield of stealing his hog. The rest, as we say, is history.

One hundred and twenty five years later, the descendants of Randolph McCoy and Floyd Hatfield gather every year in the town of Matewan and celebrate the storied feud with a pig roast, square dancing, and staged recreations of the 1887 skirmishes. Many present day McCoys are now married to the formerly feuding Hatfields and the two families relish in their storied American folklore.

Unfortunately, no such goodwill prevails between the Toledo family and the Dawson family. The illegal drop allegation pinned on Toledo by Dawson during the 2003 Funai Classic serves as the figurative modern day hog between these two families. Only time will judge if this feud will escalate to the level that the Hatfield and McCoy feud attained one hundred and twenty five years ago.

———————

After his most generous drop, Wiley stiffed his 5-iron to the green. Although Wiley's favorable drop went a long way toward improving his chances for par, the flexibility of the Red Ball People drop amendments served as a useful deterrent to prevent me from blowing his head off like Devil Anse Hatfield had done to a few of the McCoys.

Blister took two swings to reach the green before two-putting to save bogey. I yanked a 9-iron Pullooski on my third shot but received a favorable bounce toward the flag when it careened off the hump of the bunker. Both Wiley and I were able to save bogeys with good lag putts.

The big story was Jack. Jack had his second consecutive par after knocking a pitching wedge to the middle of the green. He won the first and only Wolf of the day. In fact, because it was a rollover hole, it was a double-Wolf, meaning the rest of us owed him $2 each, or $1 per hole. We would hear about it for days, since Jack winning a Wolf bet was about as rare as him shooting an eagle, which to my best recollection, had never happened.

Hole 17
Grandma Athie Buys a Farm

J ack and I walked the short distance to the par 3 seventeenth tee box
as Blister and Wiley moved the carts. Jack was in the middle of the
consummate mediocre round, but he couldn't be happier after winning
a double-Wolf rollover. As we walked to the tee box he recounted his
drive and pitching wedge on the sixteenth hole as if it were ancient
history. He asked me if I'd ever seen such a lovely drive and I agreed
that I never had. He asked me if I had ever seen such a pristine pitching
wedge and I admitted that such an immaculate wedge had never been
struck in my presence. Before asking me if I had ever witnessed such
beautiful two-putting, I preempted him and told him I had never been
so enchanted with a lag putt.

The course clogged on the seventeenth hole like a toilet at an Exxon
gas station. In fact, the sisters and the Morris' were still sitting in their
carts when Blister and Wiley eased in behind Babs and Donetta. I scanned
the green a short distance away and saw two of the players standing on
the edge of the green peering down into a waste area at their comrades
below our sight line, who undoubtedly were racking up some big numbers.

The sisters climbed out of their cart and stretched, as Wiley set his
brake. Both reached back and tugged the cuffs on the rear of their polyester shorts, perhaps aware that lose-hanging fabric refracted pings a
little better than clinging fabric. As expected, Wiley wasted no time in
showcasing his reticent mental capacity and whispered briefly to Babs
before she popped her head back and let out a laugh. Jack and I soon
joined the party as we gathered near Jack's cart while the Morris' re-

mained seated, eyes glued to the green some one hundred and forty yards away.

"Hey Chief," Babs greeted me. "Wiley said you told him to tell me— 'don't be a stranger.'"

"Evidently, he confused the message. I told him to tell you—'if I look like a dope and talk like a dope . . . then I probably am a dope.'"

The spontaneous joke wasn't that funny but the sisters gave me a courtesy laugh anyway. Blister seized their attention for a few minutes as he told them the story of how he had hit a duck with a duck hook.

As Blister continued to hold court, I began getting a waft of something foul. However, it wasn't a fart or a broken sewer main. It was much worse. It was one of those smells that often overcome me in tight quarters like an elevator where I'm often assaulted by an uninvited chemical dousing. It was overbearing cologne. I couldn't quite put my thumb on it—the odor was either Faberge's Brutal or Calvin Klein's Repulsion. In either case, I found it as welcome as a slap in the face with a soggy mop.

I shot an accusatory look at Wiley but I knew my suspicion was unfounded when I saw Wiley's nose curl and his face scrunch with a frown. Blister was flapping his arms like a mallard struck by a golf ball, when the fumes slapped his olfactory sense.

"What the hell is that?" Blister asked, interrupting his duck imitation.

Donetta rolled her hand like a hitchhiker and motioned toward Timothy Morris. "He put it on at the turn."

"Well I don't think he could smell worse if he had crapped his pants!" Blister scoffed.

"Maybe he did crap his pants," Jack offered in a hushed voice.

"What a dick!" Blister muttered. "Who wears cologne on a golf course?"

The smell was overbearing. I was surprised we hadn't smelled it at the par 3 eleventh hole but I guess we were never that close to Timothy on eleven. Now that it was in the mid-eighties, his perspiration must have activated the cologne. Blister decided to go on the offensive.

"That reminds me . . . have you guys seen that new show on Fox called—You Gotta Smell This!" Blister inquired, elevating his voice for Tim and Janet's enjoyment.

"Sounds interesting," I said, playing along. "Tell me what your keen eyes saw."

"Well it's kind of a cross between *Joe Millionaire* and the Rodeo," Blister continued as he did his best to emulate a THX Sound system. "The premise of the show is pure genius. They get a gorgeous babe who meets ten guys in a beach house. She wears a slinky bikini with a wet top for the first episode while hosting ten potential husbands in the ocean-side swimming pool. By the end of the first episode, all ten guys want to marry her. Here's the catch. For the next episode, the producers set her up on a date in close-quarter situations, but before she goes out on the date, the producers smear her with all kinds of foul smelling stuff. It could be caster oil. Other times its brake fluid. Sometimes, it's just plain ole foul smelling cologne like you find at golf courses . . ."

"Oh man, I bet she smells like a fish market," Wiley interjected.

"That's exactly right," Blister answered with enthusiasm. "Anyway . . . when the producers are satisfied that she smells like a water buffalo, they arrange to have her meet one of the bachelors in an area with no ventilation."

"Sounds like a damn riot," Jack jumped in.

"You have no idea," Blister laughed. "In the second episode she picks this guy up in a limousine where the windows don't roll down. In another episode, she goes golfing on a hot day like today and shares a golf cart with the guy. The bottom line is—get this . . . if the bachelor gags and says anything about how bad she smells—he gets eliminated."

"When do you have time to watch this stuff?" Jack quizzed Blister.

"When I'm not helping my kids with homework," Blister replied. "Which is almost always."

I peeked over at the Morris' who were out of their cart and glaring at Blister. They were seething. I couldn't tell if Timothy Morris was upset with Blister for barely disguising his contempt for his cologne or because of proletarian TV viewing habits. Wiley also noticed the pot beginning to boil and thought it best to put a cork in Blister.

"Hey, the Chief's going to break eighty for the first time today."

"Really," Babs exclaimed. "That's great Chief!"

"I gotta bogey both holes . . . so let's make sure the eggs are fertilized before we start count'n em," I said, tempering her expectations. "Besides, Wiley can break eighty if he pars both holes."

"Sounds like a real dog fight," Donetta observed.

"No not really," I lied. "I'm cheering for him and he's cheering for me."

"Right, Chief," Wiley said, with a hint of sarcasm.

"Have you come close before?" Babs asked.

"In fact I have, but my dream was destroyed on this hole when I took an Oliver," I answered.

"An Oliver?" Babs asked.

I forgot for the moment that the Red Ball People parlance was unfamiliar to outsiders. I explained to Babs that the vernacular—'To take an Oliver' had its origins in the Oscar winning movie *Oliver*. During the movie's most memorable scene, young barefoot Oliver is having supper at the dreary orphanage with hundreds of other orphans and, like the other orphans, is still hungry after his paltry serving of dumplings. He becomes an instant hero among his orphan peers when he walks up to the wicked taskmaster holding his empty plate and says—'Sir, may I please have another?'

"I didn't see Oliver," Babs informed me.

"Me neither," Donetta said. "What's the tie-in?"

I hate it when people make me explain jokes. If they didn't get the joke in the first place, what chance do they have of comprehending the scientific explanation?

"Well you see . . . you got this orphan asking for seconds by pleading to the taskmaster to give him another," I said to the two blank faces. ". . . Just like a golfer does when he's taking his seventh stroke on a par 3. In other words, like Oliver, sometimes we just can't have enough. We need another. You following me?"

"Not really, Chief," Babs replied, "but we'll go along any way."

"I've had all kinds of Olivers today," Donetta bragged.

"Now you're catching on," I commended Donetta.

Wiley wandered back to the drinking fountain behind the tee box to get a drink. Babs used the opportunity to get an update on his face.

"So when are you going to tell him about his face?" Babs asked pointing to Wiley.

"Probably never. We'll let his wife give him the good news," I replied.

"You guys are awful," Donetta said.

231

"Well I suppose your sister has told you about the split in the back of your shorts?" Blister asked.

"What!" Donetta wailed, covering her hindquarters with both hands.

"Not really," Blister admitted. "But see how much fun it would be if you actually had one and Babs didn't tell you."

"You guys are sick," Babs laughed.

I looked over at the green and saw that the foursome was walking off, which prompted Timothy to make his way to the tee box. The hole measured 138 yards on the card, and played close to that distance for all flag positions since the green had more width than depth. Although the hole was rated as the third easiest hole on the course, it created more heartache for me than any other owing to its sinister reputation as a milestone buster.

The river carved a jagged path toward the highway after the sixteenth green, crossing in front of the ladies tee box, separating us from the green. Between the river and the green was a sunken waste area about the size of the infield of a baseball diamond. Any ball that landed short and fell back into the waste area proved to be a daunting challenge and was the primary ingredient for mixing an Oliver cocktail. Although Pepe kept the weeds mowed in the waste area, it had numerous dry patches of cracked hardpan spotted with weed clumps. Worse yet, the bottom of the waste area was fifteen feet below the green and required a heap of finesse to save bogey if you were lucky enough to find your ball.

The river exited the landscape on the left side of the green and was routed through a cement tunnel under the cart path before emerging behind the green where it curled south for the length of the green before completing a hairpin around the eighteenth tee box. Two friendly bunkers on the back of the green, prevented long balls from taking a swim.

One notable eucalyptus about the size of the Nixon tree, dominated the left side of the teeing area. If Pepe was careless enough to plant the wooden markers too far to the left, overhanging limbs could easily interfere with a lofted iron. That problem rarely bothered the tribe, as we simply teed to the right of the markers to insure that the limbs were out of play.

Timothy Morris did his best to ignore us as we clustered with the sisters near Wiley's cart. His fumes were overwhelming and my nose tingled. Janet Morris stayed near her cart, as she no doubt found the thought of getting any closer to Blister repugnant. Apparently, Jack's olfactory nerves were also stimulated as he leaned his head down and clasped his nostril with the index finger and thumb of his right hand.

Tim took a practice swing as the hair follicles in our noses danced to cleanse the incoming toxins. I oscillated my eyes between Tim and Jack. Jack seemed to be genuinely bothered by the odor. He puffed his cheeks, squinted his eyes, and pinched his nostrils tighter.

"Uuuuttt," Jack groaned involuntarily, as he held back a sneeze.

Tim took his address and prepared to hit. I thought about warning him that there was a high likelihood that Jack was going to sneeze, but then I reasoned that if I did and Jack didn't come through, then I would just come off looking like a buffoon. If anyone was going to look like a buffoon, it might as well be Jack.

"Uuuuttt," Jack groaned a second time.

Jack's face turned crimson as General Cortex issued an emergency order to stockpile mucous to the rear of his nostrils and truck a load of slobber to the back of his throat in preparation for a surprise assault.

Tim launched his overly deliberate backswing.

General Cortex ordered the first line of defense—the hair follicles in Jack's nose, to gyrate until the foreign invasion could be tickled away from the breach. Colonel Corpuscle panicked and summarily rushed an over-supply of mucous to the posterior nasal cavity to shore up the defense. Slobber massed around the tonsils, as reinforcements might be needed on short notice. As he had been trained to do prior to imminent cannon fire, Sergeant Synapse flooded the eyes with saline water.

Tim finished his backswing and fired his hips just as General Cortex ordered an immediate counter attack.

"Uuuuutt, oh, uuuuutt, *ahhhhchoooit,*" Jack sneezed, as General Cortex fired his cannonade.

The ammo was sufficient to alter Tim's swing as he chopped down on the ball and squirted it into the water hazard. He spun around to search for the offending party. Without sunglasses, the rage on his face was fully exposed.

"You know, you guys are really something!" He wailed, as he searched for something clever to say but came up woefully short.

"Sorry," Jack said, as he wiped his nose of excess fodder.

"Gesundheit!" Blister said with a grin, not registering the seriousness of the situation.

"God Bless you," Babs said, siding with Blister.

Tim continued his unscheduled diatribe. "You guys ever heard of course etiquette? Or do you get all your knowledge from watching reality TV? I'd probably be six over par right now if I didn't have to put up with your crap every time the course backs up."

"Hey pardner," Wiley interrupted, "we wouldn't have fatal hay-fever over here if you hadn't poured a bottle of syrup down your pants . . . and the only way you're ever gonna be six over par—is if you quit after two holes."

The curious thing about Wiley, he never uses the word 'pardner' unless he wants to kick someone's ass. Oddly, the mud and mustard on his face was starting to resemble war paint. He looked like a guy who didn't mind what happened to his face and that was the worst kind of opponent to go up against. Evidently, Tim came to the same conclusion and he retreated to tee a second ball.

Rattled by the encounter, Tim hit his second ball into the waste area short of the hole.

"Keah, keah, keah," Blister giggled at Tim's misfortune.

Tim glared at Wiley as he walked back to the ladies tee to join his wife. Wiley glared back, fully prepared to win the staring contest. When Tim was out of ear shot Wiley turned to us and whispered—"what a prick!"

"I was gonna back you up," Blister giggled.

"Not me," I admitted.

"Me neither," Jack laughed.

"Come to think of it, I probably would have sided with Tim," Blister quipped.

"Whoa, this will make for an interesting finish," Babs sighed.

Wiley's adrenaline was still evaporating and he strolled over to the ball cleaner to check his gaskets and bathe a ball.

Although we were out of ear-shot of the Morris', we paused long enough for Janet Morris to hit her drive and join her husband in the waste area.

"Keahhhh, Keah," Blister cackled, unnecessarily at the mishap.

While I had no special affinity for the Morris', Blister seemed to be overly overt in exuding his pleasure in their misfortune. Perhaps if I were stoned like Blister I would have a different interpretation of the miscues. Babs and Donetta were also puzzled by Blister's spontaneous giggling and each gave him a puzzled look, which caused him to giggle harder.

"Keeeeeaahh, ahhhaaaa, keeeaaaahh, keah."

Proving that laughter really is contagious, a chorus of chortles inexplicably burst from Babs and Donetta. Within seconds, Jack and I were snorting for no apparent reason other than to go-along to get-along. It was an odd episode of uncontrollable cackling that went unabated for about thirty seconds.

Wiley, who was still rinsing his ball, shot us a vacant stare from several yards away and wondered if he had just missed the joke of the century. The fact that Wiley wasn't laughing with us left sufficient doubt in the Morris' minds that we weren't actually laughing at them, which I wasn't sure about either.

Finally, the sisters peeled away and retrieved their irons. Donetta hit first and pumped one into the waste area. As she had done moments earlier, Donetta bellowed at her miscue. Babs and Blister quickly formed a cackling chorus, as Jack and I exercised much more restraint the second time around. Babs ended the fun when she grooved an iron that hit the green to the left of the red flag.

"Good show Babs," Jack said as Wiley and I clapped.

Babs acknowledged our praise with a wave and a smile as she and Donetta hurried back to their cart. The Morris' blasted away before the sisters could put their irons away. As Babs climbed in her cart she held her nose with her thumb and index finger to warn us that a lingering invisible cloud of Calvin Klein Repulsion had been left behind.

"Good luck on your quest to break eighty," Babs said, as she and Donetta pulled away.

"Easier said than done, but thanks," I said with an abbreviated wave.

"Don't be a stranger!" Wiley barked as the sisters sped past him.

Wiley took his two clean Stratas over to his bag and used the towel affixed to a ring at the top of his bag to dry the balls. He wanted a recap of the greatest joke of the century.

"So what was that all about?"

"You tell me and we'll both know," I replied. "All I know is—Blister got silly after Jan dumped her ball in the waste area. As far as I know, we were all pretty appalled with Blister's irreverent giggling until Babs and Donetta joined in. Then it just got away from us."

"Ya think so?" Wiley asked sarcastically.

Grandma Athie Buys the Farm

The giggling incident reminded me of the unforeseen reaction I witnessed from two of my female high school Muses many years earlier on the occasion of the sudden death of my dear departed eighty-five year-old Grandma Athie.

I had just completed my junior year of high school, when one Friday evening our family received a call from Grandpa Mac and learned of the untimely death of grandma Athie. Although I was shocked and saddened to learn of her death, it wasn't entirely surprising since grandma Athie smoked three packs of cigarettes every day of her life for the past seventy years.

In what would become a curious and defining way of how I would forever remember Grandma Athie, my high school friends, Becki and Sue, arrived at my house to take me to a movie moments after the family learned of the death. Since cell phones hadn't been invented yet, there was no way to intercede and cancel our movie plans until they appeared.

Within fifteen minutes of being jarred by the passing, Becki ripped into my driveway in her dad's Valiant and tapped the horn like she always did to announce her arrival. Alerted by the horn, I slogged out to the car with a long face and leaned in the passenger window next to Sue and informed them through intermittent chokes, that my family had just received terrible news and they would have to go to the movie without me.

Both girls' smiles turned into frowns of dismay as they asked what the bad news was. When I informed them that eighty-five year-old

Grandma Athie had died, Becki attempted to console me by stammering—'owwww that's too bad, I'm so sorry to hear that.'

Sue, on the other hand, had a slightly different reaction. For a moment, she too looked genuinely grieved, until inexplicably she puffed her cheeks before bowing her head and staring at the floorboard. Suddenly, in what I would still classify as the most unexpected and indecorous reaction I have ever witnessed, Sue exploded with a burst of laughter that was uncontainable.

Becki was so dumbfounded by Sue's caddy behavior, she joined in and began roaring with laughter. I was so startled by the awkward and abrupt reaction of the two ingrates, I inexplicably found myself howling right along with them. For the next several minutes, the three of us wailed with such intense laughter that we could scarcely catch our breaths. Tears streamed down our cheeks as the howling continued unabated. My legs gave way as a shortage of oxygen depleted my muscle strength, and I toppled over in a heap on the driveway, holding my sides as I rolled back and forth.

The sight of me losing muscle control drove Sue to the next level. She began making that fog horn sound that some people are able to make when spasms of air shoot through an overworked larynx.

'Haaa, haaaa, haaaa' quickly turned into—'Haaa, haaaa, HOOOOOOOOUGH, HOOOOOOOOUGH'.

The foghorn was an unexpected pleasure that caught Becki and me off guard. Becki lost motor control of her spine and fell in Sue's lap causing more blares from Sue's foghorn. Inhaling oxygen became a top priority as I attempted to summon help by beating on the side of the Valiant in the hopes of receiving some medical attention. A few moments after the foghorn subsided and suffocation was averted, I managed to grab the door handle and pull myself up to the side of Sue's window and peeked in to determine if Becki and Sue had survived the incident. Both were gasping for air, indicating that the crisis had not run its full course.

As soon as Sue's lungs were replenished, she began issuing small craft warnings once again. Becki wailed even louder as she sopped her tears with Sue's shirtsleeve. After nearly five minutes of hilarity in which none of us were able to utter a single word, the unfathomable event was over.

When Sue finally spoke, the first thing out of her mouth was—'I'm so sorry' to which I replied—'I can tell'.

We were leveled by an aftershock.

'HOOOOOOOOOUH, HOOOOOOOOUGH,' the foghorn blared.

Spineless Becki once again morphed into a puddle on top of Sue's lap as I bawled right along with them.

After the last giggle faded, Sue admitted that she couldn't even begin to explain her reaction to the death of Grandma Athie, who she had never met. She had certainly experienced the deaths of older relatives in her own family without causing a melee and was stumped to explain what was different this time around.

I relived the account of Athie's death with the tribe and they found it almost as funny as Becki and Sue, though no one was able to reproduce a foghorn quite like Sue to propel the story to the next level.

"I can't tell you what I found so funny about Jan's bad shot," Blister admitted.

"I was appalled until Babs and Donetta joined in," I told Blister. "After that it just turned into a tsunami."

"Well, I'm just glad we don't have to share another tee box with Tim," Jack said.

"What a dick!" Blister agreed, summing up Tim for the rest of us.

Wiley inspected the teeing area and glanced up at the eucalyptus tree to insure there was sufficient clearance. His inspection was momentarily halted by Mr. Kim's self-propelled bag carrier, which eased up behind our cart. I offered a head-bob to the eldest Mr. Kim, which drew a big grin. He no doubt was wondering if there was any type of advice he could offer that would illicit another comparison to the Mongolian Warlord Sherlock.

"You know Chief, Pepe's done it again," Wiley said, completing his inspection.

"Tee markers too close to the eucalyptus tree?" I guessed.

"As usual," Wiley confirmed. "I'll just have to tee the ball to the right to steer clear of that big limb," he said, as he sized up the overhanging limb.

"What are you hitting?" I inquired.

"Normally I'd hit a 7-iron, but since that ain't an option, I'll just back up a little and hit a knock-down 6-iron."

"Oh, good decision," I lied.

"You still pray good?" Mr. Kim asked me.

"Five over par, but I don't know how," I said truthfully.

"Fie over!" Mr. Kim barked in disbelief.

"Yeah, I need bogeys on the last two holes to break eighty."

"No big fattie!" Mr. Kim advised.

"I certainly hope not."

I eyed the green and saw the Morris' leading the sisters off. The sisters glanced our way and when they saw we were watching, both held their noses as they waved the air in front of their faces.

Wiley teed his ball back and outside the teeing ground so that the most wicked duck hook wouldn't threaten the overhanging branch.

"How come partner out-sie box?" Mr. Kim asked me in a hushed voice.

"Safety measure."

"I make legal," Mr. Kim said, as he interrupted Wiley's routine.

To Wiley's delight, Mr. Kim scampered over to the right tee marker, pulled it out of the ground, hopped a few yards and impaled the spike protruding through the marker back into the sod.

"Good man, Mr. Kim," Wiley said.

Mr. Kim shot a half-hearted grin at Wiley but felt slighted that Wiley hadn't used his new term of endearment, Sherlock.

A moment later, Wiley creamed his 6-iron. But just as there is a fine line between stupendous and stupid, there is also a fine line between knock-down and knocked-out. Wiley's ball sailed over the flag, the deep sand trap, and the ravine leading down into the river. The ball must have traveled 170 yards instead of the required 150.

"Is that over?" Wiley asked incredulously.

"Fraid so," Jack answered. "But it sure was impressive."

Already down two clubs for the day, Wiley limited his mayhem to kicking his tee out of the ground before returning his 6-iron to his bag to live another day.

I set up in Mr. Kim's annexed teeing area.

"Think good thoughts, Chief," Jack said.

"That's right, Chief," Blister added. "Whatever you do don't thinking of something like Janet Reno in the nude."

"You may want to add Madelyn Albright to that list," Jack joked.

Rather than focus on the task at hand, I was doing everything in my power to keep Janet Reno's clothes on. But just as I got her covered with body armor, Madelyn Albright came dancing across the screen. I banished her by thinking about the Exxon Valdez slamming into an Alaskan atoll.

Gotta focus, I thought to myself. Just a simple 8-iron away from destiny. I'm the Chief. It's up to me to lead the tribe out of the wilderness.

But just about then the full sequence of the disastrous Oliver flashed before me. Hooked iron left of trap; stubbed sand wedge; stubbed sand wedge; stubbed sand wedge into bunker; shot left in bunker; sand wedge out of bunker; one putt for milestone-killing Oliver.

Please sir, may I have another? And another? And another? And another?

My eyes glazed over as I looked at my Titleist NXT. I imagined Oliver walking forward with his plate extended to ask the taskmaster for one more dumpling. The ball blurred as it morphed into a white spongy substance. When it came back into focus, it had congealed into a golf-ball-sized dumpling. If Oliver could find his way out of the orphanage to Franklin Canyon's seventeenth tee, I could have given it to him because I had no use for it. In fact I was pretty sure that the longest driver on the PGA tour, Hank Kuehne, couldn't hit a dumpling across the river. In fact, Hank's 145-MPH swing would vaporize the dumpling into a cloud while my 85-MPH swing stood a good chance to splinter a few big chunks twenty or thirty yards. Man, when word gets around that ole Chief Tit can groove a dumpling further than Hank, he'll be laughed off the tour. Poor sap.

"Still thinking about Janet Reno, Chief?" Jack asked, interrupting my dumpling driving contest.

"Uh . . . oh, ah—no. Just having a little trouble focusing on this dumpling . . . uh, er—I mean ball."

The silent movie starring Janet Reno, Madelyn Albright, and Hank Kuehne was over. I started my backswing. I had one last thought—I sure hope that's not really a dumpling down there because if it is . . . it'll never clear the river.

The jarring of my arms as my club entered the turf two inches behind the ball provided the instant recognition that an Oliver was in play. The ball lurched forward much as a dumpling would and only traveled fifty yards. It plopped down beyond the ladies tee box well short of the river.

"Oh—big fattie," Mr. Kim announced.

"Ugh—that was ugly, Chief," Wiley said stating the obvious.

"Oooh," Blister and Jack groaned.

I flopped down in the cart and barely managed to eke out a 'nice shot' when Blister and Jack followed with solid shots. Jack hit his a little left of the green but not enough to get Betty Pullooski's hopes up.

Our cart barely got up to speed before Blister had to decelerate and let me walk the short distance to my fifty-yard drive. I waved goodbye to Mr. Kim but offered no departing wisdom.

I only had to hit a comfortable ninety-yard sand wedge, a distance I practice more than any other. And, rarely do I skull sand wedges at the driving range. However, as we all know, battlefield results vary greatly from training sorties. If I bladed one now, my round would be over.

"Plant one close, Chief," Blister said from behind the steering wheel.

My left shoulder pushed the wedge away from my body as images of screaming- banana wedges and dumplings danced through my head. The weight of the albatross around my neck was too much and my spine angled caved under the pressure. I dipped down into the ball, perhaps as a safeguard against a disastrous skull. Instead I hit another disastrous dumpling.

My heart sank into the waste area with my ball. An Oliver was really in play now. I dropped my club and rested both hands on my knees staring at the divot below me.

"Oh no—big fattie," I faintly heard from Mr. Kim as he fed the play-by-play to the other Mr. Kims.

With both hands still resting on my knees, I rotated my neck and looked at Blister. Both of his arms were folded over the steering wheel. His forehead was resting against his forearm as he stared at the bottom of the floorboard. He wasn't in the mood to see any more carnage. I broke my one-man huddle and schlepped back to the cart

"Is this just a microcosm of how life kicks us in the teeth?" Blister wanted to know.

I didn't answer. I wasn't in the mood for chit-chat.

Wiley wasn't going to be confused with Chatty Cathy either. He was in the process of executing a T-Rex drop when Blister barreled in behind the other cart.

"Hang in there," Jack pleaded with me as I slogged past him toward the waste area.

I stood at the crown of the hill below the green peering down into the waste area. I didn't see my ball. Had I come up short and hit the water? It struck me—if I had to take a drop, I was staring at a Linda Tripp.

My attention was diverted by movement between my legs. Startled, I jumped out of the way.

"Crap almighty!" I heard Wiley scream.

I looked down. It was Wiley's ball passing below me. His skulled chip was on its way over the crown toward the waste area. I was fascinated as I watched it career from one weed clump to another, as its path was altered several times. I dropped my putter near the edge of the green before descending down the hill. Wiley trudged along behind me. The glee that normally accompanied Wiley's misfortune was gone.

He and I were sharing the same foxhole with inbounds approaching from all directions. I was beginning to believe everything I had heard about the foxhole experience. There is no such thing as an atheist in a foxhole. I thought about having Blister throw me his Mother Teresa medallion.

"I may set a record for broken clubs today, Chief," Wiley said despondently.

"Well I still can't find my ball so I got my own troubles to worry about," I told him as I reclaimed the mantle of martyrdom.

"I'll hit my ball and help you look Chief," Wiley promised.

Topside, the mood was a polar opposite. Jack nearly holed out his chip as both he and Blister let out a cheer. Moments later when Wiley was improving his lie under the pretense of identifying his ball, Blister sank a twenty foot birdie putt. Jubilation erupted again.

"Woo-hoo!" Blister yelled, sounding like Homer Simpson.

The starkness of the contrast between the pit where Wiley and I dwelled and Cloud Nine, staffed by Jack and Blister, made me feel even more despondent. I zig-zagged through the entire waste area of clumped weeds and hardpan as Wiley prepared to hit. I suspended my search to watch the fiasco. I might as well have been watching Isaac Newton swing the wedge for him.

Wiley swung too hard and hit his ball flush. It sailed over the crest of the hill on a low trajectory that might reach the river. Jack turned his neck as he followed the ball flight. Wiley looked to Jack for a sign but didn't get one. Wiley bent both arms and turned his palms to the sky as if commanding Jack to make the call. With less animation than a major league umpire, Jack circled his index finger above his head, signaling the homerun. He punctuated the call with a borrowed phrase from Dodger announcer, Vin Sculley.

"You can tell it goodbye!"

Wiley fashioned a helicopter out of his wedge in honor of his ruined round and did a fly-over of the green. The back bunker stopped the cart-wheeling wedge from following the ball into the river. Barring a meltdown on eighteen, Wiley would only have to order two new clubs after the round.

"I'm done, Chief," Wiley said, as his emotion vanished.

Wiley turned his attention to the rescue effort. I was quickly running out of time. If I couldn't find my ball in another minute, I would have to take a penalty and take a drop. I brushed back sweat, which was beginning to coagulate above my short sideburns in front of both ears. It suddenly dawned on me where happy-go-lucky Existentialist writer Jean Paul Sartre got his inspiration for his books. At the moment I was guessing he wrote his highly acclaimed book, *Nausea,* after a particularly disappointing round of golf. Obviously Sartre had never had a milestone round ruined on the 17th hole at Franklin Canyon like Wiley and me, otherwise we would have been reading his best seller: *Whirling Room, Leg over the Bed, Foot on the Floor, Nausea.* My conversion to Existentialism was nearly complete when Wiley gave me reason to reconsider.

"I got you over here, Chief," Wiley announced.

I felt a rush of adrenaline. He picked at a crack in the hardpan, before reaching in and extracting the ball from its subterranean hiding place.

"It's yours alright," Wiley said assuredly.

243

Wiley did me one better. He dropped the ball and nudged it with his foot until he was satisfied with its lie on top of an island of mowed weeds. He saved me the trouble of going through the charade of taking a semi-legitimate drop.

"Play it right here, Chief," Wiley advised me.

"Thanks, comrade," I replied humbly.

Wiley seemed unusually calm. It must have been the loss of tension that comes with capitulation. One more bad shot and I could join him.

"What ever you do Chief—don't leave it short," Wiley coached me.

"Right," was the only response I could muster.

"Of course, don't hit it long either," he added.

"You got any more gold nuggets?" I asked, as my annoyance with him was rekindled.

"I think that covers it, Chief."

I took two practice swings before looking up at Wiley one last time. He nodded his mustard-covered face in approval.

Not too hard, I thought to myself.

Not too easy.

Not too hard.

Not too easy.

The indecision allowed the small muscle groups in my hands to stage a coup and overpower my large muscles in my shoulder as I swung. The resulting skull, slammed into the side of the hill slowing its speed before being propelled forward out of our view.

"First cut," Blister announced.

"Nice. Oh, so nice," Wiley said with a laugh. "It's almost over, Chief."

Wiley and I scampered up the hill. I was pleasantly surprised when I saw my ball resting on the first cut of the green. The red flag was straight up a gentle slope, only fifteen feet away.

"Man I'd give my left nut to sink a putt like you did, right about now," I told Blister.

"I don't think there's much of a market for your nuts," Jack snickered.

Anxious to finish the hole, I stepped over the fifteen-foot putt I had tapped hundreds of times on the 17th green, and spanked it fifteen feet—albeit four feet left of target. The self-loathing returned.

"That's good Chief," Blister blurted.

"No it's not. I've gotta make this one."

I didn't want to be known as the Michael Strahan of the Red Ball People. Strahan, of course, was the popular New York Giants defensive end who set a single season record for sacks at 22½. During a lopsided loss to the Packers, Strahan was awarded the coveted sack crown when his friend, Packer quarterback Brett Favre, mysteriously ran a bootleg to Strahan's side of the line with two minutes to go in the season and clumsily fell down in front of him. To complete the pretension, Favre patted Strahan on the back and gave him the ball as a keepsake.

Like Strahan*, I didn't want to be known as Chief* Tit. I could see the emails already:

'Hey, how about that marvelous round that the Chief* had?'

'Did you guys hear that the Chief* broke eighty?'

'The Chief* finally conquered the 17th hole.'

When the day was over, no one would care or even remember that Blister kicked back a couple of putts or a few too many Red Ball People amendments were invoked. Picking up a four-foot side hill putt when an Oliver was in play while a milestone round hung in the balance, was a different matter. The incident would be branded into the memory banks of all four of us and would serve as the defining moment of the round— a round with a giant asterisk. As good-intentioned as Blister's offer was, I wasn't going to let him be my Brett Favre.

The tribe was subdued. After three straight pars Jack typically would have pulled his shorts down and mooned us. But, they knew what was at stake. They had seen my previous excruciating meltdowns on seventeen and eighteen.

I lined up the side hill putt as the tribe held their breath. The distance was well outside my kill-zone of six inches. I read a four-inch break from left to right. Adrenaline made my wrists twitch. All factors considered, I guessed my success rate was in the 40% neighborhood.

I pulled my putter back. Quivering hands forced the face to toe-in. To compensate, I pulled the putter outside the target line, stabbed at the ball, and was careful to jerk my head up at contact.

Two wrongs made a right. All the improper techniques cancelled each other out and the ball curled into the hole for a double bogey five. I was still a contender.

"Way to get it done, Chief," Jack cheered, as he also performed the honor of picking my ball out of the hole.

"Whew!" I sighed. "Someone get me a wiener and beer before I die."

Officially, the teams tied on the hole for the bet. What a shame for Blister. Saddled with Wiley, his birdie wasn't good enough to beat Jack's par and my double. Though it was customary for a team to win a capitulated hole, I didn't want to press the issue. If Jack wanted to take aim at Wiley, he was on his own. Wiley had found my ball and saved me a stroke and I didn't want to tip the karma cart by telling him he owed me money.

Hole 18
The Umbrella Man
on the Grassy Knoll

B efore Jack came to a complete stop, Wiley sprung from the cart and made his way to the shoe brush attached to the ball cleaner and scraped off the sludge accumulated from the waste area. Small clouds of smoke swirled about his face as he dragged on his cigar to rekindle the fire. Jack debated whether he should mount a challenge to the Wolf bet, which ended in a tie when Wiley abandoned the hole.

"Are we pushing on the last hole?" Jack asked to no one in particular, testing the waters.

"I don't really care," Wiley said somberly, still smarting from his abrupt collapse.

"Let's just roll it over," I told Jack, losing my appetite for kicking an adversary when he's down.

"You gave it a good run Wiley," Blister said trying to cheer him up.

"If you think about it . . . the Chief and I were really overdue for an Oliver."

"In fact, were still overdue," I cautioned.

"I don't want to hear any more talk like that, Chief!" Blister said. "It's bad luck. Maybe Mother T can help with a guiding hand on the final hole."

"I think I'm done with Mother Teresa for the day," I replied. "I shouldn't need her on this hole. If I can't par the easiest hole on the course, then I don't deserve to break eighty."

The par 5, final hole was the easiest hole on the course, measuring 461 yards, but playing thirty yards shorter with the tail wind. The tee box sat on a peninsula that was created by a hair pin in the river. The river flowed westerly, from the green to the tee-box, and created a lateral hazard to the left of the fairway for the entire length of the hole. On the right side, the kamikaze crawdad pond came into play on the second shot but was well out of reach from the tee box.

A small protrusion of the river bank lined with oaks and scrub brush, jutted to the south just beyond the teeing area and turned the hole into a slight dogleg left for the first seventy-five yards. The Pullooski sisters had a year-round camping permit for the area and usually overstayed their welcome. If there was ever any doubt about who the YANKee-doodle-dandy was for the round, the dogleg often settled the score.

The line of pines that separated the eighteenth and tenth fairways stretched all the way to the pond and was the most contentious ground on the course as golfers from both fairways mistakenly played the other foursome's balls. The green had three traps on the left, but did more to protect balls from drowning than anything else.

A grassy knoll created a hump on the right side of the fairway some one hundred and fifty yards out and sat between the flat fairway and a steeply sloped rise that led to the tenth green. The grassy knoll also had a little mysterious history behind it. During a springtime round a year and a half earlier we had experienced intermittent spring showers. As a result of the unstable weather, we were one of the few foursomes on the course that day. No one had been in front of us the entire day—until we got to the tee box on eighteen. Though the sun had parted the clouds, a lone person with an umbrella loomed on the grassy knoll as if waiting for a presidential motorcade. Even though the umbrella-man had a golf bag with him, we thought it was highly surreal that a mysterious umbrella-man would suddenly appear on a grassy knoll. To this day, Jack thinks the man was part of some sinister conspiracy and had lost his way to a book depository.

"I'll tell you one thing Chief, you're buying us all lunch if you break eighty," Blister informed me.

"I second that Chief, and I'm getting a little hungry," Jack added.

"Wiley should be buying lunch," I countered. "He's the guy with all the money."

The tribe knew I was dead-on. Wiley had sold a few properties lately and was loaded with cash. So flush, in fact, that he considered entirely new avenues in which to blow his load. His most intriguing proposal was to prove once and for all that baseball players really are the stupid-est athletes.

Jose Canseco Makes an Offer
Wiley Can't Refuse

Just as Wiley became committed to his quest, he stumbled upon a news story that was sure to prove his point. He read that former A's slugger and Bash Brother, Jose Canseco, was under house arrest once again at his home in Florida for yet another barroom brawl. Under the terms of the court order, the slugger was fitted with an electronic ankle bracelet and was not allowed to leave his property without his parole officer's approval. To make a little money on the side, Canseco started a web site, which advertised a novel idea that only a baseball player could think up—he offered to spend a day at his house with any fan who was willing to cough up $10,000.

Since the court had essentially relegated him to sitting on his ass and watching TV all day, why not invite a lazy fan over who had a little too much money on his hands? Canseco had already tested the adage—'a fool and his money are soon parted,' and he was more than willing to apply the adage to his fan base. Regrettably for Canseco, his plan was based on the reliability of the premise of another adage, namely—'the bigger fool theory'.

Canseco's plan went awry when the slugger failed to realize that there really is a finite supply of fools and he was already at the top of the heap. Nevertheless, Wiley considered offering Canseco a package deal for $15,000 whereby he would fly in a foursome of the Red Ball People, who would be more than happy to lounge around Canseco's pool to confirm Wiley's theory. Sadly, Wiley's wife got wind of the idea and diverted the money toward refurbishing the kitchen.

———————

Blister walked to the tip of the peninsula tee box and peered around the corner of the oak trees.

"All clear Chief," he announced. "It's your moment."

"Time to show us what you're made of, Chief," Jack added.

"I'm living my dreams through you now," Wiley said, adding to the growing list of clichés.

It was only appropriate that I start the hole off. The last thing I needed was a picnic with the Pullooskis so I adopted an ultra-conservative stance and aimed far to the right, toward the grassy knoll.

"Where you aiming, Chief?" Jack wanted to know.

"Grassy knoll."

"Good. I don't think you'll have any trouble from the umbrella-man today."

"You mind if I hit while you perpetuate a conspiracy?"

"Not at all, Chief. Have at it."

My minimum expectation was to pop a 150-yard drive and that's precisely what I did. On another par 5, I would have been in trouble but not the eighteenth at Franklin Canyon. I could still reach the green with a long iron and a wedge.

"It ain't gonna hurt you Chief," Wiley said.

Blister followed with a rocket into the Pullooski campsite for one last rendezvous with Betty. Jack was awarded the mantle of YANKee-doodle-dandy of the round when he did the same a moment later.

"Jumpin Jesus, how do you expect me to follow those garbage shots?" Wiley asked.

"You might as well join the Pullooski festivities. They're in full swing on the left," Jack encouraged him.

I could tell by Wiley's alignment that he too would be testing his ability to hit a draw around the oak tree at the tip of the Pullooski picnic grounds.

"You're aiming pretty far left," I warned him.

"No guts—no glory, Chief."

Wiley soon discovered that no glory often goes hand in hand with no common sense. He came over the top of the ball and yanked it left of the oak, warming the heart of one of the Pullooski cousins.

"Don't say I didn't warn you," I said, against my better judgment.

"Shut-up, Chief," Wiley flashed back.

"I guess that means I gotta go wolf," I announced.

"With a rollover too," Jack whined.

Wiley's threat was officially over. He could score no better than a six and I could score no worse than an eight, owing to the maximum number of beads in the Red Ball People abacus. His ass was kicked. Now if I could only break eighty, and rub his nose in the carpet!

We drove the short distance thirty yards beyond the eastern side of the bridge, to the Pullooski neighborhood. All three players threatened to make a mockery of my lateral hazard amendment and dropped fifteen yards to the south of where their ball entered the hazard. However, at this point in the round, the strokes were perfunctory since the entire attention was on me breaking eighty.

Perhaps because no one had anything to lose, all three advanced their balls more than two hundred yards up the fairway.

"It don't get any better than that," Jack said, as he gave both Wiley and Blister a knuckle press.

"It's odd," Wiley replied, "some of the best hits of the round always seem to happen when you've finally lost interest."

"It's because you no longer have tension interfering," Blister guessed.

"That's right," Jack agreed. "Tension is the biggest cause of problems whether you're talking about golf or work."

I offered my own theory.

"It's a lot like that albatross I was wearing back on seventeen. Sometimes it's just wrapped so tight around your neck—the only way you can get rid of it is by cutting off your head."

The tribe gazed at me with glossy looks. Sometimes my analogies were a little deep for them to comprehend.

"Tension's got to be the biggest problem in golf," Blister decided. "I'm kinda surprised more PGA players don't take a massive hit before they play a round."

"Yeah, it sure helps you," Wiley replied, chiding Blister.

"How about those putts on seventeen and thirteen?" Blister asked, trying to build his case.

"How about the Linda Tripp on fourteen?" Wiley asked.

"Well that wasn't tension . . . that was just lack of ability," Blister countered.

"If I could get rid of tension, I bet I could break eighty once a month," I bet the tribe.

"Yeah, but how do you get rid of it," Jack asked. "That's got to be one of the mysteries of the universe."

Jack was right. Tension was one of the biggest mysteries of the universe. However, it was nowhere near the top of the list.

Mysteries of the Universe

The largest enigma of 20th century physics was, and still is, the clash between quantum mechanics and the general theory of relativity. Quantum mechanics emerged with the discovery of the electron in 1897 but the atom remained only a mathematical likelihood for many more years since no one could empirically prove its existence. In the case of relativity, Einstein relied on the behavior of electromagnetism and gravity to extrapolate his theories of how time is unified with space to form a timespace continuum as the accurate description of the universe.

The incompatibility of the two theories primarily rests with the recognition that the laws that apply to general relativity are inconsistent with particle behavior unless the effects of gravity are ignored. In a nutshell, in quantum mechanics, particle interactions can occur at zero distance but Einstein's theory of gravity make no sense at zero distance. Einstein argued that there had to be a unifying principle to insure that the laws governing large spatial bodies (relativity) were consistent with the laws governing atomic (quantum mechanics) particles. He was so certain that an eventual unifying body of physics and mathematics would eventually be discovered, he claimed, "God does not roll dice."

Sadly, the vast majority of physicists are dedicated to tackling the problem only at a theoretical level, which will yield only modest improvements to our daily lives. A larger and more worthwhile challenge would be to use a more pragmatic approach and define a body of physics that explains and lends itself to solving the more immediate problems, like say—tension in the golf swing. Some even more pressing mysteries that pervade the day to day human experience that could use a little more scientific attention are described below.

The Blaring Television Conundrum

Not long after TV was invented in the late forties, millions of people who dozed off while watching late night television encountered the conundrum of the blaring television. Even before remote controls where invented, folks would doze off on their couches usually after a few beers only to awake to a blaring TV whose decibel level had mysteriously doubled since the observer had fallen asleep.

The present day phenomenon seems to be more pronounced on Friday and Saturday nights and often occurs when the subject dozes off while watching the Late Show or the Tonight Show. Some theorists have suggested that the TV viewer has simply rolled over on the remote control causing a layer of body lard to depress against the volume-up sound button as they passed into a state of sleep. However, this theory has too many inconsistencies.

First, the volume never goes down, indicating a strong incompatibility with the laws of probability, which would predict an equal chance for the body lard to roll on top of the volume-down button as often as the volume-up button. Secondly, the phenomenon is encountered even when the subject loses the remote control in the lining of the couch.

Other sound wave experts such as renowned mathematician, prime number expert, Gesundheitist, Nobel Laureate econometric model calibrator, and dolphin trainer, Professor Daniel Goldston, speculate that the interaction of sound waves caused by snoring somehow interact with cathode rays to create electromagnetic pressure on the TV's sound circuitry. Whatever the explanation, until scientists put some attention on this deserving problem, millions of wives across the world will continue to bop their husbands on the head and wake us from our late night golden slumbers and rudely order us to stifle the blaring TV.

Unified Sock Theory

While most physicists are concerned with finding a unifying theory between General Relativity and Quantum Mechanics, their time would obviously be better spent attempting to discover a unified sock theory. The problem of the missing sock seems to have its historical roots in the invention of the washing machine and gained even more steam with the introduction of the clothes dryer.

Since the introduction of these two ghastly devices, sock drawers across the world have been occupied with orphaned socks and mankind has been plagued with an unfulfilled expectation that the missing partner will one day materialize in a basket of laundry. But we all know that this story never has a happy ending.

In fact, to see just how pervasive this problem really is, I would encourage the reader to drop whatever you are doing, and peer inside your sock drawer. If you don't find a few orphaned stragglers—I'll gladly send you a million bucks. Many people who don't have a solid grounding in physics mistakenly believe that static-cling is the real culprit. As a result, a billion-dollar industry to eliminate static-cling with products such as Bounce, have flourished. Well, I got news for you. All Bounce does is guarantee that you walk around smelling like a peppermint stick. In fact, when I wash my socks, I take every precaution short of assigning The Nation of Islam to guard the washroom. Yet at the end of the month, I still have at least three orphans looking for their twin brother.

I suspect there is a much more sinister explanation. After eliminating the usual suspects such as static-cling, and a knotted pant leg, I think we can reasonably postulate the existence of a sock worm-hole in the timespace continuum. For the layman, you can think of the sock worm-hole as an invisible tunnel, a tear in the timespace continuum to a parallel universe, if you will.

It's not hard to imagine what this parallel universe is like. It has billions of unmatched socks and tons of head covers from all the guys you see walking around golf courses without head covers for their brand new $400 drivers. It has my baby socks; my gym socks from high school; one of my FootJoy golf socks; my missing Christmas stocking; my Titleist 3-wood head cover; my Titleist driver head cover; and of course one of the Armani socks I bought for $15 each last week to match one of my suits I had to wear for a job interview for a job I most likely didn't get because I was wearing mismatched socks.

While the sock worm-hole theory may seem outlandish to the un-initiated, it is worth noting that black holes were theoretical necessities that emanated from Einstein's General Theory of Relativity long before the Hubble telescope captured photos of light escaping from ionized dust as the particles were sucked into a black hole.

Of course it's worth noting, that while the majority of missing socks and head covers indeed dwell in the parallel universe—never to return, other socks and head covers are just lost in our own universe. To assist with the latter problem, I'd like to plug my invention—Chief Tit's Global

Positioning System SockFinder™ (GPS SockFinder™). The invention consisted of two components: a microchip that is implanted into socks and head covers by manufacturers; and GPS SockFinder™ Palm Pilot software.

The device works as follows. The microchip implanted in the sock or head cover beams its position to a geostatic satellite which in turn sends a wireless transmission of the sock's coordinates to the Palm Pilot loaded with the GPS SockFinder™ software. The victim of the lost article simply activates the Palm Pilot GPS SockFinder™ software, which sounds a series of beeps similar to a Geiger-counter that grows more rapid the closer the person gets to the lost item.

The original business model called for licensing the technology to Procter & Gamble, the company that manufactures the static-cling product, Bounce. However, after exhaustive field tests it was apparent that even the GPS SockFinder™ had limited success in locating lost socks, further adding credence to the General Theory of Sock Worm-holes.

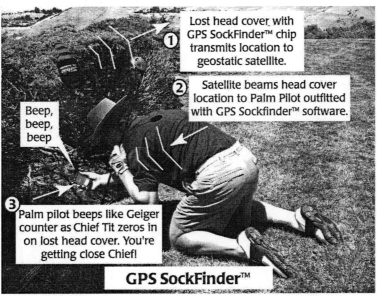

Chief Tit uses GPS SockFinder™ to locate missing head cover

Of course, in addition to modern science not putting enough energy into solving golf's tension problem, they were also woefully deficient in addressing the attention problem as well. Rather than concentrate on breaking eighty, I was suddenly preoccupied with all the money I was going to pile up with my inventions. Blister woke me from my slumber.

"Let's go Chief, what are you waiting for?"

As we drove the short distance south to my ball, Blister wanted to rehash my remaining strategy for the round.

"So how you gonna play it, Chief?"

"I think the smart play is to stay away from the pond and cream a 3-iron down the left side of the fairway. Even if I hook it a little, I think I'm too far out to worry about reaching the river."

"I agree completely, Chief," Blister said. "Just stay away from the woods and you're home free."

In the back of my mind a little shoot of concern began to sprout. Blister was no better a caddie than he was a golfer. If he liked the strategy, it probably had an inherent flaw that I hadn't discovered. A well hit 3-iron should put me at 110-yards for my third shot, the perfect gap wedge. On the other hand, perhaps I could reach the river on the left with a hook. There was a lot of dead grass and hardpan near the cart path on the left. A screaming hook could roll a long way over hardpan. And I did have a slight side hill lie—the type that lends itself to a hook. Maybe I should use a 4-iron. That would put me at 120-yards and would serve as an added precaution against getting wet. I decided to over-think the situation a little further and get my stupid caddie's opinion. I ran the various scenarios by Blister.

"I don't know Chief—It's six of one and two dozen of the other. I'd rather hit a gap or a sand for my last iron over a pitching wedge."

"Uh-huh."

"You'd have to hit a pretty bad 3-iron to hit the river from here, Chief," Blister decided.

Although Blister had a spotty track record, at best, as a caddie, I decided that he was probably right and I gave him the benefit of the doubt. I pulled my 3-iron.

"OK Chief, just be committed."

I might not get this chance again, I thought to myself, without a significant rework of the Red Ball People Amendments. I took aim down the left side. Everything felt good as I made a conscious effort to maintain a good tempo. The tension in my arms had dissipated. I was ready to step up to the next level, which is probably exactly the way Bill Buckner felt about things before letting a slow rolling grounder squirt between his legs in the sixth game of the 1986 World Series.

I immediately recognized that this was not the best of times to be thinking about Bill Buckner, and quickly banished the thought by thinking about Calton Fisk's 1975 game six World Series homer, instead. That's right, I thought to myself—think of Fisk.

All I had to do was execute one more 3-iron. I started my downswing, and thought—Fisk. Be like Fisk! He's the man. Fisk, Fisk, Fisk.

Buckner!

As I tried to keep my mental images in order, Buckner stepped in and shoved Fisk out of the way just as I made contact. I looked up in horror and saw a screaming banana hooking over the one hundred and fifty yard marker.

"*Fore!*" Blister yelled to Jack and Wiley, who were already taking cover.

"Jesus H. Christ—*Sit down! Sit down!*" I yelled.

The banana struck the fairway in front of Jack and Wiley and peeled across the cart path into the dried grass and hardpan.

"If that ball goes in—I'll kill myself!" I promised Blister. "And then you."

The ball looked like it might stop on the dry grass a few feet from the edge of the riverbank. But, alas . . . the event horizon sniffed it out and sucked on it until it was a goner. It was the biggest tragedy I had ever encountered without someone actually dying. I looked at Blister. From the look on his face I couldn't tell who was more disappointed, him or me.

"Technically—you're still alive Chief."

"Technically—you could be elected president."

What a blunder! If only I hit a 4-iron.

"You need a hug Chief?" Blister asked politely.

"A high-caliber revolver might be a little more to my liking."

I drove the cart forward to the 150-yard marker to meet up with Jack and Wiley. There was no need for Wiley and Jack to share their condolences. Their faces said it all. Jack patted me on the shoulder twice without saying a word before turning and proceeding to his ball.

"Let me buy you a drink, Chief," Wiley said, handing me a Heinie.

257

I sat in the cart and chugged the beer as the other three players stood in front of me to take turns hitting their balls. Babs and Donetta were still parked to the left of the green but stood outside their carts looking down the fairway. It appeared that we would have a gallery.

I replayed the stroke again and again. Each time I imagined that there was a gopher mound, a clump of grass, or a twig to stop the ball from rolling into the hazard.

"Swoosh," I heard coming from Jack's 7-iron.

I exited from my dream of an alternative view of history and looked up to see Jack's ball sailing to the front of the green.

"Way to finish!" Blister said, as he posed with Jack.

A few moments later Wiley hit the back of the green and Blister hit the fringe to the right. Everyone was enjoying their own little Cinderella story on the final hole except me, though I did have a starring role in the life of Humpty Dumpty.

Jack, Wiley, and Blister exchanged high-fives and patted each other on the back as I stayed in the cart and moped. After the circle-jerk was over, Blister flopped down in the passenger seat.

"Good going," I said, with tepid praise.

I spun the wheel and turned the cart north to locate the drop area. Wiley and Jack were several yards ahead trotting back to their cart when Jack sent a shock of panic up my spine.

Without warning, Jack collapsed on the fairway in a heap of agony and began clutching his left leg. Wiley was so startled he jumped away before rushing over and crouching by Jack's side. Oh my God, I thought, Jack's been taken out by the umbrella-man on the grassy knoll.

I sped over to the scene, carelessly driving over Wiley's 6-iron that he had dropped on the ground a moment earlier. Blister bolted from the cart and rushed to Jack's side. I half expected to see an entry wound in Jack's neck from a 25-caliber umbrella bullet, but in fact, there was no blood at all. I was relieved to see that Jack was not clutching his chest, but his left calf.

"Get my shoe off!" he screamed.

Blister quickly dropped to his knees and yanked Jack's shoe off without bothering to untie the shoestrings. I quickly spotted the problem. Jack's calf had ballooned to a bulging knot indicating nothing more than a painful, yet debilitating cramp.

"Ouhhh—I can't straighten my leg," Jack screamed, as he writhed in pain.

Wiley began massaging the calf as I tried to help Jack sit up. Jack slowly tried to straighten his leg by pushing on the top of his knee with both hands. Jack's grimace turned into a mild frown as the muscle stretched and receded back to its normal position. But just as we thought the danger had passed, his toes began to cramp.

"Oh Jesus—rub my toes," Jack wailed.

"Huh?" Blister asked, seeking a little more clarification.

"Rub my toes!" Jack screamed.

"You mean it?" Blister asked. "Here Chief, you want to take over?"

"I ain't rubbing Jack's toes," I said with certain finality. "I'll take the risk that he can live without it."

"I got the calf," Wiley said with a preemptive strike.

"Ouhhh—my foot's killing me!" Jack screamed, as he wondered what the holdup was. "Rub my toes, Blister!"

"Not unless you guys promise not to tell anyone that I rubbed Jack's smelly feet," Blister said, opening negotiations.

To Jack's dismay, Wiley and I began chuckling. We probably would have been more agreeable to the requested medical attention if we knew a little less about Jack's laundry habits. As we all knew, Jack's socks weren't always part of the scheduled maintenance. His golf socks often stewed in the trunk of his car for a couple weeks and were sometimes worn two or three times before they were recycled to the laundry basket.

"OK Blister, we promise," Wiley lied.

Reluctantly, Blister seized Jack's toes and bent them back and forth until the spasm subsided.

"Ah, that feels better," Jack said as his frown disappeared.

"OK that should be enough," Blister concluded as he withdrew his hand from Jack's foot.

Jack sat up on his elbows and looked down at his left foot as he continued to wiggle his toes back and forth.

After another minute, Blister and I clutched the back of Jack's arms and helped him to his feet. The crisis was over. Jack limped the short distance to his cart and leaned on the roof as he thrust his leg back to stretch out the hamstring and calf muscle.

"I was sure the umbrella-man got you Jack," I informed him.

"It felt like it," Jack agreed. "Man that sure hurt. Did you see the size of that bulge."

"Holy Taliban, Jack, I'm gonna have to piss on my hands just to get the smell off," Blister confessed, which drew laughter from all of us.

Jack eased himself into the cart as Wiley turned to find his 6-iron. Regrettably the front wheel of my cart had transformed Wiley's 6-iron into a 2-iron with fourteen degrees of loft.

"Oh—that doesn't look too good does it? Keah, keah," Blister giggled.

"Sorry Wiley," I said, unable to contain a giggle. "You've still got eleven good clubs in the bag."

"Make that ten Chief," Wiley declared. "I'm gonna take one of em and shove it up your ass."

We had a hardy laugh at Wiley's empty threat. Between the guzzled beer and the rush of adrenaline from believing we were under assault from the umbrella-man, I was feeling much better about things. Maybe I could still be the Cinderella story after all.

Blister and I drove the cart to the edge of the river, careful not to allow the event horizon to suck it over the bank. Blister peered over the side as if looking for an AWOL soldier. I pulled a second ball from my pocket and began sizing up the drop zone.

"There's a good spot," Blister said, pointing to the other side of the cart path.

"That's alright," I said, rejecting his suggestion. "I'll just drop here on these dead weeds."

"You ought to at least give yourself a chance, Chief," Blister argued.

"It don't matter anymore. I'll drop within two club lengths for once."

The patch of dead grass was about the size of a wash towel. It had a small baseball sized area of hardpan, which I covered with my left foot. I raised the ball to shoulder height and let it fall to the turf. It felt awkward to drop the ball from that high off the ground after years of T-Rex drops.

"You got a limb in front of you, Chief," Blister warned me.

"I see it."

"Have it your way, Chief," Blister said.

I backed up and selected my line. For the first time of the day I wasn't hampered by positive thoughts that I knew would morph to negative thoughts. I wasn't hampered by negative thoughts either. I didn't have any thoughts whatsoever. I was slaphappy from guzzling Heinies. I just wanted the round to be over and the fastest way to make that happen was to step up and spank the ball with my 9-iron.

"Swoosh."

The lack of sound from smacked lumber assured me that I had missed the oak limb. I mustered the courage to look to the sky for my NXT. It was a thing of beauty. I glanced down at the flag and back up to the ball. The two were converging. Blister recognized the magnitude of the moment immediately.

"Right at it, Chief!" Blister yelled as the ball began its decent. "I think you got an *out of the ass* shot."

"Be the one!" I screamed.

The ball slammed down with such force that it plugged without a bounce. Wiley, Jack, and the sisters erupted in cheer as they jumped in the air and kicked their heels.

"Three feet!" Wiley yelled. "Totally *out of the ass*, Chief!"

"Chief, Chief, Chief," Jack and Wiley began chanting. Blister joined in.

"You've done it, Chief! You pulled one right out of the ole poop-shooter!" Blister bellowed with jubilation as he locked arms with me and began twirling me in a circle.

"Woo-hoo," I yelled.

The fatigue I felt moments earlier had disappeared. In one brilliant swing, I was on the way to saving par, saving the round, and winning the coveted *'out of the ass'* bet. I floored the cart and got it up to its maximum cruising speed of 8-MPH.

As I drove by the right front sand trap I caught my first glimpse of the ball. It was certainly within three feet. It might have been closer to 2 ½. I slammed on the brake and skidded to a stop behind Jack and Wiley's cart and got an idea what Charles Lindbergh must have felt like driving down Broadway for a ticker tape parade. Wiley and Jack were still giddy. Both had been waiting behind their cart and swarmed me before I could even get out of the cart. Babs and Donnetta stood a few feet off to the side of Jack and Wiley's cart and clapped. Jack and Wiley took turns pushing me on the shoulder as Blister banged in to me from the right side. When I finally was able to push Jack and Wiley aside, Jack stepped up and gave me a NFL chest bump, his highest compliment.

"That was some shot, Chief!" Jack howled.

"I really didn't think you had it in you," Wiley admitted.

"Boy you guys really had some highlights on this hole," Donetta chimed in.

"Just make sure you don't shake Blister's hand!" I warned Donetta.

"What's wrong with his hand?" she asked.

"He's been rubbing Jack's toes for the last few minutes and it wasn't pretty."

The sisters giggled as I launched into my stand-up routine. I'm always amazed how a stiff 9-iron can transform a golfer into Jackie Gleason in a matter of seconds.

"Shut up Chief," Blister muttered from behind the cart. "Your hero's welcome is over."

I continued to chat with the sisters about my Herculean feat of breaking eighty as the others circled the green to tend to their putts. I described several key shots as well as the episodes of adversity. I recounted my birdies on nine and fourteen, and my miraculous drive aided by Mother Teresa. I was in the middle of a story about the grueling dogfight between Wiley and me on the sixteenth when my story was interrupted by Blister.

"Here you go, Chief," Blister said as he whacked my ball to me and then leaned down to repair the ball mark.

"You're not going to putt that out?" Babs asked incredulously as I leaned over to snag the rolling ball.

"Come on, Dedalus—you gotta putt that out," Donetta added. "You want to please the gallery don't you?"

"No one picks up the putt that breaks eighty!" Babs continued.

"Not even Bill Clinton?" Wiley wanted to know.

"Huh?" Babs asked, not fully aware of the former president's habit of conceding his own lengthy putts.

Suddenly I felt like a retreating marine who had just been ordered back into battle. The tribe would certainly not make a big deal out of me picking up a putt of thirty inches. In fact, I can't remember anyone who didn't pick up a putt that was much less than four feet for the entire day. What was so damn special about this putt? I was beginning to regret that Babs and Donetta had stayed behind to watch us finish.

Dumb bitches.

If I didn't putt out, I was certain I could count on Babs to spread the story around the pro shop. It was only a matter of time before they starting reserving my starting times with my new name—Chief* Tit . . .the guy who saved his 79* with a perfect 9-iron and a one* putt. The name would quickly spread to the tribe as they all had a voracious appetite for scandal. What I really needed was Brett Favre to step in and sink the putt for me.

My fate was sealed. I walked to the cart and retrieved my putter like it was no big deal. But I might as well have been pulling a battle-axe out of my bag because I felt like a gladiator stepping into the Parthenon against an overwhelming force of lions.

"You gonna putt out for us, Chief?" Wiley asked.

"Why not?" I answered, hiding my fear. "Got to make it legit," I added, not meaning a word of it.

I walked over to the hole and took a look at the distance from the hole to the ball mark Blister had just repaired. Since the tribe only cared about the encore, they hurriedly went through the motions. Jack easily two-putted, to set the Wolf betting bar at six. Only a catastrophe would force a tie of the two-hole rollover bet. Wiley followed with a two-putt for an 83, a stellar round by Red Ball People standards. Blister three-putted and broke 100 by two strokes.

The green and the glory was all mine.

Waiting to watch the tribe finish out had settled me down. It also gave me a chance to watch the break of the other three balls near the hole. I had a dead-straight 30-inch putt with no break. How hard could that be?

"Hey Chief—I forgot that you went Wolf," Wiley reminded me.

"Oh Yeah," Jack remembered. "This is for a lot of marbles, Chief!"

"Thanks for reminding me."

No question, the tribe viewed my task as more of a coronation than a putt. A 30-incher on eighteen was golf's closest thing to a victory lap. Babs and Donetta walked out to watch the feat. Blister picked up the white flag and moved to the left side of the hole and stood by Wiley and Jack.

"It's your moment, Chief," Jack said.

"Knock it close," Wiley joked, as the other chuckled.

I placed the ball a little to the left of the bruised grass where Blister had repaired my ball mark and walked to the far side of the hole to insure that I hadn't missed any aberration in the break.

"It's dead straight, Chief," Blister assured me.

"Looks that way," I concurred.

The others stood perfectly still as I stood over my ball and aligned my SeeMore putter. The distance was much too short to take a practice stroke and I knew I would look silly trying. Besides, a practice stroke only demonstrated that I had no confidence in myself. The fear had disappeared. I actually began to savor the moment.

I took one last look at the hole and reminded myself not to jerk my head up like I normally do. I started the club back as the gallery waited to erupt. After a few inches, I reversed the direction of the club toward the hole.

Contact!

The round was now out of my hands. I could do no more to screw it up. It was over. All I had to do was lean over and pick the ball up. Those were the immediate thoughts that crossed my mind before the ball reached the hole. I kept my head down in accordance with my earlier order to myself but quickly turned my eyes to follow the ball in the hole.

A surge of electricity shot through my chest.

The ball wasn't on line. I had pulled it. Now I jerked my head up. Could this be happening? The ball continued toward the left edge of the hole. Unless divinity intervened, the ball would miss the hole on the left. Just when I was sure all was lost, the influence from an unperceived anomaly to the left of the hole redirected the ball back to the hole where it caught the left lip. The extra gas I had applied, spun the ball toward the back rim and prolonged the tease.

Would it drop down or spin out?

I think we all know.

After all, this is intended to be a book about triumph and overcoming adversity. Regrettably, it's also a story about the game of golf.

The ball spun out.

I missed a three-fuckin' footer. A Yip-a-dee-doo-dah on the final stoke of the day.

"What a fuckin' disaster!" Wiley gasped.

"What the fuck just happened, Chief?" Jack blurted, with exasperation.

"What a fuckin' idiot!" Blister bellowed.

"What a Fuckhead!" I yelled as we all did our best to prove that the word fuck could be deployed as a verb, adverb, and noun equally well.

It should be noted, it was my sincere intent to keep this book PG-rated and not use cheap gimmicks like the use of the word *fuck* as a sentence-filler. However, if you have been playing golf every weekend for ten years like I have, and then miss a chance to break eighty for the first time because you missed a three-fuckin' footer, I think you can understand. Only two types of people know this agony—saps who have done the same thing and people who loaded up on Cisco stock during the first quarter of 2000.

We don't just shrug it off and say—"Gosh, we'll get em next time." No, sir. We yell *fuck* at the top of our lungs and make sure we do it with sufficient volume to insure that people like Mr. Kim who are 180-yards away are apprised of our performance so that he knows better than to ask how our round went inside the club house and risk being strangled with his own suspenders.

To appease Babs, I knocked the fuckin' ball the remaining fuckin' inch into the fuckin' hole for my fuckin' eighty. I also lost a fuckin' double rollover bet with the biggest payout of the day. Fuck me again.

I picked the ignominious ball out of the hole and launched it toward the pond, its proper resting place. But I missed that too. It came up short, though at least it didn't spin out. I couldn't even hit a fuckin' pond. Fuck me one more time.

"Oh—That's awful," Babs finally said. "If I thought there was any chance in the world you could have actually missed the putt I wouldn't have talked you into it."

"It ain't your fault, Babs," I replied, though I wasn't sure if I really meant it.

"Let's go get a burger and beer, Chief," Wiley said, trying to wring the sour taste out of all our mouths.

"Yeah, I can't get off this green quick enough," Blister announced, as he planted the flag back in the hole.

"Sorry Chief," Donetta said, as the sisters walked off the green with Blister and me. "You'll get it next time."

"Right—I'll get it next time," I uttered back, suppressing an urge to impale the center of her skull with the shaft of Wiley's broken 7-iron.

Final Score Card after 18 Holes

Hole	10	11	12	13	14	15	16	17	18	Front	Back	Total
Yardage	356	189	338	504	335	401	353	138	461	3088	3075	6163
Handicap	4	8	12	2	14	6	10	16	18			
Wiley	④	③	③	6	③->(o)	4 ^{6}	5	⑥ ^{8}	⑥	43	40	83
Chief Tit	④	③	5	⑥	④	4 ^{6}	5	5	^{9}6->(o)	39	41	80
Blister	4	6 ^{1}	5	⑤	7 ^{5}	5 ^{6}	5	②	⑦	52	46	98
Jack	5	4 ^{2}	④ ^{3}	7 ^{4}	7 ^{5}	④	④ ^{7}	③	⑥	51	44	95
Par	4	3	4	5	4	4	4	3	5	36	36	72

Notes:

/ => Signifies that player gets stroke

O => Signifies that player won bet

->(o) => Heiroglyphic for "out of ass."

[1] Blister surrenders to hole after hitting lob shot 170 yards across river, takes a Linda Tripp.

[2] 6 foot putt conceded to Jack to avoid 4-putting green. Wiley and Chief Tit pick up for impressive up and down.

[3] Favorable ruling allows Jack to save 16 strokes for clear-cutting around ball.

[4] Jack attempts to record Gesundheit score of 6. Actual score was 7.

[5] Blister and Jack are too tired to spawn after salmon run, both take a Linda Tripp.

[6] Mother Teresa blesses all but Jack's ball. All but Jack have miracle drives. Wiley tries to ice Chief Tit down.

[7] Jack wins two hole Wolf bet. Wiley invokes hyperbolic drop rule to gain 80 yards on drop.

[8] Newton's law of Reaction acts to bring Wiley's score back to equilibrium. Wiley quits hole to stop bleeding.

[9] Chief Tit wins "out of ass" bet and then ruins round with Yip-a-dee-doo-dah.

Clubhouse
Sweet Jesus, an Angel
Just Got His Wings!

W iley ordered a pitcher of beer from Steve the Bartender while Jack placed an order of four burgers with fries. As usual, he ordered the burgers without cheese since we were all watching our weight. Blister and I plopped ourselves down at one of the square tables in front of a giant satellite TV. Notre Dame was playing though we couldn't tell who their opponent was.

Blister and I debated the bets circled on the score card, which was more complicated than normal due to the high number of rollover bets on the back nine. Wiley won the most skins with thirteen, followed by Jack with twelve, who had a strong finish owing to his own Wolf bet and my Yip-a-dee-doo-dah on my own Wolf bet. I had ten and Blister finished with nine. Wiley poured each of us a dark beer as the money changed hands.

"How come everyone keeps asking—'what happened to my face'?" Wiley wanted to know. "Steve's the third person to ask."

"Beats me," Blister chuckled. "It's never looked better to me."

Blister turned his attention back to the score card and his eyes nearly crossed as he concentrated with his addition.

"Shall we see how many you would have won had you made the putt, Chief?" Blister asked with an insipid grin.

"What do you say, we pass on that one, Butthole."

"Actually it's pretty easy to tell," Wiley interjected. "It's four skins for all three of us. Chief would have had twenty-two skins—an all time high, I might add."

"That's another gold nugget of data I can really do without," I said, reproaching Wiley.

Wiley hadn't been to the restroom yet and I knew that we all had only a few more minutes to enjoy the mustard and mud collage on his face. If I guessed right, Babs was probably in the pro shop telling Nick the starter about my disaster. It was only a matter of time before Nick would make his way up the short flight of stairs to the clubhouse and give me the grief I deserved. With a little luck, Wiley would still be here and some of the attention could be deflected toward him.

"Thirty two bucks for the food," Jack announced as he sat down.

Fives and ones changed hands again.

I felt two hands on my shoulders. I turned to see Nick the starter and scratch player. His problem in breaking milestones occurred at the number 70.

"I guess you heard?" I asked.

"Tough luck, Chief. I've been there and it's brutal."

"It sure is. By the way—nice touch on combining the Mr. Kim singles."

"Yeah, I've been trying to get a Mr. Kim foursome together for a year. I've had a couple of triples, but today was the first home-run," Nick laughed. "So, I'm sure you're getting a lot of support from your buddies? They treating you OK after that tough finish?"

"Like a baby treats diapers."

"What the hell happened to you?" Nick said, turning his attention to Wiley.

"You're the fourth person that's asked me that!" Wiley scoffed. "Why's everyone keep asking me that?"

"You look like your face caught on fire and you put it out with a jar of mustard," Nick crowed.

Wiley bolted for the bathroom as the rest of us chortled at Nick's rather accurate analogy. Nick patted me twice on the shoulder before slipping into the kitchen to steal a Snickers bar.

Babs and Donetta climbed the steps from the pro shop and begged Steve to give them a free soda. After being hounded by several flirting players in the clubhouse, the sisters chose the table next to us to sip their drinks. I turned to Babs to let her know there was no ill will.

"Wiley should be remaking his face about now," I told her.

She smiled without laughing and said, "Nick told him, huh?"

"Yeah, he spilled the beans."

"I bet it was fun while it lasted?" Donetta guessed.

"It was . . . until the Chief put everybody on a downer," Blister informed them.

As Blister kidded with Babs, I spotted Jeb slipping through the side door near the bar coming in for his tenth cup of coffee. I dreaded the moment. He would be the first of many to ask me how my round went. It was only a matter of time before Mr. Kim and half a dozen other golfers I knew strolled by my table and made me relive the horror. Worse, Jeb was nosey and would insist on scrutinizing our score card. He had a gut feeling how all the players scored during the round after watching them play a few holes and often tried to validate his suspicions by peeking at everyone's score card whenever the opportunity presented itself. I found his habit very annoying but it was one of the eccentricities that we put up with. Sure enough, after picking up a cup of coffee from Steve he headed our direction.

"How'd it go, Wildroot?" Jeb bellowed.

"Missed a two and a half footer on the last green for an eighty?" I said, going straight to the facts.

"Gaaauuuuhh—are you pissing in my ear?" Jeb asked with more color than usual.

"I wish I were."

"Me too!" Blister giggled. "I'll piss in Jeb's ear."

"Aaaauuuuhh—watch your tongue!" Jeb cackled at Blister through a mouth full of yellow stained teeth. "You've broken eighty before haven't you, Wildroot?" Jeb asked me as my annoyance with him mounted.

"Nope," I said curtly.

"Oh, Oh, Gauuuuh, ha, ha, haaaack," Jeb belched as he hacked up a mouth full of flem howling at my calamity. "You must feel like a bucket full of crap—Gauuuck."

"Who was the big winner?" Jeb asked, refusing to leave us alone.

"Wiley topped us at thirteen," Blister answered. "Chief Tit . . . er, I mean Wildroot, would have had twenty-two had he not lost a double-Wolf rollover with a yipper on eighteen."

"Gauuuck, ha, ha, hooey—make that a cement truck full of crap," Jeb bellowed. "Let me see that score card," Jeb barked, as he leaned over and snatched it off the table.

Jeb was pouring over the score card when Wiley returned to the table with a freshly cleaned face.

"I got to hand it to you dickheads," Wiley started, "that's the worst little three-hour gag since Blister walked around with toilet paper hanging out the back of his pants. I couldn't figure out why you guys were calling me snowman. I sure wasn't buying that iceman explanation though."

The levity that comes with the moment when a victim discovers that he's been the object of a three-hour joke took my mind off the debacle on the last hole for a moment. Babs and Donetta joined in as we all laughed at Wiley's expense. Regrettably for Wiley, he cleaned up one major mess on his face only to expose another on top of his head when he removed his cap.

"Oh—nice hat hair!" Jack roared, complimenting Wiley on the gangly swirl of matted hair.

"You should know better than to take your hat off before you get home," Blister giggled.

"Well I'd rather have hat hair to deal with than no hair at all," Wiley retorted with a swipe at Blister.

"Hey Wildroot," Jeb barged-in, interrupting our onslaught on Wiley, "What's the deal with hole thirteen?"

Jeb tapped the score card with his cigar-stained stubby finger.

"What'd you mean?" I asked with a stern look of irritation.

"I thought you told me you had a par."

"That's right."

"Well you wrote it down as a six," Jeb advised, as the table went silent and turned their eyes to Jeb.

I shot a glance at Blister who sported a goofy Stan Laurel look. I recalled that he had written down the scores after the hole, a responsibility I normally assumed in order to avoid such slip-ups.

"And *you* told me you took a bogey on thirteen!" Jeb exhorted. He waved an accusing finger at Blister as the evidentiary proceeding continued. "Aren't you the one who sunk the twenty-footer while you were singing?"

"Yeah," Blister said sheepishly. His paranoia with authority began to rear its head.

"Well this card says Wildroot got a six and you got a five," Jeb bellowed. "Gauuuck—it looks like the best wood in your bag is the pencil—Gauuuck, ha, ha."

"Let me see that!" Wiley demanded, as he snatched the card from Jeb's hand.

Jack and I dashed from our chairs and leaned over Wiley's shoulders as we scanned the card together. Could it possibly be? Was it possible that my dear sweet stupid stoned friend had transposed our scores and my score was actually one stroke lower than we thought? My heart pounded, but I remained reserved as I fully expected some sinister discovery to nullify the correction.

"I know the thirty-nine on the front is correct, so let's start on the back nine," Wiley said with the determination of a trial judge.

Babs and Donetta rose from their chairs and hunched over Wiley forcing Jack and I to place our forearms on his shoulders while he conducted the investigation.

"OK—par on ten and eleven. I remember those."

"Up and down after a penalty on twelve for a bogey," I added. "A par on thirteen and a matching Maxwell Putt on fourteen with you."

"Check, check, check," Wiley rattled off.

"A Mother Teresa aided drive on fifteen for a par," Wiley continued. "You and me caught in a Watergate scandal with Nixon on sixteen—but we both save bogey."

"Check, check," I said, taking over the checking duties.

"Two fatties on seventeen, but a lucky double-bogey," Wiley clattered.

"Check," I confirmed.

"A Yip-a-dee-doo-dah on eighteen for a six!" Wiley said, as his voice began climbing one octave after another.

"Chief! You broke 80!" Wiley shouted, as the table erupted into pandemonium.

"Sweet Jesus!" I shouted, as I jabbed the air with punches.

"Chief, Chief, Chief," the tribe chanted as Babs and Donetta joined in.

"Gauaaaack, ha, ha, haaaaack," Jeb wailed, as he hacked up more flem.

What jubilation! While Jeb backed away, Wiley shot up from his chair. He and Jack wrapped their arms around my shoulder. Spontaneously Babs and Donetta joined the circle and wrapped their arms around the shoulders of Jack and Wiley and the five of us bounced up and down in a gyrating circle. I waved Blister over to join the dancing circle, breaking the link between Jack and me. The rotating piston circled the table as the points on the arc screamed—"Chief, Chief, Chief."

I leaned over and kissed Blister on the cheek. I felt like Jimmy Stewart in 'It's a Wonderful Life' hugging Uncle Billy on Christmas Eve. After all these years it finally dawned on me why George Bailey wanted to hug blundering Uncle Billy when the rest of us wanted to slap him.

"Gauaaaack—you ain't kissing me, Wildroot!" Jeb howled, as he backed away from the bouncing circle and returned to the bar for a refill.

Lori the cook ran out the kitchen door to see what the commotion was all about as Nick ran up the steps from the Pro shop. Six or seven players we didn't know sat dumbfounded at nearby tables with their eyes on us as the spinning circle performed a few more revolutions.

"Chief broke eighty!" Babs shouted to Nick, just as the eldest Mr. Kim came bounding up the steps behind Nick, pockets bulging with golf balls.

"Oh, Goooooo fo you!" Mr. Kim shouted, as his face nearly turned inside-out from a grin.

"Drinks around, Steve!" I screamed, as I twirled my arm in the air inciting the unknown strangers to start shouting, "Chief, Chief, Chief!"

The strangers were the first to line up at the bar behind Mr. Kim. The circle finally began to lose its steam as we unlinked and bent over with laughter. The slaps on the back continued unabated for several more minutes as each stranger toasted me with their drink. While some of them may have not been unduly impressed with our ability to add a score card, all of them were more than grateful for their scotches, bourbons, and vodkas. Mr. Kim trotted over with what appeared to be a glass of apple juice. He was beaming a huge smile as he reached into his pants and pulled out a keepsake golf ball.

"I fie ball you try to trow in pond," Mr. Kim snorted, as he offered me the divine sphere.

"Way to go, Sherlock," Wiley spoofed, as he patted Mr. Kim on the shoulder drawing an even bigger smile.

"Thanks for picking that up, Mr. Kim," I said graciously. "Let's play nine sometime."

"Ret's pray nine. Goo," Mr. Kim agreed before returning to Steve the bartender before the credit dried up.

The sisters scooted their chairs on either side of me as they squeezed into our table for four. When Lori brought our hamburgers we were too exhausted to eat for several minutes, though we had plenty of energy to guzzle a glass of beer with a shot of scotch.

Babs and Donetta sat with us for the next hour, much to the delight of the tribe, though the conversation was more dopey than usual as each tribesman tried to outflank the other to impress the sisters. For a time, the sisters snuggled their chairs so close to mine that I imagined they might have an unspoken plan to take a bubble bath with me. But alas, I realized they were simply sliding their chairs away from Jack who tends to spew slobber when he drinks and carries on.

The tribe finally got a fantasy inoculation when Babs' and Donetta's boyfriends called their cell phones and arranged for a date later in the evening. With a new plan set in motion, the sisters rose from the table, thanked me for the drinks, and scurried off toward the women's restroom, affording the tribe one final chance to establish missile lock.

Not long after, Wiley and Jack adjourned the weekly Red Ball People meeting when they announced that they had to return home to clean ceiling fans and perform other vital post-round chores. Steve's bar bill came to $125 but it was the best $125 I ever spent. Since the hullabaloo could be classified as an obvious business expense, I used my business MasterCard to pay for the drinks and got a hardy handshake from Steve the bartender after I left him a hefty tip. The four of us walked out to the parking lot together. On the way, Blister reminded me—what a wonderful life it really is.

"You know, Chief," Blister mused, "I hear every time someone breaks eighty—an angel gets his wings."

"That's right, Blister," I said to my simpleton friend, "That's right—somewhere an angel just got his wings."

So that's how Chief Tit became a legend of Red Ball People folklore. I feel a little ashamed for using that nasty burst of profanity on the eighteenth hole to illustrate how the Red Ball People really deal with adversity. However, I felt it was my literary duty to be as concise as possible and give an accurate account of just how pissed you're gonna be when you miss a milestone three-footer like I did. I could have shot a 78 for Christ's sake. Jumpin' Jesus, how cool would that have been?

Corrected Score Card after 18 Holes

Hole	10	11	12	13	14	15	16	17	18	Front	Back	Total
Yardage	356	189	338	504	335	401	353	138	461	3088	3075	6163
Handicap	4	8	12	2	14	6	10	16	18			
Wiley	④	③	③	6	③->(0)	4 ^{6}	5	⑥ ^{8}	⑥	43	40	83
Chief Tit	④	③	5	⑤ ^{10}	④	4 ^{6}	5	5	^{9}6->(0)	39	40	79
Blister	4	6 ^{1}	5	⑥ ^{10}	7 ^{5}	5 ^{6}	5	②	⑦	52	47	99
Jack	5	4 ^{2}	④ ^{3}	7 ^{4}	7 ^{5}	④	④ ^{7}	③	⑥	51	44	95
Par	4	3	4	5	4	4	4	3	5	36	36	72

Notes:

/ => Signifies that player gets stroke

○ => Signifies that player won bet

->(0) => Heiroglyphic for "out of ass."

[1] Blister surrenders to hole after hitting lob shot 170 yards across river, takes a Linda Tripp.

[2] 6 foot putt conceded to Jack to avoid 4-putting green. Wiley and Chief Tit pick up for impressive up and down.

[3] Favorable ruling allows Jack to save 16 strokes for clear-cutting around ball.

[4] Jack attempts to record Gesundheit score of 6. Actual score was 7.

[5] Blister and Jack are too tired to spawn after salmon run, both take a Linda Tripp.

[6] Mother Teresa blesses all but Jack's ball. All but Jack have miracle drives. Wiley tries to ice Chief Tit down.

[7] Jack wins two hole Wolf bet. Wiley invokes hyperbolic drop rule to gain 80 yards on drop.

[8] Newton's law of Reaction acts to bring Wiley's score back to equilibrium. Wiley quits hole to stop bleeding.

[9] Chief Tit wins "out of ass" bet and then ruins round with Yip-a-dee-doo-dah.

[10] Score card corrected for Blister's transposition error. Chief Tit becomes a legend of Red Ball People folklore.

GLOSSARY

–>(o): Hieroglyphic used by Red Ball People on score cards to denote that unexpected score was pulled out of player's ass.

3: The number that Bill Clinton writes on his score card for a par 3 hole after parring the hole with his second ball.

3-Shank Theorem: A trigonometric principle devised by Chief Tit that proves that 'Two wrongs seldom make a right but three shanks *always* make a left.'

4: The number that Bill Clinton writes on his score card for a par 4 hole after parring the hole with his second ball.

8: The maximum number of beads in the Red Ball People's abacus.

Ajax: A cleansing detergent made by the Colgate-Palmolive Company. Also the term used by President Bush to describe the inflection point on a green where the influence of gravity exceeds the influence of ball acceleration.

Apex: The inflection point on a green where the influence of gravity exceeds the influence of ball acceleration. Also a term used by President Bush to describe a cleansing detergent made by the Colgate-Palmolive Company.

Blaring Television Conundrum: An unexplained phenomenon that causes the decibel level of a television set to double when a person, primarily a male who has quaffed a few beers, dozes off watching late night television.

Blister Forehead Lie: Describes a ball sitting on dirt or hardpan that resembles the receding hairline of Blister's forehead. Blister's name may be substituted for anyone you know who has a receding hairline and a hairy back.

Blister Back Hair Lie: Describes a ball sitting in tall grass that resembles the hair on Blister's back.

Branches: The appendages that jut out from trees that golfer's mistakenly believe are translucent to golf balls.

Bye-Bye Miss American Pie: A downhill putt that rolls off the green.

Coleman Brick™: A styrofoam brick patented by Chief Tit and named in honor of NFL referee and brick head Walt Coleman. The brick replica is best used for tossing at the TV when referees make bad calls or when your favorite quarterback fumbles the ball during the game winning drive. The brick bounces harmlessly off the TV set while allowing the user to blow off steam.

Event Horizon: A gravitational field that surrounds water hazards on golf courses that acts to suck golf balls into water with the same intensity that a black hole sucks in ionized space dust.

Falwellians: A future religious sect that promotes the desegregation of church and state. The Falwellians will discover the artifacts of the Red Ball People during a religious retreat as they are having an Easter Egg Hunt in the Sierra Nevadas in the year 2503.

GEM™: An invention of Chief Tit's named in honor of former Grateful Dead front man Jerry Garcia, the GEM™ is an acronym for the Garcia Electronic Mittens. The GEM™ is used by concert promoters to insure that arm waving fans don't impede the view of the people seated behind them. The device consists of a 90-volt battery, two electrically wired mittens, suspenders, and a patented GEM™ black box, which contains an altimeter for detecting when a concert-goer has raised his arms above his head.

GEM™ (Garcia Electric Mittens)

Convenient backpack for porting 90-volt battery

GEM™ black box contains altimeter, which detects when arms are waving above head.

90-volts of current are delivered to the mittens until concert-goer drops his arms.

Suspenders for strapping on GEM™ black box

Ushers identify and outfit offending arm wavers with the GEM™ as an alternative to removing them from the concert. The moment an inconsiderate twit raises his arms over his head and blocks the view of those to the rear, the GEM™ delivers a 90-volt current to the mittens as a friendly reminder to the mutton head to keep his arms down for the benefit of those to the rear.

Gesundheit Score: A score on a hole whose sum is less than the addition of the strokes actually taken. The Gesundheit score is based on Gesundheit Perception Measurement theory developed by Professor Daniel Goldston as a repudiation of Gestalt psychology. Contrary to Gestaltists like Max Wertheimer, Gesundheitists believe that the 'whole is less than the sum of the parts'. Goldston originally named the theory Gest-Seigheil in deference to the German founders of Gestalt psychology that his theories refuted. However, before submitting his work to his publisher, he ran the manuscript through Microsoft's spellchecker and it inadvertently changed Gest-Seigheil to Gesundheit and the theory was mistakenly published under the latter name.

Global Positioning System (GPS) SockFinder™: A device invented by Chief Tit to use global positioning satellites to find lost socks. The invention consisted of two components: a microchip that is implanted into socks by manufacturers and GPS SockFinder™ Palm Pilot software. The microchip beams the missing sock's location to a geostatic satellite that inturn sends the coordinates of the sock to a wireless palm pilot. The GPS SockFinder™ software converts the coordinates into a series of beeps similar to a Geiger counter, which grow in rapidity as the searcher moves closer to the sock's location. The device can also be used to locate missing head covers.

Gut Check: A visual inspection of the waist of one tribesman by another to determine who is adding the most girth.

Hat Hair: The gangly mess on top of your head when you remove your cap after a round of golf.

Howdy Doody Time: A measure of time during a round of golf when the quality of play among the Red Ball People is particularly dreadful.

HUMDINGER: A Navy acronym for the artificial intelligence synthesizer invented by Professor Daniel Goldston that allows dolphins to talk to humans. The acronym was formed by combining letters from the formal name of the top-secret invention: HUMDINGER—(HUMan-Dolphin MimickING SynthesizER).

Hyperbolic Drop: The preferred method by the Red Ball People for taking a drop after hitting a ball into a water hazard. The drop is based on Red Ball People Amendment 2 to USGA Rule 26c, which allows any tribe member who occupies hyperbolic vector space, to take advantage of a flaw in Euclidean geometry's 5th postulate and drop on one of the infinitely many parallel lines that intersect both a favorable location on the fairway and the Euclidean line that the player used to hit his ball into the hazard.

Maduro Presidentes: A cigar made of the finest blends of hay and stink-weed, and the preferred cigar of the Red Ball People with the exception of Chief Tit who has a shine for Montecristo #3s.

Oliver: A quadruple bogey or higher. Named after the movie Oliver. Origin comes from the phrase spoken by Oliver to the Task Master of the orphanage during supper when Oliver requests an additional dumpling by asking, "Please Sir may I have another?"

Linda Tripp: An ugly triple-bogey. It's a Tripp and its ugly.

Maxwell Putt: A putt that's good to the last drop.

Missile Lock: The state at which a jet fighter has locked onto a target with radar. Also an adage used by the Red Ball People to stare at breasts or buttocks of females without being detected.

Neighborhood Watch Program: A colloquialism used by the Red Ball People to describe the habit of using range finders to establish missile lock on females around the golf course.

Newton's Law of Reaction: A physical law discovered in the 16th century by Sir Isaac Newton, a man who was nearly as smart as Chief Tit. The law demonstrates the role that equilibrium plays in golf and guarantees that a player who is temporarily playing better than his handicap—won't be for much longer.

Pop a Woody: A state of arousal that the Red Ball People find themselves in when an attractive woman compliments the aroma of the tribe's cigars.

Platinum Plan: Branding name used by marketing people to signify that their company has embarked on a new business model to simultaneously degrade service while raising prices.

Pullooski, Betty: Red Ball People colloquialism for a pulled shot.

Pullooski, Donna: The ugly twin sister of Betty. Two pulled shots on a hole gets you the twins.

Pullooski, Momma and the Pullooski Cousins: Momma and the cousins show up when a player or the entire foursome are pounding every tree on the left of the fairway. The Pullooski's get progressively uglier as you move from Betty to the cousins.

Shankazoid: An imaginary box that is used to establish a redirected target line when a player embarks on a shanking bout. When applied correctly, the shankazoid serves as a practical application of the 3-Shank Theorem and provides the shortest route with the least amount of strokes to the hole.

Sock Worm Holes: An tear in the timespace continuum that sucks socks and head covers into a parallel universe. Travel through the sock worm hole is one directional and is limited to only socks and head covers. The parallel universe is comprised of billions of mismatched socks and mountains of head covers.

Stunt Driver™: An environmentally sensitive device patented by Chief Tit that is used to augment a tirade and resembles the expensive driver in your bag. The driver is made of flexible foam rubber with a hollow core filled with thin wire resembling a clothes hanger to keep the shaft stiff. The device is marketed as a substitute for a real driver when rage overcomes the player and the player wants to wrap a driver around a tree but exercises enough reason to realize that he doesn't really want to spend $475 to do so. After the player cools down, the club can then be unfurled from the tree for reuse later in the round.

T-Rex drop: The preferred method of the Red Ball People for taking relief. Technique entails dropping the ball to the ground from close range to insure that player has flat fluffy lie.

Telecellerator™: A device invented by Chief Tit to insure that drivers in the fast lane maintain proper speed as they chat on cell phones. The Telecellerator™ contains an integrated cell phone and four electrical wires. Two wires attach to a 90-volt battery, one wire is attached to the odometer, and the other wire is attached to the ear lob of a driver. As the cell phone interferes with the driver's primary task of driving at freeway speed, the device activates upon detecting a 5 MPH deceleration and a 90-volt payload is delivered to the driver's ear lobe until the driver attains proper highway speed.

Twin Prime Conjecture: A famous mathematical conjecture that claims that there are an infinite number of pairs of prime numbers that differ by two. The conjecture has never been proven, though San Jose State University Professor Daniel Goldston worked on it for 20 years and claimed he had solved it until he submitted his proof to his colleagues who spent about 5 minutes reviewing his work before discovering numerous holes in his argument.

YANKee-doodle-dandy: A player who has accumulated the most Pullooski ladies and is king of the pulls.

Yip-a-dee-doo-dah: A yipped putt—usually a 3-footer or shorter.